A HEART OF STONE

PHOENIX BRIAR

Night and Day Trilogy: Book Two

A HEART OF STONE

Printed by Amazon

Charleston, SC

ISBN 978-0-9905631-3-6

OTHER WORKS BY PHOENIX

The Night and Day Series
A Heart of Ice
A Heart of Stone

The Beauty Series
Rose Borne

Short Stories
The Perfect Seashell

ACKNOWLEDGMENTS

When God puts someone in your life—someone wonderful—we always hope that it's for eternity. But sometimes it's only for a few years, maybe even a few months.

I knew a woman named Blenda Sing for about eight months. I was hospitalized in December of 2016 for a severe anxiety attack. A few months after was when I found my therapist, Blenda Sing. I made more progress with her in eight months than in the entire previous eight years I'd spent working through mental and emotional disorders.

She saved my life.

I am a better person, a better wife, a better mother, teacher, sister, and friend all because of her.

The last time I saw Blenda was in December of 2017. She called to tell me that she had the flu and couldn't keep our next appointment. A few weeks later, her husband called all of her patients to let us know that she'd contracted pneumonia and had been placed into a medically induced coma.

She passed away the following spring.

Most of you probably don't know who she was, and she's not alive to even appreciate my gratitude for everything that she's done for me.

So my acknowledgement is to those of you who help others walk through the darkest parts of their lives; and to those of you who are willing to let others help you when you need it.

Thank you. All of you.

For my husband.
You were my new beginning. You taught me how to live again. I love you.

A Heart of Stone

A QUESTION

A voice said, Look me in the stars,
And tell me truly, men of earth,
If all the soul-and-body scars
Were not too much to pay for birth.

-Robert Frost

PROLOGUE

One thing alone not even God can do,
To make undone whatever hath been done
- Aristotle

Chapter One
Scarlet

The Last Month of Spring
The Catacombs of Castle Karnei, Flora

I will never quite become used to the cold.

By now, it is an ever-present companion. First, in Crystalice, and now even in Flora. There is cold everywhere. It has followed me since that first time I dared to venture out into the wastelands and challenged Gabriel. Since then, I do not think that I have ever not been cold. It follows me constantly, like death looming over my shoulder, waiting for a moment to steal my life.

"Hnnn," I grunt as I shift my brow upon the damp, frigid floor. I can hear water dripping from stalagmites nearby, and the sound is soothing enough to have me wishing for sleep and yet too obnoxious to permit me rest. With a sigh, I manage to wedge my hands underneath me and push myself up into more of a leaning position, getting off of my side. My whole left side hurts and throbs, having laid in one place too long. My skin is damp and slick with water that mists the caverns and slimes the walls. Red hair sticks to my face and back in roped clumps, peeling off my skin when I turn my head to look around, only to stick back again.

I push myself through the aching weakness in order to sit up. I am naked and cold, shivering with my hands and feet bound in irons. I tuck my legs up close to my body for the illusion of warmth and for some form of stability. As much as I would like to lean back against the wall, the cavern wall is icy and jagged. So I forgo the wall and lean over my knees and tremble while my thin arms wrap around my legs to try and curl up, trying to protect the lifefire burning in my chest.

The hole in my side is burning, and it aches something fierce. I can smell infection, but it's not yet in my blood. I tried to use what little of my strength I had to cauterize the wound when I first woke up here, mostly burning it closed. But it needs proper tending, and I used all of my strength on that.

Drip…drip…drip-drip…drip…drip-drip-drip…

The droplets do not fall in a steady pattern. It is maddening, really. I have nothing to do with my time but to listen and to wait. So I close my eyes and try to sort out a pattern in the droplets. I lean my eyebrows against my slick, gritty knees and close my eyes.

How did I get here?

Drip-drip…drip…drip…

A Few Hours Later

A loud bang from the mouth of the cavern startles me, and the sound echoes through the whole place. I jump a bit, not quite sure if I'd been sleeping or merely resting my eyes. Heavy footsteps clomp and splash their way carefully down into the lower parts of the cavern, and I push myself up. I am weaker than I thought, like a new fawn, trembling and shaking all over on thin limbs

Two men approach the mouth of my little hole. I cannot see them, but I can hear them. The solid stone wall separating my chamber from the rest of the catacomb pushes away from itself with a scratching, grinding sound that has me clenching my teeth.

"Ere, lassie," an old, raspy voice growls. "Some hot gruel."

I press myself into the back of the cavern, hiding in the darkness. A shaft of light from the hole connecting my chamber to the outside world above is the only thing that offers even a scrap of vision. I stare past it into the faces of the two Flora men who stoop at the entrance, one carrying a stone bowl and one carrying a sword.

"I 'eard she's a pretty thing," the other said, younger and a bit more impish looking. The kind most women would never stop to gaze at. Or perhaps it was their own instincts that warned them away from the lecherous madness in his eyes.

"I 'eard she's quite mad," the older one rumbled dryly, setting the bowl down. "Ere, kitty, kitty. We'llna bite. Gots to report yer condition to the duke. Makin sure ye's alive an alls that."

The chains on my feet make it difficult to move too well or too quickly. The smell of sulfuric water confounds my senses. "Who ever thought to call for a tiger: 'here, kitty, kitty'?" I ask in a rasp of a voice, crouching forward on my knees with my hands bound in front of me. I move a bit more into the light so that they can see that I am bound and still quite alive, but no further do I venture.

The younger one recoils a bit and looks upon me with a mixture of disgust and fear. "She's all cut up in ribbons," he hisses to his older companion, without any sense of modesty or decency. Not that I am sensitive to either.

The older one clucks his tongue. "Aye an' aye…most soldiers are…here, pretty thing…come an' eat. We'll leaves ye 'lone." He nudges the clay pot closer to me.

"What of Alistair?" I demand, leaning forward a bit. "Has he woken yet? Is he well? Has Gabriel sent word?"

"*Duke* Alistair," the young one snarls.

The older one frowns a bit at him beyond his bushy, gray brows. "Nay, lassie." He looks back to me. "Alistair sleeps an' nay word from the prince. The duke's a'might burnt all over an' is fightin a fever…"

"Alistair…" His name is a soft sound of agony pulled from my chest, and I slump onto the ground, sinking against the wall. "It's all my fault…"

The older one sighs. "If ye are who ye says…ye've nothin to fear. Jus' wait a wee bit longer…"

I ignore the bowl of gruel despite my growling stomach, curling up against the wall again. "I am…Scarlet Anita Sön'yana mei Ka'Rose…ne Lasar…Inferno…" I close my eyes and press my brow to my knees. "Ward of Gabriel ne Crystalice Cerulean…and murderer of Alistair ne Maeghdra Flora…"

A Few Hours Later

The soldiers closed the wall and left me in the darkness of the cavern, and the hot gruel that they left me sat untouched for a while. It seems to be such tedious effort to eat, and whatever is in that clay pot does not smell the least bit appetizing.

Finally, I manage the energy to scoot my way carefully towards the pot and take off the lid. Inside smells like the scrapings of the bottom of many overnight-pots. There are different meats and burnt parts, unidentified breads, perhaps? I'm not a particularly choosy eater, but even my stomach is telling me that it's not food.

Even so, my head tells me that it is, and I lean back against the cold, damp wall once more, feeling the jagged rocks press into my injured back. My leg is beginning to turn useless on me. I've barely noticed, since having my feet bound keeps me at awkward positions that perpetually cause my legs to tingle and go numb. But now, with my legs stretched out, I can feel the numbing, burning pain in my thigh from where the arrow pierced. It wasn't very deep or damaging, but it still hurts something fierce. I bend my legs in and out idly as I eat, something small to try and keep them moving.

There is nothing to eat the gruel with, so I tip the jar up against my lips while the clumped sludge crawls its way toward the rim. I am left somewhere between slurping and biting at it to get it into my mouth, chewing and swallowing the different pieces. By the time I'm half way in, I'm almost too exhausted to finish, but I am also much too hungry to care what's inside of the pot anymore. It could be carrion for all I care, and I would still eat it.

But once the pot is empty and I lean back against the wall once more, I feel hungrier than ever. The food did me some good, and if I could just get my hands and feet unbound…I pull at my wrists, separating them. Now that I've had some food and warmth, some of my strength has returned. However, as I test my bonds, I realize that I do not have near enough strength to break them. These chains are Flora steel. At my strongest, I would struggle to break them, if I even could. Here in these damp, cold catacombs, I am better off saving my energy for something else and suffering the chains for now. I sink back against the wall and close my eyes wearily…I can hear thunder outside…it sounds like it'll rain again…

Chapter Two
Scarlet

Six Days Ago
The Karnei Forest

The first attacker screams when I crunch him beneath me, tearing into his throat. There's not much point after that, and I chase after the others. But in the seconds it took me to take the first one, the remaining six have all started their *Shift*. Black bears are significantly smaller than Alistair's brown, usually about half the size. I'm somewhere in between. I'm larger than some of the bears but smaller than some too, and fairly reasonably dwarfed by the brown bears.

One of the bears roars at me, an angry sound that isn't entirely unimpressive, and he charges me with two others at his side while the other three get around me and box me in. If I were a cat and not a woman, I would have fled a long time ago. In fact, I never would have come after them. But I am a woman and a very, very angry one at that. These men prey on the weak. They went after my Zsoka. They would have easily killed us without a thought for our goods. I hate them. I hate people who would kill others for such petty reasons. I especially hate people who would injure a child as if she were nothing. Were I any other woman and not a soldier, I would have been defenseless. I know these type of men. They would have humiliated me, raped me, used me, sold me, or even killed me. Maybe all of those. Men like this don't deserve to live.

I pinpoint the smallest one—he is one of the ones caging me in. So I turn from the assault and attack the rear, jumping on the smallest bear. I rip into his throat as my body burns, and another bear tackles me and takes me to the ground. It knocks the air out of my lungs, but the bear screams, his fur engulfed in flame. Almost as soon as he attacks me, he jumps away from me, rolling on the ground, trying to put out the fire but instead spreading it.

I notice now: the smell of burning. It is so familiar. So sweet and lovely in my nostrils, floating viciously through the air. Around me, bursts of fire jump from tree to tree, widening and spreading. The forest is wet, so the fire travels slowly, but one by one, each tree goes up in flames. Another bear attacks me, this one larger, and he takes me to the ground. Another joins in. The combined weight of them crushes me, and I struggle and roar as one bites into my shoulders.

Then, I hear a furious cry—human—and the weight leaves me. I push myself up, ready for a fight, heaving my breath. Alistair stands before me, sword in one hand, dirk in the other. He is breathing hard and covered in sweat. There is a long burn down his arm, and his brown eyes glisten with rage. The bears now at my sides groan in agony, trying to stand but unable to. Quickly, I realize that Alistair has sliced open the tendons in their ankles, crippling them.

No point in letting them suffer, I suppose.

With a bitter sound, I lunge on the first, and then the second, ripping into their throats, clawing their faces to keep their maws from clamping down on me. When it is finished, I stand, my breath heaving, and I take my place beside the much smaller Alistair as he faces the remaining three. He does not *Shift*, and I do not know why. In his bear from, he should easily overpower them. But he remains human. And the bears, considering their options, charge.

I go out before Alistair, taking on the largest one who is a good hundred pounds heavier than me and attacking. He is too big for me to take to the ground, and I have to face him in quick attacks. Crouched, I wait, and when he leaves an opening, I lunge and swipe his side. He groans and I jump back when he swipes at me, staggering forward a bit. He roars, and I hiss unhappily, tail flicking back and forth and eyes over-wide. Another opening, I charge and bite the leg then dart away, his claws grazing my back but no more.

Behind him, I hear Alistair swear and shout at the other two. He is fully capable of handling them, but why does he not *Shift?* The creature facing me roars again and this time charges me on all fours, spreading his mouth in a furious cry of anger. I charge as well but dodge at the last moment and attack his side. I jump on his back, sinking my claws into him and holding on. He rears back in a roar and thrashes around, but more and more, blood begins running down his body. He collapses, breathing hard, and I jump up for an extra foot of height and attach myself to his neck, ripping it open. It is a quick and sure way to kill someone, and one of my favored methods since it is usually so vulnerable.

Behind me, Alistair cries out. Pain.

One bear is down, but Alistair is kneeling and using his sword to hold himself up. One more opponent is left, missing an eye and hobbling badly. The last bear is nearly Alistair's size. Four and a half hundred pounds, maybe more. He pushes himself towards Alistair. I'm tired. I've been stabbed in the shoulder, bitten on the same shoulder. I've had nearly five hundred pounds crush my chest. I boast claw marks on my stomach and on my back. I ache everywhere. Thankfully, most of my wounds are superficial.

Alistair's injury does not seem nearly so innocent.

Phoenix Briar

With a vengeful cry, I race towards Alistair and his opponent, throwing my weight upon the beast who is only slightly smaller than myself. We both topple over, and his claws go into my throat, holding back my snapping teeth. I bite and claw at him as he holds me back, and with a scream of frustration, I light myself on fire. He roars and arches away from me, trying to push me off, push me away. His hold weakens, and I push past it and tear into the pulsing vein in his neck, ripping it open and spilling his lifeblood onto the ground.

He stops moving, mostly anyways, and I slump off of him, standing up and breathing hard. I take a long, slow look around to make sure that they are all dead or soon will be. None of them move. The one I lit on fire first is struggling weakly, not far away, but he's nearly expired and not worth my trouble. They will not hurt anyone any longer.

A crash beside me alarms me, and I jump, hair standing on end. But it is only the sound of a tree limb separating from the whole and slamming into the ground. I frown, curious, and I look all around me. The fire has spread quickly despite the wet leaves, and it is devouring the trees, eating them alive. I watch in surprise and interest as creatures flee, screaming and shrieking to the sky as they run from the fire. The trees all moan in pain and collapse to the ground.

This is not like my burning forest. The trees at home love the fire. It purifies them, warms them. The animals there snuggle up in its warmth, comforted and protected by its painful thorns. I look up to a tree where a bird with baby-blue wings cries angrily at the fire, standing between the burning trunk and her nest. The nest is filled with eggs, and the little bird keeps trying to fight off the fire. It burns her beak, eats her wing, and she cries, flapping furiously, trying to put it out. I watch, unable to look away as she flutters up towards the sky, her wing alight, and then, she drops suddenly into the molten lake beneath her. Her eggs are left alone in the nest. They, too, will burn.

I step back slowly, looking all around me. My ears are down and my tail low. This…this is not what fire does. The firebirds and the phoenix, they love the fire…they make their nests from burning twigs, and they preen themselves in the flames. The eggs hatch to the fire's warmth. This is not supposed to happen.

"Scarlet," Alistair rasps, and my ears jump up in surprise. I swing my head over to him and find him trying to stand. One leg is collapsed beneath him, and although I cannot tell of a wound, I can see that his pant leg is soaked in blood.

Alistair…

He breathes hard, leaning on his sword, and when another tree collapses, my ears go up and my fur stands straight. The fire will kill him. I have to get him out of here. I go to him, and he looks at me with a tired gaze. There is no easy way to carry him, especially since he is very nearly my size even as a man. So, I crouch down by him, nudging him when he stays still. "You want me…to ride you?" he asks breathlessly.

I snort, and he sighs and grabs hold of me to keep what little balance he has. His sword is discarded upon the ground, I suppose since he does not have the balance to hold onto it or sheath it. His weight is oppressive but easier than if I were human. I also cannot run quickly. If I begin moving too fast, I can feel him slip to one side or the other, and I must pause and try to help him readjust. Even so, I move through the trees, avoiding the fire. I do not know where I am going or if I am in fact taking us further from Karnei. The only thing I know is that I must get Alistair away from the greedy flames.

The flames are moving faster than I am able to run, and I cannot escape them. On my back, Alistair coughs and wheezes something. I cannot understand him. But I must get him to safety. The smoke is rising and the ground is becoming a dangerous place of falling trees and burning brush. My heart races. I cannot think. I cannot outrun the flames. They will kill him. I can feel him fading fast. Alistair!

Finally, I search out a little hill where there are not so many trees and begin to search out our only hope. There. In the hill. The foxes have abandoned it, but it is there, a little hole. It is not nearly large enough to fit him, but it tells me where it is safe to dig. Tigers are not diggers by nature, but we can. I let Alistair slide off of my back as I tear into the earth. The ground is soft and wet beneath my paws, and the deeper I go, the wetter and cooler the ground becomes. The scent of fox irritates my nose, but it should suit Alistair just fine.

I can hear the fire. It is roaring now. At least this hill and the clearing should prevent smoke from filling in. I dig out the den as deep and wide as I can until I am out of time. Fire engulfs the hill and threatens Alistair. I can control fire some, but not much, and I keep the area around him free of its flames. Even so, the ground is getting hot, and he is beginning to sweat from the sweltering heat of it. The forest will cook him even if it doesn't scald his skin.

The den is his only hope, and I grab him carefully in my jaws and pull him inside. The inside is cool and wet, and I hope that it will stay that way. I do not know if this will work, but it is his only hope. I lay at the opening of the den, warding off the fire and the smoke, sending it up and over the opening of the den. My face and side feel hot and healed by the fire's kiss, and my rump and far side are cool from the den. I do not know, however, if it will be cool enough to save Alistair. And I have not even had a chance to look at his injuries just yet.

"What…have you *done?*"

He is still awake and groaning with pain, his hands weakly pulling at his pant leg, trying to assess the damage. It occurs to me that he might bleed out before the fire is even finished, so I leave my post to slink inside.

What have I done?

The den will not hold us both very well. I did not have the time to dig out an accommodating space. Only enough to protect him. So, I Shift forms into a woman again.

What does he mean, what have I done?

With the fire to fuel me, I have more than enough power and strength to heal my wounds, and so what few marks remain are barely more than scabs and are more ugly than they are dangerous.

"Alistair?" I ask, shifting on my hands and knees to where he lay, my head just barely not hitting the top of the den. I grab his pant leg and rip it open. There, several marks bubble up blood in his leg. The bite is so deep that I cannot even see past the blood pooling. It is amazing to me that he is still conscious.

"Hold still," I warn and heat up my hand, clamping it over his leg. Fire races from my skin into the wound, sealing the injury to keep it from bleeding. I only hope that it will not cost him his leg.

Alistair screams in pain, and I wince at the sound of it. I do not know what it feels like to be burned, but I imagine it feels much like being stabbed by pure ice. I've had that happen upon occasion, and it is one of the most painful experiences of my life. Even the torture I underwent to become a Knight Protector could not compare to the very first time an ice-dagger buried itself in my arm. I would have ripped the arm off just be rid of that agony.

"I know. Just hold on," I tell him, and I turn him a bit so that I can access the wound on the other side of his leg. I repeat the cauterizing process while the fire burns at my back. I begin to channel the heat, pulling it into my body as I expel it onto Alistair's wound to close it up and ward off infection. When it is finished, and Alistair goes mute, he collapses against the ground.

Terrified, I put my head to his chest but sigh at the sound of his heart pounding.

"You're alive…" I whisper and burying my face against his chest. "Don't die, you fool." I kiss that spot and then sit up and move back over to the entrance of the den.

The heat and the flames are delicious upon my skin, and I pull them into me, sucking in the heat all around me. It keeps the den soft and moist, and it fuels me and heals me. I can hear the forest raging with the fire, trees collapsing like thunder in the distance. Every now and again, a stag runs past or a little troupe of hare or a flock of birds. They're all running from the fire as well. Everything burns, and it reminds me of my homeland.

But this fire is different. The fire at home was languid and easy, a flickering, slow warmth.

This fire—the fire that burned from my own body—is greedy and furious. I watch uneasily as it eats up the world around it. Laying at the entrance of the den, I lay my cheek upon my arms and watch the fire destroy everything it touches. Those trees that remain standing are stripped of their leaves and many of their branches, leaving them bare and scorched black. The grass is eaten away and left as burning footpaths on the ground. The air becomes warped and distorted, and I squint my eyes to see through it but cannot. Everything blurs and twists with the fire, and my gaze goes up to the canopy.

Before, sunlight had poured through beautifully. But now the treetops are red, and there is no sunlight to pierce the ground. Instead, there is only black smoke blocking out the sun. It has turned the noon day into darkness. My world goes dark, slowly, ever slowly, while my lifefire eats away this world. Laying there, I take in the heat and the fire, the offspring of the fire that had come forth from my own fur. And yet, too quickly, the world is eaten up and fades away. The fire leaves us and moves on.

The danger has passed.

Alistair brow is twisted with pain while he sleeps, and I frown at him while I think upon his words.

What have I done?

I turn and look to the entrance of the den from where I can see the blackened trees and the scorched earth. What have I done indeed…everything Flora has been eaten up, devoured, destroyed

My fire is hostile here. This place cannot survive my wrath.

"I am sorry…" I say quietly to his sleeping form, looking back to him. How far will it spread? How much will be lost? "I should have listened…"

With a heavy sigh, I lay down beside him. Refreshed in flames, I may be, but today was a long one. I am tired and sore, and I need rest. Besides, there is nothing more to do than to wait for Alistair to recover. Even so, my mind cannot sleep.

Above us, I can hear the tidal wave of flames raging and the thunderstorm of felled trees. The world has turned gray and hazy with smoke and ash, and the forest is still hot with lingering flames.

I close my eyes and smell ash and cinder and smoke. I miss home. Laying my cheek against Alistair's shoulder, I find whatever comfortable position I can and think of home.

Chapter Three
Gabriel

Five Days Ago
Marine, Cerulean

Despite the vacancy of the Marine Manor existing as a nearly palpable reminder that Cara has left my world for what will most likely be quite some time, I have managed to get almost nothing done. I had hoped that the time solitude and lack of feminine distraction would provide ample opportunity to catch up on the work that so desperately needs my attention. And yet, I seem more distracted than ever.

Once we saw Alistair's party off that morning, Enté spent most of the rest of the day crying. Heather, of course, went through all manner of strategies to appease him, and through the thin walls of the sandstone manor, I heard every one. First, she tried scolding him and taking him to task. Then, she tried distracting him with breakfast. When that failed, she resorted to coddling him and rocking him with Flora lullabies. After that came more scolding and an attempt to logically convince him to calm down. Eventually, the boy collapsed from exhaustion sometime after the midday meal—at which point I did actually manage to get several pieces of legislation annotated—but as soon as he awoke from his nap, the crying started all over again.

I set out on trips to various politicians and aristocrats in the area to pay my respects and talk politics. Of course, all anyone really wants to talk about is the White Fang. And Cara. However, once assured that Cara is on her way to Flora, most of the conversation turns to sideways attempts at prying either for information about the White Fang or plans for what the crown has determined to do about them. Unfortunately for myself and my companions, I can tell them very little because I honestly know so little.

Claque has not fared all too much better during his many investigations at home. However, with Cara now gone, he informs me that I really simply ought to just come home, which I have to agree is the better of the two situations. And yet, I do not wish to leave. Marine feels like…a world between worlds…it is not a place without Cara and yet it is one in which she is here. It does not feel as if she is *gone* from this place, and—in fact—it seems as if it is a place where she will return soon.

To return to Crystalice, however—to return *without* her—then…then, I believe I must re-enter a world in which she truly no longer exists.

But Claque is right, and the sooner I return, the more work can be done and the sooner we can form a plan against these White Fang—and the politicians. I am not quite certain which one I fear and hate more.

I put Enté and Heather in a carriage, and when I look upon the woman, I am glad to be leaving so soon. I have tried the past few days not to think too long upon the boy named Tam. I am certain that I met him once or twice, but I do not recall a face.

Even so, knowing that he is Heather's son…Heather whom I have known for years, who tended to my late wife since our marriage—all through her pregnancy and through her death—she was by our sides at all times.

To imagine the woman who was so strong and so brave, who held my hand as I wept over Catherine, she herself swallowing her tears. Even though she herself was in so much pain, she stayed beside my son and I. Although she is not Enté's nurse, she looks after him as much as a grandmother would do. She tends to Dena and to Petara. She helps the other waiting ladies and their charges. She is a good friend to my mother, and they're of the same temperament. In fact, I recall my mother often inviting Heather to her solar to ask for her advice even when she had all the sorcerers and star-seers in the kingdom to give her their thoughts.

To know her. To know what a powerful and monumental creature she has been to our kingdom. To know that she has lost something so precious and valuable to her as her own child, her youngest son. The thought of such pain upon her is an insult to my entire being and sets upon me a torrential rage such as to devour whoever has dared to harm one of my own.

Heather seems weaker than usual…frail and sallow. As she climbs into the carriage with Enté, she gives a little groan of age and sits herself down in the seat. I watch her for a moment, her muddy-green eyes downcast and her lips set in a soft frown, pensive and quiet and sad. She seems…tired…and old in ways that she never did been before.

"Enté," I call to my child, and the little boy turns his head to look at me. I meet his eyes and tip my chin down a bit, holding his stare. "You mind yourself for Heather. If you give her trouble, you will regret it, do you understand me?"

The boy looks like he might defy me for a moment, sucking up a breath to argue simply because he can. But then he seems to think better of it and lets out the air before saying softly, "Ye'sir…"

I give a single nod to him, accepting his answer. I half-expect Heather to say something. She, like Cara, can rarely let a conversation pass without having the last word.

But the old woman says nothing. She watches Enté with the aged and tired smile of one who has seen many long years and will not see many more. Enté hops up on the bench across from her and settles himself.

"Why dinna ye practice readin again?" Heather offers. "D'ye bring yer book?"

"Yes'm," Enté replies and turns to dig it out of his sack. "I brought the ones my tutor gave me afore we left."

"That's good," Heather says with a nod of her head, folding her hands in her lap quaintly. "Start again, then."

Enté smiles, and I sigh just a bit, shutting the door to the coach and allowing the footman to take over. I'd rather ride than sit, but at least this way, I can get some more work done. In my own coach, the wooden door creaks shut on tired hinges, and I sit back on the padded seat. Stacks of notes and parchment are all beside me. I won't hardly be able to write in this carriage, but at least I can read through the materials. Claque sent me a great portion of proposals concerning war funds and initiatives towards the White Fang. With a sigh, I sink back into my seat and pick up the first collection to read through. Maybe this way, I can get to work as soon as I return...

My eyes drift towards the window, and I stare out for a moment, watching the cliffs and the clear, blue skies begin to roll away.

In the far, far distance, it almost looks like smoke. But it's much too far to see.

Cara and Alistair have probably reached Karnei by now—they must have arrived a few days ago, actually. Soon, they'll be leaving for Maeghdra.

Chapter Four
Scarlet

Five Days Ago
The Karnei Forest

In the morning, I left Alistair's side to try and find something for us to eat. Most of the day was spent marking paths and scouting out food, and it was a long while before I managed to chase down a deer for supper.

It is near sundown when I finally find the precarious pile of debris that marks the den, and I sigh with relief. The rain has stopped, but I am cold and wet and muddy, and I smell like a wet cat. It's awful.

A strangled sound of anguish makes me drop the deer at once, and as it crashes onto the ground, I bolt for the entrance of the den just as a muddy mop of sandy blond hair emerges. Alistair! His head snaps up to look at me, and in a split second, he lets out a cry of anger and thrusts a dagger towards me. However, it loses force halfway through the thrust, and I lurch back.

"Scarlet!" he cries in alarm and sighs with relief, dropping the knife.

I hiss at him unhappily and Shift forms. My human form doesn't smell quite as bad as my wet-furred self, but I look like I've been dragged through mud. "What was that for?" I snarl.

He is breathing heavily, clearly straining where he's at, and he lifts his head to look at me, then swears and decides to focus back on the sky. "I did'na recognize ye at first. I've nay seen that form much."

I sigh. "I am the only possible tiger in this area."

"Quite."

I go quiet, and he lays there in the mouth of the den, catching his breath. We don't say anything for a few moments, and so I get up and go grab the deer, dragging her by her burnt leg towards the den where she can't be snatched.

"Just where in the seven hells have ye *been*?" Alistair suddenly seems to have renewed his strength and snarls at me.

I am so unused to anger from him that it startles me, and I growl low in my chest. "Where do you think, fool? I went hunting. There was nothing to eat. I was starving. You were injured."

"I had nay idea where ye *were*!" he shouts, dragging himself out of the den and finally sitting up. He, too, looks as though he's been dragged through mud—and he has—but he's significantly less soaked than I am.

The rain has softened into more of a mist and will probably be gone within the hour.

As it is, Alistair glares at me furiously, his face having regained some color. "Ye just left me here with nay clue as to what had happened to ye!"

"What did you want me to do!" I shout back at him, dropping the deer and turning to face him. Again, he struggles with looking at me and finally swears and jerks off his tunic with some effort. I just sit and watch him struggle with it until he throws it at me in frustration.

"Put that on."

"Do I offend you?" I snap. "Forgive me for not having on a suitable dress to curtsy to you with since I've been out hunting for hours!"

"Why're ye *yelling* at me?" he snaps.

"Because you're angry with me!"

"I'm nay angry with ye!" He throws his head back to glare at me but then turns it again. "Damnit, Scarlet, put the shirt on!"

I give out a scream of frustration and snatch the shirt out of the mud, pulling it on over my head. The feeling of the cold, damp, dirty thing is miserable, but it is slightly warmer, so I cannot really complain. But I cross my arms and glare at him anyways.

"There, you idiot." His tunic is huge on me. It keeps falling off one shoulder, and the hem goes down nearly to my knees.

He glances back at me and then turns to look at me fully. We both stand there and huff at each other for a while until he finally growls, "Ye shouldna just left."

"What?" I bark. "You think I'm just going to up and run off as soon as I have a chance and leave you to die in that hole in the ground?"

"Nay, I thought ye were *dead*!" he screams. His voice crams my words back into my throat, and I shut my jaw, just looking at him. He huffs, red-faced, glaring at me, and he thrusts out his arm and shouts, "I had nay idea what to think! I thought ye'd been killed! That ye were dead somewhere miles away and I couldna reach ye! Maybe those bandits had found ye! Maybe soldiers from Karnei! Chelyah's mercy, Scarlet! Ye're an Inferno in Flora! They could just kill ye and ask who ye are when they send yer body to Crystalice!"

My anger and hurt simmer down to an uncomfortable embarrassment and frustration that knots up my stomach. I clench my arms tighter around myself and look away, glaring at the ground like a sulking child.

Despondently, I mutter, "Mm surry…"

"What?" he snarls.

Snapping my head back to him, I clench my fists and scream, "I said: I'm sorry!"

He shuts his mouth and leans back a bit, although whether from the shrill cry of my voice or because of what I had said, I'm not exactly sure. He looks at me for a long minute while I take my turn to huff irately and grab the deer again.

"Do you think you can eat raw meat?" I ask him as I bring the deer nearer and then go to him. Alistair shifts a bit uncomfortably when I lean towards him, but I take his dagger and go back to the doe.

"Most liken not," he says.

I just nod and begin cutting away at the creature, pulling out the organs and leaving the meat. I can start a fire without tinder, but it's harder to maintain, especially in such a way that will cook meat without burning it. Alistair leans against the mouth of the den and watches quietly as I prepare the fire and meat.

"Art hurt?"

I shake my head. "I'm fine. Just hungry." I glance over at him, sticking the meat on the dagger to cook it so that I can continue cleaning the rest of the meat down to the bones. None of the sticks around us have the strength to hold up the food over fire anyways. "How's your leg?"

He sighs and looks down at it, inspecting it for a moment. "Hurts sommat fierce. I'll heal with rest, but I canna walk on it for now."

"Mm," is my only response, and I take a bite of the meat before sliding off the cooked strips and taking them to him. "Eat as much as you can. Wildlife is scarce. I came upon her by sheer luck."

"Thank ye." He takes the meat and starts eating it while I prepare more. A portion for him, a portion for me.

Once the meat is gone, I cook the liver and heart as well. I try not to be picky about food when I'm not sure where the next meal is coming from. In the end, it's enough to fill my stomach and satisfy me for the time, and I try not to think on the hunger that will begin soon if we don't get to better hunting grounds.

Alistair doesn't speak much. He eats the rudimentary meal I made, and when he doesn't eat, he looks up at the sky and then checks his wounds and his supplies. "It's goin to rain again."

I glance up at the sky. How can he tell? It's still just gray. "What do we do?"

He sighs. "We need to stay out of the rain if we can. Moreover, I canna tell the way to Karnei with the weather like it is and with no instruments to guide me. Plant life is all burned up too. We'll have to wait for now."

"How long?" I look to him sharply. "You need a healer, and I'll starve very soon if I don't find hunting grounds."

Alistair considers me for a bit and turns his eyes to the sky once more, rubbing his stubbled jaw. "How long can ye go without food?"

I grumble irritably. "Not long. With no food while traveling and cold, I can last three…maybe four days, and then I'll be too weak to hunt or travel. Another few days and I'll die. With small prey, I can go a little longer, but it's only a short-term, survival solution."

He nods. "We're nay far from Karnei. Afore the fire started, I noted of our direction. Ye chased those bandits northeast towards the shore. We're nay much further from Karnei than we was afore, just off the main road. If we head south, we should reach it soon enough."

The sky rumbles quietly in the distance, and I glance up to it unhappily. I consider something and glance to him. "How long can you go without food or water?"

He considers his state and responds, "Much longer without food. I can go a few weeks if I need to on nothing. Water is more difficult. I'll need water every few days."

I puff out some air in frustration. "Well, then I suppose it's good that it's raining." I stand up and add, "I can fire a clay bowl to collect some of the rain water."

He watches me as I go and collect some materials to pack together a hard enough clay. The fire is more difficult. It needs to burn hot, and that takes much of my strength. But a bowl is a bowl and it will hold water—more or less.

As the rain begins to sprinkle down, I light it with my fire, trying to let the bowl harden as much as it can before the fire is put out. I'm exhausted. I've burned through much of my energy, and already, hunger gnaws at me once more. I mumble miserably to myself and put the bowl out by the entrance to the den.

"You should get back inside," I tell him. "I'm going to move the carcass away." I actually wouldn't mind it attracting more creatures, but I don't want them sneaking up on us at night.

"Be careful." And with that, he manages to get back inside the den while I pull the deer carcass away from our makeshift home. The rain is coming down in sheets once more by the time I scurry into the den, and I shiver considerably.

"We'll leave soon as the rain lets up and I can get a sense of direction," Alistair tells me when I am inside.

I wring out my hair and try to wring out my shirt. I'm cold and wet and rather irritated about both. I hiss and growl at anything near me: the shirt bunching at my waist, my hair dripping muddy water into my face, an itch between my shoulder blades that I just can't get, my cold toes, the list goes on.

"Come 'ere, sweetheart," Alistair consoles with a short chuckle that he bites off when I glare at him. I huff, but he holds out a hand until I go to where he lays. He sighs and grabs me up, tugging me down with him. "Come get warm. Tis alright." He draws me near, and he is warm, warmer than the cool, wet dirt which had seemed like a good idea when the forest was aflame.

I shiver a bit and nestle up close to him, and I remember when we sat out on the chilly balcony together while I was wrapped up in his cloak. The thought makes me smile a bit, and I recall how warm and heavy that cloak was. "I miss your cloak," I tell him quietly.

"Mm?" His brows pinch together in pain, and he breathes slow and deep. He must be suffering. I study his features, unable to ease the torment that I caused.

"When we were on the balcony…your cloak. It was warm. I lost it chasing those men down."

After a moment, he gives a pained smirk and says, "I liked that cloak."

It makes me laugh just a bit. "I'll make you a new one."

"Mm…that'd be nice. Do ye even know how to sew?"

I snort. "Of course I know how to sew."

He smiles. "I just dinna know if Inferno taught their women to sew."

"Who else would make clothes? The soldiers?" Outsiders really don't have much of an opinion of Inferno, do they? I sigh.

He chuckles to himself and amends, "Aye, I s'ppose nay. I just find it difficult to picture ye sittin by a fire with a needle and cloth."

I don't know what is so strange about it, and I frown at him. "Well, I have. And I can."

Alistair goes quiet for a moment, shifting a bit and then sighing again. "Are ye always so defensive?"

I glare. "I'm not defensive."

"Ye are, lass."

"Well, I am only defensive because you are so very irritating."

He smiles and cracks his eyes open to look at me. "Am I now?"

"Yes. You are."

"Mm…" He smiles to himself, and it makes me want to pinch him or poke his injured leg.

I restrain myself, although only barely. I tuck my face into his side and think of something witty or at least caustic to say, but as I rummage through my head for some manner of retort, my exhaustion sets upon me fiercely, and I sink into a restless, miserable sleep beside him.

Chapter Five
Gabriel

Two Days Ago
The Crystalice Palace, Cerulean

"Hold!"

The coach jerks to a stop, and my head bangs against the glass pane. I must have been snoring, because when I sit up to tend to my injured head, I smack my tongue to the roof of my mouth and find it dry and sticky. I lick my lips and rub my tongue against the roof of my mouth while I gather up my papers which had strewn about the floor of the coach while I dozed. Glancing out the window and up at the sky, I realize that dawn has not even broken yet; the sky is dark, but the horizon bares a thin, pale light like a spider's silk thread.

It took five days with Cara to reach Ocarine with the weather the way it was. Coming back, however, the rain had long since stopped and—since this time we did not have to replace a wheel—we were home within two and a half. A week. It's been a week since Cara left for Flora.

I need to stop thinking on that. Now that I'm home, I'll have much to do, and I can't afford to be distracted at the moment. I need to finish going over the proposals and bring up the annotations I made to Claque. I'd like to have a meeting with my mother to discuss some of the funding issues, and perhaps talk with my father about initiatives concerning the White Fang. Of course, he might still be growling at me because of Cara, but hopefully he's more agreeable to working with me now. Stubborn, old bastard…

A footman pulls the door open, and I climb out, setting my papers aside. "Have someone take those into my study," I tell the footman.

"Sir," he responds, chin up and eyes straight ahead. He'll make sure to get them to the right people.

Heather is already out of the coach with Enté, who is trying to get away and hurry into the palace. I approach them both, and Heather stands, giving a ghost of a smile. "I'll get 'im in and changed, highness."

I shake my head at her and take her by her shoulders, my heart squeezing a bit. She seems so small and frail beneath my hold, as if she might shatter if I squeeze her too hard. It is painful to see her like this, and frankly, I cannot bare to look at her in this state. It is mostly for my own selfish reasons that I tell her, "No, Heather. You go and find your family. They are the most important thing right now."

She looks up at me, and her muddy eyes suddenly seem quite liquid and soft; her eyes look up into my haggard, unshaven face, and my long, white hair is tied back messily in a leather thong. I really don't look much like a prince at all, and I don't feel like one either.

"I'm fine, sire," she says softly. "I'll take care of the wee one, and then—"

I squeeze her shoulders a bit and give a very soft shake, towering over the elderly woman.

She had never seemed so old before.

"Go to your children, Heather. They need you. Enté will be fine."

That seems to nearly undo her. She blinks, and her lips turn down and writhe as they fight tears. She won't look me in the eyes. She just stares at my chest and nods slowly, giving a thick swallow before rasping out. "Aye, sire...please call on me if ye need anythin..."

"I will," I assure her, knowing that she does not want to feel useless or downcast. I kiss the crown of her head before releasing her, my own throat tight and my heart pounding. "Go on, Heather. Thank you for your assistance in Ocarine."

She swallows again and nods slowly, turning and walking away with her chin up and her walk steady and steps firm. But her shoulders are a bit slumped, and she walks slower than before.

"Prince Gabriel," Claque calls, coming out of the castle as the servants continue moving around us, unloading the coach as they go and taking everything inside, unlatching the horses and taking them to be tendered and watered.

Looking down to Enté, I tell him, "Go inside, son, and find Aunt Dena. I'll bet she's missed you."

His face splits into a wide grin. "Ye'sir!" He turns and sprints inside, his longing for Cara appeased by the love for his aunt.

Chuckling, I turn my attention back to Claque.

He is not one to smile; he is cold and rigid in public as much as any Crystalice, if not more so. He stands at attention at my side: short hair immaculately slicked back, his face shaven clean without a hint of stubble. He wears his soldier's uniform, as he always does. White eyelashes frame his blue eyes, and those eyes are locked straight at mine with a sense of urgency that does not require words to be conveyed.

My smile drops.

It takes only a sharp nod from my chin to set us both marching up the stairs and into the palace, snow crunching under my boot. "Explain."

He inclines his head and says quietly, "We've received word from Flora. A few days ago, a forest fire broke out and destroyed much of North Karnei. The Karnei Elite shot down a wild tiger roaming near the town with an injured and unconscious Alistair. They currently have her prisoner and have requested confirmation as to her identity when she claimed to be your companion and ward."

I hiss out every foul word in every language that I know, and I turn on Claque with a snarl and shout, "Well what other damned tiger would possibly *be* in Karnei! Does he honestly think that a single tiger would have somehow snuck past all of Cerulean into their territory, or have otherwise gone directly to Flora through the mountain pass simply to travel all the way to Karnei and light that forest on fire! Have they all gone absolutely mad, or am *I* the only one left with any sort of sensibility in this country!"

Claque stares back at me calmly, and I am left acutely aware of the deafening silence of the entry hall.

I don't even need to look around me. Instead, I draw in a long, slow breath, and stand up straight, tugging my tunic down and trying to control my raging heart. It feels like it might rip in pieces with the pain it causes me with every beat. I begin walking again with my hands clenched at my sides, and Claque falls into step beside me.

"I do not believe he mistook her identity, sir," he says simply. "I believe he simply mistrusts her intentions, and Alistair remains in critical condition and unable to defend her. No one quite knows what happened in the woods, as their other traveling companions have not yet been located."

"And Zsoka?" My heart drops into my stomach.

He does not respond at once. "They found her," he says when I stop to stare at him. I sigh, but his look promises more. "She's in bad shape. Scratched up and near starving. She won't eat but cries constantly and bites anyone who comes near her. If Alistair or Scarlet don't get to her soon, she likely won't make it much longer."

My chest squeezes with pain, and I swear again, standing in the hall and looking back and forth, fists clenched. I only just got back. I cannot simply mount up and go tearing across the countryside even though that is what every fiber in my body is screaming at me to do.

"Sire," Claque says at once, and in a rare gesture of empathy, puts his hand upon my shoulder and meets my gaze. "If I may. Send me to Flora. I can travel quickly and verify Scarlet's identity and innocence, and at the very least save the child until we can find out what happened."

I swallow and take in a shaky breath. It will be difficult managing this on my own without Claque on my side. Petara is ruthless and opinionated. Claque assists me in sorting through the politics and the rubbish to see things without bias and evaluate the best course of action when I cannot. Honestly, he would make a much better king than I ever would, and I am not fool enough to not value him as a confidant.

I incline my head and respond, "Forgive me for not being able to honor you with the title and respect you deserve, Claque. You act as my footman and always at my side, yet you are a count and will soon be a prince, but you are always at my call. Your loyalty and diligence are beyond value."

His fist thumps his chest in salute, and he bows at the waist. "I give my life to serve, my liege. Please use me as you will."

"Go."

He turns abruptly and leaves my side at once.

I know him. I know that he will take only whatever provisions are absolutely necessary in order to waste as little time before leaving. I know that he will not rest, that he will ride as swiftly and relentlessly as his horse will permit.

I trust him with my life.

I trust him with Cara's.

Chapter Six
Scarlet

I drift in and out of sleep in a horrible sort of way. My sleep is black and shallow without any dreams, and it seems much too often that I wake from discomfort or cold or hunger and must force myself back to sleep once more. When at last my will becomes weaker than my wakeful mind, I rouse myself to full attentiveness and sigh. Alistair has rearranged himself some in his sleep, his hand near the injury on his leg, as if he could somehow ease the throbbing pain.

I sit up, looking over at him. His face is twisted in discomfort and occasionally pain, but despite that, he still sleeps. I carefully inspect his leg and gingerly push up his pant cuff, inspecting the whole of it. That bear took a nasty chunk out of both flesh and muscle, and I may have cauterized the bleeding, but there is still significant damage. Not so much that he will not regain the ability to walk, but enough that it could kill him if we do not find Karnei soon.

I need to eat again, and he will need some food as well. However, I loathe to think of what bombardment of unwanted wrath should await me if I leave once more. I lean over, nudging Alistair carefully. He mumbles but stays asleep, and it takes a fair bit of effort to rouse him to full consciousness. "What?" he hisses with annoyance.

Frowning at him, I reply simply, "I'm going hunting."

"Fine." He closes his eyes again and shifts his weight.

I curse him under my breath and move away from his sleeping form, crawling out of the den.

The rain is lighter, and I can see the sun faintly from behind the clouds.

Most of the smell of fire and death has been washed away, but I dare not go so far as I did yesterday. The way I went yesterday seemed to be more burned than not, so I take off in a different direction and find that fresh growth begins much sooner. I find a hare with little problem after an hour or so, and I eat it raw in my tigress form before finding another and carting it back to the shelter. Cooking it is easier than the doe, and I take the cooked meat back inside with the sleeping Alistair.

The smell of it wakes him, and he groans uncomfortably while he sits up by propping himself up on his elbows. "Wha's that?" he grumbles.

"A cooked hare," I tell him, offering him the morsel, which he takes and then lays back down. He must be pretty well hurt to have lost his sense of humor and joviality. I try not to let it worry me and instead go back to his leg.

"We need to move as soon as we can," I say. "The rain should let up soon."

"Good," he replies, swallowing another bite and choking on it.

I shake my head as he manages to clear his throat, coughing and roaring out the sound. I go and get the fired clay bowl, bringing it carefully inside. "I'll help you sit up." Lifting his head, I wriggle myself behind him so that he can sit up, and I bring the bowl to his lips.

"I'm nay an invalid, Scarlet," he says after a few sips.

I mutter, "Close enough," and ignore his look of annoyance. I scoff. "For the past several months I've been in a bed more than out of it, so I'm pitiless to your plight."

"Ye're quite pitiless anyhow."

"Quite."

On the corner of his lips, I can see a faint trace of a smile tug, willing him back to health. But his smile is small and weak and quickly vanishes.

He groans, sitting up some and beginning to reach for his leg.

"Leave it alone," I tell him, shoving his hand away from it.

He glares at me. "We need to get goin. I 'ave to get it working."

"I can do it. You're useless."

"Och. I take offense to that," he says in a bit of a huff, scowling at me.

"Good. Heal faster then." He mutters to himself, and I scoot myself down towards his leg, lifting the cuff. "There are no herbs for an ointment out here. It's not bleeding, but it needs to be mended." I throw him a little smirk and tease, "Sorry. It'll leave a nasty scar. Hope the ladies don't mind."

He grumbles to himself and glares at me and says, "Ack, well, if they do, 'tis yer own fault."

I hesitate and then look back down to his leg with renewed regret. "Yes…this is my fault." I begin to clean his leg carefully, getting a better look at it while I do so. It's going to scar something fierce, but it looks like most of the functionality is still there so long as it doesn't get infected and kill him.

Alistair does not comfort or console me. This whole mess is my fault and he's not going to tell me otherwise. Instead, he merely asks through pain-gritted teeth, "Next time, wilt heed my warning?"

"Hm," I consider, grabbing the bottom of Alistair's shirt and ripping it.

He tenses a bit, seeming uncomfortable, and he looks up at my eyes once more, waiting for an answer.

"Most likely not," I say honestly and begin wrapping up his leg tightly.

He lets out a heavy sigh and lays back on the ground. "Ack. I thought as much."

I finish and look back at him with a little smile. "I'll make it up to you."

Alistair frowns at me with dubious, half-opened eyes. "Oh? And how do ye plan to do that, lass?"

It's the first time he's called me by any of his endearments in a while, so I suppose that I am—at least in part—forgiven, and I smile. "I'll find a way."

He scoffs and then moves his weight to roll onto his side with a groan, easing himself out of the den.

I crawl away from him and wriggle my way out of the opening and into the bleak, open air. It smells much better out in the open. Less of musk and dirt and soiled clothing and filthy bodies. What is best, though, is the sunlight peeking down from the gray clouds looming overhead of us.

Alistair grunts and groans from behind me, and I turn to help him out of the den entirely. He stumbles a bit and then decides to just sit, breathing hard. Sweat already coats his brow, and my stomach knots up with the prospect of trying to make it back to Karnei with him in this state.

"If you tell me where to go," I offer, "I can run ahead and bring help."

He shakes his head, and my anger coils up.

My lips pin together with insult. Does he really think that I will leave him? That I'll abandon an injured friend out in this wasteland? Does he think so very little of me?

"They'llna trust ye," he says once he catches his breath. "Ye've just burned down a good sections of these woodlands, sweetheart. They'llna be too warmly welcomin of a stray firecat running around. Even if my men have made it to Karnei and alerted the duke of our situation, I'dna trust 'em nay to kill you on sight. Tis best with me."

I release my pent-up breath, and I look to the sky, my body happy for fresh air, even if it is only a few seconds. "So what do we do then?"

He makes a considering sound in the back of his throat and looks up towards the sky. "Tell me about yer run. Which way did ye go and for how long?"

I think for a moment, and then I describe my direction and my general pace including how long it took to find food.

He nods to himself and says, "The wind was blowing northeast when the fire started. Any luck and we're a few miles northeast of Karnei. At a steady pace, we'll reach it by nightfall like as not."

I look him up and down. "Define *steady*."

He shoots me a nasty look. "I can travel just fine. Help me up, lass. Let's get a move on."

"It would be easier for you to hold onto my tigress. Do you think you can manage that?"

He nods, and I turn my back to him for both our sakes and pull off his soiled shirt, tossing it at him behind me. I take my *Shift* and stretch out in the faint sunlight.

It is still cool and crisp outside, but the memory of the sun's warmth while it dances upon my fur lends me some semblance of warmth and comfort.

I shake out my fur and look over at Alistair who has pulled the shirt back over his head and struggles to stand.

He stumbles, but I am right at his side, catching him and helping him to find his balance. Breathless, he gives a little smile and sighs, "Thank ye."

I stare back at him without blinking, my yellow eyes considering his dirty face and the shadow that has begun forming on his jaw. With a short grunt, I look towards the direction I had gone yesterday, nearer to Karnei, and I begin walking. Alistair hops and stumbles beside me. If he had a bit more strength, then he might be able to *Shift*. But even now, I think that if he could manage a *Shift* at all, he would surely collapse, and I would not be able to drag an unconscious bear through the woods.

That night, exhaustion pulls hard at both Alistair and I. My stomach growls almost constantly, and I am becoming weak for want of food. Alistair himself taxes his already worn and weary body by traveling too swiftly, and we both frequently have need to stop and rest. I consider hunting a few times, but Alistair assures me that our time is better spent making our way to Karnei as fast as we can; once we are there, we can eat our fill. The longer it takes to reach Karnei, the lower our chances of survival become.

"Why're ye stoppin?" Alistair barks at me, pain and exhaustion making his patience quite far-gone. He leans heavily on my large tigress form, practically riding on my back and letting me drag him while he hangs on to my beloved orange fur.

I'm going to have bald spots now on my beautiful pelt. Ungrateful wretch. My pretty fur...

I stop and turn my head to narrow my eyes at him.

"We must reach Karnei," he growls, panting hard, his brows knit together in tense focus.

I push him over.

He gives out a little cry and collapses to the ground, breathing hard and struggling to get up.

I *Shift* into a woman once more and stand over him with my hands on my hips. "No. We must rest. We are not far now. I can see smoke in the distance from the town. We will reach it in a few hours, but only after we've slept for the night."

"Scarlet!" he shouts at me.

I crouch down while he pushes himself up on his arms and glares up at me. My yellow-orange eyes glow in the night, locked on him, and I watch him seethe at me. "Go to sleep before I knock you unconscious and just drag you back in the morning."

He watches my eyes for a while, watching the way they glow, like a cat's, little orbs of fire in the darkness. His lids begin to drift closed slowly, and his hold slackens.

I move closer to him, and he scoots away from me, uncomfortable with my nakedness, until at last his arms collapse under him and he lays on his back. Looming over him, I give a wry little smile, holding his gaze and saying in a low, lullaby voice, "Sleep, Alistair. We will reach Karnei soon…"

His eyes struggle to stay open, focusing on mine, intent and determined, but they soon close, and he goes lax upon the ground.

Smirking, I push myself up, sitting down beside him and rubbing out my sore muscles. I look up at the midnight sky, stars peeking down at us from holes in the clouds. I smile just a bit, watching the glittering gems of white, and I *Shift* forms once more, warmer in my tigress form. *Shifting* is taxing though, especially with limited food. When I lay myself down by Alistair, I am spent, and I fall asleep almost instantly.

I wake with the dawn and stretch, looking over at Alistair, who sleeps soundly. He is so very quiet that for a moment, my heart jumps in alarm and terror; I press my head to his chest and hear his heart beat a rhythmic pulse in his chest. I sigh, the knots in my stomach coming undone.

Well, if he plans to sleep all morning, I am going to hunt. We left the scorched woods a few hours back, and now the lush foliage promises breakfast, and I am nearly starved. I should not have need to venture far from Alistair, and so I leave him beneath the tree to go in search of something to eat, hoping for at least a fat hare or a fox. I shake out my fur and push myself on into the foliage to find a meal, hoping for any small parcel, really.

Instead, I find myself a young stag wandering the woods, driven close to the town by the fire. I praise the goddess for my luck and crouch in the brush, ready to spring myself upon the creature. But just as my muscles spring to pounce, something slams into my side. Then, another. I crash onto my side and panting hard.

Two fat arrows with their feathered shafts protrude from my orange flank, and I stare at them with growing fear. The shouts of men reach my ears, and I struggle to catch my breath, pushing myself onto my feet.

I cannot stay here.

I force myself to my feet, heart pounding, and body trembling. Alistair. I must reach Alistair! My mind makes my feet move when my body screams to be left there to die. The stag has run off in fear, and I do the same. The shouts of men grow louder, but I stumble and stagger my way through the underbrush, occasionally jogging, sometimes nearly collapsing.

"Here tis!" a man shouts, much too near to me.

I veer to the side, but not before another arrow slams into me, piercing my back leg. I scream out my agony, staggering and crumpling onto my stomach. I struggle to stand, to move. Fire flickers over my form, but I cannot hold it long enough to protect myself. Alistair! Alistair!

"Hurry! Hurry!"

I hear the voices coming nearer. I can feel the pulse of the earth as their feet pound into the ground towards me.

"Tis an Inferno?"

My world is spinning and darkening. I can't breathe. I'm freezing…I'm so cold…

"'Tis a she-cat! Hurry up! Grab her! Tie her paws!"
Alistair! Ali...stair...

Chapter Seven
Scarlet

The Catacombs of Castle Karnei, Flora

A relentless cold wakes me from my slumber. Colder than before. Icy even. It's like shards of glass in my skin which even the heavy, languishing darkness of sleep cannot keep me from. I am almost grateful. Perhaps without the agonizing cold, I would not have awoken. Perhaps I should thank the cold for keeping me alive.

But what awaits me when I wake is far more frightening than the killing cold.

Water.

Thunder rolls over head and lightning occasionally fills up the catacombs with a brief, white light glistening on the water-soaked ground. I fell asleep sitting upright, and the feeling of icy water up to my mid-calf—soaking me to my lower torso—jerks me to my feet in fear. My exhaustion and weakness are forgotten in an instant as a fear-driven fire floods my veins. I scramble to try and get away from the water, but it is everywhere, pouring down like a small, sputtering waterfall from the opening at the top of the cavern. My head hits the roof of the cavern, and I crouch carefully to try and keep standing.

In my efforts to scramble away, the irons holding my feet reach their limit and lock with resistance. It stops the motion that my muscles had already begun, and—unable to brace myself—I collapse to the ground. A sharp rock slices a gash from my upper thigh to my hip, and I cry out in pain, thrust into darkness with the fading light. It is the dead of night, and I see only black. Some of the lightning is far away and casts me only in shades of gray and black. Others are very near, lighting up my world and the torrent of water pouring in.

I have never known such fear as this. The Inferno who cannot swim; we fear drowning above all else—we cannot live very long without the air in our lungs that lights our lifefires—water is our greatest enemy, the worst of our nightmares. I would sooner have the bears killed me, have died in battle. I would rather have starved or died of my wounds or exhaustion or cold. My weakness and mindless suffering beg for death, but fear of the water forces me to my feet again.

I remember the burning forest, those who are not immune to fear. I remember the scorched nest and the bird trying desperately to save her eggs. I remember the burned carcass of the deer. And I wonder if this is the fear they felt in their dying moments, to be burned alive in a torturous and agonizing death. I have never known such fear as this. It is painful and horrendous.

I scream in agony and terror, turning my voice to the opening in the chasm. I do not know if someone will hear me, if they will realize my plight. My terror is so great that I cannot even form words. I cannot even fathom coherent thoughts. I merely scream, adding to the outpour of water with salted tears that run from my eyes, soaking my misted, dirty face with desperation. I press my back to the sharp wall, feet splashing in the water as more pours in from above.

Was this the fear they felt? Fear of something so painful, so agonizing, as their last moments alive?

I am going to die.

It will not be swift.

It will be slow and painful, and I will be awake for every moment.

It will not be peaceful.

It will not be merciful.

Perhaps this is my punishment for what I have done…the lives I have taken…for all of those who have felt such a moment as this…

Chapter Eight
Claque

On the road to Karnei

I have never particularly liked Scarlet Anita. From the moment Gabriel scooped her up into his arms after that duel and made the decision to carry her back home with us, I knew that she would be nothing but trouble. It is one of the very few times—if not the only time that I can remember—when I have spoken out against Prince Gabriel. Nothing ever struck me as so damning to our entire world as letting that woman into it.

From the very beginning, she began tearing everything apart at the seams, plucking at it piece by piece, gnawing away in tiny intervals. She had the whole castle in a fit trying to keep her alive—numerous times, actually—that I am quite amazed that she was a soldier for so long; it seemed as if the smallest thing would have her bedridden for weeks. It became exhausting and tedious and, frankly, illogical to keep someone so scorned and useless to our world alive.

She was everything that a woman—and a soldier—was not supposed to be. She was rash when she should have been sensible; she was impulsive when she should have been controlled; vicious when she should have had patience; proud when she should have been humbled; arrogant when she should have been cautious; spiteful when she should have been grateful.

And yet…perhaps it was because she was everything that she was not supposed to be that…she began to change everything entirely without even meaning to. She was merciful when she should have been just; she was forgiving when she should have been vindictive; she was determined when she should have been afraid; she was compassionate when she should have been indifferent; she was honorable when she should have been cautious; she was warm when she should have been cold.

For the first time in four years, I saw a spark in my prince that I had not seen in a long time. At first, I thought that it was perhaps that she was an exotic female to have incurred his interest—although after seeing her horrendously scared form beneath the clothes, I cannot have imagined it. Then perhaps, I thought that she merely bothered him and tested his patience, or perhaps the fact that she was fond of his child.

But there was much more to that. She challenged him in ways he never had been before. Here was a woman who had faced more than he ever had—scared and broken, alone and without friend—and yet she thrived. She was fierce, and she fought. After Catherine's death, Gabriel had lived as something of a ghost, a shadow of his former self, and frankly rather useless. She taught him how to fight back. She challenged everything that he thought he knew about his enemy…and about himself. She taught him about war and about hatred; she taught him about mercy and love.

I do not think any of us expected that.

I found myself as perplexed by this woman as I was frustrated by her. And it didn't help that my lovely Dena was completely enamored with her.

I still think that she is too rash, too bold, too arrogant, and far too damn weak. She's nothing but trouble.

But we need her. I think that she is exactly what this country has been waiting for.

She's our last hope.

A Few Days Later

I ride my horse far crueler than I should. I am only gracious enough to the creature so that it does not fail me on my journey, but I have no illusions that the horse will survive this venture. His wobbling gate tells me that I have lamed him at some point of our travels, racing across the country with scarcely any rest. Each time we stop for only a few hours to rest and to eat, and each time I mount again, the horse gives a low protest of agony, not wishing to press on through the pain and exhaustion. But although I am remiss to lose such a great beast, I cannot waste a moment. Karnei does not realize how fragile the Inferno are in our world, especially the little child. And to lose either of them—Prince Gabriel's beloved or his son's *senai*—would be devastating to our relationship with the Flora.

Half way into Flora, rain begins to pour down in sheets upon my horse and I. Despite the deteriorating condition of the roads, the cold actually helps to refresh both man and beast, and my horse picks up with some speed towards Castle Karnei.

We storm into the village in the dead of night, the streets barren of any sane Flora man or woman who would not dare to be out in the storm. Lightning flashes across the sky, and somewhere in the distance, it strikes an unfortunate tree which groans out in protest and collapses onto the earth, shaking the ground with its demise.

Up to the castle and to the gate where two guards stand posted. My person is soaked and my white hair plastered to my head, the ends of it dripping into my eyes. I sputter past the rain on my face and call past the gale, "I am Count Claque of Crystalice! An emissary of Prince Gabriel Jan'tel, heir of

Cerulean! I demand entrance and counsel with Duke Karnei immediately!"

The guards shout to one another and at once push the gate open. My panting and trembling horse drags up the last remaining strength it has to push me past the gates and quickly into the courtyard. I dismount at once, throwing myself off my horse and landing with a thud upon the cobblestone ground. If I'd not been holding on to the reigns, I'd have slipped almost surely. The horse, once I stand, collapses onto the ground, legs tucked under him and panting.

"Put that poor creature out of its misery!" I shout to the stableman who has come to fetch him.

Without deliberation, I make haste into the castle as the sleepy servants wake to attend to me and determine the urgency of my arrival. "Where is Duke Karnei?" I demand at once, rounding on the steward who has been woken by a maid.

He is still in his evening robes, a simple pair of breeches having been hastily pulled over his white tunic which is untucked on one side. "Milord, Duke Karnei's asleep. 'ere an' let me get ye a room for the night, an' I'll get 'im straightaway in the morn."

"No." I narrow my eyes upon the man. "I must speak with him at once at urgent demand from Prince Gabriel."

He turns a few shades paler and bobs a quick and clumsy nod before hurrying down the hall, tucking his shirt in a bit better as he goes fumbling up the stairs. Finally, I take the time to wipe my face and push my hair back out of the way, rounding on the nearest maid. She stands by with confusion and appropriate concern.

"Where is the Inferno child? Is she alive?"

The woman jumps and nods quickly. "A-Aye, sir. Last we checked on 'er was at suppertime. She'd nay eat, but she was 'live and hissin."

"Where is she? Have someone bring me some raw meat in small strips."

The maid quickly turns to another, younger, miss beside her, who goes scurrying off to do as she was told. The other leads me, with candelabra in hand, down the hall and up the stairs.

"We set 'er up in a room near Duke Alistair. We tried to put 'er with him to see if it'd help, but we couldna tend the lord with her hissin an' bitin at 'nyone near 'er."

I do not respond to the woman, and apparently that makes her even more uncomfortable, for she hastens her pace, practically running up the stairs, all hint of sleep gone from her person. Three doors down on the right hand side, she stops and pushes the door open, leading me inside with her candelabra to light the way. She takes the time to go and light the other candles in the room, for the young she-cat is not at once visible.

Fear strikes my heart—for not only would I not wish death upon a little child, but I am also well aware of the vengeance that would ensure. And Prince Gabriel could very rightly take retribution on a man who had, through neglect, killed his son's *senai*. As light slowly floods the room, even still the cat cannot be found. Not in the empty hearth or against the chest, not by the windows.

Finally, I drop to my knees and peer under the bed. "Here," I call to the woman. "Hand me that candle."

I reach out my hand, and she places the wax candle within it. Carefully, I dip the candle under the bed, careful to not set it on fire. There, in the far back corner under the bed, a very skinny tigress cub is curled up in a ball, wedged up tight. "*Clk, clk*," I click my tongue at the child. She doesn't stir.

"Sir," the young maid calls from the door. "The meat you asked for."

I glance at her feet from under the bed. "Good. Set it there. Light that fire in the hearth and get me a mug of hot milk; hot as you can. Now!" Both women start scrambling, the older one at the fire and the younger one hurrying off.

I grab a piece of meat and stick it under the bed, wiggling it in front of the kitten. "*Clk, clk* here, kit-kit. *Schwooot!*" I let out a sharp whistle, and it seems to catch her attention.

Dull, black eyes crack open, and she turns her head to look at me. Her nose flares up in warning.

"Easy there, kit-kit," I coo gently. "Remember me? Claque...remember from Crystalice? When Thomas brought you home?"

She lets out a slow, quiet yowl. She's weak.

"*Tst, tst,*" I croon. "It's alright. I'm a friend of Lady Scarlet. I'm here to get you both."

She hisses at me, her ears flat against her head.

"Here now, kit-kit," I call, a bit more firmly. The meat is not going to work. She's too agitated and afraid; I can see her shaking from here, even in the darkness. "Do you wish to come find Scarlet with me? Come on...let's go see her together."

She pauses and seems to consider it for a moment, but then she snarls at me again.

I can't reach her from where I'm at. My arm isn't long enough. "Here, you," I call. I hear the fire behind me start crackling. "Come on. Let's go and get Lady Scarlet."

Her yowl turns into a scream, and she lurches at my wrist, biting down.

"Gotcha." I yank my arm out before she can let go, and I grab her by the scruff.

She screams and yelps, thrashing in my hand with renewed strength. I can feel icy blood trickling down my wrist and hand.

"Here, sir!" the young maid calls, shaking nearby with the mug of hot milk. It's steaming and practically boiling in the mug.

Sitting down on the bed, I pry the cat's mouth open with my hand as the women stand back with great concern. She is too cold to burn me, but I am certain that my icy touch wounds her, and so I try to move swiftly.

"Here, you. You're not allowed to die." I grab the mug from the woman, having to use my thighs to hold down the twenty—maybe thirty— pound kitten. I hold her mouth open as she chews and snarls at me, and taking the mug, I carefully pour some milk down her throat.

"Here, here, now!" I hear Karnei down the hall.

The kitten gags on the milk, coughing it back.

I pause and then start pouring carefully again while she struggles. This time, some gets down her throat.

Duke Karnei comes through the door of the child's room, looking hastily dressed and only partially awake. "What the devil's going on here!" he roars.

The duke is a rather impressive man despite his age, old and with piercing eyes, a firm set to his jaw. He is bald and with a gruffly shaven jaw, but it does nothing to diminish the fierceness of his gaze or the hard set to his frame. He might have once been a tall man before age bent him over, and what was once strength in his gait and arms is now mostly fat. Nevertheless, he is an imposing man who fills a room with his presence.

"Where is the Lady Scarlet?" I demand, looking back to the hissing cat who digs holes and cuts in my fingers with her burning fangs while I carefully pour a large mug of hot milk down her throat.

"Who are you? My man tells me you're from Crystalice." He watches me with the cat, apparently uncertain of whether to stop me or help me.

"Emissary of Prince Gabriel. Count of Crystalice and betrothed to Princess Denair Jan'tel. Where are you keeping Lady Scarlet? I do not believe you are aware of the precarious condition of Inferno in unfired lands."

Karnei seemed to struggle with words for a bit as I forced more milk down the kitten's throat. "In the catacombs. We used to use it as a dungeon before our cells were constructed, but as they are mostly wood, I didn't want her burning the whole damned thing down."

"The catacombs?" I ask, a sense of dread and urgency filling me at once. "Underground catacombs?"

"Yes, yes, naturally. Fireproof."

"You imbecile!" I roar, standing to my full height. "Have you no head to the storms! The catacombs will flood!"

The man suddenly shrinks back and pales considerably. "Oh goddess…" He snaps out of his horror and snaps, "Quickly! Quickly! I will take you myself!"

I drop the mug of milk, too impatient to set it down, and I take the writhing cat and toss her into the fire.

The women scream in terror.

"It won't hurt her!" I bark at them as I march to the door. "Keep her in there! Put up the grate!"

They look at me with fear and hesitation, and I pause only long enough to make sure that they continue to cage the kitten in the burning hearth.

Chapter Nine
Scarlet

The Catacombs of Castle Karnei, Flora

The water is rising higher and higher. Soon, it will overcome me. I've managed to push my head some ways up the shaft in the cavern, letting in both the water killing me and the air keeping me alive. I gasp in both simultaneously, coughing up the water and sucking in more of both once more. Water splatters on my face and in my eyes, and I am swallowed in the darkness of the night.

I do not dare use any of my breath to scream anymore. No one is coming. I don't know why I continue to fight, honestly. I am going to die here. I know it. Yet, I cannot resign myself to drowning. I should just give up and go under and let it be finished with, burn up my energy faster to try and make the suffering end. But I cannot. I do not have the strength of will enough to hurry along my death.

The water is at my ears now. There is no portion of the cavern left that is not filled with water. My shoulders grind against the ceiling over the cavern as I try to push my face further against the opening, swallowing in more water than air now; the skin is rubbed completely raw if there is any left at all. My heart is pounding. I don't see the lightning anymore, only darkness.

The water is at my cheeks.

My feet scramble against the floor, scratching and scraping the skin away as I desperately push myself towards the opening. I step too far and the irons catch me. I go under with a gasp, sucking in water. My body immediately tries to expel the foul liquid, but there is no air to suck in. I scramble to find my footing and push myself up, my shackled wrists against my chest as I straighten my body. I cannot tell up from down, and I do not know if it is from the water carrying me or the death overtaking me. My head slams against the ceiling and sharp shards of roof break against my skull. More blood in the water.

I can't find the opening.

I try again, pushing against the ground. My head hits the roof.

Where is it? Where is it!

I can't find the opening.

I bend my knees to try again, but I can't move them out. I try to straighten my legs, to push against the ground. One more time. I just need to try one more time…but I can't move …the back of my head brushes against the roof of the cavern.

…just one more…time…

Chapter Ten
Claque

Castle Karnei, Flora

"Here! Here!" Duke Karnei calls. He wasted no time in bringing me to the caverns and is now just as soaked as I am. He and I wade through calf-high water rushing through the catacombs, marching our way through to the cavern where Scarlet is being held. Each moment pounds away at my chest with fear and a certainty that when we arrive, it'll be too late.

"Here it is!" he says again, coming to a wall in the cavern. He calls on his *Magik* and pushes the wall away, splitting it in two. Almost at once, water comes gushing out, pouring out up to our waists. I have to brace myself to keep from falling over, but Karnei falls back. He quickly stands up, sputtering, and the water recedes to calf-level again, if not a little higher.

I hold on to the edge of the wall as the water runs out of the cavern, coming in from the hole in the ceiling that I assume was to make sure that she had plenty of air and instead may have led to her death.

"Lady Scarlet!" I call, but when Karnei was knocked down, his lantern went with him. I throw my head back behind me to the guards who had followed us. "Quick! Give me a torch!" One of the soldiers hurries up and hands me one as I step into the dark cavern.

There on the floor, beneath the slow flood of water pouring in, a pale and bluish woman lies naked and bound in irons, still half-buried under water.

"Lady Scarlet!" I rush in, thrusting the torch back into the guard's hand as he stares and watches in horror and dread while I gather the freezing cold woman in my hands. A tug of irons calls my attention; I freeze the chains until they are brittle, and they shatter with little effort. "Move!" I shout to get Karnei out of my way so that I can carry Scarlet out of the chamber.

"Air—she needs air—she needs air—" My mind races to come to a solution, and I quickly lay her on one of the shelves of the catacombs, turning her head up and opening her mouth, just as I did with the cat. I only wish this cat was biting and clawing at me. I press my mouth to hers, blowing air down her throat.

I pull back and watch her, but she remains still. Again, I press my mouth to hers, pushing air in. Nothing. Is her throat open? I press my fingers into her mouth to try and make sure her throat is clear, and then I try again, pushing air back into her lungs.

Finally, her body convulses, and she begins coughing and choking. I help her lean onto her side without falling off the shelf, and she coughs up more and more water, vomiting nearly as much up from her stomach as well. I hold her steady as she shudders and expels all of the water from her insides, retching in agony. She is so thin, grayish and twigish in my arms.

Turning my head, I shout to one of the guards hovering over me.

Even Karnei looks on with fear and concern. At the very least, his urgency to find her and his horror at her state tells me that, while he was negligent, he was at least ignorant in her suffering.

"Go and light a fire in the great hall! As hot as you can manage!" A hot bath was usually how we treated her at home but—as with the kitten—we don't have the luxury of waiting on boiling water, and she needs something hotter still. I only hope that raw fire will be just as healing for her.

With the naked woman now still but breathing, I gather her up again and lean over her as I carry her out of the catacombs and back out into the rain.

The guards and Karnei all follow, Karnei shouting orders for a room to be made with a coal pan to heat the bed and a warm fire made ready in the hearth.

By the time we reach the shelter of the castle, Scarlet's condition has not improved in the slightest. I am not sure if she is still breathing or if her abused organs have finally given up after all their years of torment. We Nephilim are hardy creatures, but we are not immortal.

Nearly all of the castle is awake now, either bustling about in the dead of night to help prepare the rooms or tend the kitten or stoke the fire; else they stand around nervously watching everyone else and trying to figure out what has happened. The fire in the hearth is not yet full, but it has at least started up.

"Keep it going," I tell the servant. "Add as many logs as you need. Get this fire as hot and large as you can…we'll pray this works."

I cannot throw the woman into the hearth as I did the kitten. The kitten was quite awake and feisty. The woman bleeds from all over, her head, her hip. There are fresh wounds in her side and leg that have begun bleeding anew. Her shoulders and her feet do not seem to have any skin left at all, dripping as much blood as water.

As careful as I can manage, I draw her towards the burning hearth. I lean my knee upon the edge and reach into the burning chamber. Fire licks at my hands first, and then my arms. I wince as it hisses, searing my flesh. My sleeves burn up, and by the time I have set Scarlet carefully in the back of the furnace, my flesh has begun melting away.

The pain is intense, a torment consuming me as I withdraw from the fire. But as I do so, I hear a sound—a soft sigh—and it is enough. The pain is worth knowing that her life is spared.

I do not know if she will live, but at least she has a chance. She's not dead yet at least.

Beside me, Karnei sinks into a chair, soaked and trembling and gazing off at nothing.

"Here, sire," a maid says, bringing him a cloth to dry his face.

He says nothing to her but huffs a few breaths and takes the cloth, dabbing at his dripping face with a shaking hand, panting hard and still quite pale.

I stand there and wait for him to recover, arms trembling with pain at my sides, the skin burned away, leaving the muscle and sinew exposed. The sleeves remaining at my elbows are melted into my flesh like a seam. I breathe a bit harder, watching him, focusing on my task at hand to ignore the agony ripping up my arms and searing every nerve.

"You nearly killed her," I bite at him. "Without cause or reason, your men injured her, and by your order, resulted in her torture and nearly her death."

He shakes his head, dabbing uselessly at his face once more. "That was not my intent. Not at all. I wanted to put her somewhere she couldn't hurt anyone. I sent her hot food. If she was cold, she could have turned back into a cat—"

"She did not have the strength to turn back."

He stops then and looks at my face, focusing on me. All around us, servants run about, adding logs to the fire, bringing charms to place upon the hearth to build it higher and protect the chimney from the rain outside.

"I did not know," Karnei rasps.

My eyes narrow into slits. "That does not matter. It doesn't take away what you did. Your actions could have resulted in a cease-aid from Cerulean if not severe military repercussions which, quite frankly, *sir*, your country cannot afford. Your intentions do not matter."

He watches me and then nods slowly, holding the rag in his hand, water running down his face as he stares intently past me. "No, no…you are right…I allowed my fear to control me without reason…"

He looks up to me then, his jaw set firmly once more, his eyes once more piercing, and he sits up a bit straighter in his chair. "Regardless of if the Lady Scarlet was responsible for the fire or under what intention, I would never condone the ill treatment she has received. Now that we are aware of her condition, she will be tended with the utmost care and caution until we can surmise the nature of the forest fire. When we have information, we will send word to Prince Gabriel with our recommendation if Duke Alistair is not yet recovered."

I incline my head to him, but before I can speak, Karnei calls out, "Good gods, man! Your arms!" He stands up and once and calls to the servants, "Go and fetch the village healer! Bring some iced water and scissors and brandy! Hurry now!"

He moves aside and gestures to the chair. "Please have a seat, Count Claque. Let us tend your wounds as well."

"I will stand."

PART ONE

It is easier to find men who will volunteer to die, than to find those who are willing to endure pain with patience.
-Julius Caesar

Chapter Eleven
Scarlet

Three days after leaving Marine
The Karnei Forest, Flora

"Gabriel's a'might fine liar, he is," Alistair says to me.

I pick up my head, jostling faintly from side to side as my mount picks his way neatly among the dirt path. We'd gone as far as we could yesterday and stopped at a little town at the border—the last town we will see before we reach Karnei. And now we've two more days left to ride. At least the weather is fair. Sunlight peeks down at us from behind the canopy of trees, speckling our faces and occasionally blinding us. It is cool in the shade, so I've left my cloak on and pulled up the hood, but the Flora do not seem bothered in the least, particularly Alistair who wears only a thin, brown shirt under his leather jerkin. Just looking at him makes me cold even with my long-sleeved garments.

"Hm?" I ask, not entirely sure I'd heard or understood Alistair.

He cocks a little smile, turning his wry gaze away from me and back to the lead. "I said that Gabriel's a fine liar."

I frown, not understanding. "How so?"

He sighs, a bit put-upon by the sound of it. "He warned me ye were a noisy creature if e'er he'd heard one and liable to talk my ear off. But I've scarce heard a word out of ye since we left Marine, lassie."

Color tints my cheeks a bit, and I feel warm again. "Would you prefer I talk you senseless?"

He laughs then, and the sound fills the whole forest.

It had been a quiet ride, and for his laughter to suddenly break through, loud and warm, is almost intrusive, but in a pleasant sort of way. Our traveling companions murmur to themselves, as if Alistair's laughter had broken whatever ban upon speaking there had been before.

"I'dna mind such a thing so long as ye'd speak. Else this will surely be a very long few days."

He's such an odd creature, and I smile just a bit, happy to leave my melancholy thoughts behind and ask, "Then what should we speak on, Alistair?"

"Ah, anything, my lass," he says, and I can nearly see the happy smile upon his face as he rides.

I smile, feeling lighter for it. "*Aye* then," I tease in a fake Flora accent. "What is Maeghdra like? Is it like this place?"

"Hm," says he, scratching the scruff on his jaw and peering up at the canopy. "Aye and nay. Tis colder than this place since tis up near the mountains, but tis also late spring now. Summer will be hotter."

"Spring…summer…so Flora has seasons? Like the Levosa?"

He nods. "Aye, lass. Summer's hot and humid, and winter's a might cold, 'specially in the mountains." He glances back to me. "Ye'll see a heap'a snow, but nay near as much as Crystalice. And we've many more hearths and thicker clothes. We'll make certain ye'd nay suffer for warmth."

I give a single nod as thanks, feeling still a bit disheartened at the prospect of snow once again. I am not looking forward to its biting chill and neither for the reminder of what I have left behind. "It's…alright." I tell him.

He frowns back at me, trying to understand, no doubt, why I have gone meek and mild once more.

I do not mean to. It is not as though I wish to draw attention to my morose state. It is simply that…everything else seems to take too much energy. Smiling, talking, laughing. It hurts. It's exhausting. I just—I do not wish to do those things. But I also do not enjoy how Alistair focuses upon my unhappiness with resolve, and I decide to continue the conversation.

"Tell me of your home. Do you live in a castle or something more like the Den?"

He chuckles a bit and says, "I've ne'er seen the Den, so I dinna ken, but tis far from a castle. Maeghdra Manor… more is like a very large home. Only family and servants live there, and many o'the servants live instead in the town and merely return at dawn and leave after nightfall."

"I see," I reply. "And what family have you that lives there?"

"Ah, just me mam," says he. "She runs the manor and the town of Maeghdra. I'm away too much to be o'much use. Flora isn't a matriarchy like Crystalice, but tis nay uncommon for women to run certain establishments as me mam has done since my father died."

"I see…what will Zsoka and I do then?"

Again, he scratches at his scruff, saying, "Well, I've nay really thought of it. Mam will know what best to do with ye. Zsoka will probably begin lessons soon. Yell like as not just be expected to stay beside her and keep her out o'trouble and to help others with her—since not many of us have ever met an Inferno. I'll warrant there are some key particular differences they'll be needing to ken."

"Like what?"

He laughs. "Well, for starters, the fact that ye can eat just as much as I can and still look like ye could eat more and yet ye're no bigger than a wee mite."

Although I have no idea what a mite is, I blush with embarrassment. There's nothing wrong with how much I eat. Inferno burn hot. We need the fuel to stay alive. The Flora eat about three times a day, average sized meals, I suppose. I eat as much or more if I can help it without being rude.

Alistair looks back at me and grins. "Och. Dinna pout, lass. I fancy ye right fine as ye are."

"Alistair." My voice drops low with warning, and he pauses to look at me with confusion before his eyes follow mine.

He brings his hand up, and our company stops.

There. Ahead of us. Three men block the road quite intently. The leader is mounted center on a gray horse, and his two companions bring up either side, thoroughly preventing passage. They are large—Flora—and dressed in browns and greens that blend in with the forested world around them. But they are not so large as Alistair who is a clear reminder that most Flora have the second form of a bear, his in particular a brown bear from what Gabriel tells me. Judging by their size, these men are more likely their smaller, northern cousins, the black bears.

"Hail," Alistair calls, a bit warily. He straightens his back and squares his shoulders. I watch his eyes skim our surroundings.

Gabriel warned me before we left not to announce my Inferno blood if I could help it, and I draw my hood up further over my head, hiding my dark skin and copper hair. Zsoka has her hood up as well, but she cannot help but look up and around with fear, announcing her presence. For now, I do not speak, merely scent the air quietly. There are more men…three, maybe four to our right, two to the left, three more behind us. Damnit.

It's an ambush.

"What business have ye?" Alistair calls.

The man ahead of us gives a wide smile. "Peace, travelers," he falsely assures us. "We're merely a company o'poor vagabonds. We mean nay harm."

Alistair inclines his head. "If ye mean us nay harm, then why d'ye block our path?"

I am a bit uncertain as to why Alistair does not announce himself by title. Or perhaps that would put us even more in danger? Most likely, if he reveals himself as a duke, it would signify they he carries something of value or that he would be of some value to someone.

"Ah, tis a toll road, ye see." says the man. "We'll just collect our fee an' be on our way."

Alistair nods. "Aye an' aye…If ye'd nay mind letting me see yer permit o'collections from the Duke of Karnei, and I'll pay whatever the fee is."

The man's smile falters, and then he grins. "Och, but we're nay under the Duke of Karnei. We's the only law on these roads hereabouts. So we'll be taking whate'er goods ye have on ye as our fee an' get on."

Alistair draws then, and so do my guards.

I've a dagger in my boot, but nothing else, and I make note in my head to find a solid bow and quiver of arrows when next I am able.

"Och," Alistair goes on, "But I'm afraid that's nay an acceptable answer, good sir. Ye'll move on now, or ye'll be a'might sorry for it."

The man grins, and Zsoka whimpers softly, "Mama…"

I glance back to her and grit my teeth. "Zsoka, stay close to me," I say quietly.

For a moment, no one moves. Nothing happens. We all sit awkwardly on our horses for the longest minute I've ever lived, and the tension in my neck begins to make my head hurt. I'm almost too tense to breathe.

But then, there's a snap of a branch beside us, and it's as if that single sound sets us all moving. Vagabonds descend upon us with shouts and crude threats, engaging our guards behind and beside me.

Zsoka screams despite herself, and I give out a furious roar as a thief grabs her horse and tries to push her off. I throw myself off my horse and land on him, taking him to the ground.

Getting the dagger out beneath a cloak and skirts takes a bit of work, but I yank it out and jab it in his neck.

Here is no different from the war. Fighting for my people or fighting for my life. I don't take prisoners. Images flash before my eyes of soldiers screaming, a forest burning. I see arrows flying overhead and a sword swinging at my face. But then the image is gone, and I am left before the troupe of miscreants again.

"Tis that!" a man screams, and I stand to my feet before Zsoka's horse. I can hear her cries, and her pony whines uneasily, jerking against my hold on the reigns.

"Look at it!"

"Red hair!"

"Them eyes!"

"An Inferno!"

My hood was knocked back in the jump, and I stand before them unveiled in the patchwork of shadows beneath the canopy of trees.

It is a strange place for a fight. The sun is so bright and peaks down on us from between the leaves. A nice breeze wafts through the branches and stirs up a sweet, whispered lullaby. It is the perfect day for a lazy nap against a trunk.

Alistair calls my name, along with some order than I do not pay any heed to.

"Give me your sword!" I shout to one of the guards. "Take the duke's ward and get out of here!"

I throw him the reigns, and he looks hesitantly at me before Alistair shouts something at him, and the man mounts his own horse and takes off at a furious speed, leading the pony with the girl clinging to its mane with him.

On the ground is the sword he left for me, and I lunge for it, knocking a man out of the way and narrowly avoiding a dirk. I come up from my crouch and slice open one man's belly. These men are pathetic.

Most of them don't even know how to hold their own weapons right and their balance is pitiful; they leave themselves wide open and can barely even block a blow. They are used to simple travelers, but not to experienced soldiers. And they are certainly not used to one of my kind.

Not all of them, however, are worthless, and there are nearly three or four for every one of our party. I may be a skilled swordswoman, but I am not entirely recovered, and I only have one sword and two eyes. I cannot fight four men who are trying to kill me at once. Those stories are only for legends, not battlefields.

A man behind me charges, and I manage to jump out of the way and let him tumble into the man I had engaged in a fight.

I bump into someone else, and he delivers a stab to my shoulder more by accident than anything—which shows just how out of practice I am. Swearing, I toss my sword—which is much too heavy for me in any case—to the side and rip open my dress.

The sight of my bared chest is enough to distract them for the moment for me to *Shift*. Stupid men. By the time they realize why I ripped my clothes, it is too late, and my *Shift* is complete. I land upon the first man and grab him in my jaws, shredding and running at the same time to avoid swords.

The man is dead in my mouth, and I drop him but miss the sound of someone behind me.

I whirl around with no way to block the blow, but a sword reaches over me and knocks the enemy blade away.

Alistair moves to my side, back to me, and he fights off the attacker. "Welcome to Flora, lass!" he calls, grinning a bit, although it's more of a grimace as he forces back the other man and swings at him.

I cannot respond in my form, but I give a low yowl and turn my attention to another of the vagabonds after our remaining horses. I launch myself at him, but rather than engage me, he runs. "Get out o'here, men! T'aint worth it!" the leader calls, and those who have horses mount up while the others follow on foot.

I snarl at them, and a loud roar echoes through the trees.

The men pour off the main road, and I hiss in rage at their cowardice. I have nothing against strategic retreats and their value in battle. But they have accosted my own and frightened my little child. They are not getting away so easily.

My rage boils over, and flame fills my fur, floating over my form.

"Scarlet, nay, lass!" Alistair calls after me, but I charge into the woods after the men, dodging shrub and tree, following the sounds of their rampaging, their fleeing.

I am faster than the ones on foot. Much faster. It takes barely more than a heartbeat to catch up with them.

Chapter Twelve
Scarlet

I gasp in a breath as I wake, stirring from my slumber. With a sigh, I swallow and clench my eyes, sitting up and rubbing my face. When I open my eyes, I see sunlight streaming in through the windows and warming my back. Alistair is still sleeping in front of me, and Zsoka too. He lays on his back on the bed, breathing slow and deep. At least some of his color's returned. The healers tell me that the infection had managed to get into his blood. They've had a time of purifying it and keeping it from killing him. The wound itself isn't so bad and has mostly healed up, but they've had to bleed him out quite a bit and use a hollow needle to put some sort of potion into his blood.

Standing up, I lean over him and smooth his tawny-blond hair out of his face to kiss his brow. "Be well," I murmur softly, leaning my brow against his. He's woken some, but never for very long and rarely coherent enough to get anything more than drugged murmurs out of him. It's best he rest now, anyways.

My little cub is happily curled up at his side. She fell asleep with his hand on her back near where he'd been scratching behind her ears. She's fattened up some, and her pelt is a little brighter now, but she—like myself—has a good deal longer to go before she is completely healed. I wish to reach out and pet her head, but I am afraid of waking her; so instead, I stand up out of my chair where I'd fallen asleep with my head on Alistair's leg.

By the time I woke from my slumber in the fire, Claque was gone. Karnei told me that he'd wanted to stay until I recovered, but after four days of sleeping and signs that Zsoka and I were improving, he was content enough to leave me and urgent enough to return home. Once I could come out of the hearth—and that was marvelous thinking on Claque's part— I was set up in a room, and Karnei only told me to come and see him in his study when I was able.

I slept for a day or so with Zsoka at my side before coming in to check on Alistair. I hate to see him in this condition, knowing that it is my fault that he suffers so. I nearly killed him with my carelessness.

"I'm sorry…" I whisper pitifully, reaching out to touch his hand once more before walking quietly to the door. I slip out carefully and shut it behind me before sighing and closing my eyes.

I am tired, and I still feel so weak and heavy. When I become too tired, it often becomes difficult to catch my breath, and at once, a panic strikes me. For an instant, I forget that I am safe and I am suddenly thrown into the memory of the flooding cavern. Even so, there are things that I must attend to before I can rest, and one of those happens to be Karnei.

A maid in the hall shows me to his study, knocking quietly and opening the door at his command, showing me inside.

His study, like most of the Karnei castle that I have seen so far, is built and designed with simplicity and functionality at the forefront of importance. The wood door is solid and square, fitting perfectly into the frame. The study itself is neatly arranged, every nook and cranny taken advantage of for functional purposes. One nook holds a collection of scrolls while a small bench holds some books stacked up neatly. There are no flowers and no paintings, neither tapestries nor decorations. Not that it isn't a comfortable and quaint room, simply one without adornment.

It is much like Duke Karnei himself. He sits on a sturdy, wooden chair with a simple, green cushion. Despite his rank as essentially one of the three kings of Flora, he is clothed only in a gray shirt and brown tunic with lambskin slacks, spectacles hinging on the bridge of a broad, straight nose. "Lady Scarlet," he greets, pushing the chair back to stand at his full height.

He is a man of impressive size, or at least one who might have been in his prime. I am certain that he is long past his prime now, and yet I pity whoever would mistake him for a simple, old man.

Lifting my chin, I respond, "I am she. You are the Duke Karnei?"

He inclines his head. For a moment, he merely watches me with those glassy, green-gray eyes, his posture neither submissive and nor intimidating. He is a man who is comfortable in his own environment without feeling threatened.

"Please," he says in a low, smooth voice, gesturing to a smaller chair beside the desk. "Have a seat."

Although I would prefer to stand, I would also prefer not to insult my host. I might very well wind up back in the caverns that way. And so, I walk quietly into the room, my eyes never quite leaving Karnei's. My blue skirts rustle faintly against my legs, and I tuck them under me as I carefully take my seat. Sitting or standing, I am still in pain. If I stand, my leg aches from the healing arrow wound. If I sit, my sides hurt from the other arrow wounds and the cut in my hip.

Once I am adjusted and as comfortable as I can be, I sit back a bit and return my attention to Karnei. He has set himself back down in his chair and rests his arms patiently on the armrests. He watches me with a quiet, inoffensive expression, waiting for…something, I suppose. But he is the one who asked to meet with me, and so I shall wait until he is comfortable. I fold my hands neatly on my lap, watching him with the patience of a cat who can sit and wait all day.

"You seem uneasy," he says, almost to himself.

I tip my head a bit to the side and reply, "I am merely trying to decide if I am among friend or foe."

He gives a slow, sad smile and a single nod, sighing. "You entered the castle as my foe, Lady Scarlet…but I should hope …that you will part from it as my friend."

After a moment, he sighs a bit and shifts some in his seat. "Lady Scarlet, to begin with…I must—humbly—ask your forgiveness."

I narrow my eyes a bit.

"When I placed you in those catacombs, I did not realize the harm I was incurring. It was not—I am rather ashamed that…"

He sighs with frustration and leans forward a bit, folding his hands in front of him. "There are no excuses for what I have done. Especially to a woman. Women are prized in our culture as ones who bring life into the world and who tend to the home with care and devotion. It is a severe crime in our world to wage war on women…and your treatment is unforgiveable."

I watch him for a while, considering what to say. "Hm… Flora and Crystalice are a good deal alike." What I said is not what I meant to say, but I suppose it will do.

He raises a brow. "Oh?"

I incline my head. "Indeed. I heard something very similar once when I was there."

"You disagree?" He asks curiously.

I tip my head a bit, considering. "Hmm...we are physically weaker; that cannot be denied. But what we lack in brute strength, we make up for in other ways. Likewise, what men often lack emotionally and logically is also made up for in other ways."

At first he seems offended, but then realizes that I am only teasing the male race, and he smiles faintly. "I tend to find that the males and females complement each other...and together, they make up for the other and form a perfect pair. Where one is weak, the other is strong. I do not see either in need of being protected or being praised in any way that the light is better than the darkness."

He frowns once more. "Is not the light greater than the darkness?"

I smile faintly and reply, "I do not think so. They are both compliments much the same. The light gives warmth and growth. It illuminates our way and provides great joy was well. But the darkness brings us rest. It brings us relief from our weary toil and torment. It gives us safety from our over-long exposure. You cannot say that one is better than the other. Where one is weak, the other is strong, and you would be remiss in denying yourself either or in making one master over the other."

He nods slowly, still leaned over his hand and considering me. "What a very curious woman you are, Lady Scarlet."

"Scarlet is fine," I tell him simply. "I have no title in these lands, nor in Cerulean. There is no need to call me any name but my given one."

"Scarlet then." He sits back in his chair, watching me. "If you would please, my dear...we have not found your traveling companions; your child-cat will not speak; and Alistair slumbers still. We are all rather ignorant as to what transpired in the woods some weeks ago. All that I know is that nearly half my territory is burned down."

"So much?" I ask miserably, looking up at him and slumping my shoulders some. I look down to my hands in my lap and begin to rub them together somewhat, my thumbs caressing the palms and backs, rubbing into them nervously and guiltily.

I shake my head and say, "We were ambushed by thieves…I *Shifted* and went after them, on fire as I went and chased them down…Alistair warned me not to hunt them; he tried to tell me, but…I wouldn't listen."

Raising my eyes, I look to him and straighten some. "The fire in North Karnei is of my own fault. It was not my intention to cause damage to your homeland, but I am its cause nonetheless. I am prepared to accept responsibility for my actions."

Karnei studies me for a long, slow moment. Then, he rubs at the stubble on his jaw and leans his elbow on the table. "It would seem, Lady Scarlet, that we are both apt to cause harm that we do not intend. I would be no more to blame to seek vengeance for the wrong against me than you would be to seek vengeance for the wrongs I have done to you."

He sits a bit straighter and continues, "Even so…none of my people, none of my crops were harmed. The loss of the woods and the animals is very sorrowful to me…but it has not caused much harm now that I am certain your intent was not malicious. However, although my intent likewise was not malicious, you were abused, tortured, and nearly killed at my hands—and that is great harm indeed."

He stands, looking down upon me, and says, "The debt between us is not settled, Lady Scarlet…for the balance between my loss and yours is not the same."

He drops slowly to the ground, kneeling before me and putting his right fist over his left shoulder. "I ask for your forgiveness, my lady. Forgiveness which I do not deserve."

I stare at him, heart pounding in my ears and throat dry, rather uncomfortable and unsure of what to say. I bite my lip a bit and try to think of something that isn't completely foolish, saying, "Please, Duke Karnei…I hold nothing against you so long as you do not place me back."

I give a nervous laugh that he does not echo, looking up at me. "I am merely grateful for the care you took of myself and Zsoka, and Alistair of course. All I ask is that we leave here in peace."

He stands, slowly, carefully and I am tempted to rise and help him, except that I would likely land us both on the floor. Even so, he manages to come to his full height without my aid, and I am left sitting in the chair rather uncertainly. "You have my word," he vows, and as I watch him there—a proud and aged man of a dying breed—I cannot help but smile, and I believe him.

Chapter Thirteen
Gabriel

The Crystalice Palace, Cerulean

It takes a sennight for Claque to return to Crystalice.

I wish that I could say that I was far too busy to notice his absence, but although I was quite busy indeed, his absence was not only a cause for great concern for me, it was also a severe detriment to my effectiveness as well. I am not completely useless on my own; I understand politics and finances quite well, but I lack the patience and tact that comes with age, and so many of these councilors—both young and old—are belligerent enough to drive me mad.

Claque has a knack for redirecting the conversation or slipping in a few choice words or statements that at least give me a few moments to collect my thoughts and decide what to say. Besides all that, it doesn't make it any easier with my father staring down at me from his seat at the end of the table, watching and waiting for me to slip up, and my sister, Petara, undermines everything that I say and do in an irritatingly subversive sort of way.

Moreover, Claque provides an excellent excuse to not have to deal with my father after the meeting when he dismisses everyone but myself—since clearly, I have nothing better to do with my time—and asks my opinion on the meeting. No specific question, no hint as to what sort of answer he's looking for, just a simple: Well, Gabriel, what did you think of that exchange?

It's not even that I'm particularly afraid of my father so much that incurring his wrath is likely to lead to a torrent of a rampage that will take far more time and effort to appease than is reasonable, and *that* is truly a waste of my time.

And even with all of that, my mind and my heart are constantly torn, filled with thoughts of Cara and the little Zsoka. I fear the worst for them and for what they have suffered. I fear for Alistair who, as I am aware, remains in a catatonic state. I am helpless to do anything for any of them, and yet I desire to do anything and everything for them, regardless of the cost.

"You are troubled, my son."

The hall is dark and quiet, and as usual, I cannot sleep. My room feels too small and too tight, particularly with the door leading into Catherine's—and Cara's—old room looming anxiously nearby. Most of the castle slumbers with the exception of the guard. I had not expected to find my mother lurking near.

It has been a long time since I have seen her so casually dressed. My mother is something of a performer, always putting on a show for those around her. It is not to discredit her that I speak thus of her, only that she is constantly watched and judged by everyone around her, and she is keenly aware of that. Every aspect of her hair, her dress, her mannerisms, her words. Everything is specifically arranged and catered to what they expect to see in her.

And so it is rather disarming to see her standing next to me, two heads shorter and dressed in only a simple nightgown and a heavy, damask robe pulled over it and tied with a golden cord at the waist. Her long, silver hair is braided and pulled over her right shoulder, no ornaments, no finery. And yet, she still looks no less than a queen to me—so regal and tall, even without the hoops and ornament and finery.

"Ah—no, I mean, yes…but do not let it trouble you, mother," I tell her, giving a tired smile.

She smiles softly at me and then looks out of the window nearest us and gives a long, slow sigh. "I find it difficult to sleep as well…come…join me in my study for some tea." Before I can protest, she adds, "I would be glad of the company."

I sigh out a little agreement and follow her to her solar. Past the double-doors, a private sitting area waits, neatly groomed and ornamented with statues and paintings, all quaint and calm and yet subtly powerful, like the tall wave in an ocean, or the fierce expression in the goddess' marble gaze.

Mother sinks into her plush chair with a tired sigh. "Come and sit, Gabe," she says fondly, sweeping out her hand in front of her.

I incline my head, settling myself in my favorite spot at the end of the fainting couch. When I was younger, I would stretch my legs out along the length of it and read quietly in there with her; we would often sit in silence, she and I, listening to the rain or the snow or the wind outside as we read our books and drank our tea. We never spoke, never needed to. But those were our times together.

It has been a very long time since I have sat in this room with her.

"You are worried for Scarlet and Enté's *senai*. You are worried for Claque and Alistair as well," she says simply.

I give a somewhat sheepish smile at her. "Yes…I am worried."

She nods slowly and considers to herself for a moment before saying, "And your father is frustrating you."

I bite my tongue, but a sardonic smile touches my lips anyways.

She does not need to hear my answer, for she gives a low laugh and nods again. "Dante is a very aggravating man at times. He is stubborn and hard-headed and convinced that he is always right." She gives a long, slow sigh again. "Ah, he is a very difficult man to live with." But despite her words, there is a fond lovingness in my mother's eyes when she speaks of my father that is rare to see and not unnoticed.

She then stands and walks quietly to the other side of the room, peering wordlessly at her impressive collection of books. "It can be maddening at times," she says, gazing at things beyond my line of sight, "left adrift in a current of fate that you cannot change…you can no more rescue your friends and loved ones than you can change your parents or your title…it is a bit like being at the mercy of the ocean, isn't it?"

I give a quiet chuckle, but my heart sinks. "Yes, I suppose so…but what are you to do then? If there is nothing you can change, then what is there to do at all? Surrender yourself to fate and let it take you where it leads? That sounds …weak and foolish. If fate is unchangeable and will take you where it will, then what is there left to do?"

My mother plucks one of the books from her shelves and brushes her hand over the front cover gingerly, dismissing all trace of dust and time.

"Build a better boat." She looks from the book to me and smiles gingerly. "You cannot change the sea, Gabriel. But 'tis far better to venture her in a brigantine than a raft." She walks to me and hands me the book in her hands, a wry little smile on her face that almost reminds me of my little spitfire, although the two seem to me to be completely different women altogether.

I study her face, and then turn my eyes to the book. With a little reluctance, I accept it and hold it in my hands, examining the fine, green cover, leather stretched tightly over its binding. It smells of dust and of old paper, the glue of the bindings. My mother settles herself back in her chair and takes up the book on her table, opening it to her page.

I smile and then kick the boots off of my feet, pulling my legs up on the chaise and stretching them out across the length of it; I crack open the book and look up at my mother to see if she'll complain. She says nothing and merely turns the page of her book, but there's a small smile on her lips. My heart feels a bit lighter and my seas a bit calmer. I open the book and begin to read…

"Sire."

I am startled awake by the sound of Claque's voice and sit up suddenly, dropping my book out of my lap. "Hn? Claque?" I am still in my mother's solar, but I am alone now—the pale, crisp light of the morning piercing the windows and illuminating the room with an ethereal, almost ghostly light. Turning my head to the door, I find that it is, in fact, Claque at the door.

"You're back!" I cry, standing suddenly and going to him. "Did you make it? How do they fair?"

He is dressed in a noble's clothes, but not his uniform— a simple doublet and slacks with boots, his hair hanging down about his face. He seems tired and ragged, silver-blue stubble on his jaw.

"They are well, my prince," he says with a single nod. "I informed Duke Karnei of their conditions and how best to treat them. He has taken my recommendations and has ordered new measures to be taken. As I left, their conditions were improving considerably, and Duke Maeghdra has been waking up intermittently."

With a sigh, I sink back onto the table behind me, putting my head into my hands and restraining the emotion I feel swelling within me. "Thank the goddess…" I rasp out, swallowing my breath. Claque stands in silence for a moment, waiting quietly.

After a moment of taking time to collect myself, I stand to my feet, a bit taller than I have felt in some time. I look straight at Claque, inclining my head. "Very well, my friend. We have much to do! Come on then, and let us go to my study. I'll fill you in on what you've missed, and we can get to work!"

Claque frowns at me with confusion as I pause to pick up my green book and head for the door. "Forgive me sir, but…work on what?"

I flash him a grin. "To build a better boat, Claque!"

His brows knit in confusion, and I merely laugh, striding out into the hall. "Sir?" he asks, no less confused as he quickly follows after me.

Chapter Fourteen
Scarlet

A Few Days Later
Castle Karnei, Flora

I have slept too much and for too long to be content sleeping in past daybreak. The little Inferno, however, sleeps at my side in her little ball and seems content to stay that way. I smile faintly, leaning down and kissing her dark brow. She frowns and furrows her brows, but she just rolls onto her other side and sighs, going back to her sleep and ignoring me entirely.

Laughing quietly, I push myself up and off the bed. The mattress is small and sleeping with Zsoka is like sleeping with a sack of foxes. My sides hurt from her kicking me all night, but at least it was not my injured side. I'm half-tempted to bind her hands and feet tonight when we sleep so she can't squirm.

My feet touch the cool, stone floor. It's been freshly swept, and the room smells of sweet air since the windows were left open. It is still cool here but Zsoka and I were given warm blankets for our bed, leaving fresh air more desirable than a warm, stuffy room.

The Lord of Karnei had a servant bring in our bags of supplies which thankfully had not been lost in the attack, although I do not know how. I change into a warm, red dress and comb my hair, plaiting it in a braided bun to keep it out of my way. I decide to check on Alistair before going and getting breakfast.

The castle is quiet as I move to the next door down; a few servants are out and about but not making much noise. I suppose most of the servants either sleep in their own quarters in this wing or outside of the castle, since there are few to be seen. Considering this, I throw the latch on Alistair's door and open it quietly. The sight before me almost brings me to tears of laughter.

Alistair has found himself sprawled out on his stomach on the floor, his blankets beneath him and his bare backside left naked for the world to see as he struggles to get up. I just pause and stare at him as he whips his head around to look at me. He opens his mouth and then laughs, his face turning a bit red. "Enjoying the sight, lass?"

I laugh then and go inside, shutting the door behind me. "You're a fool," I say, laughing again and moving to sit beside him, crouching down.

He grins at me, managing to throw the corner of his blanket over his back to cover himself. "Quite," says he with a chuckle. "And you, sweetheart, are the best thing I've seen all morning."

"You just woke up," I argue.

He merely grins. "Still the best thing I've seen." I roll my eyes and help him up and back into bed, managing to keep the blanket wrapped around him. We get him settled back in bed, and he sighs and lays back while I fix his blankets. "So, can we agree now to stop ignoring my decisions?"

I scoff and smirk at him. "Someone's feeling better." Laughing a bit, I sit at the foot of his bed and say, "You shouldn't take it so personally. I ignore everyone's orders."

He chuckles to himself and replies, "Aye, you know, I do recall hearing Gabe mention something about that."

I scrunch my nose at him playfully and ask, "What were you trying to do, in any event?"

He makes a rude noise and says, "Ah, I was *trying* to get my clothes and get up."

Shaking my head, I give him a look. "Alistair, your leg's been badly injured. Just rest." He opens his mouth to argue, but I add with a wink, "Besides, you look better without clothes."

He shuts his mouth, and I laugh until I nearly can't breathe, watching his face turn a charming shade of crimson. He mutters to himself and says, "I believe I'm becoming a bad influence on you, lass."

Unrepentant, I grin at him and stand up. "I was just going to get some food for Zsoka. I'll bring you some and inform a servant to tell Karnei that you are awake. Do you need anything else?"

He smiles wryly at me and replies, "Ah, I'm sure a kiss would do wonders for my state of health."

Laughing, I turn around and head out. "I'll be back soon."

I shut the door behind me, making my way down the sunlit halls of Karnei and smelling the crisp, sweet breeze pouring in from the windows. My steps are light and easy, soft boots thudding on the floors. There is a sound in the distance of metal rattling together harmoniously. A wind chime. Once I turn the corner, I see it fluttering there in the casement, a vase of flowers standing sleepily in the crisp, morning light. There is a motion to the air, a soft breeze wafting through the halls and carrying with it sweet smells of dewy grass and fresh rushes.

It is peaceful here, like a dream. It is neither uncomfortable, nor completely home. It is some sort of ethereal netherworld where my soul slumbers with contentment.

I can hear the faint clunk of wooden swords in the courtyard from one of the windows, and I pause in the dining hall to step out into the inner courtyard for a moment just to watch the sun break through the gray morning and fill up this place. It is peaceful here.

"Scarlet?" A servant calls, and I turn to look at a new face. He is a bit older than I, and he looks a bit shy. Somehow, he reminds me of Tam, and my heart clenches at the memory of him. This world-between-worlds reminds me of him. Perhaps because it was his home.

"I am she," I reply after a moment. I suppose I am the only Inferno to speak of, so it cannot be hard to miss me.

He smiles faintly and says, "The cook jus' sent me to see if ye an' the lassie was up yet. D'ye come to get sommat to eat?"

"I did," I say and although it would be nice to smile, I find that the motion costs too much effort from my heart to do so, and so I am unable.

He hesitates, rubbing his hands nervously together. "Ah…Miss Scarlet?"

"Mm?" I turn fully to face him.

"Art…art well, miss? Ye look a'might troubled."

I swallow and take in a breath slowly, blinking back my memories and looking at the ground for a moment. When I look up, the tears have all fallen back to their place, and the frown on my lips is a little softer, a little more resembling of a smile. "Yes…I was merely remembering a friend. Might I grab a few trays? Lord Alistair is awake as well."

"Ah," he says and nods, smiling and heading back in with me and towards the kitchens. "Ah can send sommon with a tray for him. 'ere's a few plates for ye an' the wee one. We ken ye tend to eat a fair might."

I laugh. "Yes, we do. Thank you for your hospitality."

He laughs a bit and rubs the back of his neck. "Ah, aye an' aye. We all think might fine o'Laird Alistair, an' most of us are happy to 'ave ye an' the lassie."

I incline my head to him and accept the trays, taking them back to Zsoka with thoughts of home in my mind.

Chapter Fifteen
Scarlet

A Few Days Later
Castle Karnei, Flora

"I really do not think you are healed and ready for travel," I say dryly as Alistair moves about his room. Zsoka sleeps in my room, napping away the afternoon the way I wish I could. Instead, I decided to spend my time trying to convince Alistair that a week was not enough time for him to recover.

"It takes more than a bear to finish me!" he says with a grin, throwing his things into his bags.

I cock a brow at him, sitting on his bed with an annoyed sort of expression. "Maybe. But I don't want to listen to you complain the whole ride home. And if we get attacked again, I'm just knocking you out and dragging you all the way to Maeghdra."

He laughs and turns to me, hands on his hips. "Ack! I'm nay the kind to laze about in bed, lass. I canna take much more o'this. I'll go stark raving mad, I tell ye."

I quirk a little smile. "And *how* is that different from how you usually are?"

He grins at me and winks. "I lose all o'my irresistible charm."

"Irresistible, eh?" I ask, laughing a bit and standing up. "You might want to have that looked at. You're fairly resistible, as far as I can tell."

With a hand to his heart, he cries, "Ah! My lady, ye're so cruel to me!" I grin, and he laughs and takes my hand, pulling me towards him. "We'll see how resistible I am, Scarlet."

I nudge his injured leg, and he yelps and backs away from me with a howl, sitting down and nursing the injured limb.

I laugh. "No. Still pretty resistible, Alistair."

"Mean little creature," he mutters, checking on his bandages while I smirk and leave the room, going to gather up my things since he seems so hell-bent on leaving after dinner.

I pack while Zsoka sleeps and carry our things out to the carriage. Since Alistair's leg is much too damaged to ride the full way to Maeghdra, I am to be confined to a box on wheels once more. The prospect of such an event leaves me rather sore, but by the time I return, Zsoka is awake and hugging her pillow to her chest, sitting up and waiting for me. When she sits like that, it makes me wonder what she thinks. Does she fear that one day she will wake and I will not return for her?

"Are you ready to go?" I ask her.

She looks over at me, a bit startled, but then she smiles and nods, climbing off the bed and hugging my legs. She nuzzles her face against them and just sighs, holding onto me. I look down at her for a while, stroking the top of her head with one hand, the other on her shoulder.

"It's alright, Zsoka," I tell her gently. "I'm here. I will always be here."

She nods quietly, but I wonder if she believes me.

I pull her away from me and kneel down, my leg at least doing much better. "Alright, now we're about to head for Maeghdra but we'll have to be in a carriage for a while. Do you have your things to keep yourself busy?"

She nods. "I brought a few books and my embroidery."

"Good." I stand and help her put her dress back on and get her into her boots. "I'll read to you some, but I won't be able to read the whole time. You'll have to entertain yourself."

"Yes, mama," she says, scowling while I brush her hair.

"Scarlet? Zsoka?" Alistair knocks on the open door and pokes his head in, grinning at both of us. "Art ready, lassies?"

Zsoka is still wary around most people, but she nods mutely. I smile a bit and say, "We're all packed up. Once we finish dinner, we're prepared to leave." At least the first several hours would be easy since we would sleep. That is the hope, anyways. Zsoka can sleep anywhere. I probably won't sleep well, but I can. Alistair, on the other hand, has a sore leg that will likely keep him from sleeping much at all. I wonder if he's realized this little predicament yet. More as likely not.

Still, true to his word, the man doesn't complain, and although the three-day ride to Maeghdra is long, tedious, and irritating, at least it is made slightly more tolerable by having jovial company. When my voice is too tired to read, Alistair decides to teach Zsoka and I some of the Maeghdra folk songs, and he spends hours singing. It makes me laugh and makes my head hurt at the same time, but it is mostly very wonderful.

Three Days Later
Maeghdra Manor, Flora

At long last, the carriage creeks to a stop.

"Home!" Alistair cries with great relief, stepping out of the carriage and spreading his arms wide.

"You're in the way," I complain, wanting to get out as well. I am tempted to shove him and would have were it not for his bad leg.

He turns to me and laughs, offering a hand for the little Zsoka ahead of me. "Here, wee one," he says and helps her out before offering me a hand as well.

"You're not in any state to be helping anyone," I say dryly but accept the hand anyways, stepping out of the carriage and looking up at my new…home.

Maeghdra manor is much more of an over-large house than a castle. It is nestled up into a mountain, constructed of stone and tall, tapered roofs. Two chimneys, one on either side, show signs of fire, which pleases me greatly, and unlike the large, open windows of Karnei, this manor has thinner windows with closed glass panes. I hope they open at least. The front of the manor is packed clay of a russet sort of color, and there are elegant designs etched and painted in a dark red-brown on the face of the house.

A few servants come by with greetings, unlatching the horses and taking them to the stables off to the side to be fed and tended. Several people gather around Alistair with eagerness and hearty cries of, "Milord!" and "Welcome home, sir!" Alistair laughs and grins at them, greeting the handful of servants while I stand to the side with Zsoka. I am not exactly certain where to go and what to do, much less of what to say. The entire ordeal is incredibly uncomfortable.

"Ack!" comes a low but distinctly feminine voice from the manor. "Quit your gawking and get moving! Lazy whelps!" The greeters quickly scatter about their business, unloading the carriage and horses and wheeling the carriage off. It will need to be returned to Karnei, but for now, it is ours to use.

I turn my attention back to the manor and find a woman standing in the doorway. She is old, her silver-blond hair braided and pinned up in a severe bun. She is tall, perhaps taller than even I, and thin as well. She has her hands folded neatly in front of her, but her finger taps impatiently on a round, blue ring pushed on her strong, wrinkled fingers.

"Alistair," she greets my companion with a stern voice. "What's the meaning of being gone so long? And then tarrying so in Karnei? Do you mean to take *any* of your duties seriously, boy? Or do you just enjoy wandering the countryside like a vagabond flirting with fair lasses?"

She glares at him while he approaches, and I glance down to Zsoka—who in turn looks up to me. Neither of us know what to do or where to go, but one thing is certain: neither of us are going anywhere near the woman at the entrance to the manor.

"Mam!" Alistair greets, kissing her cheek warmly and saying, "Ack, I kens I worried ye. Dinna fret so. Ye'll get wrinkles."

"Alistair," she complains, "I am *serious*. You know that I hate dealing with that imbecile. *You* are the Duke of Maeghdra. *You* deal with him. If I have to write one more letter to that sniveling wretch, I'm going to tell him exactly what I think of him and send that spoil'd ingrate into an early grave."

Alistair laughs and puts an arm around her. "Ack, aye and aye, mam. I'd be glad to see it, too. But come. I've sommon I want ye to meet." He turns her to look at me and Zsoka, and I really wish that he hadn't.

Both Zsoka and I go completely still, watching that woman turn her head to look at us and set her eyes upon us with such a dismissively punitive gaze that I am reminded at once of my father's eyes despite the fact that this woman is no more than half his size.

"Well, do they plan to stand there in the courtyard all day and do nothing?" she barks and then reaches out a hand towards us. "You there. Girls. Come here."

"I don't want to…" Zsoka says quietly.

I sigh and squeeze her hand. "It's alright, love. I won't let her hurt you. You don't have to say anything, alright?"

Zsoka still isn't happy, but she walks with me up to the manor where Alistair smiles warmly, completely unaware or otherwise uncaring of the unease between we Inferno and the piercing condescension of his dam. "What's your name?"

"Scarlet," I reply, "And this is Zsoka. Alistair's taken her as his ward due to—"

She holds up a hand in front of me, silencing my words and turning to Alistair. "Boy, what is the meaning of this? Do I not have enough trouble without these two here? A child and a wildwoman. Honestly, what do you expect me to do with these ones?"

Alarm is the only thing that keeps my mouth shut, and Alistair laughs and says, "Mam! Yer too rash. Scarlet's perfectly presentable, and Zsoka's a very mild lass. They'll nay cause ye any trouble. Besides, Gabriel needed them to come here. I canna very well tell him *no*."

"Sure you can," she snaps. "*You* are the Duke of Maeghdra. Your standing is equal with his even if you do share your throne with three others. He has no right to demand this of you."

I bite in, "He didn't demand—"

"Quiet." That's all. No glance my way, no excuse or transition.

She opens her mouth to speak to Alistair again, but this time, I cut her off.

"*Excuse* me," I snap at her, and she shuts her mouth and turns to look at me while my eyes pierce hers. "My name is *Scarlet*, miss, and I speak for myself. Now, either you have something to say to us or you can tell us where to go, but I do not intend to stand here and listen to you accost two of my friends and my charge with your words. So which is it?"

She turns from Alistair and looks straight at me, and I do not look away, not even to see Alistair's reaction. She folds her arms, watching me quietly—her lips pursed together and her gaze contemptuous. "I see. You're quite an entitled little thing, aren't you? Or did Prince Gabriel not teach you proper manners during your stay at Crystalice?"

Before I can speak, she goes on, "Yes—I know all about who you are and what you are doing here. I was not asking for information; I was inquiring as to my son's part in all of this which—by the way, lass—is no concern of yours. And the fact that I need to take the time to explain all of this to you is rather annoying, so I will be frank: I do not trust you and I am *not* happy that you are here.

"However, since you are here of Alistair's doing, there is nothing I can do about it, and I will not waste my time complaining about it. So long as you do as you are told and tend your charge and do not cause trouble, I do not care what you do. One thing I do mind, however, is rudeness and insubordination; *that*, girl, is something I will not tolerate in my home. Do we understand each other?"

I breathe slowly in and out through my nose, watching her with my jaw clenched. I know what I would like to say to the woman, but I have not yet decided if that is what I *will* say to her. Thankfully,

I do not need to, for Alistair interrupts us both with, "Mam, in addition to being Gabriel's ward and here at his own request, Scarlet is a dear friend o'mine, and ye should treat her with more respect. Or is my word nay worthy enough for yer consideration?"

She glares at me and then looks to Alistair for a moment before sighing shortly and saying, "As I have said, I will not bother her. If she is here, let her be." She turns her head back to me and says, "A room has been prepared for you and the child. I am usually too busy for formal meals unless Alistair is here, so you will need to speak with the staff concerning yours and Zsoka's meals. Tomorrow, I will introduce you to the staff and will explain who to ask for certain items of concern."

The few minutes I was afforded to be able to think over my words and to calm my racing heart soothed my seething ire, and I am able to respond with a calm and firm, "I understand. I will do my best to not impose upon you or yours. Only make known to me my responsibilities, and I will perform them."

She is quiet and watches me, and her look is not unlike the scowl of disappointment that had been there moments before, but it has changed somehow; perhaps it is a spark of interest in her eyes, something redeeming my presence to her sight.

She gives a clipped nod and says, "Very well then, Scarlet. I am Freya, the wife to the late duke, Alistair's father. Welcome to Maeghdra Manor."

Chapter Sixteen
Scarlet

Two Months Later
Maeghdra Manor, Flora

There is one thing that I love best about Maeghdra—the smell of fresh bread in the morning. It is the first thing I wake to everyday: the smell of warm, sweet bread drifting through the halls of my new home. Cali has her own family recipe of sweet bread and she only makes it for her kin and the Duke of Maeghdra. Every so often, she'll make a loaf or two for festivals, I am told, and it's always the first thing to be eaten.

This is what I wake to every morning, when the dawn is young and the sun peeks timidly in through my window. The air is cool and keeps me under my warm covers for a little while longer, but I soon sneak out from under them and dart for the chest in the corner which contains my dresses and other clothes. I dig through it until I pull out something snug, and I drag it over my chemise and tie the laces in the back.

I glance back to Zsoka who is still asleep on our mattress on the floor. Alistair said that he would buy us a bed if we wanted, but I really do not care, and I doubt the child does. A mattress on the floor or a mattress two feet up on a wooden frame makes no difference to me. It's still the same mattress.

Zsoka is sprawled out in some twisted, angled form that only boneless children seem to be able to get themselves into, let alone sleep that way. I smile and stifle a little laugh at the sight of her. She won't wake for another few hours, and I like to steal the morning for myself, my few hours before the day becomes busy and loud.

Not wanting to waste a stolen moment, I yank on my stockings and boots and quickly tie my hair behind me before hurrying out the door. The Maeghdra Manor is spacious and large, construction of solid, dark wood. It is two stories high, but most of the manor's great structure goes towards the dining hall and ballroom; there is an open area before the hearth where musicians play and couples dance or where bards sing songs of love and war and adventure. The back part of the first floor is the kitchens and storage.

Down the wooden stairs, I avoid the especially noisy ones, being as quiet as I can and sneaking down to the main floor which is much quieter with its stone foundation. The kitchen door is open, and I peek my head in to see Cali, a plump woman with dark brown hair tied up out of her face and a green dress splattered in flour.

"Good morning, Cali," I greet with a warm and happy voice. "You are looking lovely today."

The older woman turns her head to me and laughs, her bright smile showing a few missing teeth and a few other crooked ones, but it is a smile that has come to warm my heart. "Ack! Afta me bread already are ye now, lassie?"

I grin sheepishly and she waves me in. I hurry in excitedly and laugh.

"Och, but yer like a cat cry'n fer cream firs' thing in the mornun." She slices off the end of the load of warm, sweet bread and hands it to me.

"I shall take that as a compliment and shall praise the wonderful maker-of-cream who spoils me every morning," I tell her, getting out of her way and sitting on the windowsill with the sun warm on my back. I bite into the soft piece in my hands, and my toes curl while my mouth curls into a grin with pure delight. These mornings in Maeghdra are the best mornings I have ever had.

Cali laughs to herself and continues mashing up the apples for her breakfast tarts. "Aye and aye, lassie," she says with a warm smile. "And wha'abouts do ye plan to be up to today?"

"Mmm…" I think on her words as I savor the bread in my mouth, finally eating it just before it becomes soggy. "I think that I might go riding," I tell her. "I could go and pick some of those pears up at Shamen's Hill that you like."

"Ah now *tha'* t'would be wonderful!" she says with a grin. "Dinna forget that the laird of Oakensten is due to day to visit Alistair. Ah bet he'd be a'might charmed by ye and dem pears." She winks at me with a grin. Oakensten is one of the several of Alistair's lairds and a particular ornery one at that.

He is young and an illegitimate bastard child, with a chip on his shoulder the size of Mount Kaheil. His mother was one of those prostitutes in the rural areas Alistair talked about; she came forward with her son and gave him to Oakensten's father as a boy, baring in her possession the family's seal which her lover had given her. Apparently the man had been stupid and thought she was in love with him. She had been a swindler whore after his gold. In any event, all she'd gotten for her trouble was the wrath of an angry wife who nearly ran her out of Flora before Karnei stepped in. Oakensten's father, the previous laird of Oakensten, had raised the boy, but he'd spent his entire life in a culture that hates infidelity worse than any I've ever seen.

In any event, the laird always gives Alistair a hard time but he seems to favor me, and he has a sweet tooth for pears and cobblers. If I can at least keep the man appeased during his visit, it will make Alistair's life easier. Alistair doesn't show it when he thinks anyone can see, but his leg still bothers him, and all the walking and riding and traveling about this past month has made him tired and sore. When Sam Oakensten is here, it makes his condition that much worse.

"I'll be back then before the others wake," I tell her and smile.

"Well, fer sooch a heroic task, a heroine must be properly compensated. Here, lass. Take a piece fer the ride." She cuts off a hearty portion of that warm loaf and wraps it up, handing it to me.

I kiss her cheek and grin. "You're an angel, Cali." She laughs, and I head out to the stables, taking a brown stallion who is mild and tolerant of me out of his stall. I usually try to ride all of the horses and get used to them. Each has their own funny quirks. But today is a lazy day, and I feel like giving Marshal a brisk, morning walk. It would do him some good.

I mount up and ride out of the front yard and onto a worn path that will lead me east towards Shamen's Hill where the red pears grow.

That Evening

It brings me a feeling of great triumph to set a whole basket of those red pears down in front of Sam Oakensten later that evening as he sits at Alistair's table and puts up his feet cockily.

At the sight of me and the pears, he respectfully puts his feet down and smiles warmly. "Ah, the Lady Scarlet!" says he with a grin. "'ave ye brought these fer me, sweetheart?"

I might bite him if he calls me that again.

"I was out picking some today and heard you were fond of them," I tell him, standing up in the fire-lit dining hall with a smile. "Alistair always seeks to show his respect and consideration for his lairds and make them feel welcome in his home."

Alistair seeks no damn thing, and he's hiding a smile at me from behind his hand, because he knows that I'm lying between my teeth. I'm quite familiar with what he thinks of Oakensten, and there are words used in the same sentence with that man's name that even *I* would blush to say.

"Does he now?" Oakensten says, taking a pear and gesturing to Alistair as if it were something to toast. "Here then, my host. What a generous and considerate man ye are!"

Alistair laughs and leans forward on his forearms, hands clasped in front of him—a habit I wager he picked up from Karnei. "Ah, the lass gives me far too much credit, Sam. But please, eat, enjoy."

Oakensten smiles to me and says, "I'll do so and with great thanks, sweetheart." He bites into the pear, and I wish there is a worm inside of it. No such luck, however, and he devours the pear before grabbing another one.

I turn my attention to the black-haired little girl reading her book by the fire and say, "Zsoka, it is well and time for bed. Say good night to your guest and your lord and let us go."

She looks up at me with a frown, clearly uninterested in leaving her adventure, but she sighs and marks her place in her book with a piece of folded parchment before closing the book and setting it down by her chair.

Still, she stands up and curtsies to the two men at the table and says, "G'night, Lord Alistair. G'night, good sir Oak'stan."

Oakensten inclines his head to the girl, and Alistair smiles. "G'night, wee lassie. Sleep well."

Zsoka nods and comes to my side, taking my hand. I smile at her and lead her up the stairs as she glances back at the dining table a bit somberly. She sighs as she trudges up the stairs, and I ask, "What is wrong, little love?"

We make our way down the hall and to our room, and I open the heavy, wooden door for her. "I wan'ed a pear, but they're for Oak'stan, so Freya wouldna lemmy 'ave any," she mutters glumly as I shut the door.

Crouching down in front of her, I reach into the pocket of my apron and pull out a fat, red pear. "You mean, one of these pears?" I ask, and her whole face lights up. She grins and takes the pear, biting into it and smiling with a mouthful of fruit while pear juice runs down her chin. I laugh and help her out of her dress while she eats the pear.

She offers me a bite, and I take a little one, and we share a secret smile before she finishes the whole thing, core and all; I clean her sticky face and hands before tucking her into bed. "G'night, mama," she tells me, and I smile warmly, leaning down and kissing the very tip of her nose before kissing her brow, my kiss lingering there as I close my eyes and relish her company and her love.

"Goodnight, my little love. Sleep well."

She smiles, and closes her eyes. Then, I take her dress and bring it downstairs with me to wash tomorrow, putting it with the other clothes that need to be washed as well. I entertain Oakensten with fables and stories of all kind, using my fire *Magik* to create the pictures. I hadn't realized that it wasn't something others knew how to do. Alistair has said that he's tried it since watching me, and while he can create some forms of earth and stone for storytelling, it's not quite as fluid and impressive as fire.

I happen to like my fire as well, but then again, I'm rather biased.

And when the night drags on until it is more morning than night, I leave the gentlemen to their talk and laughter—mostly fabricated though it may be—and move up to my own room. Alistair will retire shortly. He cannot tolerate Oakensten's company much longer without my presence to deflect it. It's funny, really. Oakensten doesn't hardly bother me, but my presence makes it easier for Alistair to deal with him. It is likewise for Freya, I suppose. On her own, I barely keep myself from torching her. But when Alistair is there to deflect the harsh cut of her tongue, she is much more easily suffered.

I am happy to have been able to give Alistair more time to at least be productive with Oakensten. No good thing ever came from a laird leaving a duke's house feeling bereft and offended. This will make Alistair's life easier. And in turn, that will make my life easier.

And so, I creep quietly into my dark room and shut the door, latching it and wearily untying my dress before pulling it over my head and tossing it on the floor to be washed as well. The room is dark and quiet aside from a tiny, little snore coming from the child that sounds more like a squeak than a real snore. I smile in the darkness of the night and ease myself down onto the mattress with her.

The nights at Maeghdra are the worst I have ever known. I do not know why, really. But they are an awful thing.

When I lay down beside the little child, I am restless no matter how late I stay up or how tired I am. There is a cool stillness of the darkness that brings with it unease and a terrible, aching loneliness. I lay there in the soundlessness of Maeghdra nights and close my eyes, willing sleep to come, willing for the gaping hole that builds in my chest to go away. Holes are supposed to be made of nothing, and yet this one feels swollen and festering, pressing upon my chest and making it hard to breathe.

The hole is always worse at night.

I call to mind the feel of Gabriel's cold body tangled with mine in Ocarine. He would always fall asleep with his arm thrown over me and his leg tangled with mine, but by morning, he would be on his back with his arms above his head and only our ankles crossed. Even still, it would make me smile. I loved being wrapped up in him as we fell asleep together. I felt invincible and beautiful in his arms. I felt at home there with him.

Phoenix Briar

And now I am surrounded by darkness—a still and quiet darkness that scratches at my soul, picking at it slowly and slowly, eating away at the threads of it until the whole thing might very well unravel.

Chapter Seventeen
Scarlet

The Next Evening
Maeghdra Manor, Flora

"What d'ye see, sweetheart?" Alistair comes up behind me in the fading light of the day.

I stand out on a gazebo behind the manor, cut into a little section of the mountain. From the gazebo, I have a clear line of sight down the valley and further into the mountains. It is a sacred place to me, and it is one that I where do not like being disturbed. I suppose it is more Alistair's than mine, but this has been my spot every evening for the past few weeks since I discovered it.

Looking back at him, I draw the shawl around my shoulders a bit tighter before turning my gaze to the valley. "Do you not see it?" I ask him quietly. It's a bit difficult to see. You have to stand in the right place at just the right time as the sun fades before us.

"What? The sun? I dinna try to look right at it if I can help it."

I shoot him a look, but he grins innocently at me. "Not the sun," I mutter, glancing to the burning orb that sinks into the sky. "But what she shows. You can only see it this time of day."

He comes up beside me and frowns up ahead, squinting past the burning rays of twilight to see what I see. "All I see's mountains."

"Because that is all you know," I tell him with a sigh. "That is all you wish to see. That is all you look for." I bite my lip, trying to think of how to show him. Finally, I move back from my spot and tug him by his shirt to where I stood.

"Here. Stand here." I climb up on a bench behind him to see what he sees and squint my eyes to find it again. "There...look beyond the mountains." I point over his shoulder to a small space just beyond the mountains.

"There..." my voice is a low murmur in his ear, wistful and somber both. "Can you see it? The way the sky is warped in that little stretch of horizon?"

"Aye...'tis nay from the sun?"

I shake my head, leaning my chin on his shoulder and focusing on that little, burning piece of earth. "No...the rest of the horizon isn't warped like that...that is from the burning forest of Inferno."

He frowns. "Art certain, lass? There's nay smoke."

"There is never smoke. The fires of Inferno do not smoke unless they are burning bodies."

He gives a nervous swallow, and I smile faintly.

He falls quiet, and we just stand there, watching as the sun sinks below the horizon. I have to squint harder and harder until my eyes are nearly closed, that warped section of air slowly vanishing behind the mountains until I can see it no longer. Although the sight is the best part of my evening, watching Inferno disappear once more is like a knife to my heart, twisting inside of me and bringing me to suffer once more.

Had I but known when I rode to the wastelands with Jacob that I would never see my beloved home again.

Had I but known that Blaze's cocky grin when we parted ways that evening would be the last time I would see his face.

And father. Father standing there on the steps and watching me with pride and full expectation for me to return home...father.

I will never see him again.

Swallowing back my tears and heartache, I suddenly move away from Alistair. I hop down from the bench and make my way to the stairs to head back to the manor.

"Zsoka must surely be finished with her lessons by now. I should go collect her from her tutors." My voice is tight and choked with tears, but I clear it and pick up my skirts in one hand, dismounting the stairs while my other hand holds my balance on the rail.

Alistair stops me, however, with a hand on top of mine, holding it firmly still on the rail. I whip my head around to look up at him, the mountain breeze blowing my crimson hair into my face until I release my skirts in order to push it away again. He stands above me on the top steps, leaning down a bit to clasp my hand, and he stares at me with an intensity in those green eyes that frightens me somewhat.

Not for fear *of* him—for Alistair is no enemy of mine—but for fear of... something. Something that I cannot name.

"Alis—"

"Ye've worked hard the past month," he cuts me off, releasing my hand and taking a few more steps down towards me. Grinning, he says, "Tonight's a harvest festival in the town. Tis the pride o'the season; t'will be fun, lassie. Why dinna ye go and get Zsoka, and I'll take ye both?"

"I..." Swallowing the remnants of my sorrow, I think of some reason or means by which to refuse him, but I can think of none. Besides, Zsoka would be happy to go out among others...actually, she'll probably hate me for taking away her reading time, but it'll be good for her anyways.

So I sigh and smile faintly. "As you wish, my lord."

I curtsy to him, but his hand clasps my chin gently and lifts it. He smells of earth and of soot. Had he been picking at the fire with that metal rod again? He has such a habit for doing so when he's agitated.

"There's nay need for such formality, sweetheart. Nay between *us*." His voice is low and warm, something comforting and with a hint of laughter in it. But it sends my heart fluttering and my stomach twisting, and the combination of the two is entirely too uncomfortable and unpleasant.

I give a tight smile and remove my hand from his. "I am merely the nurse to your ward, Alistair. I would not want anyone to think that I had any other relation to you. Such, as we have said, would be unwise for your position as duke."

Alistair does not answer me. Instead, those green, summer meadow eyes study mine in the fading light, and he gives an undaunted smile that is as equally charade as it is sincere. I am very used to such smiles from him, however, and it does not offend me. "Aye and aye, lass. Go and fetch yer charge. I'll meet ye in the front yard."

I incline my head to him and reply, "We'll meet you there shortly then."

I pause, hesitating for a moment and watching him, uncertain if he shall say more. But he says nothing and merely watches me with those green eyes and that damnably unreadable smile. I turn from him and leave the gazebo to return down the side of the mountain from whence I came, making my way around the side of the manor and stepping in through the kitchen.

Cali has gone for the day, and so the kitchen is left clean and ready for her to begin again in the morn.

Freya sits at the dining table, and Zsoka sits at the far end with her parchment, ink, and quill. She's scowling down at the paper, making long, unsteady scratches in it with the quill.

"How are your words coming?" I ask her as I enter the dining hall.

Zsoka looks up at me with a frown, and while Freya glances my way, she says nothing. "It's very hard," Zsoka complains with a sigh. "They're a'might longer than I'm used to."

Coming alongside her, I look at the scarcely identifiable characters on her paper, overlarge and clumsily drawn. Smiling, I kiss her head and say, "You do not need to remember them all right away. Your tutor gave you these three books to start with. You practice those. That's all you need right now. Other books are for later."

She huffs a sigh and pouts up at me. "I'd like to read all of it now."

"You will," I promise the stubborn child. "But for now, Alistair has a treat for you. Come and clean up your things, and we will go."

She gets up and cleans her quill and puts the stopper in the ink bottle before collecting them all to her chest. I take the parchment so that she doesn't smear it on her dress, leaving her to hold the quill and bottle as we head upstairs. "What's the treat?" she asks.

I grin. "You will have to see."

She huffs at me and puts her things away in a box that goes on a shelf in our room before letting me help her into her boots—she does not like to wear them in the house. Once they are on, she takes my hand, and I lead her down the stairs.

When we reach the bottom, however, Freya calls out, "Where are you going?"

I pause and Zsoka moves closer to my legs so that I surely would stumble over her if I had not already stopped. Looking to Alistair's mother, I reply, "To the town. They are having a bonfire tonight."

"I see…" She considers us both and then inclines her head. "Enjoy. Be careful."

I give a single nod to her and then tug Zsoka out from her precarious position so as to lead her out of the manor.

Alistair stands in the front yard, his hands on his hips and staring out at eastern sky which has already turned a mild blue while the western sky remains gold and orange, though quickly fading. He turns to look at us both with a heartfelt grin. "Art ready, lassies?"

I nod to him and smile a bit, going to his side with Zsoka alongside me.

She looks up at him shyly and offers a little smile, which he returns warmly.

Crouching down before her, Alistair says, "We're going to a bonfire tonight, Zsoka. There will be some children there yer age as well. D'ye want to go?"

Alistair must have become accustomed to my habit of resenting being told where to go and what to do. Having asked Zsoka instead of merely dragging her along, the child seems more interested, and she gives a slightly warmer smile. "Aye, Lord Alistair."

He chuckles and stands up. "Then let us be off!"

We leave the lantern-lit warmth of the front yard for the road leading to the town. There are lanterns lining the road there as well, but they are not as bright and are spaced too wide to be of much use. They enable us to see the road but not each other so well. Even so, Alistair fills the empty space around us with talks of the town and the people there. He tells us of his adventures as a boy and all the trouble he got into; one of which involved him and Gabriel setting off fireworks at one of the festivals—except they were not properly positioned and instead went straight down the street.

He gives a loud, boisterous laugh while I stare incredulously, and he swears to me that he could not sit down for a week after once his father had gotten a hold of him.

"You would have liked my brother," I tell him with a little smile, looking off towards the town appearing in the distance.

"Oh?"

I glance to him and grin. "Indeed. Sage and Jacob would pull stunts like that. Once they enchanted the dancer's costumes so that the seams came unraveled during a performance."

Now he stares at me in alarm and mild horror. "Ye *jest!*"

I laugh, throwing back my head at the memory. "I do *not!*" But I grin wickedly. "I was one of the younger dancers, and my *Dailyn* helped me to get revenge for my sisters. Later that night, I drugged their wine and he helped me to tie them up. They woke up the next morning hanging upside down on a post with their naked backsides for the world to see."

Alistair covers his face and howls with laughter, shaking his head. "Well done, sweetheart. Remind me never to pull such a jest on ye."

I grin at him wickedly. "'Tis unwise, I assure you."

He pulls back his hand and grins at me warmly, a broad smile filled with warmth and amusement.

"Alistair!" a woman calls from the town as we approach.

At her call, several other notice our approach, and there are other calls of, "Alistair!" "Duke Alistair!" "Milord!" Just as when we first arrived, Alistair is soon crowded with people happy to see him.

He laughs and greets many of them by name, and I smile, shaking my head. I nudge Zsoka away from the crowd that is making her so uncomfortable, and we head into town together.

"Scarlet!" Alistair calls from behind us, and I glance back curiously. He excuses himself from a few of the people and smiles to one lady, kissing her hand and saying, "Aye and aye, I swear it, lass. Now ye must excuse me." He moves towards us and laughs. "Ah, dinna run off, sweetheart. I've nay mind to leave ye two alone to night."

I shake my head and say, "I do not mind. You are an important person. Do not ignore them on our account."

"Lord Alistair, who is this?" one of the older men asks, coming up beside Alistair and looking to me and then to the child with curiosity and a bit of wariness.

Alistair claps his back and says, "Evening, Scott. Tis my ward, Zsoka, and this lady here's her nurse, Scarlet. They're charges Prince Gabriel has asked me to house for the time."

"Ah," says the man, instantly put at ease, and he gives a broad, toothless smile at me, offering a thin, knobby hand.

I accept his hand, although I am not sure what to do with it.

He squeezes it and gives it a few shakes in a very odd gesture before letting go. I drop my hand awkwardly to my side, not exactly sure what just happened, but old man Scott laughs and says, "Welcome, Scarlet! War happy to 'ave ye and the wee lassie! Is this yer first time in Maeghdra?"

I smile a bit and nod. "'Tis," I tell him. "Zsoka and I have never been to Flora before."

"Och! Such a well-spoken ting!" says he, grinning to Alistair and then back to me. "Ne'er 'eard a lassie talk like that. Where ye from, darlin'?"

I'd thought it obvious, but I respond, "Inferno, sir."

"Ah!" he says and smiles. "Aye and aye, ye looks a'much. D'they all speak as ye?"

I shake my head and reply, "No, sir. I was merely educated to speak articulately as a child."

"Nobility then?" he asks while nodding his head. "Than wha're ye doin here?"

I smile a bit, somewhat awkward and uncertain of how to respond, "Ah…something of the sort, but I am not royalty, merely raised near them. And I was a…guest?—I suppose, of Ga—Prince Gabriel's."

The man hoots a laugh and claps Alistair's arm. "Might fine lass!" says he to my host. "Ye gon' stir up quite a fuss here, boy!" He chuckles to himself while Alistair laughs, and the old man says to me, "Dinna mind the sweethearts here, darlin'. They's all been for our Alistair since he was naught but a scrawny brat. If they gives ye any trouble, ye jus' come an' sit with me." He winks, and I smile warmly at him, laughing a bit.

"Thank you, mister Scott. I shall remember that."

He nods and nearly moves on before noticing Zsoka and pausing. He smiles warmly at her and reaches into his pocket, offering something to her. "Here ye go, wee one," says he, and she accepts the little token from him. In her hand is a large, bluish stone that shines iridescent in the lantern glow. "Tha's a dragon's eye," he tells her, giving a resolute nod and a secretive smile.

I look to Alistair who smiles and gives a little shrug.

"Takes good care of it and to will bring ye luck."

Zsoka's eyes go wide, and she clutches the stone before looking up at the older man with wonder in her eyes. "Ye'sir," she says and grins. "Thank you."

He winks to her and nods his head before moving past us and into the town.

Zsoka returns her attention to the blue stone, and I look to Alistair as he claps my shoulder and laughs, "Well then! Let's head to the fire!" He leads us into town, pausing every few feet it seems to greet someone and introduce us.

Most of the townsfolk are friendly and welcome us warmly. They especially love Zsoka who has refused to let go of her dragon eye and only barely pays attention to newcomers. Still, they coo over her and her shiny, black hair and her big, brown eyes and she blushes—although I doubt anyone but myself notices with Zsoka's dark skin—and she hugs closer to my legs.

The bonfire is rather literally what is professes to be. In the center of the town, a large, stone dais has been piled high with logs in a great pyramid of wood that has been lit ablaze with a tower of fire that climbs high above the tops of the houses, pouring black smoke into the sky and clouding up the night. I look up at the fire, and my heart squeezes with longing and with joy. It is the largest fire I have seen since leaving my homeland, and the sight of it is like going home in my soul.

"Scarlet?" Alistair asks, and I gasp in a breath, blinking and looking over at him as a tear rolls hot down my cheek. He clucks his tongue and reaches for my cheek, smearing away the tear and saying, "Ah, dear heart. I've nay upset ye, have I?"

I smile with trembling lips and close my eyes when I shake my head, opening them again to look into his eyes with heartfelt earnest. "No, Alistair. This is beautiful and wonderful …thank you." I take his hand off of my cheek but lean towards him and kiss his own cheek to show my thanks.

Behind us, I hear a few people hoot and call to us, and Alistair turns a shade of pink and laughs nervously.

Anxious, I tense up and ask, "I've not done something scandalous again, have I?"

He grins and chuckles nervously. "Nay, lass. Dinna fret. Kisses are'na scandalous as that. They only tease."

I sigh with relief and give an apologetic smile before something tugs at my skirts. I look down and catch sight of a little girl with golden hair tied up into ribbons on either side of her head.

She looks up at me with huge, blue eyes and grins. "I'm Sahrah," she says.

Zsoka hisses at the other girl, baring her teeth and clutching her stone tightly.

The girl blinks in alarm and looks over to Zsoka uncertainly.

Laughing a bit, I crouch down in front of them both and say, "Hello, Sahrah. My name is Scarlet. This is Zsoka. Say hello, Zsoka."

Zsoka looks to me from the corner of her eyes and lets out a little yowl in the back of her throat, her lips slightly parted in warning. I frown at her and say, "Zsoka, be nice and play or I'll take away your dragon eye until we get home."

She shuts her mouth and glares at me with a look of betrayal before frowning over at Sahrah, blaming her for my treachery. "Hallo," she says glumly.

Sahrah, undaunted, grins like a fool and grabs Zsoka's hand. "Le's play!" She yanks Zsoka away, and the dark girl looks back at me with huge, horrified eyes.

I stand and cover a laugh with my hand, hearing Sahrah say, "T'will intraduce ye to all mah friends, I will! We ca' be the bes of friends, Zsoka!"

Zsoka looks back at Sahrah as if she is considering killing her while the little girl's back is to her, but then she gives a put-upon sigh and goes along with the girl.

I watch Zsoka stand awkwardly by the blonde's side, still holding my child's hand captive while she introduces the hesitant Inferno to a band of boys and girls around Zsoka's age and a bit older.

"Let her be," Alistair says to me, and I look back to him. He smiles and says, "T'will be good for her to make her own friends. She's done naught but cling to ye since ye arrived here. They'll nay hurt her."

I laugh a bit and glance back to my little fire-child who runs off with Sahrah in what looks like some kind of game. "I'm not worried about her getting hurt. I'm worried about her setting something on fire." I look back to Alistair to see him wince and look off at Zsoka a little anxiously.

Laughing, I nudge him and say, "She'll behave…probably. Come. Show me your village." I grin and take his hand, pulling him away from the fire.

He leads from there, taking me from one group of people to the next, introducing me and allowing me to talk to them for a while.

When we reach a woman named Getara, he says, "I'm also in need o'some new clothes, Tara. D'ye think ye could get sommat for her?"

"Ack! Aye and aye!" she says and grins. "Why dinna ye come and let me measure ye, Scarlet, and we'll look at sommat!"

She heads off towards one of the buildings, and I follow uncertainly beside Alistair. "What do I need dresses for?" I ask him, frowning.

He grins and says, "Ye're Zsoka's nurse, lass. That means that when I go to formal events, she'll need to attend with me. Ye'll need to be properly dressed as well. As her nurse, ye share a social standing with her."

I purse my lips together and puff up my cheeks in frustration, letting out the breath slowly through my nose. "Please tell me you do not mean events like the balls in Crystalice."

He laughs and says, "D'ye dislike them so?"

I scoff. "Considering the only one I attended was one in which I was stabbed by a madman on order from a jealous heiress, yes, I do."

He winces at the information and gives an awkward smile. "Well, we've nay had any stabbings in quite a while, lass. Though *tis* an occasional drunken brawl out in the yard."

My eyes snap over to him with surprise, but he holds up his hands in defense and laughs.

Sighing, I subject myself to being measured and selecting a few styles from Getara's sketches, giving a slight smile as we leave her shop. "Thank you for taking the time on a celebration day to help me."

She laughs and waves me off. "Thank naught of it, sweetheart! I'm tickled red to be able to say I'm makin the dressus for Alistair's new lassie."

My words get shoved back into my throat, and I choke on them while Alistair recovers with a warm smile and a, "Thank you again, Getara. I'll send Zsoka down to be measured as well later this week."

"Och, sure. I got some estimates, so I can order the cloth for a matching style. I'll jus' need her for the final fit."

"Yer talent exceeds expectation," Alistair says with a grin, kissing her hand and chuckling as she hustles back to her group of friends.

He looks back at me to find me smiling mischievously at him, and he suddenly seems nervous. "Och, but what's a look like that for, sweetheart?"

I laugh and move away from him towards where the others are drinking and dancing. "You're a flirt," I accuse, but my eyes are watching the dancers. They do not move quite as freely as the Inferno, but their dances are lively and informal, and the sight of them makes my heart race.

"Ack!" Alistair cries and I grin back at him. "I'm nay such thing, lass!" he defends. "I'm merely polite s'all! Surely ye're nay jealous? I swears it!"

I laugh and walk backwards, taking his hand to drag him with me and saying, "Sure, sure, rogue. Now, if you will, *politely* take me over there and teach me how to dance with them."

He looks past me to the fire and grins. "Ye want to dance?"

His gaze returns to me, and I beam at him until my eyes turn into mere slits of gold. "*Aye and aye*, rogue. Now teach me!"

That Night

"Oh, but my legs are sore!" I lament as we walk the long walk home. The night is now pitch black and filled with the faint image of stars behind a veil of thin smoke that still puffs into the sky from the smoldering embers of the bonfire we left behind in the town.

"If ye can hop on my back, I'll carry ye home," Alistair promises, carrying in his arms a little dark-skinned girl with black hair who is completely lax in his hold. She's got her dirty thumb in her mouth which has long since stopped sucking and merely lags open. The other arm is thrown across Alistair's opposite shoulder from where her head bounces faintly with his steps.

I laugh and grin at the sight of the two and say, "You cannot hold us both."

Scoffing, he gives me an offended look and insists, "Come and see if I canna, lass."

"You're limping again," I tease.

He mutters something and then insists more loudly, "I dinna ken what ye mean."

"Mhm." I smile a closed-lip smile as if keeping a secret between my teeth and look ahead of us towards the manor we all call home.

The manor is quiet and dark when we slip inside. The servants have all gone for the night—many of whom we saw in passing at the bonfire. Skylar and Molly are asleep in the hall, and we step past them as quietly as we are able, Alistair carrying Zsoka into our room.

In our bedroom, I light an oil lamp by our mattress and take Zsoka from Alistair before he can try to prove to me that his leg is fine by kneeling down with her and falling flat on his face. I lay the child down and then sigh upon the sight of her dust-covered form. She needs a bath, but I'll not wake her for one this late. Still, she should at least have a clean face and hands.

Alistair still stands in the darkness when I rise. "D'ye need anything?" he asks.

My smile is weary but content, and I shake my head. "No, Alistair. Thank you." I go to him, stifling a yawn, and I kiss his cheek. "Thank you for tonight. You look after us both." I pause. "Do not think that goes unnoticed." I stand back to look at his emerald eyes—they are dark and reflect the faint light of moonglow coming in from my window behind me.

He smiles, and it is both tired and elated in one, and the sight of it nearly makes me laugh. "'Tis my pleasure, sweetheart. Rest well." He inclines his head to me, and I watch him leave my room, shutting the door quietly behind him.

I go to my charge and carefully wriggle her out of her dress, taking the thing to the window and opening the glass panes to shake out the dust. Once it is shaken, I set it by the door to wash off and do the same with my own dress. I still smell of soot and of Flora's bitter earth though and decide that Zsoka and I both shall require a bath tomorrow. I hope that it is warm so that the water will not be too unpleasant out in the sunlight behind the manor. I can boil it, but the effort of boiling a wooden tub of water leaves me tired and annoyed for the rest of the afternoon.

I will need to do what I can to wash up tonight and clean off the girl as well so that our mattress does not collect dust and soot. With a tired sigh and aching, bare feet, I trudge quietly out of my bedroom. To my left is the end of the hall where the moonlight pours in from a tall window. At the other end is the rail overlooking the entrance of the manor and where a notably awake Skylar and Molly hover near as if listening.

Frowning, I step quietly down the hall and come up behind them just as Freya whispers loudly, "Alistair, this cannot continue!"

"Mam," he rasps back, but she cuts him off.

"It is *dangerous*. Why can you not understand this? That girl is going to bring you ruin if you do not keep the lines between you clear."

"Mam, she's a friend, one whom I respect a great deal, and I'm rather fond o'the wee lassie as well."

I stop cold behind the two youths eavesdropping.

"This is what I mean!" she snaps, very nearly leaving her whisper for a flat-out snarl. "She is your ward's *nurse*, Alistair. Nothing more! Do not make her more than she is! You're *settling*, Alistair."

I can practically hear Alistair's frustration. I do not know what he's doing, but I'm sure there's some sort of exasperated expression and dramatic arm-waving—funny little quirks of his.

"Tis *madness*, all! I'm well aware o'her position here. I dinna ken what ye mean by *settlin*." He's lost his jovial, loose accent for a speech much more clipped and articulate. It reminds me of how he speaks with other dignitaries when he is annoyed, and Alistair is not easily annoyed.

"You're *settling*," his mother repeats in a hiss. "You're settling into this cozy little role as the girl's father and as Scarlet's mate." I stop breathing. "You've stepped so easily into that life as if it is so easy, but it is *not!* You're going to ruin your position here and make a harlot out of her by acting like such a fool!"

Molly sucks in a sudden breath, and from the bottom of my vision, I see her roughly nudge Skylar who also turns and steals a glance at me. She gives a little squeak and both of the girls quickly murmur something under their breaths to me before scurrying furtively past me and back to their pallets in the hall down at the end by the window and Freya's room.

I do not know if Alistair or his mother heard them, but they suddenly quiet to whispers that no longer carry to my ears.

Swallowing, I can feel my pulse in my throat, and I back away from the rail. They cannot see me there, for the dining hall where they converse is hidden from view around the corner, but they could choose at any moment to peek around to the stairs and catch me standing there like a wide-eyed doe in the moonlight waiting for an arrow to pierce her flank.

So, I turn and pad quietly back to my door. Molly and Skylar have their backs to me on their pallets as if they are asleep, but I know they are not. I do not care. I simply skirt into my room and shut the door when the stairs creak under someone's weight.

Within the quiet of my own room, I decide that the wash can wait until morning and the mattress is really not as bad off as I thought. But Freya's words echo in my mind again and again in torturous repetition. I go to the window, pushing it open and letting the cool, mountain air rush past my face and fill up the room. It does little to chase away my racing heart and clenching chest. My throat feels so tight as if I could not possibly speak if I tried. And even if I could, I would not know what to say. I keep trying to think, to decide how I feel about what I heard, but every time my mind nearly completes a coherent thought, my heart speeds up and completely erases it from all memory, and I am left dumbfounded once more.

With a heavy sigh, I fold my arms on the windowsill and nuzzle my face into them, smelling the soot and dust from the festival. After a few moments, I find my voice, though only a whisper of it, and I mourn into the night, "Gabriel...I am lost..."

Chapter Eighteen
Scarlet

One Month Later
Maeghdra Manor, Flora

"Scarlet," Alistair calls from the kitchens. I'm surprised that he returned so quickly from his ride to Tharis.

I have my arms shoulder-deep in soapy water, leaning over a shallow tub of mine and Zsoka's laundry.

"Alistair," I greet, sitting upright and smiling. Freya's warning rings in my ears, however, and my smile falters. If Alistair notices, however, he says nothing and merely smiles, stepping out into the warmth of the yard where I wash.

"I did not expect you back so soon," I tell him, standing and drying my arms on a nearby towel, turning to face him as he approaches.

He chuckles and says, "I'd nay either. But the laird's expecting his first bairn and was eager to be done with me."

I laugh and grin at him. "I have a feeling you planned that."

His smile widens into a mischievous grin, and I mimic the look. "Mayhaps." He looks past me and laughs. "Sommon's enjoying the warmer weather."

I follow his gaze to a sleeping tiger cup who is sprawled out in a spot of sunshine and napping contently. "She made her first *Shift* since the attack at Karnei when Claque found her and since then has been rather fond of her new form."

"Ack! I missed her first real *Shift?*" He seems morose at the thought and looks on her with disappointment before sighing and giving a smile, saying, "Ah well…good for the wee lassie."

I nod in reply. "Yes. I am worried, though, that she's becoming too tired to *Shift* back. She gets herself stuck and cannot return to being a girl again."

"Och, she'll learn," he assures me and then seems to remember something, turning his attention to his coat and rifling around in it until he produces a letter for me. "A carrier arrived while I was in Tharis. Twas on his way here, but I went ahead and got this from him." He hands it to me, and I turn the envelope over carefully in my hands, frowning at it and inspecting the wolf's seal on the back.

"From Gabriel."

My head snaps up to look straight into his eyes, and he smiles, although it doesn't quite reach his eyes. "Go ahead and open it. I'm going to go and let me mam know I've returned."

I incline my head to him as he heads back inside, and I sit down on my wooden stool, breaking the seal on the letter and opening it. My hands are shaking as I unfurl the parchment, seeing the black ink curling ornately on the page and for a moment, I am unable to focus enough to read it, my excitement writhing within me as if it might burst from me at any moment.

My dearest Cara,

> *I must have written a hundred letters before finally sending this one, and so if my words seem at all inadequate or lacking, know that no less than a hundred brethren to this letter lay in ruin upon my study floor.*
>
> *I have received word from Karnei concerning the events of your travels, and I am much relieved to know that the incident*

passed without severe loss. I lament my lack of wisdom to send with you an escort of my own to ensure yours and Zsoka's safety and can only hope that you fare much safer in your current habitation. Chelyah be thanked that Karnei is a prudent man who did not kill you on sight, and although I am angered as to the treatment you received, the situation could have proven far more dire than a few arrows to your flank, and Claque has assured me that he rectified your mishandling.

You must try, Cara, to use more discretion in your new home. Although the Flora are considerably more tolerant of the Inferno's liberal cultural customs, there are still considerable differences among you, and any lack of sensitivity could prove unfavorable to both you and to Alistair. I pray you to also keep in mind that many Flora have lent soldiers to Cerulean for our war who have not returned, and while many do not consider Inferno to be an enemy of their country, you have already experienced the bitterness of loss and how such pain can lead to irrational intentions.

All chastisement aside, I hope that you fare well in Flora. How has your stay been thus far? It occurred to me only after you had left that I perhaps should have warned you in regards to the Lady of Maeghdra. She is of a very particular temperament that left me uncertain as to your response to her. Bare her no ill will however, for although Lady Freya can be sharp of tongue, she is a fair and compassionate woman who has managed the affairs of Maeghdra well since her husband's death. It is my earnest prayer that her company will become favorable to you.

Has the little Zsoka become more open towards others? I heard her speak a few words to you before you left, but I am hopeful that she will become more hospitable of a person in an environment that is supportive and affirming for her. Alistair has told me of many children in the village near her age. If you have not already done so, you should introduce her and try to find for her some gentle-spirited companions.

As far as your host is concerned, I heard as to the damage done to Alistair's leg and meant to inquire of his condition. I do not trust his own judgment since he would surely laugh off having lost the whole thing and assure me that it was nothing more than a scratch. I would like to be made aware, however, if the injury is something that should be a concern to his mobility, particularly in any measure I am cautioned to take as far as reinstating him into the military.

Please relay my gratitude and appreciation to the Lady Freya and to Alistair for their courtesy. You are within my thoughts always, and I pray daily for your happiness and safety.

My deepest regards,
Prince Gabriel Jan'tel of Crystalice

I have never in my life read such a bland and lackluster letter, especially one beginning with the salutation of "my dearest". Many times I read the letter over again, uncertain of whether to be wounded, offended, or amused. I am tempted to take it to Alistair in order to have him translate the meaning behind Gabriel's formality and utter lack of sentiment, but I decide against it. I will simply reply to him in my own way and ask him plainly what he means.

I stand up from my stool, the clothes forgotten in the tub of water. Zsoka continues to nap in the sunshine, and so I let her lie there whilst I go inside.

Alistair sits at one of the dining tables—he rarely sits at his own designated seat on the dais unless he has no choice—and I make my way to him. He too, has a letter in his hands, but as he spies my approach, he folds it up out of sight and smiles at me. "And what has Gabriel to say, my lass?" he asks.

I make a face at him, frowning a bit. "I'm rather indecisive as to that myself, my friend. If I may, I would like to write a correspondence."

"Already?" he asks and laughs, standing. "Well, I'll be leavin in a few days for Karnei again. Should be a shorter trip, but expect me to be absent at least a fortnight. I can send it when I'm there." He walks across the hall to the storage room, pulling from it a spare quill and bottle of ink. He hands them to me and then removes several sheets of parchment. "If ye need more, help yerself, sweetheart. I've plenty for all the letters I need sent and contracts I write." He sighs with the irritation of the thought but hands the reams to me with a faint hint of laughter in his eyes.

I smile back at him and accept the parcel. "Thank you." And then I take my own seat on the hearth, a small fire always burning there for my benefit. I hear the sound of Alistair's wooden chair scraping back against the stone floor, and I lean over my parchment, trying to decide how to begin.

At last, I sigh and press the nib to the page.

Chapter Nineteen
Gabriel

A Few Weeks Later
The Crystalice Palace, Cerulean

The piles of parchment and scrolls waiting in my study upon my return to Crystalice were such that I could scarcely move from the doorway to my seat. I dare say that I have done little else but sleep, read, and write since I have returned. I feel some regret for not spending much time with my son except that even if I had all the time in the world, the boy refuses to talk to me.

I blame Zsoka for teaching the little scoundrel that not talking is an excellent way to stir the ire of adults without my really being able to do much about it.

Most children would not have the patience or stubbornness required to go weeks, even months, without saying much of anything at all to a particular person. My son is not 'most children'. He has his mother's resilient patience and the stubbornness that I have only ever seen since from Cara and whom I shall henceforth blame for his acquiring of the trait.

Although Cara and I both attempted to explain her going-away to the boy when we were in Ocarine, I do not think the child fully grasped what everything meant until we ourselves left to return home and Cara did not come back. The ride home had been filled with sobbing and screaming and incoherent mutterings with a considerable amount of vehemence for someone who has lived a mere four years in this world.

I lean back in my chair and fold my hands behind my head, letting out a tired sigh and closing my eyes, chin tilted up towards the ceiling. A knock on my door nearly startles me into a yelp, and I realize now how close I was to falling asleep instantly in my chair in that moment. I clear my throat and bark, "Enter."

A guard opens the door, and in walks a plump, Flora woman named Heather. I have not seen her since I returned and only heard that she had been with her family making arrangements for Tam's funeral. At once, I am on my feet, turning to face the older woman who seems but a shadow of her former self. It has barely been a few months since we received word of Tam's death, and she looks as though it happened yesterday.

Heather's skin is ashen and hangs from her frame. Her dress is loose on her in a way I wouldn't have noticed except that it indicates the amount of weight she's lost. Her hair is slightly pulled from its bun, and her face in general seems sunken and sallow. She does, however, offer a little smile at my presence and bows her head. "Highness."

I gesture to the guard, and he leaves, shutting the door behind him. "Heather," I greet gently, going to her and taking her elbow to lead her to a table and chairs, easing her down onto one of the plush seats.

She pats my hand gingerly and clucks her tongue quietly at me the way old women do, and it rends my heart for her plight.

I settle myself in the other seat after moving some papers and look around my neglected study with some embarrassment.

I am uncertain at how to proceed. I remember when Catherine died and how very tired and almost angry I became at all of the condolences and apologies. Most of them were sincere, and for that I am humbled, but having to graciously respond to each piteous comment becomes very taxing upon the soul. I do not wish to burden Heather any further.

And yet, I do not know what to say to the grieving mother. Surely there is no pain so as to lose a child, especially one whom she had already feared dead once before. When Cara chose to spare Tam's life, it is as though the boy had been marked for life and would continue to live. To suddenly be struck down in spite of everything…it seems cruel.

"Ah wish…to continue to work in the service o'yer majesty," she says at last, quietly and slowly, as if each word is a figment in her mind and grasping a hold of each one in order to find the means by which to utter it is painful and trying.

I look to her eyes, but she is staring down blankly at her hands. "You are always welcome here, Heather," I assure her. "And you may take all the time you need with your family. You need not worry of returning so quickly. Whether two months or two years, whatever amount of time you take, you will be welcomed into the Cerulean household."

She looks up at me then with tired eyes, and her smile is worn but heartfelt. I find myself smiling back at her, sadly and with fading hope. "Tha's a'might kind o'yer highness…I've much joy to be able to work here an' serve yer family. I ken gay fine that ah came here as Catherine's nurse an' many thought ah shoulda gone home when she passed…but I've lived here nigh six years now, an' I'm happy to serve ye."

She takes in a long, slow breath that rattles in her lungs, and I wait patiently for her, feeling as though she has more yet to say and just needs time to find the words. "Tis nay safe, though…I kens well…I'm sendin me bairns home to Flora— away from this mess."

I nod to her, a slow bob of my head as a means of buying time to find my own words. "Of course…does your family have what they need to make the travel and return?"

She closes her eyes with a nod and opens them again. "Aye an' aye, majesty. They'll be jus' fine…"

I nod again, still at a loss for words and both comforted and unnerved by Heather's presence. It occurs to me that now she will be alone in Cerulean with her family gone. She has friends here among the staff so far as I am aware, but it is another thing entirely to become completely bereft of those she loves so dearly and who have no doubt supported her greatly through her loss. I am not entirely certain it is a healthy decision for Heather to stay here with her family gone.

"How does Scarlet fare in me homeland?"

I look back to her, my gaze having drifted to her knobby hands which rub themselves wearily. Smiling faintly, I say, "She's doing well as far as I can tell—I sent her a letter a few weeks ago. They had some trouble on the trip, but she is safely in Maeghdra now and has not had trouble since."

She frowns at me and says, "Och, an' wha' trouble ha' she on the way?"

"Well, she did burn down several miles of the Karnei woods," I tell her, and Heather sucks in a breath before it bursts back out of her in a hoarse laugh.

She leans over and cackles, and I chuckle in unison over the sound. "Ho! Ho-oh, me! Ah goodness!" she rasps, her laughter dying down, and she holds her stomach as she sits back up and chortles to herself. "Ma goodness…ah canna believes it. Och! Troublesome lass. Where'd she go an' do that fer?"

I lean my chin on my hand, elbow propped up on the table, and I smile at the old woman. A bit of the tension leaves the room, and I am left feeling tired but more relaxed. "They were attacked by bandits, and even after they chased them off, Scarlet hunted them down and spread the fire everywhere."

"Och!" she clucks and shakes her head, smiling to herself and sighing. "Ah, lassie, lassie," she sighs, and we both smile a bit brighter.

Silence stretches on before us for a while, but it no longer feels strained and perilous, although a bit of the awkwardness remains. Still, I am content to sit in companionable silence with her and let her gather her thoughts and share in what is most likely the first conversation she has had in two months that is about something other than the fate of her youngest son.

"If ah may, highness…ah ken well that ye love the lassie…" Her statement startles me a bit, only because I did not expect it.

I swallow a lump in my throat and give a wan smile past my hand, choosing not to say anything at all.

Heather reaches out towards me and pats my knee, leaving her cool, wrinkled hand there and squeezing a bit. "Ah, tut, tut, dear…ah ken ye love'r." She sighs and sits back. "Ah'm might fond o'the darlin' meself…sooch a dear, wee lassie."

'Sweet' is among the last words I would ever use to describe my little spitfire and probably first among the words that would surely earn a curse from her if ever I called her such, but Heather can always get away with such things.

"Tha's why…if ah may…ah'd as like to go to Maeghdra an' tend 'er an' the wee fire-lassie."

I am relieved at the prospect of Heather returning to her homeland away from the danger and loneliness here, and Cara will certainly know better than I how to console the old woman's grief. And yet, I am uncertain with sending her away. I had not known what to expect when I sent her to Flora. I half expected the first letter I received from Alistair to be informing me that she and Zsoka disappeared into the mountains to return to Inferno. I am uncertain how sending Heather to Maeghdra will affect Cara.

I nod and reply, "I have no thoughts against it, but I will need to write to Alistair and the Lady Freya. After all, Scarlet is more of a servant there than a guest, and she will like as not require no tending as you have done for her here. But I will write and see if they would be opposed to an extra household member. I am certain that Scarlet would be grateful for your company."

She watches me for a long moment, her eyes regaining some of their sharpness as they look into mine. Her eyes are more gray than green, but I can still see some color there as she watches me, trying to discover what I am not telling her. After a moment, she says, "She's a'mind to go home...back to Inferno."

Speaking it aloud makes me anxious.

While Scarlet slipping away from Maeghdra and running away could scarcely be considered the fault of the Cerulean crown, my foreknown knowledge of such intent could be. "I do not know what she plans, Heather," I tell her honestly. "I do not think she knows what she plans to do either."

She frowns at me, clearly hoping for more of a complete answer, and I can at least share in that sentiment.

I also wish that I could understand Cara's thoughts a little more deeply and thoroughly, but it is very hard to understand what a woman wants when she herself does not even know. It's hard enough reading a woman's mind when she knows what she wants and expects you to know it too. It's another thing entirely when her mind is a jumbled mess of indecision and anxiety.

At last, Heather clucks her tongue and nods her head slowly. "Write to Lady Freya if ye please, highness." She leans forward with a hand on the arm of her chair, and I stand, helping her up. This time, however, Heather shoos me away and rasps, "I'm nay a cripple, boy. Shoo. Ah'm jus' fine." I smile to myself and step back to give her room, escorting her to the door.

"I will send word as soon as I receive a correspondence. Until then, please take care of yourself, Heather."

I open the door, and the guard there turns and stands at attention, offering a hand to Heather—who shoos him away as well. The old woman nods and clucks her tongue and says, "An' yerself, highness. An' yerself…"

When the woman is gone and I am shut again into my office, I am both relieved and burdened. I rub the bridge of my nose, moving over to the window and looking out at the courtyard, lost in thoughts of Cara.

…I never know what to expect from her.

Chapter Twenty
Gabriel

A Few Weeks Later
The Crystalice Palace, Cerulean

With another tower of legislation reviewed and addressed, I decide to stretch my legs and perhaps grab something to eat in the dining hall. The winter landscape outside gives no indication as to the time, but it feels somewhere near the afternoon. No wonder I'm so famished. I rub my face as I walk down the hall, looking like I only just awoke in my shirt and slacks, my hair left in a mess on my shoulders.

A crash and a scream down the hall alarms me, and my head snaps up to my son's door when the guard standing by opens it cautiously and calls to the nursemaid inside. When the door is open, I can hear my child screaming at the top of his lungs past his sobs, as well as the resolute sounds of thumping that is most likely his tiny fits beating on the floor or whatever he could get his hands on.

Muttering a curse, I trudge towards the room, unsure if I will make matters worse. The nursemaid, a young girl with white-blue hair and gray eyes scurries out in a huff, her hair all pulled from her braid and her hands shaking. She notices my heading her way and catches her breath, dipping into a quick curtsy.

"Highness," she greets quickly and stands, her eyes filled with tears. "I apologize, my prince, but I am afraid that I can no longer tend to the young prince. You should find someone more suitable to attend to him." She bobs another quick curtsy and then flits past the guard and hurries down the hall in a huff of frustration.

I groan into my hand and mutter a few curses beneath my breath, rubbing the bridge of my nose and considering what to do with the inconsolable brat on the other side of the door. The guard shuts the door and returns to his post, wisely remaining silent and looking ahead of him.

Cara would know what to do with him. Heather would know.

Hell, it seems like I and the numerous nursemaids I have hired in the past four months are the only ones who simply do not know what to do with him.

Dena tried once, but she lacks the command of a mother to reign him in and merely tries to appease his whims, which she is unable to do. Petara is too short-tempered to tolerate the sensitive brokenness he feels at being abandoned to actually deal with what is bothering him, and I am both too insensitive and lacking in parental confidence to do either.

Another few minutes of muttering and listening to the storm in the room, and I finally move from my spot to his door, opening it and unleashing the full force of rage coming from a shrill-voiced child who has thrown himself onto the floor of a room he has quite thoroughly destroyed. He's red faced and flailed out on the ground, his eyes pinched together in rage and his cheek pressed against the cold ground.

I sigh.

"Enté," I call in the pause he takes to suck in another breath of ammunition. He swallows the gulp of air but then sucks in a few more in rapid succession and shifts from screaming to sobbing, tears running down his face and pooling on the floor beneath him. He's a pitiful sight to behold which helps to abate some of my growing frustration with him.

I sit down on the floor near him and just wait. There's no use in trying to shout over his sobbing, and I'm not about to console him when he is the one who upset himself in this manner. It takes several more minutes, but he finally calms down enough that I can hear my own thoughts, and the silence of the room is filled with watery snorts and short rasps of breath that come in clusters and then fade with a sigh before starting up again. He has his face turned away from me, but I can tell that he is at least still awake from where I sit on the floor, one knee drawn up and the other leg straight. This wasn't exactly what I had in mind when I planned on taking a break and stretching my legs.

"Enté," I repeat, letting my voice sink into his conscious. His breath picks up for a second and then settles once more, both acknowledging and—for the moment—accepting my presence. I consider how to proceed for a moment before deciding to start with a mild conversation, "I thought you liked that nurse...she played games with you more than the last one..."

Silence.

He swallows a watery gulp, snorts, then goes back to his patterned breathing.

I sigh. "Aunt Dena is going to have to look after you until I can find another nurse..." still nothing, "...do you want an older nurse? Someone like Heather? Or...do you want someone who will play with you? ...I can try and find you a playmate your own age..."

The child remains silent, and I shift a bit to look over at him and see if he is even still awake. He is. He's reverted to sucking on his thumb and staring blankly across the room at the far wall. I settle myself back down. At least he hasn't started screaming at *me* yet. "Enté...you can't act like this. I know you're not angry...you're sad because Cara left."

"Go away!" he screams suddenly, his voice slurred and muffled past his stuffed nose and his thumb in his mouth. Well, there's the screaming. I can't decide if it's better than silence or not.

"Son...Cara had to leave."

"Go away!" he screams again, his breathing picking up. He still lays on the floor, not looking at me.

"She was in danger here, Enté...do you know what that means?"

A few hiccups and then, "I don care!"

"You don't care?" I repeat. "Son, there are bad people here...remember I told you that they hurt Cara's friend? They want to hurt Cara too. Cara had to go away so they couldn't hurt her."

"No!" he screams, this time louder.

"You want them to hurt her?" I challenge.

He sucks in a breath and then, "No!"

"Then she had to go."

"No!"

I begin rubbing my temples. This conversation is going nowhere...perhaps that is what I deserve for trying to rationalize with a four-year-old. But Enté surprises me by speaking again, "Ina go with her!"

I open my eyes and look back to him. "You want to go with her?"

"Ina go!"

I sigh. Well, this is progress, at least. "You can't go, Enté...you're a Cerulean prince."

"I don' care!" he screams. "I dun wanna be'a prince! I wan Cara!"

I lean my cheek on my knee, watching him rub his face and sniffle and cough a bit before asking, "What about me, Enté? You want to leave me?"

He sucks in a breath again and shouts, "I hate you!"

I know that he doesn't mean it—that he's hurt and angry and tired and young—but the words still cut. I'm fairly certain that I told my father such things when I was younger. Every child does. But it is still the first time my son has ever said such things to me, and I am at a loss of how to respond. "Alright then…" I say quietly and stand up, not sure of what else to say.

I turn towards the door, but Enté pushes himself up on his arms and screams, "No!"

I pause and glance back at him. "No? I thought you hate me."

Tears begin anew and he sobs, "Don go!"

I wish I knew what to say to him, something to make him understand, to help him. But I am completely at a loss. All I know to do is to stay by his side. So I turn around and kneel down in front of him. "Okay, Enté…" I say gently, lowering my voice and softening it. "I won't go. I will stay right here… alright?"

He watches me, and the tears build and build until he begins crying again, holding himself up on his arms and clenching his eyes.

I am caught somewhere between weariness and relief as I reach out for him and pick him up under his arms. He does not fight me, and I sit down on the floor again, bringing my son to my chest and holding him to me.

Enté cries louder, but his cold little arms go around my neck, almost choking me, and he gathers up fistfuls of my shirt, sobbing into my neck.

My breath leaves me in a rush, and I'm unsure if I'll get it back with the way he's squeezing, but a little smile escapes me, and I glance at his hidden face from the corner of my eyes, hushing him quietly and holding him to me.

"I miss her too…" I tell him softly, and a sudden stab of pain and loneliness grips my chest and threatens to tear me apart. This must be what he feels all the time. Enté is too young to know how to distract himself from pain, how to lie to himself to make it better. He does not know how to put the heartache away and deal with what is before him. He is left open and vulnerable to that pain and is at a loss at what to do with it.

So I hold him, and I let him cry for both of us until his throat goes hoarse and he completely exhausts himself. I'm exhausted as well, and it is with lead steps and a heavy heart that I pick us both up off of his floor and I carry him to his bed. I kick off my boots and shift onto the bed, not even bothering with covers as I lay down, the sleeping boy on my chest. I sigh and lay my head back, one arm beside me and the other draped over my child. I fall asleep like that, holding onto my little hope.

Chapter Twenty One
Gabriel

That Night
The Crystalice Palace, Cerulean

A knock on the door wakes me from my deep slumber. I must have been soundly slumbering, for when I wake, I feel heavy and uncomfortably warm, and it is difficult to breathe.

"Highness?" a man calls quietly from behind the door. "Your serving man bade me to remind you that your council meeting is in an hour and that he has a meal for you in your room."

I grumble to myself and sit up on an unfamiliar bed, rubbing my face and taking in slow, steady breaths, slowly dragging myself from the dredges of slumber. The room is fairly dark now, and I quickly recall that I had dozed off in my son's room; I glance beside me to find him curled up in a ball on his side and snoring quietly.

To the guard, I reply, "Yes, thank you. I will be there shortly."

Damn.

So much for getting more work done today. I cannot even recall what this meeting is supposed to be about. The nap should have made me feel more refreshed, but instead I feel even more exhausted and more irate to go with it. I do not have the time to read the materials for the council meeting today, and I cannot remember in any event if I had already done so. I like to read the agenda ahead of time so that I can more effectively establish arguments, counter-arguments, and a surplus of materials and evidence relevant beforehand. I have done such for a number of topics that I have been informed of since my return, but I cannot remember which ones are due for debate today.

When I make my way back to my own room, my lord-in-waiting is there laying out a set on the bed. He glances to me and smiles a bit but winces. "Did you not rest well, milord?"

I sigh and begin pulling off my shirt and tossing it into a corner. "Unfortunately, no," I grumble with annoyance. My best bet tonight would be to say as little as possible to avoid the risk of accidentally offending someone with my tone. These councilors can sometimes be incredibly sensitive to even the slight lilt of a tone they do not find to their liking. I'm usually aware of and considerate of such things, but I am afraid that even if I try tonight, I simply will not be able to manage it effectively. Best to let father do most of the speaking tonight then.

"Do you recall the agenda for tonight's meeting, Na'tak?" I ask, pulling on the fresh shirt and buttoning it up before trading my slacks for a fresh pair and tucking the shirt in.

Na'tak stands by and hands me the doublet when I am finished. "I believe, milord, that the focus tonight is recent documented actions of public disturbance and whether or not these are to be attributed to the work of the White Fang. There is also the matter of general public unrest and the grievances that have been brought forth on behalf of the commonfolk."

The name of the White Fang sinks like a hot stone into my belly, and it knots there darkly, leaving a bitter taste in my mouth. I say nothing on it, however, and finish buttoning up my doublet while Na'tak combs back my hair and ties it at the nape of my neck with a blue ribbon. "Are mother and the princess attending?"

"As far as I am aware, sir," he replies.

Mother usually attends the council meetings, and Petara used to but has been absent more as of late with her newborn son. I tried to counsel her to rest longer and let Kale take care of the council matters, but she is eager to be involved in the country politics once more. Dena, little slip of a girl that she is, could not care less for politics. She is probably the only member of my family with whom I can hold a conversation for hours and not have to hear a single word about legislation or bureaucracy or politics of any kind. There are some manners of public affairs which I find interesting and can be roused to passion. But taxes and social welfare are not usually among them. It is not that I do not care or do not recognize their importance. I just personally find them uninteresting matters to discuss with a room full of opinionated old men and their wives.

Several Hours Later

Unfortunately, the meeting is worse than uninteresting — it is unsettling and turns my stomach sour. Account after account is given of recent disturbances: vandalisms, abductions, public protestors, threatening letters, missing food and supplies. Even if these happenings are not the work of the White Fang—and there is so very little known about them that it is nearly impossible to decide what can be attributed to them—they are still a grave reminder that our people are not happy, and I am not in the slightest mind as to how to resolve these issues.

"The people need to be reaffirmed of their confidence in the aristocracy and the monarchy," Duchess Cilla of the

Wetlands calls, leaning forward a bit in her seat. Having survived two other wives to the old Duke Eden, she decided that her attention was more safely spent in politics than the childbearing that killed the other two. I haven't yet decided if she is actually invested in politics or if she simply wants an excuse not to return home to the old duke.

"Which they would have," argues the young Count Vari, giving me an annoyed look, "if they had something to be confident in."

I raise a brow to him and retaliate, "Anything in particular come to your mind, Vari?"

"That's enough," Lord Jan, the Baroness' son from Brooke says with a sigh. "That issue," which, if there is any doubt, refers to my former Inferno guest, "has already been dealt with and is unnecessary to bring up in this conversation."

"I think it is quite necessary." That would be Cilla again, glaring at Jan because she does not dare do so to me. "Since the actions previous have a very obvious correlation to the inferences made in future actions."

"If you could please be more specific, Duchess Cilla," Petara says patiently. "Generalizations are going to leave us all chasing our tails."

I watch them all bicker with waning frustration, sitting at the long table in the meeting hall. My father sits at one end and mother at the other one. The remaining princes and princesses attending—Petara, Kale, and Claque—are distributed evenly down the table according to our rank and patronage of the other members. From the corner of my eye, I catch Claque's twitch of a frown. He is clearly as annoyed as I am, and I sigh quietly, sitting back in my seat and folding my hands in my lap.

At last, my father tires of the same conversation that seems to come up at every meeting and growls, "Be *silent*."

He mutters to himself and then gestures to my mother—who inclines her head and speaks up with, "The matters for this meeting have been properly addressed. We shall now discuss what topics should be placed upon the agenda for the next meeting a month from today." She gives a glance to Count Vari and emphasizes, "We are discussing *only* what to address in a month, not to hash out old debates and waste the time of the attending."

A Few Hours Later

I leave the meeting and suppress the urge to rub my temples. Four days' worth of meetings, and I am not sure if anything has actually been accomplished. Sometimes it does seem tempting to just declare myself War Lord and do whatever I please. I doubt the Inferno have to deal with such matters. Then again, the path to tyranny is not far with that model, and although these meetings are vexing, they do help to support the monarchy and to offer wisdom and discretion where it may otherwise be lacking.

"You look far too tired, my prince."

I glance behind me to see Ame, Jan's sister, leave the counsel hall as well and give a little smile to me. I return the gesture and say, "I hope that my weariness has not offended you, lady. I merely seem unable to keep pace with my current responsibilities. I do not wish to place my incompetence as a burden upon the counsel."

She laughs, clearly not offended, and she shakes her head. "Burden us as you see fit, highness." She glances to her brother as he comes up beside her and then says to me, "These are very difficult times for Cerulean, Crystalice most especially. If Jan or I can be of any assistance, please do not hesitate to call on us." She smiles a bit brighter. "Ah, and the Duchess Marissa asked me to relay her support as well. She does not involve herself with the politics of her husband, but she told me that she has the highest hope for you as a king and that you should not concern yourself with others."

"'Bigoted, arrogant bastards' I believe were the words she used," Jan corrects. Ame blushes and laughs, and the two of us join in as well.

From the corner of my eye, I catch sight of my father who is watching me in a way that alerts me to his desire to speak with me, and so I close our conversation with a smile and say, "I appreciate the relay of her message, my lord and lady. Are you leaving tomorrow?"

"Indeed," says Jan with a nod. "Now that the talks have concluded, our mother will be expecting us home to assist her in Brooke."

I incline my head and say, "Very well. If I do not see you at the dining hall in the morning, please go with my blessing."

"Many thanks, my prince," Ame replies, and they both bow before moving past me to leave for their rooms. I sigh and give a shake of my head to Claque when he approaches me, going instead to my father.

"My king," I greet, bowing at the waist when I stand before him.

He gives me a tired look and inclines his head. "Prince Gabriel. Join me for a moment." He turns and heads down the hall, and I'm not fool enough to think that he was asking.

I rise and follow after him, stepping quietly into his study when the guard opens the door.

He moves deep into the well-ordered and pristine office, books neatly organized on shelves, papers in particular stacks, and parchment neatly rolled and stacked in cabinets—all, I am certain, with a certain arrangement known only to my father.

"What did you think of the meetings this week?" he asks me as I inspect his private room.

I turn to look at him and see that he has settled himself into his stuffed chair, lounging back and leaning his elbow on the arm, his fingers tapping idly at his chin. Well, he is seated and not leaning towards me like he wants to eat me, so I suppose this conversation couldn't be too terrible.

I shrug idly and turn to him. I'm not comfortable sitting in his room, so I lean back against the door and cross my arms. "I think that they were, at least in part, productive."

"Oh?"

So no half-answers tonight, it seems. I bite off a sigh and elaborate, "The counsel is taking the White Fang matters seriously, and the majority have come to an understanding that we need more information on them so that we can put an end to their rebellion. I think that we have also effectively come to solutions for the problems of food shortages and trade that are affecting our people and their attitudes towards the crown."

He nods slowly and has changed to stroking his beard instead, looking down at the table in front of his seat and frowning down at it. "And what of today? The conversation today."

I don't really know what answer he is looking for that I have not already given, but my stomach begins to knot up as if I am a mouse inspecting the cheese on a trap and trying to decide if it is worth it or not. Except, unlike the mouse, I have a cat holding me at sword-point ordering me to take the cheese. I just need to figure out how to do so without getting killed.

"Could you be more specific, sir?" I ask, standing up a little straighter. It's late. I'm tired.

King Dante sits back in his seat and looks directly at me now. "Duchess Cilla and Count Vari brought up some significant arguments, Gabriel. The meeting was not the time or place to discuss them, but their concerns are no less relevant."

"Concerning...the Inferno woman, sir?" To my knowledge, father does not even know Cara's name. Every time I have ever heard him speak of her in a manner that was not foul, the most accurate and considerate name he has ever given her is 'the Inferno.

He nods. "Yes, the Inferno," he says and now leans forward and clasps his hands together, looking at me like he's going to eat me. So much for pleasant conversation.

"Although she is gone and dealt with, Gabriel, the fact remains that for nearly half a year, you brought the enemy here and gave her more or less free reign of the castle, allowed yourself to be made the fool in public on numerous occasions, and in general completely upset the trust our people have placed in us."

I swallow the tightness in my throat and venture, "To be perfectly fair, father, I put her in the dungeon when she arrived. I had every intention of leaving her there."

"Do *not* put this on your mother," he snarls at me, and my voice is shoved back into my throat. There is something about staring down a man who for years you have equally admired and feared and having him look back at you with contempt that seems to steal any and all thoughts of rebellion.

Dante leans back once more. "I'm concerned, Gabriel. I'm very concerned..."

He's back to rubbing his beard again. Finally, he looks back to me as if coming back to our conversation and not whatever is occupying his thoughts. "Your suitability as the Crowned Prince has been called into question. You have yourself to blame for that." He takes a moment to let that sink in.

I never wanted to be Crowned Prince, never wanted to be king. But the thought of having that title forcibly taken from me leaves me raw and defensive. I clench my hands and bite back protest. Shouting like a child will help nothing.

"You need to prove to me—to the people—that you are worthy to be called king. And if you cannot, Gabriel…I will take the title from you."

We stay in silence for a moment, and I do not know whether he actually expects me to speak or not. He seems to expect something from me, and at last, I simply stand straight and bow. "Understood, sir." My voice is short and clipped, all emotion stripped from it and hidden from his view.

I stand again, look him straight in the eyes, and then incline my head. "Good evening, King Dante." He does not respond, and I turn from him, leaving the room.

My bedroom is dark when I return. A blue lantern glows to light the way, but it is only just enough to see by. I stand in the doorway for a moment, quite uncertain of what emotion I feel. I can feel tension and anger rising up in me along with the desire to destroy something with my own two hands. But I am also very tired. My body is tired, and my soul is worn.

Part of me, despite the anger and insult I feel at my father's threat, also wonders if perhaps he is right. Perhaps I am not prepared to be king. Perhaps I would not be a good one at all.

And so, my decision is to sigh and sink down onto my bed. I peel off my shoes and my stockings, leaving them on the floor. I unbutton the doublet and deposit it as well. But as I pull my shirt out from my pants, I notice something that does not belong—two letters sitting on my bedside table. Had they been for matters of my princely duties, they would have been left for me in my study. But these must be personal letters, and my heart jumps a bit at the prospect of hearing from a friend, or maybe even from Cara.

I pick them both up and consider the Maeghdra seal on the back of each. I sit back on my bed and reach for the blue lantern dangling overhead, murmuring a command to brighten the room; the enchantment obeys, and the letter comes more clearly into view.

I break the seal and unfold the letter, giving a little smile at the name of the sender. Alistair.

Gabe,

Karnei tells me that he sent you word concerning our rocky trip to Flora—and what he might have missed, I am sure Claque informed you of—so I won't bore you with the details of it. All is as it should be. Scarlet suffered no ill, and the lassie is just fine. I suffered only a minor injury, but it is already healed. The only thing remaining is a scorch of woods that will have to be tended. I promised Karnei that I would hold Cara responsible for the matter, but I've not actually decided on anything. I should perhaps think of something before that non-action comes back to bite my arse. Any ideas that won't end in my house getting set on fire?

In any event, the lasses have settled here just fine. Zsoka has begun her lessons and although she is behind where she should be, she's taken after it rather intently. Scarlet tells me that the girl always has her nose in a book. I didn't even think bairns could read that young. I highly doubt that I did. Scarlet says that she thinks the girl mostly likes to look at the illustrations. Zsoka barely speaks to me, so I wouldn't know, but at least she's talking to Scarlet, and she even seems to have made a few friends in town, rather unwillingly I might add, but friends all the same.

Scarlet gets along well with the house staff and seems to have developed an amicable relationship with my mother. She doesn't venture out to the town much, though, and generally doesn't seem interested in meeting anyone. It leaves me to wonder if she is trying to keep from forming permanent attachments to anyone here. Has she said anything to you on the matter? If she intends to return to Inferno, I've no mind to keep her locked up in her room—besides the fact that it's wood and she'd burn my manor to the ground if she had to—but I would also rather know than not what she intends to do.

How are those old bastards in the counsel treating you? I hope that things have settled down now that you can focus on your tasks. Let me know if you require anything, old friend. You always wait far too long before asking for help, and you really should not.

Don't die,
Ali

I do not even know what to make of Alistair's letter, but for whatever reason, it provokes me to laughter. Perhaps it is because I am so tired or because Alistair seems to be under the impression that Cara tells me any of the things that are on her mind. I just laugh to myself and rub my face wearily, sighing and shaking my head.

Setting his letter aside to answer tomorrow, I smile a bit and pick up the other letter, breaking the seal as well. I'm not exactly certain what I expect, but as usual, what I see is not what I expected at all.

Ice Prince,

What exactly did you mean by sending me such a vacant and lackluster letter? I do not know whether to be offended by your utter lack of concern or emotion or not, but I am not happy over it. If you are happy to have sent me away, then say so. If you miss me, then tell me. But do not, Gabriel Jan'tel, insult me by writing to me in such a cold and unfeeling manner or I simply will not read your letters, nor will I bother myself with the thought of them.

I miss you. And now that I have said it, you must either tell me the same or to the contrary, but you must say something. Your absence is very trying upon my heart, and that of your little Enté as well. I had not expected it to cause me such pain, but the lack of your cold skin and Enté's pale eyes have caused me much more chill than when you were both near. How does the child fare? I hope that he has not been too difficult for you on your own, for I know that Heather most likely has been tending to her own affairs as well. Just be patient with him. He's a stubborn child, but he does think highly of you and seeks to please you. I am certain that he needs you very much right now.

As to the rest of your letter, I am barely going to address your rebuke other than to tell you that you are wrong for chastising me so and I shan't pay you any heed. I clearly had no intention of burning down the woods, and they were not your woods in any event, so I will not apologize to you for it. I have handled the matter myself. I will, however, keep in mind the circumstances of my new home. I have and will continue to be considerate and sensitive towards others to prevent any future complications.

Alistair on the other hand is quite another matter. He says that he is alright, but I am beginning to suspect that he has done serious damage to his leg. He limps when he is tired or when he has been riding too much, and he rubs the leg when he thinks that no one is looking. I have tried to advise him to call for a healer, but he will not listen to a word I say. Will you, perhaps, counsel him? He listens to you.

As to Zsoka, she is adjusting as well as could be hoped, I suppose. She seems interested in her studies but she does not have much patience with herself for the time it takes to learn. Still, she is learning quickly, and I do believe that she will exceed all of her tutor's expectations by the end of the year. The child has even managed to make a few friends. Or rather, a little girl in town declared that they are now friends, and Zsoka has not said to the contrary. I plan to take her back to town soon so that she can have a chance to play with the others. I might start taking her every day after her lessons. It will be good for her to have others her age with whom she can play and talk.

Lady Freya has been welcoming to me in her own way. She is a very strong woman and has a very particular way about doing things, but she manages her estate well and seems genuinely concerned for those around her. Whenever I find her, she is always busy writing to this person or that, or attending meetings with other duchesses and ladies. The men and women act very separately here, but she is quite diligent in all of her affairs. I have a great deal of respect and admiration for her.

Which is why, I suppose, I am so disturbed by a conversation I overheard the other night. Please do not say anything of it to Alistair or Freya, for it was not a conversation I was meant to hear and in fact did not mean to hear it at all. But the fact remains that the other night after Alistair escorted Zsoka and I to a bonfire, Freya warned Alistair that he was settling into a family role with the pair of us, and she warned him that he would damage his political and social standing. This concerns me greatly, Gabriel, as I do not think Freya would have said so if she did not consider such to be a danger.

She is a discerning woman if not a sensitive one, and I trust her judgment.

I really do not even know what to say or do. It's not exactly like I can just ask Alistair about it, and I do not wish to wound him either. Flora is a charming place, and I have thus far enjoyed my time at Maeghdra Manor. It is an incomplete and perhaps lonely existence, but I do not dislike it, and I do not wish to cause trouble here. To be perfectly honest, though, I do not even know if I wish to stay.

I can see Inferno at dusk from the mountains, and my heart misses my homeland so much that it feels as though it might break. And yet, I am frightened to return. I do not know what waits for me there, and I feel as though returning there would completely undo everything that has been done. Does that make any sense to you? For it barely makes any sense to me.

If I return home, I feel as though I will be branded once more with the pain and hatred that led me to the battlefield at the start. My entire life there was based around war and fighting. I have no friends, no family, nothing outside of the military. I do not wish to go back to that life. I do not wish to kill the Cerulean men I care so much for. I could not run a sword through Ckai'ten or through Kale. Tam is dead because of me, and his loss is so heavy upon my heart as if I had been his slayer. I do not think I could bare to wear blood on my hands again.

Here, at least, no one knows who I am. They do not see a soldier or a widow or anything at all. They know nothing of me except that I am an Inferno and Zsoka's nurse. I feel as though I have a chance to start over, to let go of the pain and the hatred and become something entirely new. I did not even realize how much I wanted such a thing, as if I had forgotten how much pain I was in until it was gone, and I do not want to take up that pain again. To take up a sword for to fight means to take up my anger and my hatred and to submit myself to that suffering once more. I do not think I can.

Forgive me for burdening you with my thoughts. I do not wish to speak to anyone else on my inmost contemplations, but I doubt they are of much use to you either. I hope that you at least have been well. Have things become easier since I left? Perhaps now your people will see you as the compassionate king that you are. I believe in you.

Forever your companion,
Scarlet Anita Sön'yana mei Ka'Rose

I know even less of what to make of Cara's letter. The power of it shoots straight through me and pierces my soul. It leaves me shaken and deeply disturbed. And yet, a quiet peace settles over my mind that had not been there before. It will forever startle and surprise me the way she bares her soul to me, open and unafraid and without hesitation. Somehow with her own vulnerability, she strips me bare and leaves me defenseless to her, and I am always at a loss as to how to guard myself. And yet, even if I knew how, I do not think that I would.

With a heavy sigh, I sink back onto the bed, reading through her letter once more. A smile tugs at my lip. Even when she is so far from me, when I read her letter, I can hear her voice in my heart. It is low and smooth and it fades in and out with her thoughts. I can picture her writing this letter, biting her lower lip the way she does when she is frustrated, or the way she scrunches her nose when something disturbs her either for the better or for worse. Even so far away, I can hear her laughter as though she is beside me, and that petulant frown on her lips when she calls me to task.

I miss her.

I read the letter again and run a hand through my hair, pulling out the blue ribbon and ignoring it. I sit up once more and get up from my bed, going over to my desk. Upon it is a quill and ink and parchment, and I draw them out to begin my correspondence to my little spitfire.

PART TWO

Hope is the thing with feathers
That perches in the soul
And sings the tune without the words
And never stops at all.
-Emily Dickenson

Chapter Twenty Two
Scarlet

A Few Weeks Later
Maeghdra Manor, Flora

As much as I dislike the rain, it makes such pleasant sounds. I am alone in the manor, sitting in the dining hall with the fire blazing in the hearth. A charm keeps the sweep cleared of rain so that it does not snuff the flames, and the fire brings warmth to the home. Outside, a storm rages. It had been nothing but a gentle pitter-patter a few moments before, but the past little while, it has picked up in intensity and strength. The rain pelts against the windows and bellows against the stone walls. I can hear it on the roof, and in the distance, thunder roars like a mighty sky-god.

Outside, I can scarcely hear the sound of pounding hooves and the shouts of a man, along with the wiry stableman who lives in the loft above the stables. Lifting my head, my eyes go to the door as a great beast of a man throws it open, the dark storm at his back as his rain-drenched form plods into the foyer.

I stand up from where I had been sitting in the dining hall and turn to watch Alistair grin warmly at the inside of the manor before stepping within, pushing back his cloak hood. It's been raining all week, and apparently Alistair has had to travel in such horrible weather. Likewise, Zsoka and I have been trapped inside for quite a while, and it's beginning to make us both quite edgy. She does her best to sleep her time away, but I am too restless to slumber. It's been weeks, but I have not yet heard back from Gabriel. Of course, if the weather really has been so miserable across the lands, then it is no wonder that I have not heard word yet.

"Welcome back," I greet quietly.

"Ah, stuck inside, lass?" Alistair greets me, shaking off his wet cloak and hanging it by the fire to dry before moving over to where I sit with the kitchen knives and a sharpening stone, keeping myself busy.

I scoff at him and say, "Cats do not like the rain, much less fire-borne ones."

He chuckles. "Not even out to the gazebo?"

My face falls, and I look up at him morosely. "I tried, but I could not see the border." He seems surprised to find that I ventured the rain at sunset to catch sight of the burning forest, and it leaves him speechless for a moment before he sighs and gives me a little smile. Suddenly, however, I recall my anxiousness and ask with earnest, "Have you a letter for me?"

"Ah," he gives me an apologetic look and say, "Nay, sweetheart. The roads are much too miserable for any carrier to be out. Dinna fret, though. I'm sure t'will be here soon." He reaches into his coat pocket, however, and procures a piece of parchment, handing it to me. "Mayhaps this can interest ye, though."

"What is it?" I ask, unfolding the thing and reading the script.

Before I can finish, Alistair explains, "An invitation to the Autumn Dance. Tis more a formality since I'm more or less required to go, but t'was curious mayhaps ye and Zsoka wouldst enjoy it. Has Getara finished yer dresses yet?"

I nod. "Indeed. They are lovely. Thank you. Zsoka is very fond of them." That is something of a lie, but I cannot very well tell him that trying to get that squirming creature into a fine frock was a nightmare, and she complained the whole time and just wanted it off.

He grins again and says, "I'm glad to hear it! I'm sure ye'll both be the envy of the dance."

I give a little smile, but I am not quite certain what to stay, and I sit there somewhat anxiously as he warms himself by the fire, his boots still muddy and soaked. "Ah...Cali has gone home and Lady Freya has gone to meet with Lady Sheona Barclay with Molly and Skylar. She said that she would most likely stay a few nights with the weather as it is, but she will return soon."

He nods to himself and sighs wearily. "Tis just us and the lassie, then? Where *is* the wee thing?"

The sudden realization that the manor is completely empty except for we three suddenly makes me alarmingly uncomfortable, and I hope that Zsoka wakes from her nap sooner than later.

"Upstairs resting," I tell him, turning back to the knives and sharpening stone to give myself something to do. I look back down and explain, "We do not do well in the rain and cold."

"She's nay ill, is she?" he asks at once, and I glance to his face, finding concern and fear there.

I smile just a bit and shake my head. "No, Alistair. Do not look frightened so. She is merely tired and miserable. Once the sun is out, she will be running around again."

He returns my little smile and says quietly, "I'm rather fond o'the lassie. I'd hate for anything to happen to her."

"The Inferno are strong," I assure him, returning to my knives. It will please Cali to have them sharpened and cleaned for her.

A moment of silence stretches between we two, and I can feel Alistair's eyes on me. I do not look over at him, ignoring him as best as I can while I work carefully. For a moment, I thought as though he meant to leave me to work, but he breaks my precarious silence with, "Sweetheart…what is it? Why d'ye hold me distant so?"

I had not expected him to be so blunt, and it startles me just a bit. My fingers slip on the oiled stone, and the knife slices my thumb. I swear and bolt up and away from the knives, as if they might somehow lurch towards me and bite me.

Alistair is at my side in an instant, taking my hand in his and inspecting it quickly before saying, "Here, lass. Let's get that oil off yer hands." Still holding my hand carefully, he pulls me into the kitchen and pumps some water into the basin. I sit by the counter feeling my heart race and my limbs go numb, my voice somehow muted. The whole while, Alistair says nothing, washing my hands clean of oil and blood so that he can look to my thumb once again.

"It's nay so bad," he assures me and glances up at me from where he is bent over my hand, giving me a wry little smile. In the distance, thunder gives a mighty cry, and the windows turn white with the strike of lightning so nearby. I jump a bit but then turn my eyes back to him.

I frown at him. "I wasn't too worried over a prick. If I haven't died yet, I doubt the little kitchen knife poses much of a threat."

Alistair laughs a bit and finds some cloth, wrapping my thumb carefully until I can feel my heartbeat in the tip. "Aye mayhaps, lass, but if ye're wanting to keep those fingers, ye should be more careful."

I smile just a bit, standing in the kitchen with him as he presses against my thumb to stop the bleeding. I look up at him and wish that I hadn't, for those green eyes are focused down on my golden ones with an intensity I do not expect. I look away, turning my attention back to my thumb and feeling my heart jump.

"I…" I try to speak, but I cannot seem to find the right words, and I do not really want to go blathering on like an idiot. "I, ah, was simply wondering why you decided to leave your face unshaved."

Alistair gives a sudden burst of laughter, throwing back his head. Well, I had wondered why he'd come back with a jaw of short, blond hair. He grins at me and the sight eases some of my tension. "I think it looks rather handsome." He throws back his head in a little pose, and I laugh, shaking my head at him.

"Indeed," I tell him. "As long as you think so."

He winks at me and asks, "And yerself?"

I wrinkle my nose at him but smile and say, "Aye. I like it well enough."

Alistair chuckles quietly to himself, and I give him a wry look before turning my attention back to my thumb. I take my hand back from him and remove the cloth, cleaning it carefully and finding that it has stopped bleeding. "There…tis naught but a nick."

I glance to him to find him watching me with an exasperated sort of look, and I laugh. "What's that look for?"

"Ye," is all he says and sighs, getting up and going back to the dining hall. I follow him, watching him sit by the fire.

"If you are cold, you should go change," I tell him, but I sit beside him, feeling the anxiousness I felt before fade away. My friend has returned home, and I am happy to see him.

"I missed you," I tell him suddenly.

He looks surprised and turns his attention to me with a little smile. "D'ye now?"

I nod. "The manor is quiet with you gone."

He laughs to himself and murmurs quietly as he looks back down to his hands, "That so, eh?" My smile fades a bit because I can tell that there is something on his mind that he is not saying. I frown at him, curious. He peeks up at me and then smiles a bit before asking, "Ye ne'er answered me, lass. What irks ye so?"

I consider him for a moment, this time not so startled. Finally, I say, "I am not irked…merely unnerved." He raises a brow, and I give an apologetic smile. "I overheard your conversation with Freya before you left. I hadn't meant to eavesdrop, but…"

He seems confused at first, but then his eyes widen with realization. "Ah lass," he sighs. "She'd nay hurt ye, did she?" He puts an arm around my shoulders and squeezes.

I look up to him with a little smile and say, "No, it is not that. Freya does not dislike me; I know that. It is merely…" I do not know how to explain, and I bite my lip thinking of how to do so.

Alistair places his thumb upon my bottom lip, however, pulling it gently from between my teeth and away from the abuse.

I look up at him, feeling his warm touch linger on my lip, and now anything I had thought really has disappeared.

He does not smile, does not speak, merely leans down and replaces his thumb with his lips. His lips are warm and calloused, and the prick of his beard and mustache tickle the soft skin around my lips. He smells of cedar trees and of horses and of the sour, Flora earth. It is not unpleasant, his kiss.

A shock of warmth shoots through me, and I freeze still for a moment before pulling away and frowning at him.

"I wish you wouldn't do that when I am trying to speak."

He laughs a bit and sits up straight. "Then speak, lass. What've ye to say to me?"

I sigh, my face feeling hot and my hands trembling a bit. I rub at them to give myself something to do and I look down at my lap before murmuring, "I do not…I do not wish to cause you ruin. Freya seemed...very insistent that my presence here would only bring you trouble."

Alistair touches the bottom of my chin and lifts my face to look on him. He watches me in a moment more serious than I have ever seen him look, but he breaks it with a wry little smile. "Ye've nay done a'thing, sweetheart. Dinna fret so. She's but warnin me against actin unreasonably."

I sigh, lowering my eyes in thought. "She accused you of settling into a family with Zsoka...and with me."

"And if I do?" he asks.

My eyes snap back to his, and I watch him, feeling anxious and cornered. It makes me want to run.

Outside, I can hear the storm beating upon the side of the manor, pounding against the brick and clattering on the glass panes. The manor is so dark except for the fire at our backs even though night is still several hours off.

"Mama?" a sleepy voice pipes up from the top of the stairs, and I jerk my chin away from Alistair to look up at the black-haired child rubbing her eyes wearily. She stands in her night dress, her hair all askew. She yawns and then peers down at us sitting there, saying nothing.

I smile faintly at her and say, "Zsoka, come downstairs. Lord Alistair is home. Come and greet him."

The child murmurs something and trudges step by step down the stairs before coming to the fire. She snuggles up into my arms and murmurs a tired greeting to our host who smiles and pats the top of her head gently. She yawns and gives him an annoyed look before snuggling up to me further, lethargic.

"Cats really do hate the rain?" Alistair asks.

I nod. "Indeed."

A Few Weeks Later

The Autumn Dance is held at Castle Flora. Each of the three dukes—Maeghdra, Karnei, and Gaelen—reside in the three corners of Flora: the northern woods, the western mountains, and the southern grasslands. However, in the center of Flora near the Fauna Lake is a castle in neutral territory. It belongs to neither of the three dukes and thus is a place where there exists no hierarchy of guest and host between them. They can gather as friends and colleagues in mutual arrangement. It is there where the annual Autumn Dance is held. It is also the largest estate in Flora, Alistair tells me, five stories tall and cylindrical, the middle of which is open underneath the sky. For our sake, then, I am glad that the rain stopped and seems to have gone for good.

Each of the three territories receives a floor of the castle. The first floor is all open dancing and dining area. The second floor is filled with meeting halls and smaller convention rooms. The top three floors are bedrooms. Alistair informed me and Maeghdra will be staying on the fourth floor as a courtesy to allow the aged Duke of Karnei to be closer to the ground floor—along with two of the Karnei ladies who are expecting children—while the oldest member of the Gaelen clan is in good health and does not mind an extra flight of stairs. The Den is an equally tall structure, and so the stairs do not concern me.

"We canna wait to hear of the dance," a woman says to Alistair with a grin.

Another young woman beside her says eagerly, "Aye! You mus' come home quick, milord, an' tell us all about it."

I help Zsoka onto her horse and get her settled before looking back at Alistair with a laugh. He's surrounded by no less than ten young ladies all here to see him off since we will not be back for at least a month. They've all brought things for Zsoka as well, which I am grateful for. Zsoka is not used to presents, and while it makes her nervous to receive gifts, I think that she's fairly fond of many of them and unused to the rare treat.

"Alistair!" I call, rescuing him from the bombardment.

I can tell the difference now between when he wants to be social and when he is trying to get away as politely as possible. Right now, he has his hands up as a symbolic barrier between him and the others and his smile does not quite reach his eyes. Every few seconds he takes a little step back, scooting nearer and nearer to the horses. He's ready to get out of here.

Whipping his head around to look at me, he grins and calls, "Aye, lass!" He turns to the ladies and excuses himself, kissing a few of their cheeks and then bowing out gracefully. I'm laughing when he climbs onto his horse.

"Have I annoyed ye, lass?" he calls to me, grinning as he gives the command to his horse and starts down the road, giving a final wave to our departure party.

I stop laughing and ask warmly, "Do I sound annoyed? I just find it funny is all."

"*I* am annoyed," Freya says, climbing into her carriage with Molly and Skylar behind us.

"They all love you so," I tease Alistair. "It is cruel to lead them all on. The poor town boys must all hate you."

Alistair laughs and shakes his head. "Ah, I mean'na harm. They ken I've nay mind to be wed now."

"Do they?" I ask with a cunning little smile, equal parts serious as I am teasing.

He gives me a surprised look and then rubs his chin, scratching at the new growth on his beard. "Hm…mayhaps I *do* flirt a wee bit too much."

"Ha!" I say, and he looks to me. "You admit it. You *are* a flirt."

He laughs warmly, throwing back his head and then having to fix his hat, chuckling while he does so. "I'd nay say such thing!"

I smile to myself as we ride side-by-side out of town, Zsoka riding between us, Freya's carriage behind us, and an escort both ahead and behind.

"Why don't you marry one of them?" I ask. "I've met several of them, and many of them are wonderful ladies. They're clever and kind and lovely. Surely one of them would make a fine wife?"

He clucks his tongue and considers the road ahead of him, smiling to himself and thinking on my words. He sighs after a bit, although his jovial spirit has not yet fallen. "Aye and aye. Any one o'them wouldst make a fine wife. But…tis all they could be."

I arch a brow at him with a bit of a frown. "Well, what more do you want?"

He casts a smirk my way and says, "Ah, but there is more than that, lass." Another heavy sigh as he thinks. "Any one o'them could keep a good house, raise some fine bairns, and mayhaps even be witty enough to keep a mind o'the other dukes and politics in Flora…"

When he doesn't continue, I prod with a, "But?"

He gives a crooked smile and then it fades before he says, "But t'would always be one-sided. I've seen too much. None o'them kens what it means to face down the enemy. None o'them kens what it means to lose a dear friend, to watch them die. They dinna ken how it feels to know that the decisions ye make in a council room affect the lives o'people who are under yer protection…and what it feels like when ye fail."

I consider him and then look ahead. "I think you underestimate them," I say. "Many have lost ones they love. They've lost brothers and fathers…some of them may lose sons as well. And in Gaelen, they are constantly under attack by the Levosa. Many of them have had to defend themselves."

He nods slowly, thinking to himself and rubbing at his face again. I think the new beard annoys him and I wonder at why he doesn't just shave it off it is so bothersome. He shakes his head then and says, "Aye, mayhaps. But, in any mind, I've nay found a one who I can share those things with and who'd understand with more than an 'aye dear, tha's nice'."

I laugh a bit and say, "You're too picky."

He scoffs and tosses his head in my direction. "Says the pot calling the kettle black!" He makes a rude noise, "And what o'ye, lassie?"

I frown at him. "What *of* me? I've been married. I do not wish to be again."

"Ye'd marry Gabriel if ye could," he says bluntly.

My teeth snap together and I glare at him, looking at him sitting upright on his horse and watching the road ahead. "You'll mind your tongue if you know what's good for you, Alistair. You know nothing of me."

He looks to me from the corner of his eye and smirks a bit, but then it softens into a little smile, "Ah, lass, dinna be so sore. I'd nay mean offense, but ye wound me."

"How so?" I've stopped glaring, but I'm still frowning.

He smiles. "I ken ye better than ye say. And I dinna much like bein lied to, even if ye're lying to yerself too."

He turns his head to actually look at me, but I break sight and focus ahead of me, scowling. He chuckles and looks ahead of him. "Ye're angry. Ye dinna like it when people ken how ye feel. It scares ye. I find that funny since the Inferno art oft so forthright with their feelings. Why'na ye?"

I take in a slow, steady breath, not really wanting to have this conversation. "Because words have power. What is real can be changed by what is said and some things do not need to be changed and should not be said."

He scoffs. "Tis'na answer t'all."

I do not reply to him, and he just lets out a long, slow sigh, staring ahead of him.

"All's I meant…is ye've got yer own reasons for holding out…I do as well. A Flora only takes one mate. I want to ken that the one I take is sommon I want by my side. Sommon who—even if I lose her…the memory t'would be enough to last me a lifetime."

I look over at him, and my anger fades away, watching the somber and somewhat wistful look on his face. I reach over and tug on the feather in his hat, teasing him.

He looks at me with a curious expression, and I reply with a little smile.

"You put too much faith in one person, Alistair. It is good to love, but to give someone the responsibility of all that weight…when you do lose them, you will find yourself unable to move on. Sometimes it'll destroy you…Trust me…your mate wouldn't want that."

I look back ahead of me and release my pent up breath with a little sigh. "Trust me…I know that all too well."

Alistair follows my gaze to the road ahead, letting a companionable and yet somehow heavy silence fall between us two. "We'd make a good pair, we would," he says mildly, and I cannot tell from his voice whether he means it or is only in jest.

For some reason, a faint smile tugs at my lips, and I do not feel as anxious as I had before. "Aye," I say, as equally mild. "We would."

Chapter Twenty Three
Scarlet

A Few Days Later
Castle Flora

"I've never seen such a beautiful place," I murmur quietly. The ride had been long and uneventful—trees can only be interesting for so long; but the sight of the palace before me halts my breath.

Alistair looks over at me and gives a wide grin as I shake Zsoka awake so that she can look as well. It is late afternoon, but Zsoka was tired and decided to ride with me on my horse so that she could nap. She murmurs sleepily and rubs her face before sighing and looking up at the great structure before us.

The castle is made of a pale, cream stone and is nestled amongst tall trees, some of which are nearly as tall as the castle itself. It looms high up into the sky, cylindrical and beautiful. A stone courtyard boasts arches that cast flickering shadows upon the ground, and the palace is so entirely open. The first floor is almost completely bare to the outside world. There is a ceiling over all but the center and columns here and there for support, but there are hardly any walls. What stone walls exist are cut into with large, arched openings that hold no panes or shutters of any kind. The other floors have smaller windows with glass panes that can be shut during the rain, but it is all very unusual and yet impressive.

"It is beautiful," I whisper, drawing up my horse to stop within the courtyard. People are bustling about excitedly, numerous servants bringing in horses and luggage, shouting to this person or to that, directing them all on where to go.

A few children run about, laughing, and Zsoka eyes them curiously and warily at the same time. Although she's not in her nicest gown, Zsoka is Alistair's ward and so is dressed in a beautiful riding dress of heavy damask embroidered with beautiful, red flowers on a gold background.

"Tis, isn't it?" Alistair asks, and he reaches up to grab Zsoka from my horse.

I look to him and tighten my knees on the horse so that I can help lower her down.

Once the child's feet are on the ground, he reaches up to help me off, and I give him a snide look and throw my leg over, hopping down on my own. He laughs at me as I shake out my skirts and then sigh, looking to my charge.

"It's always so busy the first day," Freya says, leaving the carriage and coming up beside me. We haven't spoken of her conversation with Alistair, and she has continued to treat me as she always has, with an attitude of mild disdain which I have come to recognize as her way of showing respect. Strange woman. If she didn't like you, Alistair told me a little while back, she'd be nice to you and would be polite because she wouldn't find you worth the time to speak frankly with. For whatever that's worth.

"Well, let's head inside. We're on the fourth floor." I look over to Alistair as he hands off our horses to the servants who came with us and throws one of his bags over his shoulder.

Here, it's not uncommon for the gentry to do some of the work themselves, carry things and such. It's also not uncommon for proper ladies to know how to cook and to help with chores. In Flora, they don't care as much for things like tea parties and embroidery.

Up four flights of stairs, Alistair shows us to our rooms. Zsoka and I will be staying in the same room with a few of the household servants. There are several townsfolk who, while they don't generally work at the manor, accompany Alistair on extended trips where he would be less able and have less time to take care of things himself. Despite not really knowing any of the others, I enjoy company and find it much more soothing to sleep with others near than in a room alone or even with only Zsoka as company.

Inside, I begin to help the servants unpack. The clothes have all been stuffed into chests and crates, and so I pull out mine and Zsoka's nicest dresses first and shake them out, laying them out on the bed once the women have made it up with the bedding we brought. I smooth down the fine skirts and then unpack the jewelry boxes and combs, laying them on the dresser. A knock on the door calls my attention as I help set up the rooms. There is no castle host or castle servants, so we do everything ourselves.

I look up to find Alistair at the door and give him a curious look.

"Oy, lassie," he greets. "I'll like as nay be gone most of the next few days in meetings. If ye take the wee one downstairs, Karnei said the nurses and gentry bairns to will be on the first floor and in the ballroom playin."

"Is that an order or merely information?" I ask. I am not too certain about suddenly shoving Zsoka into a room with hundreds of children. She frightens easily and doesn't play well with others. I was hoping to be able to spend some time with her on her own letting her get used to this place first before suddenly shoving her in front of people.

Alistair grins at me and says, "I'd nay be fool enough to give ye any orders. Do as ye wilt with her. I merely thought ye'd enjoy company as well. Most o'the nurses are yer age."

"So now you're setting up playdates for me as well?" I challenge, not entirely certain if I am amused or annoyed, arching a brow at him as I straighten out my riding hat and set it on the dresser.

He laughs, although there is a slight uneasiness to it, as if he is aware that I haven't yet decided to be bothered by him. "I'll take my leave now afore ye get to throwin things at me." And then he disappears back into the hall, ducking passersby to head down to the second floor where the gentry would be gathering.

"He's daft," Zsoka says beside me, startling me.

I look over at her in mild alarm and then laugh and say, "Don't say such, Zsoka. It's rude. He's not daft. Mama just does not play well with others."

She looks up at me with a frown but then sighs and agrees to let me lead her down to the ballroom so that she can at least see the other children even if she does not wish to play with them.

All in all, there are a dozen children of the gentry, not including the youths who no longer require close supervision. There are others as well, though, servant children who came with their nurse mothers and who are playmates to the little lords and ladies.

I stand by with Zsoka in the ball room, watching a group of crawling children sit and play while the older ones run around. I hadn't really planned on talking to anyone, but a young woman with red hair approaches me nonetheless, holding on her hip a little girl about Zsoka's age and size.

"Ye moos be Scarlet." She smiles at me, her green eyes warm and her smile bright. "I'm Clara. This is Kenina; she's Laird Barclay's daughter."

Barclay, he is one of the Maeghdra lairds. I've not met him, yet, but I am familiar at least with the five Maeghdra lairds: Oakensten, the annoying bastard child; Barclay, the old, gentle peacekeeper; Erskine, the stern conservative; Tadg, the accomplished self-made man; and Micheil, the hopeful youth. Of all of them, Laird Gavin Barclay lives the farthest away, and Laird Archi Tadg is something of a recluse since his wife died a few years ago with the birth of his only son, Rory Tadg.

"It is a pleasure to meet you, Kenina," I tell the little girl who hides her face shyly against her nurse. I laugh a bit and say to Clara, "I am Scarlet the Inferno, nurse to the duke's ward. Zsoka, say hello, my love." I put a hand at Zsoka's back and she looks up to the woman uneasily before dipping into a little curtsy.

She doesn't speak, and I do not make her. She went mute for years out of fear of others. I will not force her to speak if she does not wish to so long as she is polite.

"Ye've nay been in Flora long, 'ave ye, Scarlet?" Clara asks, and I shake my head.

"No. Less than a year."

She nods to herself, putting Kenina down while she and the little Zsoka stare at each other uneasily. "Ah've 'eard stories from the laird aboot ye."

My stomach churns a bit, somewhat annoyed. Gossip is something universal to all societies. The only thing that changes is the environment in which it is spread and the degree to which it can affect a person. "Oh?" I ask warily.

She gives me a little smile and assures, "Nothin bad. Well, nay really. Other than ye settin the forest on fire. But e'eryone kens t'was an accident. I'm jus' happy to finally meet ye."

She seems sincere, and I smile faintly, inclining my head to her. "You as well, Clara." Getting to know someone always starts out awkwardly. But by the end of an hour, we sit together on the stairs and laugh while our two charges take turns hiding and finding each other below us in the courtyard. "Ah! Zsoka's filthy now. I'll need to get her bathed for dinner."

"Och, 'ave ye seen the baths?" she asks.

I shake my head.

"Well, the baths are communal here. They're on the second floor. One for the lasses and one for the lads. I'll shows ye. Jus' bring her clothes an' meet me on the second floor. Kenina needs a bath anyways."

After wrangling the little child away from her newfound friend, I grab a change of clothes for the pair of us and then meet Clara on the second floor. There, she smiles cheerfully and shows me through one of a set of double doors into a stone room.

"Ha' ye e'er had communal baths, Scarlet?" she asks.

I nod a bit, looking around at the large, open room with a pool of water in the center. "Not like this though," I reply, looking back to Clara. "We usually go down to the stream to bathe in groups of ten or twenty girls. The waters are hot there. I've never seen a bath in a room."

Beside me, Zsoka hisses, and I looked down at her with a little half-smile. Cats don't really like water, especially not deep water. Large cats like tigers are always hit-and-miss; some of us love water and some of us would rather just bask in the dry sunlight.

Zsoka seems to mostly be the latter—that and she is a young child for whom bath time is her greatest disdain for no other reason, it seems, than to drive me mad. The bath looks like it covers most of the women to their stomachs, so it will probably be fairly high on Zsoka.

"It's not so bad. Baths are nice." She gives me a cold look and then bares her teeth at me.

Clara heads off to the side with Kenina and set down their things on one of the benches, and I follow suit. She bends and helps Kenina out of her dress and then pulls off her own. "Dinna worry aboot modesty in this room. All the lassies are quite used to jus' walkin'round without a stitch on."

"How very different from the Cerulean indeed," I say quietly, bending down to unlace Zsoka's dress.

"I dinna need a bath," Zsoka mutters, sulking quietly.

"Is it now?" Clara asks me, ignoring the whining child.

Zsoka pulls away from me, but I drag her back. She hisses and I continue with the unlacing, pulling off her outer dress and then working on her petticoats.

"Aye," I say, for the first time noticing my lapse into a more colloquial speech and finding myself somewhat discomforted by it. "Yes. Other than the day they're born, I'd be surprised if mothers ever even see their children naked."

"How funny!" she says with a little laugh.

With Zsoka now unclothed, I fold her gown as she crosses her arms over her chest, clearly uncomfortable with all the naked women and children running around, and she scoots closer to me.

"I thought so too," I tell Clara and look up at her with a smile to find that she's disrobed as well and takes Kenina's hand, leading her to the bath.

"There's a shallow end where ye can sit doon," she tells me. "Hurry up and come'n."

"Alright." But when my fingers go to my laces, I freeze suddenly. Looking down at the front laces of my bodice, I can see the very top of a scar curling around my shoulder to my collar bone.

It's where Gabriel bit me. His fangs, rather than merely piercing my flesh, ripped the skin from my muscle as I struggle, and so there are several jagged tears from the top of my breast up to my shoulder where his fangs found sure footing and sank in.

Those aren't the only ones either, nor the worst. The scar around my neck is mostly unnoticed, but there are stab wounds and slashes in my belly, numerous bite marks and cuts on my arms. Not to mention that horrible gash in my leg which nearly cost me the limb and has henceforth left it slightly disfigured since some of the muscle never regrew and the long scar running down my thigh is somewhat caved in. And those are only battle wounds. All down my legs, arms, and chest, an intricate network of scars in the old language and sacred patterns are carved into my flesh. Moreover, my skin is like burnt gold—dark and warm—and my scars are all a pale pink and shine when the light hits them.

I am not particularly vain. Well, not usually at least. But although the women in the room range from sickly skinny to obscenely fat and from homely to radiant in appearance, none of them bear the sort of scars as I do on my flesh, and I do not particularly wish to draw attention to them. Perhaps if I can disrobe quickly and go into the water…the bath looks as though herbs and oils treat it, for it is more opaque and milky in color than it is transparent. It should do well enough to hide the marks if I stay mostly submerged.

"Come'n, Scarlet!" Clara calls, giving a little wave to me from where she scrubs Kenina's back with a soapy sponge while they kneel on the little shelf she'd been talking about.

Zsoka lets out an unhappy yowl, going over to where they are and crouching down, glaring at the suds and the water. It's not as though she's never had a bath before. But usually we bathe together in a tub outside in the sunshine. The largeness of this room and the number of women in it is a bit unnerving.

"Come'n," Kenina says and laughs at Zsoka. "I'll wash yer back, Zsoka, if ye'd like."

Zsoka makes an unhappy noise but seems to consider it…at least until Kenina giggles and tosses some water on her. The cat-child yelps and scrambles back before suddenly taking her *Shift*—and I'm not entirely sure she meant to—and bolting for the door, claws scraping and clattering on the stone floor desperately as she slides this way and that in her attempts at escaping the bathing room.

Women start screaming and bolting out of the way of the little tiger cub running past a woman's legs and out the door she'd just opened.

"Zsoka!" I cry out, forgetting the lacings and the scars and taking off after her. I had already kicked out of my slippers, so my feet are bare on the stone floor as I tear down the hall after the girl.

In human form, I can catch the little scamp in an instant. But as a tiger cub, she's faster and sneakier and smaller than me, which leaves me ripping my laces off so that my dress doesn't strangle me when I *Shift* and take off running down the hall after her. People scream and lurch out of the way, and a few of the men *Shift* into bears, uncertain of my intentions. My attention, however, is focused upon the little cub who turns a sharp corner and darts into a room down the curved hall.

I yowl out at her and charge into the room, throwing the other heavy, wooden door open and scrambling into a large meeting room.

The men in the room had already jumped to their feet when the cub burst in, so they are standing and shouting to each other and trying to figure out what's happening.

Alistair, laughing, offers his hands in gesture to try and calm them all.

My eyes graze over them but then land upon the little cub hiding under the table as if that can somehow hide or protect her from me.

She curls her lips back in mean hiss, and I do the same.

"Scarlet," Alistair greets once the noise settles down.

"Wha'n the name o'all tings holy's goin'an 'ere!" one of the men shouts, and I snort at him before looking to Alistair.

I cannot speak, so I merely snort and walk towards the table.

"Gotten herself into trouble again, has she, lass?" Alistair asks, and I nod my head with a glance his way.

I do not particularly want to go crawling under a table, and cub or not, the little girl can still scratch out my eyes whether by intent or accident. It's never very good to force a cat out of a corner they've backed themselves into.

Alistair crouches down to look at the little girl. "Need help?" he offers me.

I scoff at him and give him an annoyed look, stalking the little one who hisses again.

Fire begins to spark on the tip of her fur. She doesn't really hate baths this much. Now, she's just responding from instinct to my chasing and stalking her.

I make a few noises at her, sitting down and watching her, trying to coax her out, but now the men start muttering to themselves, and we are intruding. I'm tired of playing games with this child.

So, without warning, I dive under the table and snatch the little thing by the scruff of her neck.

She lights herself on fire, but that doesn't bother me in the least. She might leave some scorch marks on the underside of the table, but she doesn't burn near hot enough to set it ablaze.

I drag the cub out clawing and shrieking, a little fiery ball of wrath and wounded pride. Turning around, I duck my head to Alistair and the others out of apology.

"Ack, dinna fret, lass. All's well," says a man, and I look to him. Judging by his similarity to Kenina with that golden yellow hair and hazel eyes of his, he must be the Laird Barclay.

Another man chuckles and says to Alistair, "Aye, laddie. 'tis a good ting ye bringin that fire-maid with ye. The wee lassie'ed scorch any o'er maid sky high, sh'would."

Alistair grins at him and says, "Aye, I'm pleased to hear ye say, Master Craig. She's a'might handy to have around."

I tilt my head in Alistair's direction and give a little snort, but then I carry the mewling kitten out of the room and back down the hall from whence we came.

Those who'd seen us before now pause to giggle or laugh a bit at the sight, and now the cub who has thoroughly embarrassed herself stops her fussing and hangs in defeat from my mouth. I drop her straight into the bath and follow after in my cat form.

Chapter Twenty Four
Scarlet

Castle Flora

Clara and Kenina are still in the bath, and they laugh at the sight while I *Shift* and come up a woman, pushing my hair out of my face. "Ah see ye found her then," Clara says, and I look over at the cub paddling her way to the shelf where she too *Shifts* and sputters out some water, pushing her black hair out of her face before shooting me a nasty look.

"Next time, don't run," I tell her without sympathy, looking over at Clara and laughing. "Naturally, she went and found the meeting room where everyone was."

"Nay!" she cries, and we both laugh when I nod. "Ack, well. This'un can pull some nasty tricks of her own, can'tcha?"

Kenina gives a little grin and swims over to Zsoka. The water isn't really deep enough to warrant swimming, but the child seems content.

I, on the other hand, sink into the water until it is up to my neck, watching as Zsoka permits the other girl to scrub her back with the sponge, which apparently feels nice, because the little cat makes a happy sound and leans forward with a little smile and closes her eyes peacefully.

"Wouldst like help with yer hair and back, Scarlet?" Clara offers.

I look at her with an appreciative smile, but I shake my head. I really don't want anyone around my scars, and I suddenly find myself quite anxious to get home and take semi-private baths once more. "No, thank you. I'm fine."

"Ack," says another nurse, coming over to us. She looks to be a bit younger than Clara, more my own age, her warm, brown eyes still over-large and full of innocence. "Oy, lassie. Tis good to finally meet ye. I'm nurse to Una, the Laird Tadg's missy. Ye can calls me Maria."

We are all Maeghdra nurses then, it seems. Maria gestures to where a trio of girls around ten years of age talk at the far side of the pool.

Clara greets the new woman and then says to me, "That one there next to Una tis me other charge, Seonag—Kenina's older sister—but she's oft with Una an' Lindsey, the other lass."

"Una just twas married a few months back," Maria tells me, and I look to her.

"So young?"

"She's eleven," the woman says, "and of age. But, aye, tis nay usual. In Flora, tis oft'na encouraged to marry young."

"Because of the one-mate rule?" I ask.

Both women nod, and Maria continues, "Most o'the time, the men get married aboot Duke Craig of Gaelen's age."

"And how old is he?"

Kenina replies, "Mmm close to Duke Alistair's—thirty years some odd."

"Ah."

Maria nods. "But tis oft to marry older too. Ye've met the Duke of Karnei—Hector—aye?"

"Aye," I say, and then find myself annoyed at the word again. My father would have been crossed to hear me speak so.

She nods and continues, "We was all just to think he'd ne're marry—for he'd turned gray afore he found Eithne."

"She was younger though," Kenina informs me, and then proceeds to tell me all about the rather romantic courting Karnei did for his bride, Eithne, who was orphaned in the south by the Levosa and had grown up fighting them. She'd been about my own age when she moved up to Karnei after the Levosa destroyed her town. He'd fallen in love with her and had gone to great lengths to please her and impress her, but it still took almost five years before she agreed to marry him.

It is sweet, and I enjoy hearing about it, along with many more stories about the gentry in Flora. There is Gavin and Sheona Barclay, lairds under Alistair and parents to Kenina and Seonag, who had met under rather different circumstances when Sheona gave her not-then-mate a sound verbal lashing for frightening her horse and making him run off, and she'd made him give up his own horse in exchange to go and track him down, neither of them realizing that she and her father were to be guests in his home. She'd had no idea who he was when she'd stolen his horse to reclaim the one he'd frightened off.

And then there is the Laird Gordon Carsen from Gaelen who rescued his mate, Malvina, from a Levosa raid and then married her the next month. Everyone still coos over them since they're young and Malvina not much older than Una, although Gordon just reached his twenties as the second youngest laird in all Flora, second only to Logan of Karnei who is a year younger.

I like these sorts of stories, and I put my chin on my arms over the side of the bath and listen quietly, smiling to myself. It's not that Inferno women don't love romance stories—the young ones especially are incredibly romantic—but there's a certain sort of excitement over it with the Flora. Although there are, of course, many disheartening stories of men who marry young and find themselves hating their wives a few years later or vice versa. There are stories of others being deceived and marrying for only title or money when what they thought was desired of them was love. I'm not fool enough to know those stories don't exist. But what is the use in hearing them beyond as a tale of caution? It is the love stories I like best, the ones that fill me with hope and laughter and warmth.

"Ah, we'd best get out an' get ready for the ball," Maria says to me, and I smile at her and laugh in agreement.

"Zsoka, time to get out."

She and Kenina sit on the shelf, kicking their feet in the water and trying to see who can make larger ripples. She looks at me and grins warmly, having thoroughly warmed up to her new little friend.

Laughing, I pull myself up out of the water and say to Clara, "I shall have to speak to the Laird Barclay about Kenina visiting us."

As she helps Kenina out of the bath, Clara replies, "Ah! Aye! Ah bet she'd like that gay fine, she would! There's two other bairns aboot Zsoka's age. I'll introduce ye tonight. Moyna of Karnei tis heiress of the Laird Sorley Greig and she's expectin her second babe. The other one's Hallwen. The lassie's a wee bit younger, but she's sweet and no squeamish aboot playin with the older ones."

She wraps a towel around her and then bends to dry Kenina. "Gregor's most like her age. He's a Gaelen lad belongin to the Laird Sorley Evander an' his mate, Gwen. He's a trickster, he is, though, so—" Clara suddenly stops talking, and I look up from trying to squeeze the water out of Zsoka's hair to look her way.

Clara stares at me with a bit of alarm, and I am suddenly afraid that there is something wrong. "What is it?" I ask, looking over Zsoka and then to my own naked form kneeling beside her. I realize very quickly what she is concerned over.

"Ah, beggin pardon, Scarlet. I'd nay mean to alarm ye. Tis just…are ye 'right?"

My stomach sinks, and I want nothing more than to *Shift* or to hide. "Ah…yes…eh…I'm fine. They're all old." Mostly.

I glance around the room uneasily and find that Clara is not the only one to notice the damage my body has taken over the years of being a soldier.

They stare, some openly and some furtively, whispering to one another. Some either do not notice or do not care to hide the looks of alarm and disgust.

At least no one laughs. I don't know why they would, but somehow, laughter seems too often be the cruelest of insults.

"Excuse me," I say quietly and wrap up my charge in her towel before grabbing my own. I'm shaking as I wrap it around myself and feel stupid and angry at myself for doing so. I've nothing to be ashamed of. No reason to be afraid. So why does it feel like I want to cry? They've no right to make me feel like that.

"Oy!" Clara calls, glaring across the room. "Mind, ye own, ye nosey biddies! Ye 'eard me! Mind ye own!"

"It's alright," I say quietly to Clara and give a little smile. "Please do not bother. I know it must be unsettling for them."

Clara scoffs and says, "It dinna make it right to stare an' carry on. Loots o'the women from Gaelen ha' scars from the border wars. None quiet so," she gestures to me, "so many or bad mostly, but they've seen'em. An' some o'dem lassies ha' lost arms or legs and sooch too. They've nay business staring like that. It's nay polite."

"It's fine," I say, and once Zsoka is dry, I stuff her into a pretty golden gown with yellow trim and embroidery before pulling on my own gown.

The sleeves, however, of the shimmering, violet thing, refuse to stay on my arms, and Clara finally laughs and says, "They're nay s'pposed to stay on yer shoulders. They're s'ppose to hang off. Tis the fashion."

She comes up to me and laces up the back of the dress good and tight but not uncomfortably so.

The short, silken sleeves of the purple dress hang off my shoulders completely uselessly, and I mutter, "How entirely pointless." At least the dress has a silken feel and is not too tight. It is comfortable to wear, and I can move easily. Much better than the stiff Crystalice dresses and their damnable corsets.

"Tis pretty, tis," she chastises, and I smile at her.

I don't feel very pretty at all, however—not with the afore mentioned scars stretching out up under the dress and over my collar bone. Looking down at them however, I frown and decide quite resolutely that I am not going to let them bother me. I can't change them, and there's nothing wrong with them. Besides, there's no point in being pretty anyways, not for me. If the scars bothers others, then let them stare. What a stupid thing to worry about anyways.

"Seein we're on the same floor an' all," Clara says, "why dinna ye an' the wee one come by an' get ready?"

"That would be nice," I reply, looking to Zsoka for confirmation, and she smiles at me. I look back to Clara and add, "Just let me grab her hair ornaments and drop off our old clothes."

"Aye an' aye," she says, waving me off and heading out with Kenina.

"What's all this?" I ask Clara as we enter the room she shares with Kenina and Seonag who has returned to her own room to fix her hair as well, briefly separated from her friends. I pause to greet her politely, and she gives me a cheerful little smile.

"How'd my cosmetics look, Scarlet?" Seonag asks me, thrusting up her little face with cheeks dusted in pink powder, eyes lined with black kohl, and lips smeared with a pink stain. "I thought I might need more powder on me face. Clara says I dinna need any white powder for me face t'all."

"White powder?" I ask.

"*Och*, tis the newest *trend* in Cerulean," Clara tells me with a roll of her eyes.

"Ah." I bend down in front of Seonag and inspect her critically enough to make her feel as though I am taking her seriously before nodding and saying, "Clara's right. Your olive skin looks beautiful with that pink powder and stain. If you had white face powder on, you'd look like a ghost."

Seonag laughs and says, "Ye think so?"

"I do," I reply with a nod. "Your olive skin is beautiful without the powder."

"Aye," she says, satisfied, and begins to go and pick out a hair pin for the ball. In the mirror, Clara mouths "thank you" to me, and I smile at her.

"Anyways, what's all this?" I ask again, gesturing to the table of food.

"Ah!" Clara is reminded and smiles as she pins Kenina's hair up neatly. "Durin the feast, we'll be eatin in the kitchen with the babes whilst the servants dish the meal. But tis oft enough very busy and excited, and ye'd be surprised how soon the meal is over. I figured it'd be best to try and eat sommat now."

"Good idea," I tell her and then ask Zsoka, "Do you want me to fix your hair like Kenina's?"

She nods, and so I set her up next to Kenina and try to imitate what Clara does. It proves difficult, however, since Kenina's reddish blond hair is curly and thick, while Zsoka's hair is straight and like silk. It hates staying in the pins and slips out almost as soon as she turns her head.

With a defeated sigh, I say to Zsoka, "Sorry, love. But I can't get your hair to do what Kenina's does."

"But I want it to look like Kenina's!" Zsoka cries in frustration, and tears begin to well up in her eyes.

I shake my head. "I know, but your hair just won't do that. I'm sorry, love. There's nothing I can do. I bet I can pull the front of it back into a pin. It should do that. So then you can still wear a pretty bauble in your hair. Do you want me to try?"

Zsoka looks up at me forlornly and then nods miserably.

I smile and kiss her brow before brushing out her hair and pulling some of it back for the pin which does, thankfully, agree to stay. I will probably have to fix it several times tonight, but it should not prove too much trouble.

As I work, however, I noticed Kenina and Clara talk quietly, and within a few minutes, Clara has pulled out all of Kenina's carefully-placed pins—which I do not doubt took the better part of an hour—and pulled the top of her hair back into a single clip just like Zsoka's.

"Look, Zsoka," I say, and the little kitten turns to see her friend with the matching hair style.

She smiles and looks like she might cry again.

"Now we match!" Kenina cries, and Zsoka grins widely with her while Clara bemoans her ruined work.

"Ah well," she says with a huff of a sigh. "Wouldst like me to fix yer hair, Scarlet?"

"No, thank you, Clara," I reply and smile. "I prefer my hair down and unadorned. I brushed it before I left."

She nods and then expertly braids her length of hair and coils it up, pinning it in place and tucking it under a coif.

As the girls wait for the meal, Clara and I sit on one of the mattresses and eat, watching them all inspect each other and praise each other, Seonag showing off her new slippers with an embroidered lily on the side.

Eventually, a serving man comes by and knocks on the door. "Ladies, the meal is set."

"Alright, let's go," Clara says, stuffing another bite of chicken in her mouth as she gets up and brushes off her hands, guiding the two little girls and one older one out the door.

Down we go to the first floor where Clara and I part ways from the children. She did not exaggerate on the state of the kitchens. Several maids and a few servants sit around a long, wooden table. Food is passed constantly, drinks sloshing, the hum of conversation filling up the entire room. It is rather overwhelming, actually.

But Clara sits me down and introduces me. I shout my introductions over the other conversations and shake greasy, food-speckled hands before fixing myself a plate and beginning to eat, stopping every now and again for more shouting dialogue.

Sure enough, by the time everyone scrambles up, I assume for the end of meal and progression to the ball, I have barely eaten anything at all and I am incredibly grateful for Clara's thoughtfulness of providing food or else I am certain that I will have been faint by the end of the night. We all scramble up out of our bench seats and stack our dishes on the counter by the wash basin. Clara shouts at me that tomorrow we will worry about scraping the plates clean and washing them, but no one bothers with it tonight.

Then, we make our way down the hall and out into the open courtyard at the center of the palace where the floor is covered in a fine, polished stone and beautiful vines crawl up the sturdy pillars in their own adornment. There is no lace, no finery, and no trimmings. There is only the blanket of dark blue sky twinkling with stars over our heads and flowering vines all along the walls and pillars. Torches are lit at each window and entrance, standing tall and circling the courtyard. They fill the place with warmth and light, and the glow of their fire fills me with a bittersweet longing for home. There is music and laughter and celebration. It is the first night in Flora that I have not felt quite so alone.

I stand with the other nurses as we watch our charges, waiting a little off to the side. The little ones seem to care little for the formality of the thing. Most of them don't even dance. Kenina introduces Zsoka to Hallwen, and the little trio have since linked hands and are sort of hopping around in a circle. They seem to be having more fun than anyone else here, though, so we let them be. Una is with the adults dancing with her new mate, leaving a slightly put-off Seonag and Lindsey to stand off in a corner and look on with jealousy. I can't tell who they're jealous of, though: Seonag for having a mate or Cormag Erskine for having stolen her away.

"Your charge looks quite cross," I tell Clara, and she seems confused before noticing Seonag and she laughs in response.

"Wha's the matter with her?" Tajan, Hallwen's nurse, asks quietly, looking over at the trio-turned-duo.

Maria laughs and shakes her head. "Ack. They're vex with the wee master Cormag for taken their friend."

Ah, so that's the reason. I wondered.

"Och," Tajan replies with a sigh. "I'm right glad, I am, that me wee lassie tis far off from sooch nonsense."

"And what nonsense would that be, Miss Tajan?" Alistair asks with a warm little smile.

I hadn't noticed him approach since he came from around behind us, but I turn to him and smile a bit.

He's all dressed up for this event and looking rather uncomfortable in it. He always seems the most at home in slacks and a shirt, maybe a leather jerkin if it's a crisp morning. But stuffed into the doublet and hose, he looks uncomfortable and edgy.

"Master Alistair!" Tajan greets, and she smiles shyly.

"Evenin, Lord Alistair," Clara adds in, giving a familiar smile.

He chuckles warmly and asks, "What nonsense then is about?"

"That of men," I reply, and he gives me a sheepish look. I laugh and say, "Una's friends are put-out with her attention on her mate."

He turns about and scans the party for the young couple, and when he spots them, he laughs and rubs the bridge of his nose. "Aye and aye. To be quite honest, I was a wee bit concerned with the match and told Archi myself, what with his lass bein barely woman and all." He sighs. "Ah well. Archi and Steaphan are fine friends and Cormag's mam will make a fine example and teacher for the lassie since Glenna passed."

I smile a bit and look off at the pair. "I was about her age when I married. Inferno do not really have a restriction on remarriage the way Flora do, but it's uncommon in any event since we're betrothed at birth. We don't really have a formal ceremony for remarriage. I knew of some who had lovers who lived with them and they would have children together, but there is only ever one *Dailyn*."

He looks to me, and I explain, "I only mean to say that it is not uncommon in my homeland to be wed young, and with proper guidance and support from their families, they should be just fine."

He flashes a smile my way and inclines his head, "Aye, so we'll pray."

I stretch my lips in another slight smile, but Alistair does not speak again and Tajan, Clara, and Maria merely watch the two of us with peculiar expression that are not overt enough for me to comment upon.

As the silence stretches a bit, I consider asking Alistair why exactly he has come to visit us when he suddenly speaks up and says, "In any event, lass, Zsoka seems rather entertained with her own friends. Do ye think I could steal ye away for a dance?" He winks at me, and I hear Maria say something to Clara, but I cannot catch it.

"Ah, I suppose," I reply uneasily. Alistair offers his hand, and I accept, letting him pull me out into the lively courtyard. These dances are not like the Crystalice ones. They are lively and quick, and although they follow a certain pattern, it is generally a short pattern that is repeated throughout and is easily memorized after performing it once or twice.

"How d'ye favor Castle Flora, sweetheart?" Alistair asks when he stops and bows to me before taking me by the waist.

I laugh a bit at his devilish grin and reply, "It's beautiful, and I've enjoyed my time."

The music is boisterous and the dancers laugh and chatter through the eager steps and twirls. I have to raise my voice a bit, and our conversation stalls for a moment as we launch full into the dance, beginning with Alistair swinging me around and the lifting me up and twirling me. That doesn't last for too long, though, or else all the women would surely faint of dizziness, and we dance together with my hands on his shoulders and his on my hips.

"I ken ye'would," he says at last when he can catch a breath to speak.

I give a single nod and say, "I am not as homesick as I thought I would be. This place is…very different from my homeland…but it still feels similar enough that I am not uneasy here."

"Tis now?" he asks and grins, looking pleased.

He seems happier than I would expect someone to be from such a statement, and as such, I quirk a brow at him. "Aye. It is. These dances, for example—" I pause to let him spin me one by one arm and once by the other before we are rejoined. "—they're fast and fluid like ours. Not quite as…I suppose you would probably use the word 'vulgar' or 'scandalous' but I would say not as graceful or sensual."

"I'd like to see them." He surprises me with his words, and I must have shown my thoughts in my eyes, for he laughs a bit and smiles warmly. "Wouldst dance for me, lass...a dancer from yer own world?"

I scoff, having meant to jest with him but suddenly feeling heavy and burdened. "No," I tell him. "I only danced *those* dances for my *Dailyn*...I would not dance for you."

"Yer mate?" he clarifies, and he slows our steps until we stand together in the midst of the fanciful chaos, ignoring the dancers around us.

"Yes," I say, looking up at him, "Jay'let...his name was Jay'let."

Alistair's smile falls, but he does not seem unhappy. He merely watches me, thoughts in his eyes that he does not say to me, and his slightly parted lips seem on the verge of saying...something. And I do not know if I wish to hear what he has to say to me.

I look away from him, my eyes catching sight of the dancers once more as they spin and twirl around us. "He would have liked this...these dances..." I look back to him again. "I think he would have liked Flora too."

Alistair closes his lips and then sighs out his nose. "Ah, lassie," he says to me, and he leans down, kissing my brow.

My hands are on his arms and his on my waist, and I cannot think of a delicate way to move away from him without seeming unnecessarily repulsed. I am not...opposed to his affection, per say...merely discomforted by the state of my mind.

"I swear to ye," he says to me, quietly down by my ear, "I'll do whate'er it takes to take away the shadows I see in yer eyes. That's my vow, sweetheart."

He grabs me then before I can speak, my heart suddenly beating with a great pain in my chest. He spins me and lifts me off the ground before pulling me back to the dance at hand. Somehow, it is as though he pulls me straight out of my thoughts, dragging me away from my sorrows, spinning the fears off of me.

I laugh when he draws me near again, my belly to his, and I say, "You slip into your accent when you're home."

A laugh breaks from his chest, and he says, "Does't bother ye, sweetheart?"

"No," I say, and I smile at him. He releases me to shift steps, but I step apart from him when a little black-haired creature bounces her way to us, dodging the heavy boots and fluttering skirts.

She laughs and grins at us both, crying, "I wanta dance! Show me! Show me!"

I echo her laughter with my own and say, "I am certain Alistair will dance with you."

I do not think she intended to dance with him, but she looks to him a bit hopefully anyways, willing to try. There are some dances that do not matter the partner, but some are made for pairing with a lighter match—a girl, usually—for the twirls and lifts.

"Wouldst honor me with a dance, my wee lass?" Alistair asks, bowing to Zsoka. She lights up with a giggle and accepts his hand.

I grin at them both, pleased to see her so happy, and I give a little wave before skirting my way out of the chaos where I am less in the way and can find a space to catch my breath and rest my feet. Clara and Maria are not far off from myself, and I turn and make my way towards them, stopping not far when I hear Zsoka cry, "Mama! Mama!" I catch sight of my girl and grin as Alistair hoists her up in the air with a spin. She waves to me, her mouth spread in laughter. "Mama! Look at me!" And then she is placed back on her feet and out of my sight.

I laugh with warmth and then turn my attention back to my newfound friends.

The warmth and welcome I had expected in their expressions, however, is absent, and I find myself looking into two disturbed and uneasy faces watching me with quiet unrest.

I hesitate then and we stare at each other, they two and I, completely unabashed and without excuses. I do not know what they are looking for, and I do not entirely know what I seek to find in them. But their disquieted looks do not leave, and I am hesitant to rejoin them.

They are not the only ones, either. My eyes turn to Tajan who has found another nurse whom I have not been introduced to but who addresses Lindsey as though responsible for her. Both of them are talking quietly to themselves and looking at me and then again to Alistair and the little Zsoka. Their expressions bother me greatly because I do not know what to make of them. They do not show jealousy, nor even surprise or scandal. They do not appear alarmed or particularly nosey. They merely watch, uneasy. I cannot think of what would disturb them so.

The dance has finished, and the partakers clap while the musicians set down their instruments, probably to rest and allow for some time to talk. A harpist takes up the task of filling the air with music, although not the kind to be danced to. It allows for rest and easy conversation. "Mama, didst see me?" Zsoka asks as she hurries to my side, attaching herself to my legs.

"She's a lively one, the lassie," Alistair says with a laugh, coming up alongside Zsoka and grinning at me. "The minstrels are taking a rest to let everyone spend some time…but they should start up again if you would like another dance."

I open my mouth to reply but then consider the women again and shut it, shaking my head. "No…I do not think so."

Alistair notices my hesitation and frowns. "What's the matter, sweetheart? What's upset ye?"

I shake my head again, trying to think of words to say. "I …do not know…something is wrong. I do not know what or why…but it would be unwise to continue in this manner."

"Ack," he says with a frown, probably no doubt thinking that I have conjured some reason to evade him without cause. "Tis naught amiss, Scarlet. Tell me what bothers ye, and I'll put it to rest."

I frown at him and say, "No. I do not think so. I cannot think of how to explain it, and I do not think you would understand in any event." He seems a bit offended then and sighs, frowning at me. "Besides, it is late. Zsoka has been up far beyond her normal hours…we should retire for the night."

"Ack, lass. There's nay need for—"

"Goodnight, Alistair."

He sighs again and looks on me for a moment while I take Zsoka's hand.

The child has gone silent, watching us both and looking around us. She, too, seems unsettled by what she sees and holds my hand a bit tighter.

"I am sorry, Alistair," I say. "We will talk. But not now. Goodnight."

He gives a half-smile and inclines his head. "Aye, rest well, lass. Ye too, wee one. Good rest to ye both."

I incline my head, but Zsoka says nothing, staying close to my side as I lead her out of the courtyard and back upstairs to our own rooms.

Chapter Twenty Five
Scarlet

Castle Flora

The next morning, I hear the boisterous thrum of voices before Zsoka and I even reach the kitchens. I slept in more than I meant to, but Zsoka did as well, so it is not such a bother. Still, I feel lazy waking up long after the sun has risen, and I find myself missing Cali's bread. Oh, they have bread here, sure. But there's something missing. Some herbs or something in Cali's bread that is distinctly different, and this morning, I really do want nothing more than to go home and eat a fresh, warm piece of bread while watching the sunrise. Maybe take a nap in my tigress form in the sunshine.

I push the door open to the kitchen, and a few laughing faces catch sight of me, do a double-take, and then quickly stuff food into their mouths. Those who had not seen me at first quickly notice me, and the roar of voices that had scarcely been contained by the door has now dulled into a low murmur. Clara clears her throat, Kenina sitting in her lap, and she calls, "Here, Scarlet. I've saved ye a'seat."

I give a little smile and sit beside her, Zsoka squishing her way on the bench to fit next to me. There are nine nurses total, including myself, along with seven small children, eleven housemaids, and thirteen footmen, all making for a very crowded kitchen. And yet, for the first time, I can hear myself speak.

I fix a plate and sit quietly as I debate my choices and then finally come out and say, loud enough, "All right, everyone. Someone tell the foreigner what she's done this time."

A few girls find my slight humor and easy tone amusing and they giggle, a bit of the tension leaving the room. Maria chuckles nervously and says, "Ah, well…eh…"

"Tis aboot las night," Tajan says, and Megan beside her shushes her and jabs her elbow.

"Dinna mind her," Megan says. "Tis naught."

"Seems like something," I say, eating bites every now and again to keep my manner calm and controlled.

Clara finally sighs and says, "Well, ah, lassie." She sighs. "Has…has Master Alistair spoke with ye?"

"Not since I left last night," I tell her.

She nods and continues, "Well, tis aboot the dance."

"Can people not dance together?"

She holds up her hands defensively and says, "Och! Nay, nay, that's nay what I meant. Tis jus'…that *particular* dance…tis only for the mated folks. And he asked ye quite specifically to dance with him."

I pause in my eating and look right at her, feeling a sense of dread. "Someone please tell me that I have not unwittingly married myself off last night."

The table bursts with laughter, and the thrum of voices gets louder once more, not quite to its usually, deafening roar, but enough that the threat of danger passes.

"Oh, bless ye!" Clara cries, holding her stomach while Kenina looks at Zsoka as if to ask if she has any idea what is going on.

Zsoka merely shrugs and looks up at me past a mouthful of fruit.

"Ah, nay, nay," Clara says when she can speak again, and I sigh. She smiles warmly, but what was laughter turns sympathetic, and she says, "But…it means sommat. Ye see, by Alistair askin ye and ye agreeing and all…ye've announced to the Flora that yer courtin."

"Courting?" I clarify.

"Aye," says she. "Tis nay permanent and sooch as a mate, but tis a'might serious. It means Alistair's lookin for a mate…and that ye are too."

"Oh, I have had enough of this!" I shouted, suddenly off my appetite as I slam my wooden cup back onto the table.

I'm glaring at Clara, but in a huff, I try to apologize, "Forgive me, Clara. It is not you whom I am angry with, but this whole thing is nonsense! I do not see why my fate is somehow dictated as to whether or not I am married! As if *that* was the most important thing a person could be defined by! And in any event, it *doesn't* matter because I have no intention of marrying! Ever! Not to Alistair, nor to any other Flora, nor to any man at all! I have been married once and once is quite enough for me! I do not wish to go through such torment again!"

I had said more than I meant to say, particularly about Jay'let, and when I finally quiet down, the whole room is very quiet, such so that my shuddering breaths trying very hard to push back sobs can be heard. The whole of the room, however, is not looking at me, but is in fact looking behind me at the door to the kitchens.

A sinking feeling sets into my stomach, and I turn around in my seat to find a very sheepish looking Alistair standing half way into the kitchens.

He clears his throat and says, "Ah, I'd nay think my dancing was *that* bad, lass."

I open my mouth, not quite certain what I had expected to come out of it, but what does, in fact, emerge is a little laugh.

The whole room lightens with a bit of laughter and Alistair's easy grin.

"Good morrow, Alistair," I greet gently, standing up from my seat and facing him with my hands clasped in front of me, feeling a bit sheepish myself. I meant what I said, but I do hope that I had not hurt his feelings. Part of me thinks it serves him right for having asked me to such an important dance, but either way, I do not want him hurt.

He gives a warm and hearty laugh and claps me on the shoulder. "Ack! T'was my fault! I'd paid'na mind to the song when I asked ye. I merely dinna want ye cooped up in a corner with the wee one. I dinna mean'na harm."

The chatter in the room starts up again, signaling a safe passage—once again—out of peril, and I sigh, shaking my head at Alistair. "*Do* try to be more careful," I say.

He chuckles and winks at me and says, "I canna make *that* promise. But I truly dinna mean'na trouble. I'll set it rights first thing."

I nod to him and reply, "That would be well. Thank you. When are we leaving?"

"Och," he says and scratches the back of his head before rubbing the back of his neck. "Ah, there's a bit more to be done among the gentry." He grumbles a bit to himself. "A few more days, at least. But then we'll go."

"I'm in no rush," I tell him and go to the counter, taking out a cloth and putting on some bread and cheese and fruits before wrapping it up and handing it to him. "Good luck." I wink back, and he seems surprised by the gesture and then smiles. But his smile…it is different somehow…it seems sad.

"Aye, lass." He inclines his head and then disappears back the way he came.

I stand for a moment just staring at the door and wondering if I should run after him, make sure that he took no offense at my words. It is not that I dislike him or do not think he would be a good husband, just that marriage is something so permanent and binding…and I feel very transient and fleeting, as though I am never quite sure where I am or where I am going to be. My thoughts, my decisions. I have never been so wayward in all my life. I hardly consider it wise or fair to talk of such serious things as a mate when I can scarce decide if I will even remain in this country at all.

"He seemed sad...didn't he?" Maria says, and I am not sure if she speaks to me or not, but my heart feels heavy.

"Aye..." Clara says softer, and I sigh, turning away from the door and taking my place at the table.

There is nothing to be done about it now. He is busy.

And I have many things on my mind.

A Few Days Later

"Scarlet." Alistair catches my arm as I make my way through the gardens on the outer perimeter of the courtyard.

We are leaving today, and there is much to do. Even with all the maids and the footmen, the nurses are still required to do much work, particularly for themselves and their charges. I've loaded up all my things and Zsoka's into our own trunks and brought them down to the carriage. Now all I've left to do is gather up the pallets and shake them out before loading them as well.

Alistair's hand is a sure and steady force, however, and it snaps me not only from my path but out of my busy thoughts and plans and lists and preparing for the journey back to Maeghdra.

I look up to him, my eyes more red than brown, flecks of gold shining brightly in the morning sun. "Aye?" I ask warily.

He smiles a bit, rueful almost, and he asks, "D'ye have a minute, sweetheart?"

"I do...I suppose," I say. I really do not, but if Alistair wishes to speak to me, then I shall make time for he would not interrupt me if it were not important.

"It's just that we'll be leaving soon and we'll not have a bit of time together again for a while…and I'd like to say what's on my mind."

I turn towards him, facing him and looking up at his green eyes. I give a single nod, preparing myself. "Alright then. Speak your peace."

He laughs a bit, looking down at his hand on my arm, and his thumb brushes back and forth over it. "I…am always afraid o'ye, lass."

"Afraid?" I ask, incredulous. Surely he does not think me so dangerous. He could snap me in half with barely a thought.

He laughs again, and I am beginning to realize that certain, little laugh he does when he is quite nervous and does not really feel like laughing at all.

"Alistair…" I beckon, trying to get him to meet my eyes.

He finally does so and gives a little smile. "Aye, lass …afraid. Afraid that one day, I'll wake up, and ye'll be gone. Ye and the wee one…nay letter, nay goodbye…just gone, gone back home to that burning forest ye wait for every evening when the sun sets so."

I open my mouth to speak, but he holds up a hand.

"Just a moment, lass. I've got to speak my mind before I change it." He sighs and struggles with words for a while. "Gabe…he was enough to keep ye."

I shut my mouth promptly.

"Ye love him. I kens that. Ye probably always will. Tis well. He's…a hard man to love. Even Catherine hated him sometime. I just…" He sighs and rubs his face with his hands, letting go of me to do so.

When he stops, he looks back at me and says, "I'm nay asking ye to stay…Inferno's yer home…and if ye've mind to go back, then I'll nay stop ye."

I watch him for a moment, watch him struggle with his words as he looks at me, tawny hair blocking out the morning rays of the sun and yet seeming to glow from it.

He sighs at me, and I give a sympathetic smile. I really do not know what he wants me to say.

"Then…what is it you want from me, Alistair?"

He sighs again and shakes his head. "Just…tell me what I can do…tell me how to convince ye to stay. To make a home for ye here. It's nay just ye, lassie. I'm quite fond o'the wee one as well, and I'd be might sore to see ye both go. Tell me what I can do…anything, and ye have my word I'll try."

And that, I do not know. I make a little sound of contemplation and turn a bit away from him. I lean back against one of the open, stone windows of the first floor. It is low enough to lean upon or to sit upon if I choose to hop up. But I merely lean and stare out at the gardens and the flowers growing there, the colors of every kind. There are brilliant lilies and violets and even shrub roses blooming beautifully.

"I do not know," I tell him at last, and I look back to him standing there with his arms at his side and his eyes set on me.

I look away once more and continue, "I've been asking myself similar things since I arrived…I have no reason to stay here—Inferno is my home—and yet…I do not know if it *is* home anymore." I look back at him with a wounded expression. "Isn't that terrible of me, Alistair? Not to acknowledge my own homeland?"

I sigh and look back to the gardens before closing my eyes and dipping my head back to feel the morning rays and imagine that they warm me despite the cool, crisp breeze. Autumn is coming quickly now. "I…do not know who I am …I do not know what I want…To go home means to take up the sword again…against people I have come to love and vowed to protect. To stay here means forever to be a foreigner, a woman without purpose."

Quietly, I murmur, "But sometimes…if I close my eyes and smell the sweet Flora air…I can forget. I can forget that there is a war. That there is death; it never comes so close as to wound the dear Maeghdra. I can forget that it is even there at all. For the first time in my life, I feel safe… and I never knew that I wanted it—to feel safe—until I did."

Looking back to him, I can tell that he is frustrated, trying to find some sort of answer, some sort of solution out of my musings, "I do not know who I am or what I want, Alistair…I have no answer to give you."

He releases a breath of air and comes to my side, standing near to me and looking down at my leaning form with tenderness and honesty. His fingers reach up and brush my cheek. His skin is not hot to the touch like mine, but it is warm, and it is pleasant. "Then I'll stay by yer side til ye find out…I only ask that…if ye decide to go…wilt tell me goodbye, sweetheart?"

Looking at him, the shadows in his emerald eyes, I smile softly, and I feel at peace there with him, as if I can finally rest and not be afraid to fall. "Aye…I will not leave without saying goodbye and letting Zsoka do the same."

A look of relief crosses his face, and he leans down to kiss my brow, whispering to me, "Thank ye, my lass."

I look up at him and smile just faintly, watching him. I wish that I could give him some assurance, some comfort to his lonesome soul. But I am not the sort of person capable of doing that sort of thing, so I merely give a single nod of my head and turn from him, heading out of the gardens and up the stairs to my room.

On my way back to my room, Clara comes into my view, looking just as harried and rushed as I am to try and get on the road. But she grins at me and gives a breathless laugh, stopping in front of me.

"Och, there ye are!" she says and sets down a small trunk to draw me into a hug, and she squeezes me tightly, robbing my breath. "Ah! Ah's afraid that I'd no get to say goodbye."

She withdraws, allowing me to breathe again, and I laugh a bit as she grins and says, "I've spoken with ma laird, and he's agreed to let Kenina and I stay the winter with ye and Zsoka. So I'll be seein ye soon."

"That would be wonderful," I tell her sincerely, smiling and taking her hands, squeezing them both.

She smiles and squeezes my hands back, but she pauses and looks me in the eyes, as if something is on her mind. Her next smile is a little more shy, and she says quieter, "Ah've been thinkin aboot what ye said the other day: that folks are more than who they're married to…"

I grimace a bit and say, "I did not mean offence. Please forgive me if I have."

She smiles and shakes her head. "Ack, nay, nay. Tis jus'— I dinna think tis the status of marriage that's so important— tis jus'…well…tis an awful long life to live alone, dinna ye tink?"

I am a bit surprised by her words, and I do not quite know what to say.

She smiles a bit at me and squeezes my hand once more. "A mate's more than a status…they're sommon who kens ye better than ye know yerself…they see all the worst parts of ye…and they love ye anyhow…isn't it better to face all of this… with sommon by yer side?"

I watch her for a moment, looking at her hopeful face, and I give a little smile at last, feeling my heart squeeze. I remember my Jay'let, his warmth and company. I remember my dancer sisters, their laughter and trust. I remember my mother—Estaire—a long, long time ago when I was still a babe. Companionship. Someone to cure the *aloneness*.

"Yes…" I say at last, squeezing her hands. "It is much better with someone by your side…"

A Few Days Later
Maeghdra Manor, Flora

I am tired when we reach the manor. The sky is overcast, meaning that Zsoka and I are both moody and miserable. She sulks in the carriage with Freya and her waiting ladies while Alistair and I ride up ahead. "Ah, good," says he. "We'll get inside before it starts raining."

Autumn is at hand. The air has a sharp crispness to it now that ensures I leave my cloak on. Not much longer, and I will need to pull out velvet and wool gowns to keep warm, and when winter comes upon us, I will more or less be confined to the manor and the hearth, as will Zsoka.

Unfortunately, Dena's wedding is in the dead of Flora winter, so the trek to Cerulean is guaranteed to be miserable, and I'll be stuffed into a carriage, not that it will matter much when we get to Crystalice. Unfortunately, it will also be more difficult to send letters in the miserable cold.

I mumble a response to Alistair, and he chuckles warmly, asking, "Art sulking because of the weather, Scarlet?"

I glare at him and give a little hiss. Yes, I am miserable. It is cold and the air is wet with the threat of rain. He only laughs at my hiss, however, and draws his horse into the manor courtyard, hopping down. I lean down over my horse, not quite wanting to expend the energy to get down. The carriage rolls to a stop, and the footmen we hired for the event hop down and assist Freya and the others out.

Alistair comes up alongside my horse and grins at me, completely undisturbed by the general gloominess of the weather. "Wouldst like help, sweetheart?"

I growl at him, watching him with my tired, golden eyes, and he just smiles at me, reaching for my waist. I sigh and shift on my horse to make it easier for him to grab me and pull my miserable, pathetic self down off of my horse. I hate rain. I hate cold. He decides against setting me down, however, and carries me from the courtyard to the manor. "What are you doing?" I grumble at him, starting to squirm. "I need to get Zsoka."

"She's asleep," he says and adds, "Skylar has already got her and is putting her to bed."

"That's my job," I complain, glaring up at him.

Inside, he takes me to the hearth and sits me down on it. The stone is cold, and I hiss at it, not at all happy at being set here. Alistair ignores me and begins piling wood up into the fireplace. "It would get warmer faster if ye light it," he tells me, and I huff a sigh and set the logs ablaze before snuggling up next to the fire.

"Ack no!" I hear Cali cry, coming out into the dining hall. "Is she ill?"

Alistair stands and grins at her, saying, "Nay, lass. Just grumpy is all. Cats are like that." I give a low mumble of obscenities directed his way, which he ignores and asks, "How was the manor, Cali?"

She clucks her tongue and says, "Oh, jus' fine. We had nay problems. Ah!" She turns away from us both and heads back into the kitchen. Coming out a moment later, she brandishes a few letters. "But these came a few days ago."

I pick up my head, suddenly quite interested, and Alistair glances over at me and gives a slight smile before leafing through the letters. He hums and haws but says nothing to me about the recipients or senders, his back to me as he shifts through them all, opening one of them quite leisurely.

"Alistair," I bark, and he looks back at me with a raised brow. "Are you going to tell me if one of those letters is mine or aren't you?"

He gives a curious look and glances back to the letters in his hand. "Oh these?" he teases me. "Ack, lass. Ye're much too ill to be reading and bothering yerself over this. Just go to sleep."

"Alistair," I say with warning, getting up off of the hearth and frowning at him, hands on my hips. "You give me that letter, you hear me."

He grins at me, no longer able to contain it, and he laughs and says, "I dinna think I will, lass. Ye're much too ill."

"I'll show you ill in a second!" I say and charge after him with a laugh.

Cali yelps and clears out of the way as I chase Alistair down the dining hall, up and down the tables, ducking this way and that before I finally catch him as he makes a break for the stairs. I pounce on him and take him to the ground, he having turned a bit to judge how near I was and winding up with a face full of red hair when we topple over onto the entry hall.

Panting, I lean up and toss my red hair back, glaring down at his mischievous green eyes filled with laughter. I huff a sigh and frown at him, but the corner of my lips are fighting a smile. "Give me my letter, Alistair Ruairidh."

He chuckles to himself and offers me the handful of letters. "Aye and aye, lass!" He sits up, pushing me back, and I sit on the floor, supported by one of his legs as he sits beside me and waits patiently for me to sift through each parchment to find the one addressed to me.

There is none—not one—for me, however, and I look back at Alistair with too much heart in my eyes, my expression filled with disappointment and hurt.

He winces and says, "Och, dinna look so sweetheart," and procures a hidden letter from behind him, offering it to me.

My face lights up, and I accept the parchment addressed to Lady Knight Protector Scarlet Anita mei Ka'Rose. I grin at the sight of my title. Gabriel has added the "Knight Protector" from his last letter to me. I look up at Alistair who is watching me with a playful smile and a bit of hurt in his own eyes. "Thank you," I tell him, and I kiss his cheek before getting up off the floor and scurrying up the stairs to my own room in order to read my letter.

Zsoka is quietly snoring when I step inside, and I smile a bit, shutting the door and going to the little table by the window so that I may read.

My beloved Cara,

Your words are a coarse blade in my chest. You are unkind, dear one. Do you not know that I love you? That I miss you? I had thought I made my intentions clear, but for your sake, I will say them more directly. I miss you, Cara. I am so tired of the half-truths and even bold-faced lies that surround me every day. I wish that if someone took ill with me that they would at least have the decency to come before me and say so. But there is none of that here. I miss the way you spoke clearly your mind. I miss the way you made me laugh. I miss your fire and your passion. I miss the rare moments of gentleness and weakness when you trusted me enough to show them to me. Do not doubt that you are missed here, Cara.

Enté especially misses you. He's run off every nurse I can find and has given himself up to fits of rage and sorrow. Sometimes he will listen to me and allow me to console him, but others he merely rages at me. He blames me for your absence and wishes to leave here in order to stay with you. I know that he does not entirely know what he means, but his words are painful when I alone have loved and cared for him all these years. I find myself constantly torn between caring for him and trying to manage my country.

The White Fang have grown bolder and are no longer content with vandalisms and the occasional robbery. Aside from Tam, they had been mostly innocuous. But now they are attacking royal caravans, killing crown supporters, raiding villages. They've become their own terror upon the land. Moreover, our council cannot properly agree on what to do about it. We have only just agreed that they are a legitimate threat and have been declared enemies of the crown. The council is hostile towards me for the most part and in general cannot agree on anything. How many more people must die? How many more goods stolen and lesser nobles frightened and harassed before the council can finally take action against them? It seems that every time we come close, one councilor or another advises against attacking 'our own people' as they say. How can we claim them as our own when they attack us? When they kill innocents? Those are not my people. Those are monsters and beasts who must be put down.

And that is not all, my love. My father has apparently refused to forgive any misgivings regarding my dealings with you and has henceforth informed me that he is reconsidering my position as Crowned Prince heir apparent. He has declared that unless I can somehow prove myself worthy of my own title that he will revoke it from me and, I assume, declare Petara and Kale the heirs. And although I am angered and wounded by his clear lack of approval for his last son and his complete neglect to see everything that I have done for my own country, I cannot help but wonder if he might be right.

I was never brought up to be king. Kale is a natural born leader and Petara already assists mother in managing the household as well as attending the council meetings. They are both capable and competent rulers, and yet...I am resistant to relinquishing my throne to them. Perhaps if Dena was older and Claque a bit more prepared, I would be content to surrender my throne to them. Petara makes me uneasy, however. She is too quick to blame the Inferno for our troubles. She even declared that the White Fang were a direct result of their actions. I am uneasy with her, and I cannot put words as to why.

Am I being selfish on insisting for my own? Or perhaps I am no longer able to see clearly the threat our enemies pose because of my love for you?

On a slightly lighter note, Heather has expressed an interest in returning to work, but she has requested to be sent home to Flora to tend to you. I told her that you did not particularly require a maid or nurse, but could you speak with the Lady Freya concerning a position there? Heather is familiar with her, I believe, so she should be agreeable.

In any event, as to the fears you relinquished to me, I wish I could be of more help. I know who you are, and I love you for it. But you must decide that for yourself: who you are and who you will become. Alistair is offering you a life, one of safety and freedom and comfort. Although it brings me pain to think on it, Alistair is a good man and would make for a good mate, but you must decide your own reasons for choosing to stay or to go. All that I can tell you, my love, is that inaction is still a choice, and it is very painful for everyone involved. Do not try to hide from Alistair or from Inferno because you are afraid. You know better than to resort to such pettiness. Decide what you want and then make a choice. I only caution you against returning to Inferno too soon because once you leave, you will never be able to return. Alistair is patient, but as his friend, I must ask you to not make him suffer.

I will always love you no matter what you decide, and I only wish that I had anything to offer you aside from war and pain.

May you find peace and everything your heart desires,
Gabriel Jan'tel, Prince of Cerulean

Gabriel's words offer me little comfort, but I hug the letter to my chest anyways and close my eyes. I imagine his voice, the low, sweet sound of it, and the way he would say these words to me. The way he would tell me that he loves me. But I can remember the words he did say to me, the words he spoke in Marine when he told me that I must go away from him. This is not a world that was made for us, and love is a stupid reason to start a war.

Love should lead to things of joy and laughter and warmth. Love is made for babies and innocence. Love should not lead to more death and pain and suffering. So there is no place for us. And I know that. But it still leaves me empty in the fading light.

Moreover, Gabriel did not leave me any sort of idea of what to do, other than words of caution against being rash. I had hoped that he would have some advice for me. That he would tell me what he wants me to do. Then again, do I really want to be told what to do? Is that what I have become? Someone who cannot decide for herself what she wants, who must depends on others to lead her this way and that?

No. I refuse to be such a worthless creature. To do such a thing would only be to excuse myself from responsibility for my actions, and that I cannot tolerate. I did not accept death; I did not accept imprisonment; I refuse to accept anything less than what I have decided for my own life.

I stand and leave the paper on the table. I will return to it another time, but for now, my heart is in pain and staying in this room is only increasing my sorrows and discontent. I will go and find Alistair and see if he is still awake. Perhaps we can play a game or drink some ale by the fire together. I would enjoy that.

So I turn my back on the letter and the table and the window pointing towards the mountains, and I leave that little room.

Fate is for the weak.

Chapter Twenty Six
Gabriel

One Month Later
The Crystalice Palace, Cerulean

"Where are you going?" Petara asks curtly. It is the middle of the night and she is in her night dress, a robe pulled over her. It is a rare sight to see her hair down; she usually keeps the white-blond mass tied up in so many intricate knots and loops it's a wonder her head doesn't hurt.

I sigh and pause after sheathing my sword, taking her by her arms. "Petara, if we lose the battle at the wasteland, it could change everything. The Inferno will come into Cerulean. Into our villages and our homes. I cannot allow that. I must go and take the remaining troops."

"Sire," Claque calls for me at the entrance to the castle. He is dressed in his battle gear as well and is trying very hard to both rush me and not insult Petara.

"I must go, sister," I say to Petara and squeeze her arms before letting go and turning around, starting down the stairs.

"Wait!" she calls after me, trying to catch up with her skirts as she descends the stairs. "Wait! Wait! Gabriel, you *can't* go! Claque, you can't either! You're the Crowned Prince, and you are about to be an heir, Claque! You can't go!"

"Don't worry!" I call over my shoulder, much faster than her down the stairs as I make my way for the door. "You have Kale as back-up! Father likes him better anyways!"

She stops on the stairs and gasps. "Gabriel!" she cries. "That's not funny! You hear me, Gabe! That is *not* funny!"

I laugh despite myself as I leave the castle, going out into the courtyard where my horse has been made ready for me. I mount on back and adjust myself carefully, getting steady on the horse as Petara comes out and watches us both. The soldiers are waiting for us at the outskirts of the city. Quietly, I can barely hear Petara say, "Come back to us, baby bother... we can't lose you too."

I look back to her and incline my head. "I swear, Tara."

She huffs, her eyes filling with tears, and she crosses her arms, looking away from me.

I sigh and look to Claque. "Let's go." We both ride out of the castle grounds and down through the city. Many others are awake this night. We do not usually round up so many troops at this hour. They can see the fire on the horizon. It is brighter than any other night. The red and orange glow eats up the sky in the distance. War is on the horizon.

Claque and I race through the night and into the next morning, we come upon the wastelands with the soldiers. Our men scream as they charge into the fray, coming up alongside our soldiers who have been fighting for hours in the darkness, tired and weary and too quickly slain.

My horse charges into the fray, and I give a resounding cry of war to alert my troops that I have come. I cut the Inferno down as I sit on the top of my horse, one fiery, burning mass after another falling by my blade. The wasteland is dry and feels both hot and cold, the ground hard and kicking up dust, the air filled with mist from the fiery heat meeting our cold.

I look at all of them, I search for signs of red hair and golden eyes, even though I know that she is not here. And yet she is. I can see her among them. With them. Fighting at their sides in her absence. I see her eyes looking back at me.

A man stares me down with his golden-brown eyes, charging at me for the kill, and yet all that is in my eyes is the way those golden eyes of hers watch me, half-closed as she kissed me. A man's red-brown hair hangs scraggly about his face once my sword rips out of his chest, and I am reminded of the curtain of red hair that laid across her shoulder, glowing faintly in the morning light as she lay by my side.

My horse screams, and I am yanked from my thoughts, cursing myself for them. It is the first time I've been back in battle in almost a year, and if I am not careful, it will be my last.

But there is something odd about the field when I look upon it. The Inferno are retreating, pulling away from the heat of battle and racing back across the wastelands to the burning forest where we cannot follow, at least not without guaranteeing the death of every one of our soldiers. We do not have that much the upper hand. Even with the additions, we are outnumbered. There was no reason to call a retreat, and Inferno generally do not do so lightly. Why then?

"Hail!" a man calls. He is on horseback, offering up a hand and trotting slowly onto the wasteland. I call out for a halt from my men, and they oblige, dragging the wounded away behind our reinforcements to be tended and to heal in the snow.

On my own mount, I move deeper into the wastelands to meet the man there. He looks familiar. His hair is brown, his skin a light brown, even his eyes are brown. I frown at him, trying to place him. Why should an Inferno face be familiar to myself? But then I remember.

"Jacob," I greet, and he seems a bit surprised before glaring at me. "I nearly did not recognize you for the scar on your face." He bears across his left cheek a deep scar running from temple to the corner of his mouth where it split his mouth open. It looks painful.

"Indeed," he calls, and he stops his horse far enough away to be able to defend an attack but not so far that we must shout to be heard. "And you are Prince Gabriel, are you not?"

"I am."

He nods to himself. "I thought as much. We'd hoped to lure you out."

"Oh?" I ask. "You could have sent a letter." Any messenger would have been killed on sight, but that's not really the point.

He frowns at me. "You have something of ours. We want it back."

"If by 'it' you mean Scarlet mei Ka'Rose, then I'm afraid you're too late." His face is struck with horror and then rage, and he grabs for his sword. "Peace!" I cry, holding up my hand. "Peace. I'd not like to strike her companion down right here, but I will if I must. She's not dead, Jacob. I merely do not have her."

"Then where is she?" he snarls.

I frown at him, watching him for a moment. "First, you tell me why it's taken you over a year to come after her."

"That is no business of yours," he bites back.

"It is my business," I growl, "If you want her back."

He grinds his teeth, and I can see him seething all the way from my horse. "We were waiting," Jacob replies. "We weren't sure as to your intentions, if you meant to ransom her or kill her. You did neither, it seems. And we were waiting—"

"To see if she could escape," I reply. He frowns at me, and I add, "So you left her alone in the frozen city to see if she could handle it herself."

"She is a Knight Protector!" Jacob shouts, and then more quietly, adds, "We have faced far worse than that."

My nostrils flare with rage, and I bite out, "I am aware. I have seen the scars."

He raises his brow and says, "Oh have you? Tell me, do you know who makes them?" When I do not answer, he replies, "She does. And if she does not make them deep enough, then her teacher will make them much, much worse."

"That's barbaric," I snarl.

"That is war!" he shouts back at me. "Our Knight Protectors must be able to withstand anything! Now tell me where she is!"

I consider not telling him, but I have no doubt that more men will die for it, and so I say, "She is in Flora with a friend of mine. But she is there of her own volition."

"Lying bastard," Jacob accuses, and I sigh.

"Write to her. Flora and Inferno are on neutral terms, are they not? Write a letter to her. She is staying with the Duke of Maeghdra. You can get a messenger through to her. I will tell him to be expecting one and to treat the messenger with fairness. I warn you, however," I add, dropping my voice, "should you attack Maeghdra, you will have not only my people to deal with, but all of Flora crashing down upon your heads. Not to mention the wrath of the woman you mean to save."

For a while, he does not speak, his horse sputtering a sound and tossing his head, stomping nervously as it waits for a command.

At last, Jacob replies, "I will do so…and mark my words, Gabriel, if she is harmed, there will be vengeance. We will send a message through Flora to seek her own mind on this…" He seems as if he wants to say more, sitting on his horse and watching me anxiously. "I came here tonight to kill you…but it seems that there is information I yet lack…if Scarlet has not killed you yet—and I am quite sure she could—then I will leave you alive for now…"

I do not answer, watching him with resolute eyes as he hesitantly turns his mount away and rides back into the flames.

I turn and trot into the snow, abandoning the wasteland between our worlds.

Claque is not been far behind me, and he looks at me with a severe expression. I will need to send word to Alistair at once to inform him what to expect. Hopefully this will not end in more bloodshed than would have been wrought today. But to have lied or refused him would surely have meant the death of many more of my soldiers, Cerulean and Flora alike.

"Let us return home," I say quietly to him. "There is much to be discussed."

He nods mutely to me and then goes to check on our resources and to get the numbers of the injured and dead.

Chapter Twenty Seven
Gabriel

One Week Later
The Crystalice Palace, Cerulean

"You scared us all near to death," Petara complains, sitting back in her chair and holding her tea cup in her hands. She frowns at me. It seems as though she is always frowning at me lately. Dena lounges on her chaise, a book in her hands. With it, she can hide her face from Petara and occasionally give me childish little looks of mischief. Claque and Kale are ignoring both sisters and have busied themselves with a board game by the window.

I sigh at my sister and sit back in my chair, crossing my ankle over my knee and lounging back. "And what would you have me do, Petara? As the Crown Prince, it is my duty to go out with my troops in times like those. What good am I to my people if I am cloistered up in these walls? Besides…the whole reason they attacked was to draw my attention anyways. Many more men would have died if I'd not gone."

Petara sighs at me and snaps, "Well you *could not* have known that, and you *should not* have gone."

"Petara…" behind her, her mate calls her name in a dull sort of 'please chose another subject' sort of voice, although he hasn't look up from the board.

"This is serious, Kale," she says to him, frowning curtly. He only sighs and looks to Claque with a bit of annoyance. Claque, ever stoic, wisely does not look at either of them.

"How's Scarlet doing?" Dena asks suddenly, putting her book down in her lap and looking over at me. "Weren't the Inferno here for her?"

"Indeed," I say slowly and sigh, looking over at her for a while as I gather my thoughts. "They said that they came to reclaim her, and I told them I don't have her. Inferno and Flora are on neutral terms politically speaking, so they should be able to get a letter through."

"Hm," Dena says, not quite sure how to respond, I'm certain.

"Well, how is she in any event? Still sick?" Petara asks.

I shake my head. "She's fine. She recovered shortly after leaving Marine. Although with winter coming, she'll likely be ill again temporarily. But they have the means to care for her there."

"Well that's good," Petara says with a sigh. "I think that's the best place for her, and I'm glad she's doing well."

"I should write her a letter," Dena says, more to herself than anyone else, looking down at the book in her lap.

"Whatever for?" Petara asks curiously.

Dena looks to her and frowns. "Because I want to, that's why. And I do miss her."

I smile a bit and say, "She will be up in a few months for the wedding."

Dena grins at that, and she blushes shyly. "I can't wait. It'll be so beautiful, and *everyone* is coming." Her smile fades though and she seems lost in thought for a moment before saying, "I heard such an odd thing from the florist yestereve. She said that I needn't worry about having babes too soon since we had plenty of heirs about to make."

The room goes fairly quiet, and Claque looks up from the board to Kale, but Kale does not return his look. "What a silly thing to say," Petara replies curtly and sips her tea. "Gabriel is the heir and Enté is his heir. There is no need for such talk."

"I thought so to," Dena said. "And I told her as much. But the woman just brushed me off and said 'things happen'."

"What a thing to say!" Petara cries. "It is bad enough that Gabriel has lost his wife. Do they really think to threaten the little Enté's health with such ill wishes!"

"I do not think she was wishing for Enté's death," Dena says mildly.

The whole while, I sit by quietly, watching the two of them bark at each other the way they've tended to do lately. It is not untrue that Enté is a shaky heir at best. For one, he is a half-blood, and for another, he has not even neared the ten-year mark when an heir is officially named after the likelihood of childhood death is much decreased. Even so, to have others speaking in such a manner unnerves me and angers me. My son will not die. I will not allow for him to die. He is all that I have left. He is the last thing in this world that I love which has not been taken from me.

"I still don't like it," Petara snaps.

Dena sighs and explains mildly, "I think they were concerned that should anything happen to Enté, there would be no heir for Gabriel and no wife either. Don't forget, Gabe," she adds to me, "you men may take a lead in the military matters because of the war, but the country answers to the queen. You won't have one."

"And what is your point, exactly?" I ask low. It is not like Dena to question me or to even attempt to take me to task.

But she gives a sweet smile and says, "No point, brother-dear. I was merely telling you what I heard. I thought you should know. If they're saying it to me then they're likely talking about it amongst themselves." She gestures to Petara.

"Petara could be queen and have more heirs, a girl perhaps. It's only because father is so insistent that the heir be male that he chose you instead of Petara."

"Dena, that's enough," Petara says and sighs before looking to me. "Do not let them concern you, Gabriel. Kale and I support you. You do not need a queen to rule. It is only tradition. After mother dies, I can manage the castle affairs and other such necessities that would not be proper for a king to manage. You needn't bother yourself with it."

I might have been more comforted by Petara's words if I did not feel as though she *was* mother trying to tell me to keep my little nose out of adult business. I do not know when that condescending nature of Petara's started or if it has always been there and only become more irritating with time.

Before the conversation can continue, however, a servant knocks and says, "Princess Denair, the seamstress has arrived with the dress to have you fitted and to show you the alterations she made."

"Oh, joyous!" Dena cries, hopping up out of the chaise without a hint of grace and scrambling up. She laughs and grabs Petara's hand, pulling her up. "Come with me! It'll be fun! I want my big sister to help me! Please, Petty?"

"I hate that name," Petara sighs, setting down her teacup before it's knocked out of her hand with Dena's happy bouncing and allowing herself to be pulled up. She smiles at the baby of the family, however, and she laughs a bit, leaving the parlor with her to go and help the last of the Jan'tel children prepare for her wedding.

Three Weeks Later

I've not heard from Scarlet all winter, and it has begun to worry me. With little time left before the wedding, I had hoped to hear from her by now. Alistair, at least, sent me a letter explaining Cara's situation to me.

Gabe,

In regards to your last letter: for the last time, will you stop insisting that I see a healer? My leg is quite fine. Scarlet exaggerates. If it gives me any trouble, you have my word that I will call a physician to tend to the matter. I am quite fine.

Otherwise, the ball went quite well. I managed to persuade the other dukes to at least consider amending the Flora code. I do not know if they will go so far as to actually change it, but it is a start. And by 'they', of course, I mean Karnei who continually insists that women must not be harmed in battle. But Karnei's men are not the ones being raped and slaughtered by hordes of them in nightly raids on the southwestern front. If you remember, it was only ten years ago that my father managed to convince Karnei to permit the killing of women by other Flora women or in self-defense. But so long as the fight is fought on our own soil, we will never get anywhere.

Speaking of, thank you for the forewarning about Scarlet's people. There is not much to be done in this winter, but I have made certain that the locals and the mountain peoples are aware that should they spot Inferno, it may not necessarily be an attack. I doubt, however, that they will brave the mountain winter to deliver a letter.

The Inferno are much more sensitive to the cold than I realized. It really is a wonder Scarlet did not die in Crystalice. She and Zsoka more or less spend all day in their room. They come down to eat and sit by the hearth or nap on the hot stones. Zsoka even crawled into the fire the other day. They really do hate this weather. And here I thought bears were the ones who were supposed to hibernate.

I should also let you know that I spoke with Scarlet at Castle Flora concerning her decision to stay in Flora. She's told me that she has not yet decided if she will stay or not but that she will at least tell me when she does. I wish I knew what to say to her. I'll not torment you with my thoughts, but it is frustrating to sit and wonder how you managed to capture her heart and loyalty when her position here seems so very tenuous at best.

In any event, we will be leaving early for Crystalice since I imagine it will take some time to make it there with the two sick Inferno. My mother will be going on ahead. You can expect her to arrive a sennight ahead of us.

Lastly, Gabe. I'm aware of the troubles you've been facing. I do not think your sister the kind to make a play for power, but if she unnerves you, there must be reason for it. Perhaps it is all of the pressure you now face as Crowned Prince. I wish I knew what to tell you, friend. All I can say is that you are in your rightful place and should remind those around you of such.

I shall see if I can encourage the Lady Scarlet to write back to you. She will be pleased to know that you inquired of her.

Strength and honor, friend,
Alistair Ruairidh IV, Duke of Maeghdra

Sighing, I set the letter down once more and look out into the darkness beyond my window. I've read that letter a hundred times it seems, and yet it brings me no peace. I wish that I knew if Scarlet and the little Zsoka were well. They should be traveling by now.

I sink back into my chair and close my eyes. How exactly am I supposed to assert my birthright? Just walk into a council meeting and declare it? It seems so childish and petulant. The White Fang, at least, have been somewhat quiet over the last few months. I would like to say that brings me some sort of peace, but with Dena's and Claque's wedding drawing nearer, peace is the very last thing I feel.

It is the quiet before the storm; the thought of them bringing trouble to the wedding—which will be heavily guarded by not only Cerulean but Flora forces as well—seems absurd and suicidal. But then again, I am trying to rationalize madmen.

Enté.

I should go and see him. He has still been in a fit lately, and although I'm just as like to be met with a temper tantrum as I am with a hug, I wish to see him, to look upon my son and know that he is safe and well and to remind him that he is loved.

So, I pull myself up out of my chair and out of the room, heading across my sitting room to Enté's room. He went to bed not long ago, having refused supper because of another fit. But, about an hour ago, he was hungry, and so I sent for a glass of milk and some bread to tide him over until breakfast. I'm not about to serve him a roast and potatoes after the fit he threw, but there's no use in starving him either.

"Enté?" I call softly, knocking quietly on the door before cracking it open.

The room is dark, and it takes my eyes a moment to adjust to the dim light. He has his window open to let in some fresh air, and I go over to it and shut it quietly before looking to the little lump on the bed. There's a full moon which gives me plenty of light to see the room despite the darkness once my eyes adjust. His toys are strewn everywhere, and tomorrow, I think, I will start the day with making him pick up every one of them and putting them away so that I don't kill myself trying to get over to him.

Sighing with relief, I finally sit upon the bed in relative safety and lean over the little lump. "Are you cold?" I ask.

The cold does not often bother him, but he does occasionally get chilly, and he has no blankets or coverings aside from his nightdress.

"Enté?" He does not answer me. Not so much as a murmur, and I turn him from his side onto his back. The sight of him makes me sick with fear. I can see his veins from under his pale, white skin, blue and purplish. His lips are dark violet. Poison.

"Guard!" I scream, my voice cracking with fear.

The door opens at once as I drag Enté into my arms to hear for a heartbeat.

"My son has been poisoned!" I scream at him. "Get a healer! Wake the castle! I want anyone who was anywhere near his room at once!"

"Sire!" he cries and quickly leaves me in the darkness once more.

I press my head to Enté's chest, unable to hear his heartbeat over my own which is pounding so loudly in my own ears. "No, no, no," I whisper frantically, putting my fingers to his neck, trying to find even a semblance of a pulse. "No, no, no! Enté! Enté!"

"He is not dead."

The voice is so calm and soothing, like the strength of the ocean tide as it rolls onto the surf, a crash of sound that while loud is not unpleasant or frightening. With my son in my arms, I turn my head to spy a woman on the other side of the bed. She is pale and black-haired with blue eyes the likes of which I have only ever seen once before.

"*You!*" I rasp, holding my son tighter. She watches me, completely undisturbed and still wearing that same, white dress I saw her in almost a year ago. "Who are you? You were there the night Cara was attacked. You brought me to her."

"*Who* is not important," she says quietly to me, her voice leisurely and unhurried as my heart pounds in my chest. She moves around the bed to where I kneel with my son. She moves as though in water, slowly and carefully, every movement graceful and smooth. Her hair shifts of its own accord, floating over her shoulders and down her back. Her white dress ripples across her legs, making a soft, whispering sound the way satin or silk might.

"He will not die," she tells me and reaches for Enté.

I hold him tightly to me, but she looks up at me with those rich, blue eyes, and I lower him a bit so that she can touch him.

She cups his face and coos gently to the boy, "You are still needed, little one." Then, she puts a finger to his forehead, and I watch as a pebble of white light flows from her finger into his forehead, and the veins vanish beneath his skin once more, some of his color returning with the opaqueness of his skin returned.

"He will be weak for a time," she warns me, withdrawing her hand and looking up at me. "But he cannot die. Not yet." She glances behind her to the door and says, "It is not safe here for him. Crystalice will seek to kill your son again. If you want him safe…you must send him away."

The door bursts open, and my eyes snap up to it to watch as several healers rush in, along with Heather and Petara. But when I turn my eyes back to the woman in front of me, she is gone and nowhere to be found within the room.

"Is he breathing? Is he alive?" the healers demand, taking Enté from me and laying him out on the bed. The lights go on in the room, brilliant white-blue orbs of light to illuminate the messy room.

"Enté…" I whisper softly, backing up helplessly so that they can work on him. The boy coughs and then turns onto his side, vomiting up the remnants of bread and milk that had not yet been digested. The healers all begin shouting orders and making notes, inspecting his stomach contents and food to try and figure out which medicines to get him.

"Gabriel," Petara calls softly, approaching me quietly and putting her little hand on my arm. "Father wishes to see you. Let them work on Enté."

All at once, the fear and the agony in my chest turns from ice cold to raging hot, and rage consumes me. The White Fang. They have dared to come into my *home* and attack my *son*. My *son!* I will hunt down every last one of them and string them up as a garland around my castle so that no one even thinks to threaten this home again.

"*Gabriel.*"

"Leave me, Petara."

She frowns and sighs softly, "Gabriel, go and speak with father. I will sit with Enté."

I turn my head to her, and with controlled power in my voice, I reply, "Petara, you forget your place. I will stay here with my son. *You* may go and tell father that if you wish. But this is *my* home and *my* child who has been attacked, and I will do as I see fit."

Looking past her, I shout to the guard, "You there! Send word to the councilmen that we are convening in four days."

He nods and says, "Yes, sir. What should I say if they cannot make it?"

"They *will* make it," I snarl, "because their prince has ordered them there, and those who cannot be bothered will no longer be *on* the council. Make that perfectly clear."

The guard, at least, does not argue with me, and he bows his head and leaves at once.

This is my homeland, my birthright. I will not be cowed here. Not by the White Fang, nor by my family, and certainly not that silly bureaucratic excuse of a council.

That Evening

Whatever the black-haired woman did to my son, it saved his life. The healers brought him some medicine and gave me instructions as to his care. For the meantime, Heather has decided to take over his care until arrangement can be made for her to return to Flora. It is just as well, I suppose, since I will most likely be sending Enté with her. But it is late, and I am tired and have been through a cruel evening.

I am not in any state to be making such decisions now.

Sitting beside Enté, I rub my face and sigh, trying to stay awake and yet incapable of falling asleep either. My eyes slide to the door when there is a quiet knock, and it cracks open.

"Sire?" I give a grunt of a confirmation, and a courier steps quietly inside, watched by my guard as he approaches me with a stack of letters. "Shall I put them on your desk, sir?"

"No. Give them here," I tell him and accept the letters from him before he gives a hurried bow and darts out of the room.

I flip through the envelopes, categorizing them from most important to least important to the 'I might throw you in the fire and pretend I never received you' category. My hands stop, however, when I come upon the last one. From Scarlet.

I sigh with relief, glad that she's not dead or too ill to even write. I look to Enté and smile quietly at his sleeping form. He will be happy to see her soon. I bet her appearance here will do much for his mood and his health, and hopefully he will do the same for her. Sighing, I break the seal and brighten the little lamp some so that I may read the letter.

Dearest love,

When you sent me here, you did not tell me how terrible the winters are. It is not like Crystalice where there is a quiet and near constant snowfall with an occasional rain. Here, there is much wind and torrents of snow. Everything is icy cold and wet as well. There are blizzards and storms of hail the size of your fist. At least the winters are only a few months long and they have a very large hearth here to keep Zsoka and I warm. The little one is not as familiar with the cold as I am and so these last few months have been very hellish for her.

I am sorry that I have not written sooner. I have no energy to do anything at all but eat and sleep. You would think with how much I sleep that I would be full of energy, but I only seem more tired for it. Cali is treating me well though with plenty of fresh bread and hot meats and stews. I'm spoiled, I am. I only thought that it was bears who hibernate, not tigers. This weather is miserable.

As to Freya, she said that she welcomes Heather and that she would certainly be of use. One of the girls, Skylar, might be moving with her family to Karnei, leaving only another girl to tend to Freya. She also said that Heather is welcome to stay as a guest. Apparently they're old friends.

I am sorry to hear that Enté has been so unreasonable. He's a very spirited child. Do not let him guilt or shame you. You are his father, and I know that you do not feel as though you know what you are doing, but you love him, and I trust that you will do what is best. Be firm with him and reward him with gentleness and affection when he needs it; there is no use in condoning a tantrum. Be patient. He'll come around; I'm sure of it.

I am glad, however, that your council has finally conjured sense enough to take the White Fang seriously. I am familiar with your politics, Gabriel, and I am sure that although the council would like to think that they are part of the monarchy, they are not. They are advisors and representatives from each sector. You do not answer to them. And feel free to tell them so. At the end of the day, thank them for their input and then declare what you mean to do regardless of who agrees or not. It's simply silly to waste all of that time chattering about when others are risking their lives. I would not be surprised if that is what your father is waiting for from you.

Speaking of, your father—

I am forced to stop reading for a moment in order to laugh. I had not expected to laugh. My heart is so heavy and worn, and I had doubted if there were any words Cara could say to ease my burden. And yet, she has surprised me again, and I laugh through every vulgar insult and threat she makes towards my father. Her words consume almost one-third of a page with what I am certain is every insult that she can think of. Some of them make no sense to me and must be an Inferno insult, talking about killing him and burying him a hundred feet deep in the ground. Last I remembered, burial is something of an insult among her kind, so perhaps that is harsher than it sounds to my own ears. Finally, I sigh and shake my head and continue on.

—and you can tell him I said so, too. He is an absolute idiot if he cannot see what you mean to your own country. I hate to speak ill of others when I like them personally, but I do not trust Petara or Kale. They seem far too supportive of you despite the fact that the support for them grows. This means that it is being encouraged from somewhere. Your mother supports your reign, and I'd thought your father had as well. So unless he is encouraging support for them secretly, I would suspect them of privately encouraging their own favor. I would say to ask her outright about it, but I understand that such things would not be met with forthright answers from your kind, so it won't be of any use.

I suggest speaking with your father. As you said for me: I cannot choose for you. You must decide if you want your crown or not. And if you decide that you do, then go to him and tell him so and that you do not need to prove anything to him since it is your birthright and your own honor, and if he insists, challenge him for it. See what he says to that. I know that it is difficult to stand up to your father. My own, although I love him deeply, is a very intimidating man, and the fear of disappointing him can be painful. But you are no longer defined as his child. Now, you are a man, and you must answer for your own actions, as you well know.

Thank you for easing my mind, Gabriel, with your words. I have not yet decided who I will be, but I think that I am at least figuring out who I am and what I will do. I will find my own way, and no matter where I find it, you should not worry for me.

We are leaving in a few days for Crystalice, and though I'd rather some place warmer, my heart is filled with warmth at the thought of seeing you and your son again. I miss you both.

All my love,
Lady Knight Protector Scarlet Anita

I feel a bit more at ease than I had before. I fold up the letter neatly and tuck it back into the envelope before looking over at my son. Enté sleeps soundly, and I smile quietly at him. He is alive. He is safe. I rub my face again and release another breath before I decide to try and get some sleep. I kick my shoes off and climb into bed next to him, checking his temperature and just listening to him breathe for a few minutes before I finally find myself capable of sleep. Not long now…soon I will see her again…

Chapter Twenty Eight
Scarlet

Six Weeks Later
Maeghdra Manor, Flora

Lightning and an explosion of thunder shatter the night. I come awake with a gasp, throwing the thick blankets off of my form and swallowing gulps of air. I can feel the phantom water at my neck, my throat. I can feel the burning pain on my feet and shoulders, scraping against the cavern to find more air and gulp down as much of it as I can.

I am trembling and soaked in sweat as I curl up on the bed and put my face into my hands, breathing in slowly and softly, shaking. I have these nightmares often now, but they are always worse during the storms. It has rained on and off for a few weeks now, but the torrential rain only just started this afternoon. It beats against my window in sheets, the wind howling outside.

At least the little one is untroubled by it. She snores quietly on the other bed, breathing in deeply, half of her blankets thrown off and one foot dangling from the bed. I smile wearily, and I manage to sip in a calming, steady breath that eases me some.

I do not think that I can go back to sleep, but I do not want to wake up either. I will be so very tired tomorrow if I do not get some rest, but I am sure that same dream awaits me if I dare to close my eyes.

Pulling myself out of bed, I move over to the wash basin and pour some cool water from the pitcher into it. With my hand on the edge of the cool ceramic, I heat the water enough to be pleasant and cup it in my hands to splash my face. It helps some, driving away the memories of icy cold and darkness.

White lightning flashes in the room, and my heart stutters. I clench my eyes tightly, my chest burning with pain.

Faintly, a low and quiet sound murmurs through the thunder, and I open my eyes in the pale darkness, listening for it. With the thunder at my left, I hear the murmur at my right, and when I turn and walk to the door to open it, I realize that it is the sound of the lute.

I leave my room and shut the door quietly behind me, clothed in a simple nightgown with bare feet that pad soundlessly on the floor. Down the hall and over to the banister overlooking the main hall, the low glow of a little fire in the hearth lights up the room. And there on the stone hearth, Alistair leans against the side in his nightshirt and breeches, strumming away slowly and quietly on his lute and mumbling lyrics that I cannot hear.

I've no wish to wake the house by calling out to him from the banister, so I set a hand to the rail of the stairs and walk down slowly, holding up the end of my gown as I go. Somewhere along the way, he must have noticed me, for I hear him cease to play, and when I look up, he is watching me with a small smile and a curious look in his eyes.

"Didst wake ye, lassie?" he asks quietly when I walk a little closer.

I shake my head and greet him with a gentle smile, watching the low light play across his features. "No. The nightmares woke me."

"Nightmares?" he asks at once as I shuffle myself up onto the other side of the hearth and lean back against that side, drawing my legs up to my chest.

"Mm," I confirm, looking back to him with tired eyes. It doesn't look like Alistair has even gone to sleep yet, so I must not have slumbered long. "Of being trapped in the cavern."

His face falls, and a flash of anger crosses his eyes. "Ah... aye...Karnei told me about that. I've never struck that old man, but I came very close to changing that." He gives a growl of a sigh and looks to the fire. "I canna imagine what that was like...Claque said ye were'na breathing for a good while... I'm sorry I was'na able to stop it, lassie..."

I follow his gaze to the fire. "It was...the worst night of my life. I've never been so terrified before—all the times I thought surely that I would never see the next morning, I accepted it. I was ready to welcome my fate...but that night, I felt a desperation that I have never felt—and with it came true fear that I have never known. I suppose death has a different meaning when you have something to lose."

He watches me, but he says nothing more, looking back to the fire and watching the flames instead. He reaches over and grabs a log, propping it up against the others to build the fire higher.

I smile faintly for his thoughtfulness.

"Ye should ken, lass...that the Inferno contacted Gabriel."

"What?" My head snaps back to him, but his eyes are still on the fire.

He sighs, a long, slow sound, and he nods his head in the same way. "Aye...some lad named Jacob. Told him they was looking for ye. Wanted ye back."

I sit in silence for a moment, letting the new information play through my mind. "And...what was Gabriel's answer?"

Alistair turns to me with a little smile and says, "Told him where ye was. Said to send a letter here if he did'na believe him."

"Hm." I relax back against the hearth, eyes downcast as I think quietly to myself. After all this time, I no longer expected to hear from my people. If they came looking for me before, Gabriel never said a word to me about it.

I am not surprised, really. My father is a very practical man and would never have risked his men in the freezing Crystalice cold for one soldier, not even his daughter. And I am not sure that I would have wanted him to at any rate. I would not want to have been responsible for the men who would surely have died in order to retrieve me.

"D'ye think he will?" Alistair asks, and at my frown and confusion, he clarifies: "Send a letter?"

"Mm." I nod slowly, thinking to myself. "I'm not sure. Inferno are neutral with Flora itself, even though we have fought your soldiers in the Cerulean armies…I do not think that they would wish to provoke Flora into an outright war. They may not be able to defend an eastern and southern war. Then again, Flora cannot really afford that either. I do not know what Jacob will do."

He gives a little grunt of annoyance. He sighs and sinks back against the hearth as well, his gaze going back to the fire. He seems to be as enchanted with it as I am, and that thought is a small comfort to me.

"Were you playing the lute?" I ask, although the answer is obvious.

He seems startled out of his reverie and looks to me. "Aye," says he, brandishing the thing for me and grinning.

"I didn't know you played." I sit up, leaning over my bent legs.

"O'course I play! I'd be daft nay to." He chuckles to himself and begins to strum on the thing, which is made to seem small in his large hands. He looks to me with a boyish grin and begins to play…

> *Oy, come ye lassies, come ye lads*
> *Come hear the tale of Cariad*
> *A boy as bonny as he was fine*
> *As the richest king these hills could find*
>
> *Cariad, this fine young man*
> *Aimed for the heart of Teimiad*
> *He loved her deep an' he loved her fine*
> *The finest lass these hills could find*
>
> *But when he chanced to come her way*
> *Wi' flow'rs in hand an' smile so gay*
> *Oy, this poor ol' Cariad*
> *Ta see her bathe in the mornin' rays!*
>
> *This lassie red as she was mad*
> *Chased 'im out w' a fryin' pan*
> *Her clothes up round her ample bust*
> *She beat 'im down out to the brush!*

At this point, I am doubled over with tears in my eyes, hand clasped over my mouth to try and keep from waking the others. Alistair grins at me cheekily and finishes the song with a slow flourish.

> *An' here comes poor ol' Cariad*
> *Cov'r'd in burs from 'is feet to 'is hands*
> *Up the hill oh he did climb*
> *The sorest sight we e'er 'ave had*

I'm snickering and snorting under my hand clasped to my mouth, tears rolling down my cheeks as Alistair chuckles and grins at me, clearly pleased with the reaction he inspired. Once I've finally caught my breath and wiped my cheeks, I grin at him and say, "I rather liked that. Did you write that yourself?"

"Ack," he says with a laugh. "Nay, lass. That's an old, old hearthsong. The wee ones always think it funny—tis'na bawdy as the others, so tis one o'the ones we play afore they're off to bed."

I laugh a bit more and smile broadly at him. "Could you teach me?" I ask.

"What? The song?" he asks.

I shake my head. "No, the lute. Could you teach me to play?"

He grins warmly and inclines his head. "Aye, lassie. I'd like that."

Sitting up, I scoot over to the other side of the hearth.

Alistair watches me with confusion and then a bit of surprise, spreading his arms out as I tuck myself up against his chest, sitting in front of him between he and the instrument. He keeps his arms spread out for a moment, as if not quite sure what to do with them. And then he brings them around me once more to place the lute in front of me.

A glance at his face reveals cheeks and ears as red as Cariad's when he spied his lady in the bath.

"Put yer left hand here, lass," he says with a little smile, peering over my shoulder. He adjusts my hand on the lute—which is much bigger in my grasp than it was in his—and then places my other hand over the strings.

"Here," he adds, hand over mine. "Like this." With his guidance, he leads my fingers to strum over it and create the different notes.

He takes me through a rough version of Cariad's Ballad, and I murmur along with the lyrics, giggling softly and smiling, the storm and the nightmares fading away to the back of my mind.

After an hour or so of this, I begin to feel heavier and slower, leaning my head back against Alistair. "I do not mean to keep you up…" I say softly, hands draped over the lute.

"I dinna mind," he replies in a soft murmur, looking down at the lute with a contented little smile.

I study him for a moment, the wry softness of his gaze, that quirk of a crooked smile, tawny hair hanging in front of his eyes. "Thank you, Alistair," I say, leaning up to kiss his cheek. Instead, he turns to look at me, and my lips land right on his.

I'd not meant or expected to kiss his lips, but once there, I freeze, eyes flying open and cheeks heating.

Alistair seems startled for a moment, but in the heartbeat of a moment I take to begin to move away, he leans towards me and sets his lips more firmly.

If my cheeks were warm before, they're blazing hot now, and I tremble faintly, completely surrounded by him, trapped in his and the lute's embrace by my own design. And yet, despite my racing heart, it is a soothing sensation—to be held, to be kissed—and I sink against him for a moment.

I am not sure who pulls away first, but I slowly move back from him, my golden eyes lifting to his face. He watches me with an expression that I cannot name, one of guarded curiosity and also uncertainty. Looking at him, I want to say something, but for a moment, his eyes seem blue—crystalline blue—and his hair, a snowy white.

I am struck at once with a sickening twist of my stomach, and I turn my eyes away. "I should get to bed," I tell him, and at once, he parts his arms in compliance to allow me to slip off of the hearth. "Tomorrow will be an early morning."

"Aye…" he says softly, sitting up with one leg draped over the hearth and watching me. "We leave for Crystalice soon for the princess' wedding. Try and get as much rest as ye can. I'll take care of the rest."

I cast a little smile, stuck in my place before the fire as I look at him, the warmth and scent of him still on my lips. "Goodnight, Alistair."

He inclines his head slowly to me and echoes, "Goodnight, my lass."

Chapter Twenty Nine
Gabriel

A Few Weeks Later
The Crystalice Palace, Cerulean

Even with her weakness of the winter, she still looks better than when I left her last in Marine. Her skin has returned to its olive-gold hue, and her eyes are more yellow than brown. She stands alert and aware, and she is even smiling. Standing by the carriage, she laughs at something Alistair says and shoves his chest, leaving him with a grin on his face.

She's dressed for winter this time, wearing a heavy, velvet dress and underneath it many more layers of wool and cotton, I am certain. The violet color suits her dark complexion and her red hair, making her yellow eyes seem almost to glow. She has not noticed me yet; I came out into the courtyard to meet her and stand stupidly on the steps, just staring at her.

"Cara." Her name leaves my lips before I can even stop myself, and it leaves my chest like a sigh of relief.

She gives a start then, her smile fading and her eyes suddenly attentive when she tosses back her hair from the wind and looks right at me. For a moment, she seems frozen, her wide eyes just locked. But then, her mouth spreads into such a wide grin the likes of which I have never seen her wear. I wonder if Alistair taught her how to smile like that.

"Gabriel!" she cries, and Alistair follows her gaze to look at me and smiles with amusement.

Cara picks up her skirts in her hands and hurries across the courtyard as if she might very well pounce on me with an embrace, and I half think that I would not have cared. But behind her, Alistair calls her name in warning. She pauses then and glances back to Alistair who watches her with a carefully guarded expression. "We're nay in Flora anymore, sweetheart," he says, having retained some of that Flora accent, I see.

I want nothing more than to throw a snowball at his face, but he is right, and when Cara looks back at me with a frustrated expression, I smile warmly at her. "Welcome back, Cara," I greet quietly, and she smiles again, this time taking her steps more carefully and making her way to me at the bottom of the stairs.

Her eyes are filled with laughter and warmth. They look right into mine, and I want nothing more than to drag her to me and hold her. Her chest is heaving slightly with her breaths, and plumes of fog float from her mouth where her hot breath touches the cold air. Her golden cheeks are flushed, and her eyes are locked onto mine with full attentiveness, lips slightly parted and curled in a little smile.

Chelyah, I have missed her…

"It is good to be back, Gabriel." She shrugs, giving a curt laugh, and adds, "More or less." And then, she smiles again. Her brows furrow some and she tips her head a bit to the side, her expression turning sad. "I've missed you."

My breath leaves me, and I wonder if her chest is heaving from breathlessness of her run or if she feels as I do when I look upon her. "I've missed you as well. Come inside out of the cold."

"Mama!" Zsoka calls from the carriage, and Cara looks back at her with a little smile. The tiny she-cat is crouched in the carriage, glaring at the snow on the ground. "Come get me!"

"I will not!" Cara calls back. "You have boots on. You'll not feel the snow at all if you hurry. Come along."

Zsoka whines and fusses, mewling unhappily, until Alistair goes over to the child. Cara watches, and Alistair speaks softly to the girl, and Zsoka listens to him with a frown. Finally, the girl nods, and stands up, stretching out her arms. Alistair grabs her up and holds her to his chest, carrying her across the snow.

When he reaches us both, Cara laughs at him and says, "Alistair, it'll do no good to spoil her." Cara reaches up and pinches the girl playfully, making Zsoka giggle.

"Ack, what can I say, lass?" he says with a grin at her. "I canna refuse either o'ye."

Cara shuts her mouth and smiles a bit shyly, a look that I have also never seen on her before. I did not think my little spitfire knew the meaning of the word 'shy'. But she shakes her head at him and looks back to me with warmth. "Inside then?" she asks.

I suddenly remember myself. "Of course! Come inside." I laugh a bit and lead the way, beginning to understand what Lady Freya meant when she said Alistair was settling into a family. The way he dotes on Zsoka, the easy manner between he and Cara.

How much has changed in these many months? I had known his care for her and had done my best not to discourage either of them when it would have been selfish to do so. But to have them both here and to see between them what she and I can never have...it is more painful than I expected, and I suddenly feel as if I cannot take in a full breath.

"Gabriel..." Cara's voice is quiet behind me when we reach the second floor, coming up the top of the stairs.

There is not much privacy to be had, but it is the closest to alone we have been in a very long time.

Cara's hand is warm when she touches my arm, and it robs my breath. Her eyes look straight into mine, soft and powerful.

I am swallowed up in them.

"Gabriel, I—"

"Scarlet!" Dena's cry of joy fills the castle halls, and I turn to see my over-eager sister practically bouncing down the halls to us. She stops at my side and takes Cara's hands, squeezing them tightly. "You've come back! Oh, I've missed you so! There is so much I wish to tell you! Oh, and I have a gift for you too!"

Cara laughs and grins warmly at her. "Aren't the guests supposed to bring gifts for the bride?"

She smiles and says, "Well, yes, but I had to buy it when I saw it. I *knew* you'd love it!"

"I cannot wait," Cara replies and then looks to see Alistair and Zsoka coming up the stairs.

"Oh! Is this the little Inferno girl?" Dena asks warmly, smiling at Zsoka. Once they reach the hall, Zsoka eyes her warily and half-hides behind Alistair. "Hello, little one," Dena greets, crouching down and smiling at her. "I'm Dena. What's your name?"

Cara smiles at the little one and says, "It's alright, love. She's a friend. This is Gabriel's little sister."

Alistair murmurs something to her as well and nudges her out from behind him.

Zsoka doesn't look much too happy with either of them, but she at least stops hiding, although she is still clinging to Alistair's leg. "Zsoka," she introduces softly. "Are…are you the one gettin married?"

"I am," Dena says with a girlish grin.

Cara smiles at them both and then looks to me. "Where is my little Enté?" she asks. "I had hoped to see him as soon as I'd arrived."

I give a half-smile and then sigh, not quite sure how to tell her. She will no doubt be murderous. "Well, Cara...he's resting right now..."

She frowns at me and studies my face severely. "What is it, Gabriel? What has happened?" She looks to Dena, and as I see the rise of panic in her eyes and the stiff way she stands, I reach out to her.

My hand grazes her arm, and I see red fur rise up on the back of her neck, rippling up from under her skin.

Her eyes are pure yellow when they lock on mine. "What happened!"

"Cara," I say gently, and she looks to me, her hands balled into fists. "He was poisoned a few weeks ago."

Her look of horror and rage coupled together makes me almost sorry for whomever poisoned my son whenever she gets ahold of them.

I am reminded of what Jacob said to me about the self-inflicted torture she had to put herself through and wonder just what she would do if she ever got ahold of that person.

"What!" she rages at me, and I can see flames flicker in her hair and along her arms. "By who? Who has done this!" But we both know who, and she doesn't really have to ask. She just stares at me and my blank expression before shaking her head slowly and crying, "No, no, no, *no!* Let me see him!"

She storms past me, and I sigh and move to go and get her before Alistair skirts past me and grabs her arm.

"Let me go!" she snarls at Alistair, rounding on him with wrath in her eyes.

"Lassie, let the wee prince rest," he tells her, pushing some hair out of her face and holding onto her forearm. "He's tired. I'm sure ye can go see him soon."

"No!" she snarls and tries to wrench her arm away from him. "Alistair, let me go! I want to go see him!"

"Scarlet," he says more firmly, "Yer exhausted from the trip. Ye're weak and tired and need to sleep."

"I am not an infant to be coddled!" she shouts at him, and he grabs her other arm then, causing anger to boil up in my chest, but Dena reaches out and lays a cool hand upon my wrist, giving me a level stare.

"Aye, yer nay," Alistair says firmly, holding her by both arms and looking down right into her eyes. "But Zsoka needs ye, and ye'll frighten Enté if yer sickly near him...There's plenty o'time. But for now, ye need to rest."

She sucks in a breath, grinding her teeth and glaring at him past the tears in her eyes. "They...they tried to kill him, Alistair..." she whispers quietly, and my heart wrenches at the sight of her.

And yet somehow, I am also pleased, if slightly. She is just as worried, just as angry, and just as guilty as I feel now. To know that the woman I love and admire cares so deeply for someone I treasure so much, it fills me with a sense of peace, as if my burden is not as heavy as it was a moment ago.

"I ken it..." Alistair murmurs and lets go of her arms, pulling her to his chest. "I ken it, lass."

I half expect Cara to push him away and shout at him again, but she buries her face against his chest and cries.

"It's my fault," she snarls quietly. "I should have been here. I should have protected him! I should have been here!"

However much I hate seeing Alistair hold her the way I cannot, I do not want Cara to feel this way. "Alistair, perhaps the Inferno ladies should rest. Dena can show you to your room."

He looks up at me over Cara's red hair and nods. "Aye. Many thanks, Gabe. I'll do that." He looks to Zsoka and smiles gently. "Come on, Zsoka…tis alright…come take a nap with yer mam."

Zsoka glances to me and to Dena before hurrying to Alistair's side.

Cara reaches out and strokes her hair lovingly before allowing Alistair to put his hand on the small of her back and guide her down the hall, away from me.

"It's better this way," Dena says quietly to me when they are beyond the point of hearing us.

I give a gruff sigh and mutter, "Says the one about the marry to man she loves." I give her a curt look, and she replies with only a gentle, sad smile before turning away from me and heading back down the hall as well.

"I'll call for some hot soup and warm ale for Scarlet. Heather will want to know she's arrived too."

I watch her go and then sigh and say quietly, "I'll…do nothing, I suppose." My sardonic mutterings remind me of my little son's sulking, and that annoys me, but I also mostly don't care because no one can hear me anyways.

The Next Afternoon

If there is anything good to be said about weddings and all of the chaos and convolution they bring, at the very least, there are fewer meetings. The prerogative of the council and the royal household has shifted mostly to the social and casual and away from the political. It has given me more time to catch up on my work and to visit with my son.

I had not expected, however, when I entered my son's room to check on him that evening, to find a little red-headed Inferno curled up in bed with him murmuring sweet lullabies. Her golden eyes jump to mine when she sees me walk in, but she brings a finger up to her lips even as she continues singing. I smile gently and incline my head to her, going and sitting down in a stuffed chair by the window. The sun casts a golden evening light upon the white snow, and I glance away from the window to see Cara's snow-covered boots tucked away by the window along with a snow-dusted cloak.

I bite my tongue for the moment, however, and wait until she finishes her song. She hesitates, watching Enté. I lean over to look at him and find him lying on his back with his mouth slightly parted and his eyes clenched a bit. His face slowly relaxes, however, and I sigh softly, watching him slip into a deeper slumber. Cara smiles gently and then looks to me where I sit. Her golden eyes are filled with warmth, and the sight of her once more fills me with a peace and comfort.

"Cara," I greet with softness.

She smiles in response and settles next to Enté, watching me. "Good afternoon, Gabriel. I tried to find you earlier, but you were busy."

I nod slowly and sigh. "I've been quite busy as of late." I gesture to the boots and cloak. "You went outside?"

She nods and replies, "I did. Ckai'ten took me out to the village and I spoke with some of the Cerulean people."

"No incident?" I ask warily. The thought of her out in that city again with only Ckai'ten to protect her…my stomach knots uncomfortably. Surely Alistair had not known or he would have never permitted her out in the streets. What was she even thinking after what happened the last time?

She smiles wryly at me, as if knowing my thoughts, and perhaps my thoughts are quite clear based on my expression. My hands are clenched, and I might have been glaring at her. "I am much stronger than I was last time, Gabriel. Everything was fine." I lean back in my chair to try and force myself to relax, but I raise a brow, challenging her assertion. She laughs. "It was." I mutter something, but she just smiles at me and keeps watching me, her head propped up by her arm.

"In any event, we should talk." I look back to her. I never trust a woman when she says that she wants to talk. It never means anything good for me. I sit up a little straighter, and look back to her, but she starts laughing at me and covers her mouth, trying not to be too loud.

Beside her, Enté shifts with the noise, and she quiets herself, slowly slipping out of bed and sitting on the edge. She pulls her boots back on and bundles her cloak in her arms, coming to me and taking my hand. Her touch is burning to mine, but I clasp her hand regardless and let her pull me up and into the sitting room. The sitting room is empty and quiet, but I go to the hearth and place a few charms inside of it which starts a fire going.

She settles herself on one end of the couch and pats the other end. I sigh and go sit across from her while she pulls her legs to her chest like a child might, watching me with a small smile. I have missed her presence here, her easy smiles and her mischievous, golden eyes. Her laughter dispels my sorrow, and her smiles release the weight from my chest.

"I spoke with your people today."

"So you've told me," I reply, reclining back against the couch and stretching my legs out before relaxing them. She kicks my leg, however, and I make an unhappy noise before glaring at her.

"When was the last time you walked among them, Gabriel?"

I suddenly feel as if I'm subtly being scolded, and I shift, giving her an annoyed look. "I've been a bit busy with running their country. But next time I have a free day, I'll take a stroll. Or would you rather me ignore my lawmaking and tax amendments to go for a walk?"

She gives me an annoyed look and kicks me again. "Ow!" I complain and glare at her. "Would you stop that?" I grab the offending foot and pull off her boot and sock before tickling the sole of her foot. She yelps and jerks, and I lean my head back to avoid a broken nose before releasing her.

She laughs though, and I am smiling again. She pulls her foot away from me, and I lean over to her. "Behave," I grumble at her, my hand moving to her side and pressing there. She laughs a bit and squirms, scrunching her nose. "And stop being so hateful." She pushes me away from her, warmth in her eyes. "If you've something to say, Cara, then say it."

"I thought I had," she says with a sigh, sitting up again and this time leaning over me as I recline on my couch, a scolding little smile on her lips. "You're neglecting them, Gabriel."

I scoff. "I thought I just answered this, Cara. I am not neglecting them."

She replies, "I do not mean to say that what you have been doing is not important. But you must take time to talk to them. Because what you and the other aristocrats may think is important and valuable to the country may not be what they actually care about. And they do not see everything that you do for them in here. You must *help* them to see it. In a way that they can understand."

I sigh in defeat and lay back against the arm of the chair. "I am not about to listen to an Inferno tell me how to run my country."

Like a cat, she slowly makes her presence more and more oppressive so that I cannot ignore her. She starts from leaning over me to laying on me, moving so that even though I am staring up at the ceiling, she lays on me and looks over at me; her red hair dangles into my face. I huff and push her hair out of my face, and she sits back, pushing her hair out of the way. "You are not listening to an Inferno. You are listening to me. Or has what I say become inconsequential to you?"

"No," I sigh with annoyance as she sits back, and I reach for her, cupping her cheek. She leans her face against my hand and closes her eyes. To hold her cheek is like cupping fire, and it only reminds me of the stark difference of when she had first arrived. Back then, I'd thought her skin to be hot, but that heat was nothing compared to the healthy glow and warmth she radiates now. "I am listening, Cara. Tell me what you have to say."

"Mmm." She does not speak immediately, instead nuzzling her cheek against my hand and sighing contently.

Finally, she opens her honeyed eyes and looks to me. "They are unhappy, Gabriel." She sits back. "Many of them are suffering for food…and they are becoming unhappy with your war. They think that they are losing to my people, and they blame you."

I sit up, leaning over my legs and clasping my hands together.

Cara slides off the couch and goes to the fire, staring into it as she sits down before the hearth. "They think that you sit comfortably in your palace with all your feasts of food and no battles seen, and they resent you."

She looks back to me as I think on her words, and my eyes lift from my hands to look at her. "I know that it is not your fault. And the last thing you need to do is jump into battle and get killed."

She sighs. "But they need to be reassured."

"And what would you suggest?" I ask, watching her.

She blinks and looks back to me once more. She bites her lip and falls silent for a moment before saying, "Announce that the castle is cutting back on food consumption. After the wedding, naturally. Speak with Alistair concerning trade for food. They have plenty but they are lacking in other materials you could provide."

I nod slowly and consider her words.

"I know that you can do nothing more than you already are with the Inferno…but spend time among them. It does not have to be for a whole day. But an hour or two…go walk among them, purchase the food they make, the toys they buy for their own children. Take Enté and let him play with their young boys."

My heart clenches at her words, however, and I look up at her with annoyance. "Enté is far too sick, and he has already been attacked once."

She sighs patiently and does not shy away from my gaze. "Gabriel, he is Crystalice as well. The cool, fresh air would do him some good. Take your choice guards if you must. But I sincerely doubt that they would attack the child in the open." She shakes her head. "Besides…they always see you from a distance as some great ruler. Let them see you as a man, as a father. Let them see Enté weak and ill. Let them feel anger for you. The White Fang attacked a *child*. Not a faceless heir, not a spoiled prince. They attacked a *boy*, a *son*. Let them see *that,* and they will hate the White Fang as you do."

"No." My heart begins beating harder, faster, and my eyes harden on her.

She opens her mouth again, but I cut her off, "Cara, I will not do it. My son is not a pawn. He is not something to *use* in order to win my people's sympathy. He is my child, and he needs to be protected."

"And how will you protect him?" she snaps at me, glaring now. Her chest heaves a bit, and she watches me with spite. "How will you protect him when your people hate you?"

She shakes her head. "You forget, Gabriel, that your people come first. Before you. Before your son. That is what it means to be a ruler." She stands carefully and then looks back to me. "I told you: you must decide if you want your crown or not. But understand that if you do accept it that it means to put your people first."

I stand as well, facing her. "And what if I do!" I snarl. "Enté is all I have left, Cara! Not only is he my son, but he is my heir. What if I were to lose him! He is still so young. How can you ask me to endanger him! He is the only heir I have, and I've no bride by which to sire another!"

"Then marry." Her words are sharp and painful. She stands before me, trembling. Her hands are clenched at her sides, and her golden eyes pierce mine. I can hear her breath hiss out slowly between her teeth. She is waiting for me to answer her, and yet I cannot speak.

"Marry?" I ask her, watching her and feeling my chest clench. I know that she cannot mean herself, and so I cannot understand what she is asking of me.

She gives a frustrated sigh and gestures with her hand before slapping it against her leg when she drops it again. "Yes, Gabriel. If you are afraid of losing your heir, then marry. Then, at least you will have the chance to sire another. Why do you think Petara has so much support even though you are the Prince and have a son? Because she has Bronx and because she can have more children. In her, there is security. And so if that is what you are looking for, then take a *wife* and be done with the matter."

I cannot think. I cannot even form my own thoughts, my own words. Every thought I had was abruptly thrown into my throat once again, and I can do nothing but repeat her last words bitterly, "Be done with the matter..." I scoff and bring up my hand, rubbing my face. Finally, I draw in a slow, steady breath and say, "Cara, leave me. I am finished with this conversation."

Cara does not speak, but she does not leave either. She merely stands before the fire, watching me. Finally, she shakes her head, and she says with a voice much softer than it had been a moment before, "Gabriel...I do not mean to say that I...that I do not—"

"Leave me, Cara." I do not want to hear what she has to say. Whatever she might say would only make what she has already said much more painful. My chest clenches and my stomach is in knots. It is one thing to know that I cannot have the very thing of my desire and love. It is quite another to have that same woman tell me to choose another. Whether she is right or not, I do not care. I cannot deal with her right now. I cannot hear these words. Not from her. She has no right to speak those words to me.

"Gabriel, I—"

"Leave!" I snarl at her, finally taking my hand away from my face to look at her, my blue eyes sharp and piercing against her golden ones which go wide, and she draws up an arm between us as if alarmed.

Again, another look from her that I have never seen before. She is not quite afraid—I have never truly seen her afraid—but it is startled and wounded and lost. But then, she clenches her hands and draws them down to her sides, her eyes hardening on me.

"Do as you will, Gabriel." Her words are sharp and biting. There is a moment between her casual anger and her utmost rage that is alarmingly still and composed. This is that moment. "Clearly my words are of little consequence to you."

Her pupils have shifted to that of a cat's, and she stares me down with those eyes before finally snatching up her cloak and storming past me, her boots thundering on the hard, icy floors. I move to face the fire, my blue eyes watching it as I had watched her. The door behind me slams.

But there is no peace. Almost immediately after, I hear Alistair's voice. "Scarlet? Where've ye been? I'd heard ye'd gone to the village. What were ye thinking? I've been beside myself trying to find ye."

"Do *not* touch me!" she shouts suddenly, and I can practically see Alistair's surprise and confusion. "I am surrounded by fools! You are all complete imbiciles! Do not touch me, Alistair. Do not say another word. I have had enough! You are all *daft*, I tell you! I am returning to my room now. *Excuse* me."

I do not hear anymore from Alistair, and I almost feel guilty. She is angry at me, not him, and yet he received the daggers meant for my heart. I growl and rub my face again, anticipating the hesitant knock on my door.

"Enter," I grumble just loud enough to be heard before sinking into my couch once more.

The door opens and then closes quietly. I hear Alistair's footsteps, much quieter than Cara's had been, move towards me and around the couch. I watch him out of the corner of my eyes, my hand covering my mouth from where my elbow is propped on the arm of the couch. He settles himself into a stuffed chair and then leans back with a sigh.

For a while, we do not speak. He watches the fire, not looking at me, and at last, I follow his gaze until we are both staring at the yellow and russet flames dancing in my hearth. The fire pops and crackles for a while, eating up the *Magik* of the talismans until their power is all drained. With its nourishment finished, the fire becomes smaller and smaller until it is no more than a little flicker surrounded by stone, and then even that too dies away into nothing.

I release my breath and move my hand away from my mouth, letting it drape casually over the arm. Turning my eyes to Alistair, I find him watching me now, and I tell him, "Cara told me to remarry."

His eyebrows shoot up, clearly not having expected those words.

Neither had I. "She suggested I use Enté as a pawn for my own public relations. She suggested spending time out in the towns—like she had today—and taking Enté with me to garner sympathy and support."

I rub the bridge of my nose, clenching my eyes as I do so, and I continue, "When I told her that I was appalled as a father and as a prince since Enté is my only heir, she suggested I remarry for the stability to my throne."

Alistair makes a silent 'ah' of a sound and nods slowly, beginning to scratch at the beard on his face.

I watch and am suddenly very tired. "Why have you not yet shaved that off?" I ask quietly. "You always hated a beard. Said it made you look old and it itched."

He smiles to himself and changes from scratching it to rubbing it thoughtfully. There is a warmth and intimacy in his eyes at whatever steals his thoughts that I can guess well enough why he hasn't shaved it yet. I make a rude noise and turn my head away.

Perfect.

The love of my life has told me to remarry, and my dearest and oldest companion in arms is in love with her.

What a glorious way to end my day.

Alistair sighs at last and says, "What Scarlet says makes good and practical sense."

My eyes snap to him, and he holds up his hands in defense.

"As a prince! As a prince." He smiles a bit and leans back. "But aye…as a parent, tis irresponsible and borders neglect."

I grunt and lean my chin on my hand, frowning at the empty hearth once more.

Alistair leans forward and clasps his hands together while his forearms rest on his legs. "Tigers are'na wolves," he says. "Have ye ever seen wild tigers?"

I raise a brow at him and do not answer.

He nods a bit and continues, "Wolves live in packs, always do. And the most important thing to the entire pack tis the pups, the offspring. Tigers are'na like that. The dam raises her cubs, but as soon's they're grown, they leave. They'd nay join her in her life, and rarely does their sire. Sometimes the sire stays 'round for a while, but she's usually alone."

I drop my arm with annoyance and say, "Alistair, you cannot honestly compare us to our feral counterparts."

"And why nay?" he asks, spreading his hands. "D'ye *truly* think the only thing we take from them is their second form?" He brings his hands back together. "We're nay feral, nor animals in the strict sense. But consider how the Inferno and the Cerulean live. The Inferno are a great bundle o'wee families in one place; they live together, but they fight and die for their kin, nay their country or king.

"Cerulean tend to focus on a pack and where ye'd fit in that hierarchy. The Cerulean place their highest heart on the whole pack, and every wolf has to know their place in the pack and do their part for the whole to work; why else d'ye think the White Fang undermine ye so easily?

"Consider then why'd she say that the Cerulean whole come afore the child."

He waits as I think on his words and then fills in for me, "The *best* way to protect the individual is to protect the whole—the best way to protect the pup is to protect the pack. She kens how yer people work. She kens her enemy. Tis her strength."

He leans back. "Tis'na say she's only looking out for herself. Remember she's a vested interest in Enté. She loves him deeply. Scarlet would'na endanger him lightly. She would'na suggest it if she'd nay think that there was greater danger in nay doing so."

I mutter something under my breath, but I do not answer him. Instead, I rub my mouth and my jaw, just thinking quietly. I do not know what about Cara's words anger me more, and I do not really wish to think on it. I do not answer him, however, and instead merely sulk in my seat while I consider not only what I think of her words but how I will respond to them.

After a moment and apparently realizing that I am not going to answer him, Alistair gets up with a grunt and sighs, moving around behind the furniture and heading for the door.

"Alistair," I call, and I hear the footsteps stop. It takes a moment to form my thoughts and to arrange them in an order that makes any sort of sense. "What is your relationship with her?"

My companion sighs and mutters something, shifting around in ways I cannot see but can hear by the sound.

I turn my head to look at him and find him rubbing the back of his neck.

"I dinna ken myself, to be quite honest," he tells me and looks over at me, dropping his hand. "Sometimes I'd warrant she's fond o'me…and sometimes I'd warrant she's bound to just leave and go back to Inferno… She's promised to tell me afore she does…but sometimes I dinna ken if she'll say 'I love ye' or 'I'm leaving and will'na return'."

I understand that feeling well, and sometimes I wonder if she does it on purpose or if she's as much a foreigner to her own thoughts as everyone else seems to be. She's told me as much that she does not know what she wants to do or even who she is. I can imagine such. She has spent her entire life with the single-minded purpose of hating and killing anything and anyone who was not Inferno. And somewhere along the way, she fell in love with the object of her hatred, with Enté. And then with me.

Truth be told, I don't think she ever hated Cerulean at all. I think she was hurt. I have never been so hurt and as angry as when Mit'an'av was taken from me. She must have felt the same. She was angry. Furious. People she loved were gone. She was angry that they were gone. But I don't think she ever hated the people who took them. Or at least, I don't think she could ever look at Enté and see someone who had killed someone she loved.

But what do I know? I clearly know nothing of her inmost thoughts.

"Do you think you would wed her?" I ask.

Alistair seems as surprised as I am that I asked. I had not really meant to. It was just the first thing that came to mind, and I spoke it aloud.

He rubs at his beard again. "I dinna ken…" He drops his hand and looks to me with a sort of determined resolve that I rarely see in him. "But I'll do whatever it takes to make her stay."

Chapter Thirty
Scarlet

I had not meant to fall asleep. Zsoka had been awake when we'd returned, and we'd played and taken a meal together, but the warm meal and a fit of coughing had her back in bed again. I sat with her until she fell asleep once. Then, I went and sat by the fire. I hadn't known how tired I was sitting there and suddenly felt so heavy and worn.

I wake when the heavy door creaks open, and I yawn, rolling onto my back and rubbing at my face. "Freya?" I call. She'd left to go and speak with the queen over tea and had invited me along, but I'd declined. I have no idea how much time has passed to know if it is anywhere near time for her to return or if she already has and I've slept through it.

"Nay, lass."

My heart jumps, and my stomach turns, but as I turn my head to look at him, Alistair is already at my side. He eases down beside me, sitting and putting a hand to my head. His hand is strong and heavy on my brow, his palms rough and calloused. They almost remind me of my father's hands, the hands of men who have wielded swords for many long years. "Art ill, lass? I canna tell if ye burn a fever."

I laugh a bit and smile at him and his cool hand on my skin, looking up at him from where I lay on the plush rug.

"Inferno do not run fevers. We burn hot if we start getting sick to try and burn up whatever is hurting us, but if we're truly sick, we go cold to try and keep from burning too much energy or food."

"Mmm tis so?" he asks, taking his hand off of my head and just smiling down at me with that mischievous little look on his face. I purse my lips together and smile at him in spite of myself. "I'd best nay let ye get cold then." He stretches out beside me and props himself up on his arm, watching me.

I laugh and continue laying on my back, feeling an unusual heat on my cheeks. "You're scandalous."

He grins unrepentantly, but he keeps his hands to himself, just watching me. I smile back. "So ye went to the towns today?" he asks suddenly.

I wrinkle my nose under his scrutiny and sigh, laying my hands on my belly. "Yes, I did. Does it concern you?"

"I'm yer guardian," he says darkly, stealing a lock of my red hair and bringing it to his lips, all while watching me. "Tis my business to be concerned."

I do not speak a word, just watching him and barely breathing.

He finally breaks eye contact and looks down to the piece of hair he is playing with. "D'ye at least take someone with ye?"

I make a rude noise and frown at him. "I'm not a fool. I went armed, and I took Ckai'ten who is one of Gabriel's best men, thank you very much." He tugs on my hair as a little punishment, and I pull it away from him. "Play nice," I mutter.

"Well," he says with a little chuckle, "twas yer visit, lassie?"

I look over at him as if not trusting his words, but his gaze is calm and his smile easy, so I smile and decide to tell him about my trip. I tell him of the different shops and the people I met, the conversations I had. "All in all," I tell him, "it was a beneficial experience if not entirely pleasant. I've learned many more insults and curses than I knew before."

He groans and rolls onto his back. "Perfect. Just what ye need."

I laugh and sit up a bit, leaning over him so that I can see his face. "It is indeed," I tell him. "My old ones are being overused."

"I canna take ye anywhere," he teases me, and I laugh.

"Do you mean to threaten to lock me up in my room?" I tease, and then realize that I should very much not have when he grins wickedly back at me.

"The thought's a'might tempting."

The heat burns my face again, and I make a rude noise to hide my embarrassment, pushing myself away from him and laying on my back once more.

Alistair rolls over again to look at me and smile teasingly.

I give him a look, and he laughs.

"Mmm...art still cross with Gabriel, lassie?" he asks quietly, and I look to see that he's stolen a piece of my hair again and plays with it between his fingers idly.

I sigh. "Is he still cross with *me*?"

He sets my hair down, instead taking the hand on my belly. He laces my fingers with his, and I reluctantly close my fingers around his hand. He gives a thoughtful smile, staring at the place where our bodies meet and bringing our joined hands to his lips. He kisses the back of my knuckles chastely. He does not quite seem himself.

"He's nay cross, sweetheart...He's hurt. He loves ye. And ye told him to marry someone else. And ye told him to put his son's life in danger...He thinks he's safe here inside these walls...Cerulean's never had problems like the White Fang afore."

I look to him before putting my arm over my eyes and closing them, just breathing and thinking for a moment. I curse under my breath and just try to think. And yet I cannot.

I miss him. I miss talking with him. I miss his passion for his son and for his country and for me. I miss his sharp wit and clever tongue. I miss his rare moments of gentleness and transparency.

"Gabe's a good man," Alistair says to me. "He's more like his mother…brilliant and demanding but nay a cut-throat. He canna sacrifice his humanity in order to do what he must."

I move my arm away from my face and stare up at the ceiling. "I gave up my humanity a long time ago…"

"Hm," is his only reply, and he takes up a piece of my hair again, playing with it and studying it carefully.

I watch him as he does so, watch the way he studies the copper piece of hair and rolls it between his fingers carefully, finally bringing it to his lips and kissing the lock gently. "Alistair?"

He keeps the lock pressed to his bottom lip, but his green eyes flicker to mine.

I look into those green eyes for a moment, the fire dancing within them, and I try to find the answer for myself before giving up and asking, "What is it you want from me?"

He sits up a bit more, dropping my piece of hair to put his hand on the floor in front of him to keep his balance. "Ah, Gabriel asked me near the same thing."

I roll onto my side to face him, my back to the warmth of the fire. "And what did you tell him?"

He looks back to me, his face not far from mine. "I told him I dinna ken."

That's not much of an answer. I watch his green eyes while they study me.

He seems about as lost and frustrated as I am, and although I am normally such a person who has always decided what I will do, I am left completely at a loss now.

"Alistair…"

His eyes return to mine.

"What do you want me to do?"

He does not speak at once, just looking at my golden eyes as if he does not know himself. Finally, he lays on his back, staring up at the ceiling. "I dinna ken," he replies gruffly. "All's I kens…that I wish for ye to stay… but I will'na ask ye to…tis yer own choice."

I lay on my side as I watch him, but he will not meet my eyes again.

He stares up at the ceiling with an intensity that makes me wonder if he thinks to find the answer there.

At last, I lean over him, catching his gaze once more before I press my lips to his before I can change my mind. I feel his breath leave all at once, soft against my cheek, and his arms go around me, slowly and carefully—hesitating —one across my back and the other against my shoulders so that his hand can tangle in my hair and hold my head to his.

Our kiss is slow and sweet and followed by another, less tentative one.

My stomach knots up painfully, and yet my heart is filled with a sweet contentment, as if it had been clenched all this time but finally released. There is a disoriented, giddy sort of feeling in my head, and I enjoy that moment there with him, his lips against my own and that beard of his tickling my chin. But after that, I pull away and look down at him and those dark, green eyes.

"I will stay for now…"

"Fire's a fickle thing," Alistair complains softly, his voice a low rumble.

I give a little smile and reply, "So are women…but I am your friend. And this I promise to you."

I shift a bit to scoot down and lay my cheek against his chest, settling down at his side. My hearts still hurts, and my stomach is knotting in pain. I want to cry, and I am completely unsure of weather I am pleased or aching, love-sick or heartbroken.

Perhaps I am all of them.

Alistair gives a heavy sigh and puts an arm around me, kissing the top of my head before laying his head back down. I close my eyes and echo his sigh, feeling my body go heavy against his. He is cooler against me than an Inferno would be, but it is pleasant enough to have him there. It is comfortable enough and late enough in the evening that I fall asleep once more.

That Night

A slamming door is what wakes me the second time, and someone shouting Alistair's name. I am laying on my other side now, curled up in a ball and facing the fire. It is so warm and comfortable, but that voice is grating in my ears.

"I have been patient!" Freya snaps. "I have waited! I have talked! But I can abide this no longer!" I mumble to myself and rub my face as I feel Alistair's presence beside me suddenly leave.

"Mam, what's—"

"Enough!" Freya snarls at him, and the urgency of her tone is finally getting to me and startling me awake. I turn and look at her and find the old, fiercesome woman staring her great bear of a son down. "You have always been rash. You act without thinking and think that your cute little smile and a jest will spare you from harm. And mostly, it has. But not any longer. Alistair, you listen to me. You get rid of that woman or you do something with her. But I will not sit here and watch you destroy yourself with her."

"Mam, that's quite enough," Alistair says in a low voice, and it surprises me because I have never heard him take such a tone with his mother.

I stagger to stand, my back to the fire as I watch them and try to think of what to say.

"No!" Freya snarls. She looks to me with anger and then looks back to her son. "People are *talking*, Alistair, and you cannot laugh that off. The gentry take that *seriously* and with the Levosa encroaching into our country more and more, the *last* thing Flora needs is a scandal involving one of their kings."

She gestures to me and continues, "Do something with her! Get rid of her! Marry her! I do not care, Alistair, but you must do *something* or you are going to lose *everything!*"

She looks to me then and points an accusing finger, "If you care for my son at all, then stop this! You are going to *ruin* him! Do you hear me, Scarlet!"

"Enough!" Alistair roars, and the whole room shakes with the sound of it. I watch fur ripple over his skin, dark brown in color. In his chest is a low, guttural sound of warning.

I cannot think of what to say to either of them, but this is really not something I have much business in taking part of. "Excuse me…" I whisper. I feel small and wounded. I have always valued Freya's opinion and had come to think of her as a friend. She can be coarse at times and painfully honest, but she has never yelled at me, and she has never accused me of something so horrible.

"Scarlet, wait," Alistair calls as I move past him and his mother for the door. "*Scarlet.*"

I ignore him, leaving the suite and shutting the door behind me. I hesitate outside of the door, breathing slowly and feeling sudden tears burn my eyes. But when shouting begins again behind me with my name peppered in their words, I give an annoyed sound and push myself away from the door, giving myself up to wander the halls for the remainder of the evening.

Chapter Thirty One
Alistair

That Night in Alistair's Bedroom
The Crystalice Palace, Cerulean

I cannot sleep. Not anymore. I dozed for a few hours after night set in, but my mind is restless and wanders constantly.

So many things.

The White Fang, although they do not threaten my country, threaten my friends, and they have shown no discretion in who they kill.

Gabe's soldier, Tam, was one of my own men. I consider that enough of an attack on my own to warrant retribution. But it is difficult to know who the enemy is now, and I am beginning to think that my best course of action would be to revoke our troops for the time being and focus our attention on Flora affairs. We've managed to hold the Levosa off thus far, but the border cities are still facing dire circumstances, and military reinforcements would help. Still, I've no wish to have to tell Gabe that we are removing our support and soldiers. That could be the final snowflake to send an avalanche rolling down a mountainside.

And then there's Scarlet…

I rub my face and turn onto my side, trying to convince my mind to sleep. But a noise begins to tickle my ears, stealing into my head and causing quite a stir there. I had almost become used to noise. The Crystalice Palace is a busy place, especially with a wedding afoot. The halls are never entirely quiet. But this is a new sound, a strange sound, and it is not coming from the halls.

My body is heavy and tired and does not want to get up, but my mind is awake and itching with curiosity at that noise. There is not one in particular, just a collection of sounds—a slight whipping of wind, a gasp, a short grunt of sound, a foot landing too hard on the ground.

Someone must be awake. Perhaps Zsoka playing.

I force myself up and rub my face again, scratching at the yellow beard on my face. Damn thing annoys the seven hells out of me. I scratch at it some more as I pad my way towards the door, wearing a pair of lambskin slacks and a wool tunic.

I push the door open and find the parlor alight and looking not at all as I had left it when I retired hours ago. The hearth is blazing with fire, talismans hanging from the mantel and feeding it eagerly. All of the furniture—the tables and chairs and sofas and such—all pushed against the far wall. And there, in the middle of the now open parlor floor, a little Inferno woman thrusts a sword into the air.

I don't know when she managed to do so, but she's stolen my nightclothes—a pair of slacks rolled up to her ankles and a cotton tunic that is much too large for her and yet still does not disguise the peaks of her breasts when she stands up tall before ducking and slicing at the open air.

She's out of practice. Even in the low, dim light, I can see that. Her muscles have become small and weak without use, and she lacks stability. It has been over a year, I believe, since her last true fight. Her mind may remember the steps, but her body has forgotten how.

"I think ye got them all," I tell her, and she yelps and turns towards me, pointing the sword accusingly and pushing her rampant, red hair out of her face.

"You," she says breathlessly, lowering the sword and watching me. She's defensive; I can tell by the set of her shoulders and that look in her eyes. "What are you doing awake?"

I flash a grin and say, "Just making sure ye got them all." She is heaving in her breaths, her lips parted and her chest rising and falling with exasperation, red hair wild and falling down her shoulders and back.

"All of what?" she asks, furrowing her brows in a frustrated manner while her golden eyes watch me.

"The pixies, lass," say I, shutting my door quietly and moving into the parlor. "There's naught else ye could be aiming for with those blows. Ye'd never hit a man."

She frowns at me and gives a little huff. "Come a little closer and see if I don't."

I grin wider, and laughter fills my eyes. "Aye an' aye, lass. Soon's ye tell me whose blade ye've swiped."

She looks down at the sword, a rapier, in her hand, and she says, "I borrowed it from the armory."

"When d'ye go there?" I ask.

She shrugs. "Many times. But today, I went whilst everyone slept. No one bothered me, really."

"The guards just let ye into the armory?" I ask, quite disturbed.

She smiles at me and laughs a bit. The sound is warm like honey, but with a spice to it that reminds me of whiskey. Then, she says, "All of the guards on this floor are ones who know me. Gabriel must have seen to that."

"Ah."

"Wilt join me, Alistair?" she asks suddenly, and I look up at her, a bit alarmed. She watches me with a wry little smile and mischief in her eyes. "I've not had a partner in some time, and I've never fought you. Well...I don't think so. My apologies if I have."

I consider her and then smile just a bit. "Nay, lass," say I. "I'd remember ye."

Her mischievous arrogance dims into something softer and sweeter, and my smile grows at the sight of her. When I'd first met her, she was coarse and hard, facing everything and everyone with anger and resilience. But she is softer now, somehow, and her eyes speak of gentleness and a subtler strength that cannot be seen.

"I'll fight ye," I say and incline my head. "But nay here. We'll wake the others and there's nay room anyhow."

I hold up a hand and then slip back into my own room. I pull on a leather jerkin and boots and return to the living room to find that Scarlet has changed, pulling on another shirt and a damask bodice along with fur-lined boots.

"Ye'll nay freeze now, wilt ye?" I say, going up to her and giving a little smile.

While she fights to contain that wild, red hair into a bun, she replies, "My fire is too warm. Last I was here, this place saw me weak and frail. Now, I am strong and bold. I will not be defeated again so easily."

"Is everything a battle?" I ask her with a small laugh and head for the door.

She follows and says, "Anything worth doing is."

The castle is dark but not empty. Servants pass by now and again while guards stand by at attention. Scarlet greets a few of them with smiles and occasionally a silly look or an outrageous comment. It is a wonder she did not start a civil war quite on her own.

I merely shake my head and tug her along when she lingers, teasing her until we reach the armory once more and borrow a pair of wooden practice swords before making our way into the ballroom.

"It is beautiful," she says quietly, walking out into the very large and very open room. Tables have been set up and lined with fine cloth. The drapes on all the windows have been changed to white and pale blue. There are ice sculptures which have begun to be set-up, flowers arranged and placed just so. Flora do not have wedding ceremonies. Occasionally, a party or feast is thrown for those newly wedded, but nothing quite like this.

"Shall we begin?" I turn to find the little vixen looking at me and pointing that wooden sword my way.

I laugh and say, "Aye, lassie, but I'll be warning ye. That wee toothpick o'yers will'na stand against my broadsword. Ye'll have to find some other way."

"I am not afraid," says my lass, sinking into a fighting stance and watching me with a veiled expression and a confident little smirk.

To her credit, she holds her own pretty well, but only because I keep myself in check. She'd like as not kill me for doing so, but—in the beginning, at least—she would not have stood her own against my sword, and I'd have shattered that little wooden toothpick of hers.

Gabriel may have barred me from the front lines of his war, but I have my own wars to fight. I tend to not be in the midst of battle simply because of the way in which the Levosa engage our armies, but I keep myself trained. The lass, on the other hand, has not held a sword in quite some time—wooden or otherwise.

An hour passes, then another, and I find myself having to move faster than I had before, having to deflect her blows, to dodge her. She pants and gives a shout of frustration every time she launches for a blow, but each time, she comes closer and closer to landing one.

"Hold!" I cry at last, and she stops herself and then hangs limp, teetering on her own feet. Breathless, I grin at her and find my own wind before saying, "That's enough, lass. Ye're near about to fall over, and I canna breathe."

"Frightened?" she gasps out and grins at me, not at all serious.

But I laugh and grin back, leaning on my knees. "Aye. Very much so." But I am not as tired as she, and I straighten myself, hoisting up my sword and going to her. "Stand up, lassie, afore ye fall on yer pretty face."

She sighs and does so, looking up at me breathlessly and grinning. "I enjoy fighting you," she says, and she leans against me when my arm goes around her, guiding her out of the room and down to the stairs. "It's certainly a style I am not used to."

A warm, slow laugh bubbles in my chest, and I reply, "Aye. Flora are fast, but not as fast as the Crystalice. Our strengths lay in a solid defense and fewer but more powerful attacks. If a Flora hits ye—if ye're nay already dead—ye'll be going home with one short a limb."

She laughs, and the sound is breathy and tired. She sighs at the end of it and leans her cheek on my arm as we walk. "Mmm. It makes me wonder," says she. "I often switch forms in battle. I just wonder if the percentage of Flora fighters among the Crystalice had an impact on the likelihood of my *Shifting* forms."

My mind turns over her words a few times until I give up. "I've nay a clue what ye said."

She laughs and clarifies, "I wonder if I had to use my tigress form more often when there were more Flora soldiers —in order to account for the greater size and strengths of my opponents."

I give a silent "ah," but we reach the stairs and she places her hand upon the icy railing, she snarls and retracts her injured flesh at once.

Her fingers shrink back from the cold, and she prepares to mount the stairs without them.

I smile a bit, just watching her. Stubborn creature. "Here, lass." I put my hand on her back when she looks back at me, and I scoop to hook the other arm under her knees and pull her up into the air and settle her against me.

She lets out a little shout of alarm and curses my name, but I laugh when I look down into those over-wide eyes that just stare at me with alarm. "What are you doing?" she barks while I climb the stairs.

"Carrying ye," I reply.

She shuts her mouth and glares at me. On her golden skin, I watch her cheeks and nose begin to turn a color more matching that of her red hair. "I can see that. Why?"

I flash a grin. "Ye're tired and canna get up the stairs."

"I can so." I quirk a brow at her, and she scowls harder at me. I reach the top of the stairs, and she starts squirming. "Alright. We're at the top. Now put me down."

I had planned on doing so, but she puts up such a fuss over it that I decide against it. "Ack. I think I'll hold ya a wee bit longer."

Her eyes snap right back to mine again, and now her face is quite nearly the shade of her hair. "Alistair, you put me down!"

"Hussssh, lassie," I scold, stifling laughter. "D'ye wish to wake the whole castle and have them all come and witness me carrying ye to the rooms?"

She gasps and hisses out, "You *wouldn't*."

I just smile at her as she sulks in my hold. "I'm nay the one shrieking."

Somewhat to my surprise, the little Inferno woman goes quiet and crosses her arms, settled in my arms somewhat agreeably.

I raise a brow at her, but she is no longer looking at me, her eyes glazed over as if she is thinking quite seriously on something. That or she is closer to falling asleep than I had thought.

We reach our suite, and I manage to get the door open, kicking it closed behind me. Scarlet has awoken from her sulking stupor and turns her head up to me. The parlor is quiet except for the grumbling of the fire, and I carry her to its warmth.

Again, I had planned on setting her down the moment we had returned, and yet when it comes time to do so, my arms do not seem to be in accordance with my will or else my will is not my own, for my arms hold to her.

Scarlet does not complain. She watches me with golden eyes as I hold her by the fire.

My arms are tired and sore and burn from the abuse, and yet they still do not seem inclined to release her.

"Alistair…" Scarlet calls gently, resurrecting me from my own thoughts. Slowly, I tilt my arms to set her feet upon the ground, and she holds onto my arms for balance until her feet are firmly on the floor. Even so, her warm, little hands remain on my arms, and mine remain on her waist.

She looks up at me and studies me, but I do not know what she is looking for or what she finds there.

I can never tell what she is thinking. I can tell when she is angry, but even so, there are times when she seems angry but is actually hurt or merely excited. Sometimes she seems sad but she is in fact ill or tired. But especially the times like this— when she is quiet and her eyes just study mine in the same pensive, unblinking way of a cat—I can make nothing of her thoughts. I cannot tell if she is angry with me or is hurting for some reason or if she feels at all tender towards me. There is nothing to tell from her face.

But her hands hold more firmly to my arms, and I take that at least to mean that she is not angry with me—hopefully. "Art cold, lass?" I ask quietly, and she blinks a few times. Of all the things I could say...I ask if she's cold...perhaps this is why I do not have a mate.

She gives me an odd little look but a wry smile and says, "Ah...a bit."

My hands slide from her waist and move to her back, pulling her a small bit closer. She doesn't feel cool, at least not to me. Her body is warm nearly to the point of being too hot to hold. But as I move to hold her closer, her hands slide from my arms to my chest, and my breath catches in my throat. For a moment, I think she means to put me away from her, but she does not. Her right hand lays over my heart, and I can feel the traitorous organ pound within my chest.

Her eyes turn away from my face to look at her hand, and she says, almost surprised, "Your heart beats so fast. Do all Flora have swift hearts?"

I give a nervous laugh and clear my throat, thinking of how to respond. "Ah...no. That, ah, tis, eh..."

She watches me and then gives a little smile. The shadows of the fire behind her make it impossible to tell the color of her face, but it seems redder than before. "I see..." She then moves her left hand and pulls my right one from off of her.

My heart sinks, and frustration wells up in me at my own stupidity. I should not have said anything. When I am out in the villages or even at dances, I always seem to think of something clever, something charming that makes the lassies laugh. But I cannot think of anything around Scarlet, and her laughter is so rare and a challenge to win from her.

But Scarlet does not release my hand. Instead, she guides it up to her, and for a moment, I am sure fit to die if she lays it upon her breast that I might feel her own heart. I can feel heat in my face, and it spreads all the way to my ears. The lass, however, takes my hand higher and puts it to her throat. She tips her head to the side so that her beating pulse is pressed right against my thumb.

The pace of her racing heart alarms me. Even in my greatest fear, my heart could never keep pace with the beat against my thumb, and I hold gently to her neck, my other hand resting on the small of her back.

Her throat is so thin and small. My hand against it seems so large and so easily capable of injuring her that it frightens me. It has never occurred to me before how much smaller she is than Flora women or how easily one of my kind could wound her. And to make matters worse, I can see the sheen of her scar on her neck—thin like a stretch of a spider's silk across her throat. And there are rough rips in her skin across her collarbone that catch the light with each breath.

My thoughts go back to her racing, hummingbird heartbeat. "Is that—do all—"

She laughs softly, and I can feel the hum of it in her throat. I brush my thumb slowly over her skin, and her eyes open a bit wider, watching me. She smiles and says, almost in a whisper, "Yes. It's something I noticed in my time at Crystalice. My heart beats much, much faster than others. Zsoka's does as well. I've never noticed it before since the Levosa's hearts are a similar pace. But Zsoka's heart beats almost thrice what Enté's does when they are both at my side."

My eyes move from hers to my hand at her throat once more, my thumb moving slowly back and forth over her skin. She closes her eyes and tips her head a bit more to the side. My own heart jumps. I notice the rhythm of her heart and say quietly, "Cerulean have much slower beating hearts even than Flora...but yer heart is racing almost three beats to my own."

She smiles slowly and her eyes do not open, black lashes resting contently against her cheeks. Instead, with her eyes closed and her neck in my hand, she murmurs, "That is because you are holding me, and I cannot tell if you are planning to kiss me or not."

Her bluntness is something I will never become completely accustomed to. It startles me right out of my skin, and I nearly jump away from her. I probably would have had my lass not opened her eyes and pinned me in place with them. I swallow the dryness of my throat and ask roughly, "Wouldst have me do so, lass?"

She does not smile, but she does not seem displeased either. She has returned to that infuriatingly unreadable stare, watching me quietly. "I've not decided that either."

I do not know how to answer her, and she does not speak again. She stands there with her hands on my chest and my hand at her throat and back. I guide her closer to me, and she does not pull away, but she does not move towards me either. It is not until the hand at her throat moves to cup the back of her head that her arms go around my neck, and as I hold her to me, she pulls me towards her.

Her kiss is like whiskey and honey. Her skin is hot to the touch, painful even, but I mold my mouth to hers as if I might devour the sun, my arms going tighter around her. She makes a sound in her throat, and I am undone, gasping in a breath and stealing another kiss from her, my coarse beard rubbing against the softness of her chin and cheek. Her fire soaks into my lips and into my body, setting me alight and threatening to burn me up in that parlor with her.

Her kiss becomes more withdrawn, however, and I leave one last, small kiss upon her bottom lip before pulling my lips from hers and looking upon her. Her arms release me, and likewise, mine fall limp from her frame. I can nearly hear her fluttering heart and her short, shallow breaths, while I am left nearly gasping at the sight of her.

She takes a step back, finally pulling us completely apart, and I am left feeling cold and lost with her absence. She stumbles, and although a strike of fear shoots through me, I am not quick enough to catch her from falling into the fire.

I cry her name in alarm, but she lands in the hearth and sits there, her hands having caught her from behind; she does not seem overly alarmed, unharmed by the fire. The flames tangle in her hair and lick her skin like little golden tongues eager to consume her. The fire is her lover, her comforter. It caresses her with tenderness and a familiarity formed by years of companionship. It is of no harm to her.

"Ow…" she mutters, rubbing her rump where apparently the stone hearth was less loving to her backside where she fell.

I sigh with relief and watch her sit with the flames as she gathers her balance, her golden eyes glowing as if made of fire itself. "Art harmed, sweetheart?"

"Only my pride," she says and looks up at me with a wry little smile. She offers me a hand, asking for assistance, and I do not know what surprises me more—the fact that she asked for my help or the way a spiral of fire winds around her arm as if trying to beg her to stay. Around her, the fire seems alive in ways I did not know fire could be. It responds to her as if alive.

I grasp her hand and close my fingers securely around her feverish skin, pulling her up.

She staggers to her feet, leaving the lonely fire to withdraw into the hearth while the lingering flames and sparks on her skin and clothes die away.

We set the parlor back in place, and then Scarlet stands with a tired sigh. "I am worn…I shall see you in the morn, Alistair."

The effort to put the room in order at the very least drained the lingering heat from my body, but when I look to her again, I feel a spark of it in my gut. She smiles at me, and that smile is soft and flighty, almost taunting me, although she probably did not intend for it to. "Goodnight."

"Goodnight, my lass."

She hesitates by her door at my farewell and looks to me. I have called her such many times, but it has changed somehow. The words are the same, and yet something has changed about them, and she seems to notice it as well. I swallow a bit and watch her, but she gives me a gentle smile.

"Sleep well, my lord." Her words are neither intimate, nor uncommon, and yet they strike me through and through and ring in my ears even after the door to her room has been closed.

I move back and sink slowly into the chair behind me, releasing a heavy breath and looking to the fire blazing in the hearth. I remember the way she had looked lingering in that fire and how it had greedily loved her. I am jealous of those flames now, and I glare at them with frustration before sighing and leaning back in my chair. I'll be getting no sleep tonight...

Chapter Thirty Two
Gabriel

Several Days Later
The Ballroom of the Crystalice Palace, Cerulean

It has been a very long time since I have seen such a beautiful wedding. Petara was the first to be married, being the oldest. But as I recall, the last time the castle saw a wedding such as this was my own wedding with Catherine many years ago. The hall is filled to the brim with people, servants squeezing themselves between them expertly to collect dishes and bring more wine.

The new bride stands on the dais with her husband who looks as uncomfortable as I have ever seen him. Claque stands up straight and solid beside his wife, one hand on the small of her back and the other stiffly at his side. He looks like he wants nothing more than to throw Dena over his shoulder and get out of the banquet hall. I laugh at the sight, catching his gaze and offering my glass as a toast. He glares at me.

Laughter catches my ears from the throng of dancers in the center of the room. My red-headed siren is at her best tonight. Her copper hair is neatly curled and pinned up in an elegant array. She wears a golden dress that flutters with her movement and shimmers like fire when touched by candlelight. Her lips are red and her eyes lined with black kohl. She grins at Alistair with whom she is locked in a dance. They both hate Crystalice dances, so I do not know why they are even bothering unless to make fun of the custom for amusement's sake.

With their right hands palm-to-palm, they turn slowly, talking between themselves, and I wonder at their conversation, wishing that I might listen in. The few times I have enjoyed the company of the pair of them together, their easy banter and casual conversation always entertains me. They both have such a carefree attitude and a sharp mind that makes their company as equally delightful as it is unbearable.

The dance concludes, and the dancers stop in order to give a quiet clap of applause—which, when there are as many hundreds of people as there are in the hall, is fairly loud. I make my way between the throngs of people and up behind my golden faerie. "Good evening, Alistair, Cara." Alistair had seen me coming, but Cara turns with surprise in her golden eyes, and she does not respond. I bow to them both, and Alistair does the same, but Cara merely stands still, watching me quietly.

"If I may," I say just loudly enough to be heard by the both of them. "I'd hoped to enjoy the next dance."

Alistair inclines his head and smiles warmly at me. "O'course. There's a wee one around here somewhere who's been wanting to dance with me if I can find her again."

"Good luck," I reply, laughing as he ducks back into the crowd to find Zsoka.

I stand before Cara, but although the music starts up again, she remains still. She does not seem angry with me, but she says nothing and she merely watches me, as if waiting for something, and her eyes seem almost…ashamed. I clear my throat and offer my hand. "Shall we? Or would you like to be the only pair standing in a crowd of dancers?"

"Ah." She accepts my hand, coming out of whatever thoughts had trapped her, and she gives a small smile, beginning the dance with me. "Forgive me. I was merely thinking of the first time we danced," she says, her hand on my arm and the other in my hand.

"You mean the night you were daggered?" I ask dryly.

She laughs, and her smile widens. "Aye. That night."

I smile at her. Whatever tension had been between us dissolves, and I am left at peace in her arms once more. I twirl her slowly and then bring her back to my hold as we continue the dance. She has relaxed from what little I can tell from my touch. She moves with more fluid ease and does not hesitate before touching me. Thankfully, she wears gloves tonight which makes her hot touch more bearable.

"Cara…" I begin quietly between the pair of us, and she gives me a curious look, attentive. "I ask your forgiveness… for shouting at you the other night."

"Gabriel—"

"No," I sigh. "Let—let me finish, Cara."

She closes her mouth and gives a disheartened smile.

"I want to thank you." I spin her away from me and bring her back slowly, turning with her. "I do not know yet what I will do but…I am grateful to have someone in my confidence who can see what I am blind to and make decisions that I cannot."

She gives me another little smile, but it is a sad one. She shakes her head as I face her once more. "Do not thank me for that, Gabriel…I would rather be of your mind. I only think of what I must do to achieve my goal. I do not stop to think of who might be harmed or if…if the cost may not be worth it." She sighs and looks down uneasily. "I am too much like my father and that is why I have lost my humanity—and become too much like a tiger and too less like a woman."

I break the formality of the dance to tip her chin back up and smile gently as we move. "You are far from too less like a woman, my spitfire."

She gives a slightly braver smile, but she shakes her head and continues, "I have forgotten who I am."

I smile at her and shake my head, spinning her once more and turning with her before bringing her back to my hold. My hand is only supposed to barely be touching her side, but I have placed it at the small of her back and drawn her nearer. "I know exactly who you are."

She gives me a dubious look, but she does not ask. Instead, she follows my lead once more into another turn and allows our few spoken words to sink from the air into our bodies. "I believe that Alistair means to ask me to marry him," she tells me, looking back to me.

I am not surprised, for I have guessed as much myself despite his words to me. But the sound of them aloud, the fact that she has greeted this information with anything but refusal—my whole being rejects it. I want to demand that she refuse him, but what right have I? I cannot bring her back here. And if she does not marry Alistair, then she will destroy both his life and hers there in Flora. All I can say is, "And what will you say if he does? You said that you would not wed a Cerulean…but would you wed him, Cara?"

She surprises me when, as I watch her golden eyes, tears fill them. "I will," she says, and the sound of those two words robs my breath. "I will wed him when I do not love you so very much."

Everything in my whole body goes still. There, in the midst of the dance, we stop, she and I, and I stare as tears begin to roll down her russet cheeks. I cannot speak, not even to say her name. I draw her nearer to me, and her arms go around my neck as I cup her head and pull her close, leaning my brow against hers. Even though the need is there, I do not kiss her. I do not dare. If I kiss her, I will not let her go. I could not. So I lean my brow against hers as she trembles in my arms, and her soft little breath breaks through the sound of music and laughter to become the only torturous melody to my ears. There is nothing else. No one else. There is only she and I in that room.

Chapter Thirty Three
Scarlet

The Ballroom of the Crystalice Palace, Cerulean

"What is that sound?" I say suddenly and pick up my head. He hears it too. A cracking sound. We turn our heads to see the blackened windows turn white with frost and shatter. The guests in the hall scream in alarm, and already people begin to run, getting away from the windows.

All at once, where there was once glass becomes filled with men dressed in white and boasting silver swords. "White Fang!" several people scream in disharmony, and the screams become shrieks as people begin shoving, running, falling, trampling, trying to get away from the soldiers who cut down anyone near to them.

"Dena!" I shout, and Gabriel releases me.

"Go!" he calls and draws his sword. "Get her out of here!" I have no weapon, no armor. Nothing but piles of skirts and hoops. As much as I want to stay by Gabriel's side and protect him, I am more hindrance than anything. He charges to meet the first of the attackers, and I rush towards the dais.

"Move!" I shout at the people nearest to me, but they slam into my body. I swear and call up my *Magik*, lighting my body afire. There is more screaming, but at least people stop touching me, and they part easily to permit me through to the dais.

Claque has drawn his sword as well and cuts down a few of the men, Dena behind him, trying to stay out of the way. "Move back!" I shout to him, and I throw up a wall of fire around the dais. The White Fang scream and withdraw from the fire as I go through it and land on the dais quite ungracefully. I pull myself up, stepping on my skirts, but I do not even have the time to remove them right now. Past the fire, the White Fang are murmuring spells to remove my barrier.

"We don't have time!" Claque shouts. "Get her out of here!"

"No!" Dena screams. "I'm not leaving you here!"

"Enough!" I snap to her, grabbing her arm. "We do not have time for romantic speeches. Let's go!" My fire packs a punch, but these are Cerulean, not Flora. It will hurt, but it won't stop them. They won't go up in flames so easily, not before I collapse from exhaustion. That's not an option right now until I can get Dena to safety.

I have to lower the barrier to get Dena through. I jump down with her and drag her off to the side as Claque blocks off the White Fang from following.

We go through the kitchens, Dena sobbing behind me. Some wedding this turned out to be. I knock down the kitchen door and drag her up the servant's stairs to the second floor.

As soon as we emerge out into the hall, however, we are surrounded by Cerulean and I can hear the sounds of more coming up the stairs.

"We're going to have to *Shift*," I tell her quickly. "My form is larger and we have no weapons. *Shift* now!" We both drop to the floor and take our *Shift*. I stand in front of Dena as she finishes her *Shift*, so I am the first one greeted with a weapon when they take advantage of our lapse of time. The sword cuts across my arm, but then I am on the man and ripping the sword from his body. The others wisely take their *Shift* as well, but they don't stand a chance.

Among the Cerulean, only the royal family have a disproportionately large second form. My tigress is easily two or three times the size of these canines. Gabriel is the only one who matches me in size. That is why his family has always been the ruling class. Theirs is the only bloodline with the abnormally large wolves. These ones don't stand a chance, and I pounce on them. Even with the five of them, two are gone quickly, and then a third, always keeping Dena between myself and a wall.

Dena is miniscule in size. Apparently the females do not carry the same largeness as the males. She's easily a quarter of mine or Gabriel's size. More like a puppy than a wolf. One of the two remaining pounce on my hindquarters while the last one goes for my throat. I roar in anger, swinging around. Three wolves come out of the stairs, and one goes for Dena.

The princess gives a shrill yelp and tries to run, but they take her down, and one gets to her throat. I scream, throwing the two off of me and grabbing the one on Dena, pinning him down so that he cannot rip her neck and crushing his head with my teeth. In death, his jaw slackens, and I turn to grab another one who launches at me, swinging at him with my massive paw and knocking him back.

Dena isn't moving, but when I take out a coyote, I look over to find that she is breathing. She is merely paralyzed with shock, but she *is* losing blood.

I don't have time for this.

I knock back another wolf as more come up the stairs, and I turn, grabbing Dena as carefully as I can in my mouth and bolt out of the hall. They cannot catch me, but I do not know what I will do when I arrive at a dead end or even reach my destination. I cannot simply keep running in doors.

Thankfully, as I reach the third floor stairs, an army of palace soldiers meet me and move past me to intercept the White Fang. I rush past them and up the stairs, carrying the injured princess to the royal chambers where ten guard are waiting with swords drawn. I approach slowly, hanging my head and giving a grunt of a sound.

They open the doors and permit me inside where the queen is sitting on the fainting couch, her hands in her lap. She gasps and looks up at once at me when I enter. Petara gives out a frightened sob from where she is curled up in a corner, holding her wailing, infant son to her breast and rocking slowly. "Dena!" the queen cries, recognizing her daughter's wolven form, and I set the princess down quickly.

I *Shift* and kneel beside her. "Dena is alright. Get a healer at once, though. She is bleeding from a wound in her neck, and it must be closed." I stand and look down at the trembling, crying mother as she lovingly runs her hand over her daughter's pelt. "I must go and help them defend the castle. Do not leave this room."

"What can you do?" the queen asks, her head snapping up. "You've no weapon. Your fire cannot burn the Crystalice."

I narrow my eyes. "I do not run. Weapon or not, I can fight, and I have my tigress. No more of my loved ones will die."

I *Shift* back into my tigress and run out of the room, past the guards at the door and down the hall. On the second floor, the palace guards are overrunning the White fang, so I jump over the banister and land on the second floor in the causeway. I move down the hall and burst into the banquet hall once more.

Even now, more White Fang are pouring in from the windows. When did their numbers grow to such lengths?

Gabriel? Where is Gabriel?

I jump onto the dais, but Claque is no longer there. I do not see him, nor Alistair. Finally, I catch sight of the trio at the far end of the hall. They are trying to keep the rebels from going out into the main hall. Right now, they are limited to going up the narrow flight of stairs to the second floor if they cannot get out the main doors.

Relief floods me, but it does not last.

Zsoka? Enté? They were both here, at the party. I danced with Enté for my first dance and Alistair was supposed to have been dancing with Zsoka. They were here! I scan the bodies on the floor, but most of them are White Fang or those who were cut down immediately when they entered. I do not see any children, let alone my own. But I still cannot find them. Where are they?

Zsoka!

Enté!

No! I won't let anything happen to them! I will protect them! No one else will die! No one else will suffer!

I will protect them!

Chapter Thirty Four
Gabriel

The Ballroom of the Crystalice Palace, Cerulean

From the far side of the room, there is a sound the likes of which I have never heard. It is a shrill and agonizing sound that stretches into something inhuman, something frightening. The final morph reminds me almost of the cry of a dragon, for the whole room trembles and the stone cracks. But what I find when I look to the dais is the remnants of a red tiger *Shifting* forms. What it turns into, however, is not Cara.

On the dais, a brilliant burst of fire takes form. At first, it looks like one great flame, as if the sun itself had settled itself into my palace. Even from the far side of the room, I can feel the sheer brilliance of its warmth, hotter than any fire I have ever known. The fire moves, however, and I slowly recognize two distinct legs, and two arms. The top of the fire moves like hair, flickering upwards towards the ceiling with its violent heat.

Then again—that sound—that shrieking, horrible dragon -sound. The sun goddess moves, launching herself from the dais and throwing herself into the throng of White Fang. In her hand, a long spark resembling a sword emerges and pierces them through and through as though solid. She slices them clean in half, and their screams fill the hall.

"The hell's *that*!" Alistair shouts from beside me, cutting down his enemy. The numbers of White Fang have left us to engage her or to try and go up the stairs.

I glance to him and call, "I think that's Scarlet!"

He looks at me with alarm, apparently not having seen the tigress before the woman of fire emerged.

"Hold the entrance!" I shout to him and the other guard, and I charge towards the woman cutting down the White Fang. Getting near and nearer to her is agonizing to my body. She radiates heat like dragon's fire so that it is difficult to even get within ear-shot of her. The other White Fang have begun breaking off from its assault and head back for the windows.

"What is that thing?"

"A beast of Hell!"

"Chelyah! Chelyah has come to kill us!"

"Get away!"

"Fall back! Fall back!"

I cut down one man still charging at her, and she runs another through. Standing before her, I feel as if I might go up in flames from the sheer closeness of her body. Up close, I can tell that it is in fact Cara, for although she is pure light of fire, within it, the body of a woman can be found.

Her eyes glow as radiant, white light, and what can be called her face turns towards me and looks me straight in the eyes.

I feel as though I stare at the sun, and it becomes physically difficult to breathe. I feel so hot, faint, just standing so close to her.

She turns her face again to look at the White Fang who are trying to flee through the windows. There are still hundreds of them filling the banquet hall, engaged with my soldiers who have come in from the main hall. She stretches out a hand towards them, and from the ground, a wall of fire bursts from the tiles and stretches up as a wall, covering the windows and burning up the Crystalice who sought to pass through them.

Screaming fills the banquet hall and some White Fang step back away from the wall while others decide to jump through.

From what I can tell, there is not even so much left to be considered a corpse. It is as though that flaming wall devours them whole.

And then, just as the White Fang begin murmuring to themselves, the wall begins to lean, and like a tidal wave, it crashes down upon their screaming forms and drowns them in its burning wrath, consuming any who remain. All that is left is myself and my soldiers.

Again, she moves, and I turn to stare at her, panting and taking a step back away from her insufferable heat. She looks at me, or at least it seems as though she does, those twin slits of white light where eyes should be turn straight for me.

And then, a hole of white light erupts as a mouth, and from it, that agonized, dragon-scream rips out of her burning form. A burst of warmth hits me and knocks me back. My skin feels raw and blistered, and some of my clothes have burned away.

I sit up at once, dazed and panting, and I watch her body dim until it is ashen, the fire dying away and leaving a ghostly pale body behind. She crumples to the ground.

"Cara!" her name bursts from my lungs as I scramble to my feet and grab her naked body. Her skin feels cold even to mine. "Cara!" I scream again, giving her body a shake, but she's completely limp.

"Fire!" Alistair calls, racing to my side and collapsing beside me. He lifts Cara's head and murmurs her name in a broken voice.

"We need to get her to a fire," he rasps, remembering his urgency. "Now!" He helps us both up since being so close to her burning form had sapped much of my strength. Together, we stagger into the ruined kitchen, and he goes to the oven, throwing in logs and trying to get it started.

I stand in a part of the kitchen that hasn't been completely destroyed from soldiers pouring through it, and I hug Cara's body to mine, trembling.

"Mama?" a quiet voice whimpers, and I watch a little, brown face appear in one of the lower cabinets too small for an adult to crawl into.

"Zsoka!" Alistair cries, going to her and grabbing her, hugging her close. She hugs him and looks past him to Cara.

"What's wrong with mama?" she whimpers. "Mama? Mama!"

"Sh-sh," Alistair says, taking her face in his hands. "Mama will be okay. Zsoka can ye help me start the oven fire?"

She keeps trying to look at Cara, but he finally jerks her face towards the oven and she nods.

"Okay. Good girl. Let's go. Quickly." He takes her to the oven, and she gets the fire going, but it won't be hot enough. "Here," he calls to me. "Go ahead and put her in. Quickly, Gabe. She's going to die if we canna get the heat up."

I take her over to the oven, feeling nothing and everything at the same time and not knowing what to think. I just don't want her to die. It's a good thing Cara is a small woman, for she barely fits into the stone oven. But it is better for her to be alive than comfortable.

Zsoka gets the fire going more and more.

"I'll go and get talismans," I say, but I pause when I hear a little voice call, "Father?"

I stop in my tracks and look to see Enté peak out of the cabinet as well. My heart stops and then leaps. I had assumed he'd been with my family upstairs. I had not thought he'd gotten separated. "Enté!" I cry and scoop him up, squeezing him to my chest and kissing his brow.

"Gabriel, go!" Alistair barks at me.

I nod. I'm wasting time. Enté is safe. Cara is not.

So, setting Enté down, I get him to a guard to send him up to my family and send another guard to go and get talismans for the fire. Soon, the oven is blazing hot and Zsoka can finally rest. The last thing we ask of her is to reach into the stove and find Cara's pulse. She does, and when Zsoka tells us that she is still breathing, we all seem to just collapse where we are.

Alistair, Zsoka, and I just sink onto the floor of the ruined kitchen, and Zsoka curls up against Alistair and cries while he drapes a heavy arm over her and presses his face to her black hair. His shoulders tremble with tears.

PART THREE

Being deeply loved by someone gives you strength, while loving someone deeply gives you courage.
-Lao Tzu

Chapter Thirty Five
Scarlet

Two Months Later
Maeghdra Manor, Flora

Everything feels heavy and warm. It is so very warm. Almost like home. And for a moment, everything seems like a dream: a wonderful, horrible dream. I stir slowly, my mind beginning to wake and my body shifting in accordance. I feel stiff almost at once, and my chest feels sore and tired as though there is some weight on it, even though I am laying on my side. I roll onto my back and just lay there for a while, closing my eyes and feeling the heat all around me. I can hear the fire whip and flutter in my ears, and beneath me, the stone is warm and soothing to my skin.

Vaguely, I can hear sounds other than the fire, like voices, except they are muffled and warped to my own ears. I turn my head, and beyond the golden warmth around me, I can make out the figures of people moving about. "Gabriel?" I murmur wearily. I put my hand to my head, trying to remember where I am.

It wasn't a dream. Those are memories. Gabriel. Enté. Zsoka. Alistair. Everything. But I can't remember what happened last. Sighing with frustration, I think back to Crystalice. It was cold. Why was I there? A wedding. Someone was getting married. Dena. Dena was getting married. And I went to the wedding…there were…men in white…soldiers

…White Fang. That's right. I took Dena and ran…and she… she was attacked.

"Dena!" I cry. I left her with her mother. But what am I doing here? I have to find her!

I sit up quickly, but my head slams into the roof of the stone hearth. It is a large hearth, but it is still only meant for wood, not for a woman. I glare at the top of the firebox, turning my head past the roof to see the long, dark chimney and the bright glow of daylight beyond. "Ow…" I mutter, and I shift carefully, moving out of the fire and onto the hearth. "Dena?" I murmur softly.

"Oh Chelyah!" a woman cries.

"Mama!" Zsoka tackles me from the side. I think she might have been sitting on the mantle reading, because a book goes flying in the air as she launches herself at me, wrapping her little body around me.

Suddenly, it feels cold despite her warm, little body, and I realize that I'm naked and sitting in the dining hall of Alistair's home. Thankfully, the only people about are Cali and Skylar who both start screaming their own way and hurrying to me.

"Oh bless me! Bless me!" Cali cries as I wrap my arms over my breasts self-consciously. She grabs me by the shoulders and squeezes. "Och! I thought ye'd ne'er wake!"

"Madam!" Skylar shrieks towards the second floor of the house. "Master Alistair! Lady Freya! Hurry! Scarlet's awake! Hurry!"

My head is spinning between the little child squeezing my waist and sitting in my lap and the plump cook squeezing my shoulders and then cupping my face and then pulling me to her bosom and crying against me. I just stand limply and wonder how in the hell I wound up in Flora and why in Chelyah's name I'm naked.

A door slams open, banging against the wall, and as footsteps thunder down the stairs, I hear another door bang open. "Move! Move!" Alistair's low, rich voice fills the hall, and my heart squeezes and sinks into my belly where it sits like a warm coal that makes me both uncomfortable and giddy. Alistair pries Cali off of me and nearly knocks Zsoka over to finally get a look at me.

I just stare up at him in alarm and confusion, not really understanding what's happening. "Ah...eh...I..."

"Scarlet," he rasps out, and then he grabs me and pulls me up off of the hearth, his arms going around me and his mouth fastening onto mine.

My eyes fly open, and I just freeze stiffly as he holds me. His lips mold against mine, hard and thorough and desperate.

His tongue invades me and brings me to gasp which only further serves his purpose. His kiss is not clumsy but filled with some sort of panic that consumes me and leaves me feeling somewhat like a puddle as I lay open to his frantic joy. It might not have been so bad were I not acutely aware of his cotton shirt and lambskin breeches against my bare skin.

"Alistair!" Freya calls, and Alistair breaks away from his desperate kiss to look back at her. Freya stands on the stairs, leaning over and shouting, "Alistair, you set that woman down! You'll hurt her! Skylar, grab that throw there and wrap her up until we can get her dressed!"

"Aye, Lady Freya!" Skylar calls and snatches a throw off of a stool and brings it to me.

I look back to Alistair and find him staring at my face as if he'd seen something astonishing. "What?" I complain and wriggle away from him, crossing my arms over my chest. "What are you looking at?" I snap.

"Here, miss," Skylar says, handing me the throw. I sigh and thank her, wrapping it around me. It covers me, at least, and I hug it to me once it's wrapped around me up under my arms.

"Ye've been gone far moonths," Cali says with a sob, wiping at her face. Her breaths come in short bursting sobs that wrack her whole body. "Tha master brought ye back in this stone oven and put ye in the hearth. An ye didna wake up."

I just stare at her blankly for a moment and then look to Alistair. "What...happened?" I ask. "The last thing I remember...is the wedding...one of the coyotes bit Dena's neck. Is she—"

"She's fine," Alistair assures me, holding up a hand and giving a little smile.

Freya comes from around him and smiles gently. "You must be tired, dear. Zsoka, why don't you take your mother upstairs and help her get dressed?" Looking to me, she says, "Zsoka has been such a great help. None of us could go into the fire but her. She tended to you all this time."

I look down to the little black-haired creature beside me waiting to be noticed and crying quietly. "Oh, Zsoka," I murmur softly, kneeling beside her and taking her into my arms. "My poor little one. You must have been so frightened. I'm sorry, my love." All of those months that I had not woken and she was on her own, not knowing if I would ever awake again.

In my arms, she cries a little louder and clings to me with her whole body, nails digging into my skin and tiny, boney arms locked around my neck.

"I'll fix ye sommat warm," Cali says with a smile and heads back into the kitchen to cook before I set Zsoka down and walk with her upstairs. Winter has left Flora, and spring has brought with it warmth and newly blooming buds. It is still not especially warm, but it is better than winter.

In my room, I pull on a long-sleeved chemise and a set of skirts, pulling on a green, cotton dress and lacing up a brown bodice with it. Once I have stockings to keep my toes warm,

I return downstairs to find everyone but Cali sitting at the tables.

Alistair turns his head to look at me and smiles warmly. He still watches me for too long, as if waiting for something, or afraid of something. What is he afraid of?

I move slowly down the stairs, feeling stiff and sore. I don't have much energy which probably has much to do with the fact that I haven't eaten in some time.

"There's some bread to hold you over until Cali finishes," Freya says with a gentle smile, and I go and sit at the table with them. Alistair takes my hand from my lap and squeezes it gently, brushing his thumb back and forth over it.

I look to him, a bit startled and unnerved. I do not understand what has him so upset. I remove my hand from his, much too uneasy to be comfortable with his affections. Instead, I set myself to putting some marmalade on the bread and eating it quietly, resisting the urge to stuff the whole loaf into my mouth. "Can someone please explain what has happened?" I ask quietly.

Freya sighs and says, "Ah, well…none of us quite know exactly…the guards say you brought Dena up to the queen's suite and then went back to the banquet hall." She glances to Alistair to pick up.

He shakes his head and says, "I'd nay see it, but Gabriel did. He saw ye change from a tiger into… sommat else. Ye had arms and legs…like a person, but… ye were solid fire— well, I mean, as solid as fire ever can be."

I frown, putting another piece into my mouth and chewing it slowly before asking, "You mean, I was lit on fire?"

He gives a nervous laugh and rubs the back of his neck. "Ah…nay…nay. There was'na *body*, Scarlet. Just fire…very, very hot fire. It—ye—killed anything ye touched. Twas so hot I could feel it from across the room. It made all the Cerulean ill. Gabe was in bed nigh a month with a heat fever."

I just stare at him, unable to understand, and I look to Freya for some clarification. I shake my head, looking back to Alistair. "I…don't understand."

He struggles with how to explain and sighs. Finally, he thinks of something and says, "D'ye remember back in Marine? When ye told that tale o'the sun and moon?"

"Yes…" I nod slowly.

"And ye made the fire in the form o'the story, aye? Like the people and the princess and—aye?" He nods his head for me and gestures with his hand as if showing me something. "'Twas like that," he says. "Ye had the form o'Scarlet, but ye were solid flame."

I shake my head slowly, looking between him and Freya. "But…Inferno can't do that…we can light ourselves on fire, but we don't—we can't turn *into* fire."

"But ye *did*," Alistair says slowly. "And nay just any fire. 'Twas like the sun'd came down and settled herself right in the banquet hall. It burned everything. Nay corpses. Naught. Everything was burned up. I've never been close to anything so hot."

I finally look away from them both to put marmalade on another slice. This doesn't make any sense. There is nothing about this in my homeland. Not even legends or stories. There is absolutely nothing about people being able to turn themselves *into* fire. Fire has to exist off *something*. When we create fire, we give it our energy, our *Magik*. There is no such thing as fire without anything, and certainly not a *sentient* fire.

After a few more bites, I finally look back to him and say, "Alright…then what?"

He shrugs and says, "After that…ye attacked them. And when they started to run, ye put up this wall o'fire over the windows, and it burned them up. Then it came down on their heads and swallowed them all." He rubs his face as I stare at him, trembling slightly. "I'd say two…maybe three hundred o'them. All dead." He looks to me and smiles warmly. "Because o'*ye*, sweetheart. Ye saved our lives, even."

"Earned yourself quite the name in Crystalice." Freya takes a piece of bread and begins putting spread on it as well, a little smile tugging at the corner of her mouth.

I feel my stomach drop. "Oh no…what is it?"

She looks up at me with a wry sort of look. "The Queen of Hell."

My mouth opens, and I feel a sinking dread. "Ugh no…" I moan and drop my head onto the table, bemoaning the name as Alistair laughs.

He cups my shoulders and squeezes before patting my back. "Ack! Tis nay so bad, sweetheart. They sees ye as Gabriel's secret weapon. Nay man'll be daft enough to go after the royal family or their ilk anytime soon with that name spinning about."

"Here! Here! Let the wee lassie eat!" Cali calls, bringing over a pot of stew that has my mouth watering.

I can smell the meat and spices in the stew, and Cali barely manages to fill a bowl before I've taken it and have begun shoveling it into my mouth. Thankfully, Inferno do not worry about burning their mouth with hot food or else I surely would have. It's quite amazing that I do not make myself sick with the sheer volume I manage to put away in my belly in such a small amount of time. But I do, and I manage to keep it down before yawning and making my way back to the hearth.

"I still do not feel well…I think I'll rest some more." I say softly.

"Ah, yes, yes," Freya says, getting up and brushing off her skirts. "It was clever of Alistair to think of the oven after you collapsed. He says you turned almost Crystalice white and weren't breathing. They got you into the oven and it most likely saved your life…now we'll know if anything happens to stick you in the hearth. That fire kept you alive."

I turn to look at her and smile a bit. "My people never leave their forest—everything in Inferno burns and is filled with fire. Even if we are not in it, we are surrounded by it. Claque placed me in the hearth when I nearly drowned…I thought just warmth alone would suffice, but you're right. Staying in the hearth feels much better."

She nods and says with a little smile, "I'll see about finding some talismans to keep a pallet from burning so you need not suffer the stone heath, however."

"Talismans?" I ask softly, having glimpsed them and heard of them before but never really asked about them.

She smiles and says, "Aye. Do they not have them in Inferno? They're these little wooden charms for all sorts of things—heating a fire, keeping flies away from food, helping dry the laundry."

"Ah…" I murmur softly, my eyes half open. "Yes, we have something like that in Inferno. Charms. Little metal coin-like objects that dangle from strings. They're fairly common. Does Crystalice have something like that as well?"

"No," she shakes her head. "Their *Magik* lay more in potions and sorcery, but they purchase ours at times. But you rest now."

"Thank you," I say sincerely.

She nods and adds, "We'll get out of here so that you can rest. Zsoka, would you like to stay with her?"

Zsoka nods quietly.

I smile a bit and say, "Zsoka, you'd be much more comfortable in your bed. Are you sure?"

She nods, having gone mute again, it seems.

I am furious and guilty that I am the one who cause this in her. I sigh, but I look to Freya as she takes her leave, heading back up the stairs to the second floor.

Alistair remains at my side, however, and I look to him. He smiles gently but still watches me with that strange look. I frown at him, and he asks, "Ah…might I stay a while and speak with ye?"

I give him an odd look but nod slowly. "Well, it seems you saved my life, so I suppose it is the least I can do," I tell him. I nudge Zsoka and say, "Go wash up and change for bed. Then, you can join me."

She seems unwilling at first, but I nudge her again, and she finally heads for the stairs.

I look to Alistair and then go and sit on the hearth. "Why are you looking at me so strangely?" I ask him as he moves towards me, and he glances up at me and smiles.

"Am I?" he asks and laughs nervously. His eyes shine in the light of the fire, and I look on him with surprise. "I…" He clears his throat and then sits by me. "I'd…I'd nay think ye'd wake," he says softly, quietly, and I watch as he takes my hand and clasps it in both of this. "When I knelt beside ye in the banquet hall…yer skin was pale and gray…I'd see yer veins underneath…ye were'na breathing, and I could'na feel your pulse…I thought sure ye'd never wake."

I watch him with widening eyes as he looks up at my face and takes my hand. He pushes back some of my hair and cups the back of my head. "I thought I'd never see these golden eyes again…I canna lose you." His voice softens to a whisper, something hoarse but quiet. "I canna do it, lass…I could once, but I love ye now, and I canna lose ye. Dinna ask it o'me."

He pulls me towards him, and I just stare in mute astonishment until his lips press to mine.

I blink a bit, slowly realizing that the world is still moving and only I am standing still. His touch is gentle and trembling as he touches my face, his other hand running up and down my arm, as if to just assure himself that I am here.

He withdraws only a bit and looks down at me with those dark, green eyes, and I look back at him, speechless. He searches my face for some sort of answer, but I cannot even think to speak, much less to form any sort of a coherent answer. He waits for me, for me to say something, for me to move away.

But I do not move. The only thing I can think to do is what comes naturally to me in that moment, and I close my eyes and lean into him. He sighs and cups my face, drawing me nearer to kiss me again, and this time, I return his affection.

It is not until I hear soft steps on the stairs that I pull away from him, putting my hands to his chest and sitting back.

He stares at me, stroking my hair a moment and then touching my cheek once more. "I'll nay do it, lass," he says softly. "I'll nay let ye go…nay anymore."

I give a little smile and take his hand from my face, placing a kiss on his palm before letting him go. "Goodnight, Alistair."

He clears his throat and nods, standing. "Scarlet…I've announced that I'm courting ye…formally. Tis nigh the closest thing we have to an engagement. I wanted to speak to ye first but…we had some accusations at the last meeting, and I could'na afford to—"

I shake my head and smile softly. "I understand…it's alright."

I welcome Zsoka back to my side, and she snuggles up into me. I look to Alistair as he searches for words, finally saying, "I…twas only sommat for appearances but…if ye would'na mind…I'd like it nay to be. I'd like to court ye, lass."

I watch him for a long while, my little child at my side, and I finally give a hesitant nod. "Al-alright…" I say slowly, watching him. "We can talk more later about what that means, but…I do not object."

He seems relieved, as if he had not known what I would say, and he smiles gently as the tension leaves his body. "Aye...goodnight, my lass."

I smile softly and nudge the child into the firebox to sleep. "Goodnight, my lord."

Chapter Thirty Six
Scarlet

Two Months Later
Maeghdra Manor, Flora

Spring is passing quickly and will soon become hot summer, taking Alistair with it as it leaves. Summer is the busiest time for Flora, and especially for Alistair, and he needs to prepare. The roads are finally decent enough for regular travel, and the planting has begun for the year.

During this time, Alistair regularly travels about his own territory, meeting with his local lairds and his people as well as with the other two dukes. Even when he is home, I rarely see him, for he stays in his study looking over charts or numbers or reading through ledgers. I visit him at times, bringing him some cool, sweet water to drink and helping to tidy up his room.

Unlike the Flora who frequently find the summer to be hot and insufferable, I do not mind it so much, although it is rather humid in parts. In the mountains of Maeghdra, however, there is usually a crispness to the air and a cool breeze. It makes Alistair less miserable but also keeps me wrapped up in a shawl.

At least with the hearthfire to warm me, I was not made to suffer weeks on bedrest again and was soon up and about with Zsoka. Her lessons have resumed, and with Skylar now having returned home, I have taken to training and strengthening myself once more. The manor usually keeps a guard or two, and from them I found some old equipment.

Against Freya's better advice, I borrowed some of Alistair's clothes once more and took to the courtyard with the local soldiers. At first, they mostly humored me, and I do not particularly blame them, for I was quite out of training. But my mind never forgot, and my body quickly remembered. Soon, I was putting them on defense once more and holding my own in our fights.

The sun is almost oppressively bright, but its warmth comforts me as I knock back one of the local soldiers, Krei, and he lunges back at me, locking swords with my own. I grind my teeth, basking in the hot, summer sun and using it to fuel me. I step back to create an opening and then turn to the side, knocking the man back until I am poised over him, sitting on his chest and pointing the sword at his throat.

He breathes hard, looking at the sword warily before turning his eyes to my face. He laughs warmly, and I grin, climbing up and offering him a hand. "Nay bad, lassie. That's the first time ye've put me on me arse."

I laugh and reply, "Well, expect more times, Krei. I've got to pay you back for all the times you knocked me down."

The sound of pounding hooves and a clattering cart come clamoring down the road, and I turn my head to listen, watching the cart pull into the courtyard. "Mornin, miss," the courier greets, an older man with a cap on his head. He sits at the front of the cart, tipping his head in my direction and laying the reigns of his horse on his lap so that he can rifle through his bag.

I smile softly and inclined my head. "Good morning, sir. More work for my lord?"

He laughs warmly as I approach the cart, grinning at me over his shoulder. "Aye an' aye, as always. And a letter for ye as well, miss." He hands me a stack of letters and a few rolls of parchment.

I thank him and smile, taking everything inside and setting it all on the table before sorting it. Some is for Lady Freya, and I set that aside, and there is a letter for me from Gabriel and one from Dena as well. Smiling, I bid Krei good bye and take those and then gather the others and carry them up the stairs to Alistair's room. I knock quietly and then step inside.

At his desk, I find my Alistair hunched over with his tawny hair all a mess from him running his hands through it too much with frustration. He's growling at whatever he's working on and glaring at it. I would offer him help, but I am much less familiar with Flora policy than he is; although he's asked me my opinion on matters, I am not of much use.

Laughing softly, I greet, "Alistair, the courier has arrived."

He swears and lifts his head, looking over at me with a scowl. I just grin wickedly. "Ye can put that lot right there," he growls, pointing to the hearth.

I laugh and set the new letters down on the far side of his desk before going to him. "It was like this last summer, wasn't it?" I ask him, coming up behind him and gently combing my fingers through his hair.

He mutters something and sighs, closing his eyes and leaning his head back a bit while I comb his hair and tie it back at the nape of his neck and out of his way.

"It will be over soon enough," I tell him. "Summer is nearly finished and the harvest is upon us."

"Mmm." He takes my hand, bringing it around in front of it and kissing the palm sweetly.

I blush faintly, never quite used to such affections from him, but I give a small smile.

"Speaking of...the beginning o'the harvest festival is tonight."

"Oh?" I ask, and he places another, soft kiss on the inside of my wrist. It sends little shivers up my arm and into my belly.

He chuckles softly and looks up at me with those dark, green eyes. "Aye, lassie. Wilt ye and the wee one go with me?"

I nod and smile quietly, taking my hand from him and saying, "But in the meantime, you have work." Laughing to myself, I move over to a fainting couch in his room and settle myself upon it, pulling my legs up beside me. I open Gabriel's letter, feeling Alistair's eyes on me as I begin to read.

Beloved Cara,

Forgive me for not writing to you sooner. I know it has been several months now since you'd woken, and I must have started writing to you a thousand times but only now could finish my thoughts.

There are not words to describe the fear I had seeing you so ill, nor the joy I felt when Alistair sent word that you were alive. So many times have you flirted with death in my castle, and I thought for certain this time that you had lost. I am relieved that you are well and fully recovered. Please continue to take care of yourself. You are needed here.

As for me, the castle has been in something of a fit. After the attack at the wedding, I was ill for some time and had to rest. When I awoke, I had councilors calling for your head and others wanting to erect a statue in your honor. It has been a very trying last few months. Enté, at least, is fully recovered, but I am still afraid for his safety. I do not trust myself to put into words what transpired the night I found him near death and poisoned, but we must speak on it sometime, you and I. I will be sending him to you shortly, for that night has made it very clear that he is not safe here in Crystalice. Besides, my late wife was Flora, and I think it would do him some good to see the homeland of his mother.

And as for you, my little spitfire, you have earned quite a name for yourself. I am sure Alistair has told you by now, but they are calling you the "Queen of Hell". I've never heard anything like it. Mothers call on your name to get their children into bed and to mind their manners, and even the older ones are afraid, saying that Chelyah has sent an emissary to protect the Cerulean crown. I think you will be quite surprised upon your next visit here.

I have also heard word that Alistair is officially and formally courting you. I only wish that I'd had more time to speak with you before the events at the wedding to be able to tell you my thoughts. Now that I am writing to you, all that I am left with is to tell you that I love you. And because of that, I wish for you everything that I can never give you. Alistair is my friend and a good man. And for his sake and your own, I wish you both joy and peace.

Either way, your choice is decided now. You must marry Alistair or return home to Inferno. I would never have wanted this forced upon you. I could not have foreseen it when we were in Marine a year ago. For that, and for much more, I ask your forgiveness.

Forever yours,
Gabriel

I smile with warmth because of his words and how much they mean to me and because they have come too late. I have already made my decision.

"What pleases ye so?" Alistair calls, and I look to find him watching me from his desk.

Smiling softly, I stand and shake my head, keeping my letters with me. "Only the thought of the festival tonight."

He looks to me with a dubious expression, but I merely smile and pass him by, pausing to kiss his cheek. It surprises him, and he watches me with questions in his eyes, still not entirely accustomed to me or knowing my thoughts.

I think I prefer it that way. "Hurry and finish your work so that we may go."

He chuckles to himself and says, "Aye, lassie. Soon enough." He watches me go, and I shut the door behind me, going to finish my work.

Alistair does not take much longer, and he comes down the stairs as Zsoka finishes with her lessons. Her tutor left a while ago, but I sit with her at the table and help her to write her letters, freshly changed into a dress suitable for the event. Zsoka can read the words well enough, but her penmanship still needs work. She works carefully on the parchment as I look up to greet Alistair with a smile. He is dressed differently than when I saw him earlier, having put on a nice doublet and slacks.

"Alright, Zsoka, that's enough for today," I tell the child, smiling softly and putting the stopper in the ink bottle before showing her how to clean her quill

Once finished, the child scrambles out of her seat in a fit of giggles. Usually she enjoys her lessons, but tonight is the night of the festival, and she is excited. She squeals with laughter and runs to Alistair, hugging his legs.

He chuckles and pets her hair gently, looking up and waiting for me as I come around the table and join them both. Our eyes meet, and he smiles, watching me. Perhaps he can feel it, something from me, something that warns him of my intent. But he does not know, and he will not ask.

So I merely smile and let him wait just a little longer.

"Och, alright, lassies. Let's be off." He offers me his arm, which I accept, and Zsoka walks at his other arm, holding his hand. She is taller than she was at the last festival a year ago, and she grins with excitement instead of hiding behind me with fear.

Along the way, we talk quietly, Alistair and I. The dirt is soft and easy under our feet, and I listen as Alistair complains about the letter he received from one of his lairds. With a smile, I tease him, and he merely scowls at me, bantering back with me easily until we are both laughing once more.

"Ah, look!" Zsoka cries when we come into sight of town, and we both follow her gaze to the sight. The village is all alight with fire. There are little lanterns filled with fire hanging down from rooftops and cords running between buildings. People throng in the streets, their laughter infectious, and the sound of eager music pouring out into the open streets.

I look to Alistair and find him watching me, and I smile softly at him. "It is even more beautiful than last year's."

"Aye," he says, looking back to the decorations with a warm smile. He leads me into the village, and it does not take long for us to be noticed.

"Lord Alistair!" a woman calls, noticing him, and she along with several others approach.

Zsoka tries to hide again, so Alistair picks her up and holds her in his arms while he greets his people.

Smiling, I step aside and let him spend time with them, heading towards the great pile of logs in the center of the village where a few people stand by muttering and arguing.

"Hail!" I call, approaching them, and they turn to look my way.

"Ack," one man says and smiles at me. The villagers are familiar with my presence now from my frequent visits. "Miss Scarlet. How're ye, lass?"

"Well," I reply, smiling back. "What's the matter here?"

"Agh!" another man grumbles. "The wood will'na catch."

I notice him with a smaller pile of burnings trying to ignite the whole bonfire. I smirk. "Well, why don't I see if I can be of some use?"

They seem surprised by the idea, and I do not know if that brings me joy or pain. It either means that they would not have considered me capable or that they have become so accustomed to my presence here that it no longer occurs to them that I am an Inferno.

With a little smile, I step forward and hold out my hand, drawing my *Magik* to me until it pools as heat in my palm. I send that heat out onto the stack of wood, fire leaping off my fingertips to spiral into the wooden pile. The wood goes up in flames, and soon, the bonfire is roaring and alive with heat.

Looking around me as I step back, I see faces of surprise and alarm, and at first, I am uncertain. But then, a small crowd starts up a cheer that the whole village joins in. My racing heart relaxes, and I smile, hearing the joy and elation from the townsfolk. Smiling, I turn to them and step into the throng once more, greeting those I know and introducing myself to those I do not.

"Scarlet!" one of the children calls, and I look over to a young boy and smile. "D'ye make the fire? Can ye make other things with the fire?"

Laughing, I look to him and ask, "And what would you have me make?"

The boys' eyes light up. "Anythin!" he cries, his friends around him grinning and eager. "Somethin amazin!"

"Amazing, eh?" I ask and grin before stepping back a bit from them so as not to burn them. I call my *Magik* to me once more, drawing it into my hands to channel it.

Above their heads, the form of a bear emerges, and it stands on its back two legs and gives a silent roar. The children call out in alarm, drawing the attention of the others, and I smile when they ask for more, obliging them. The bear of fire turns into a dragon and soars across the sky. Balls of fire shoot out from my fingertips and explode like stars in the sky, lighting up the village.

An old woman laughs and says, "Ah, how beautiful. It reminds me of the tale and Kaegnalaugh, an old, old story."

Looking to her, I smile and ask, "Would you tell us the tale?"

She has a smile in her frosty eyes and gives a wan smile. "I certainly would." Someone finds the old woman a chair, and she settles herself in it carefully before giving a long, slow sigh and starting her story. As she begins to weave her tale, I weave my fire. It spirals from my hands to take the form of her words, creating a fire display for the villagers as the woman talks in her old but powerful voice. Together, we spin the tale of Kaegnalaugh and his lover and the wrath of the gods, and I keep my back to the fire burning in the center of the village, drawing upon it for strength.

Yet even with the fire, once the story is done, I am worn, and I breathe a bit harder, catching sight of Alistair and grinning at him over the crowd. He smiles at me, that boyish, impish smile that turns my heart and sets it fluttering.

"Here now!" Alistair calls when villagers begin to ask me to continue the display. Laughing, he shoulders his way to my side and puts his arm around me, grinning at his people. "Ack, enough! Ye've stolen me companion enough for one night!" He laughs, and they laugh with him.

"Och! What'd ye expect, Alistair, with the Queen of Hell as yer mate!" one man says, grinning at Alistair and bringing us both a pint of ale.

I take the mug with both hands and sip it carefully as Alistair turns red nervously, not looking to me.

He clears his head and says, "Ack, nay. She's nay my mate just yet."

"And why not?" I answer.

Alistair chokes on his ale and has to turn away to wipe his mouth and clear his chest.

I just laugh, smiling at him warmly as he gathers himself and looks back at me with wild, green eyes. "Don't tell me you're afraid to have the Queen of Hell as your mate, love."

His eyes grow wide, and he licks his lips a bit, clearing his throat one last time and saying, "Och. I'm nay 'fraid o'ye nor anything else, my lass, so long's I've ye at my side."

My heart pounds fast while I hold the mug in my hands. I cannot stop smiling, watching him stare at me with the most peculiar of looks in his eyes. "You play with fire, Alistair. But if you're sure…I'll accept the challenge. Let us see how well you handle the Queen of Hell as your mate…and wife."

Alistair doesn't move even as the whole town goes up in cheers, his dark green eyes catching the glow of the fire and staring straight at me.

I can see his chest move with his breaths, strong and sure. I laugh, and that seems to wake him up.

He grins at me, taking two steps to me and plucking the ale from my hand, handing it off to someone before his arms go around me and his mouth is on mine.

I cry out in alarm and laughter, which only pleases him that much more to open myself to his kiss. My arms go around his neck, and he bends over me, devouring me with his lips, his tongue, sending that fire straight into my core until I am gasping in my breath, feverishly returning his attentions.

"Mama! Papa!" Zsoka cries, and Alistair breaks from me as a little black-haired girl attacks his leg.

He laughs warmly and picks her up, setting the child on his shoulders as she giggles. He looks to me, and his eyes are filled with warmth and his smile with laughter. His arm goes around me once more, and he draws me near, kissing my brow with tenderness and care in such contrast to his powerful kiss, and his hand trembles on the small of my back. I smile gently and lean into him, resting my head by his jaw.

"To the Duke and Duchess o'Maeghdra!"

I look out at the village and smile softly.

In small crowds, people press in to congratulate us and to wish us blessings. Some bring food or ale, others small tokens of gifts. The harvest festival turns into a wedding celebration filled with dancing and laughter and music.

Alistair keeps me close, stealing kisses and spinning me by firelight until I nearly fall from dizziness.

Late That Night

We do not return home until late, and half of the village goes with us. The villagers cheer and dance and sing as we make our way down the street, a sleepy Zsoka refusing to go to sleep as she sits on Alistair's shoulders. His hand holds mine as we walk, and I look up to find him smiling down at me.

There is no sorrow here.

There is no war.

Here in this place, there is only laughter and joy and love. It is the first time in my life when I have ever truly felt safe, and I squeeze his hand as if somehow I could convey all of the thoughts in my mind, the hopes in my heart. Instead, I only smile and follow my husband inside of our home. The villagers give a final cheer before slowly beginning to disperse either back to the village or to their own homes.

I can still hear them outside, and I giggle softly, Alistair leading me through the dark and empty manor by the hand.

He draws me up the stairs, hushing me with laughter in his voice, for he can feel the tired child on his shoulder slump forward, sound asleep.

I grin at the sight, and when we reach our room, I help him pull the girl off of him and lay her in bed. I pull her out of her bodice and gown, leaving her in her chemise. There is cold water in the basin, and I use it to clean her face, her hands, and her feet, before finally tucking her in and letting her rest. When I look back to the door, Alistair is leaning against it, watching the pair of us with a gentleness in his eyes that turns my heart. I smile.

"D'ye mean to leave yer new mate to sleep alone, sweetheart?" he asks me teasingly, but there is a shyness about him.

My heart seems suddenly to stop, and where once was overflowing joy and warmth, fear steals in like ice. It sets my heart pounding and drives me almost to panic. I had decided now for a while that I would accept Alistair's proposal. I know that I love him and that I would be happy by his side. But somehow the actual realization of what it would mean to be a wife had completely escaped me.

"I...I am worn and tired," I say at last as he shifts in nervousness. I am not ready. Not yet. The thoughts of being alone with him, of being made naked and exposing my scars, my fears. I cannot do that yet. I smile softly, apologetically at him. "I am afraid I would only steal your covers and kick you out of your own bed."

He watches my face, not quite sure what to make of my words, I am certain. But he smiles and shakes his head with a little laugh, coming to my side and kissing my cheek sweetly. "Goodnight, Scarlet...sleep well." He rises, and I smile gently at him, wishing that I was stronger, that I could follow after him and climb into his bed without fear...but I am afraid.

He shuts the door behind him when he leaves, and I sigh, looking down at Zsoka. I go to the basin to wash up, my movements slow and heavy, working through the thoughts and fears in my mind. When I am finished, I lay down beside my little child and close my eyes, torn with fear and uncertainty.

Chapter Thirty Seven
Scarlet

One Month Later
Maeghdra Manor, Flora

Alistair will be leaving soon. He always does. With the summer harvest now underway and the autumn soon to come, he will need to make his last rounds throughout the countryside. After that, he won't typically leave during the winter unless he has to. I barely remember the last winter since Zsoka and I more or less stayed in our beds the entire time.

For now, the people of Maeghdra are happy that their duke is home. And I am happy too.

In the morning, Zsoka and I wake as we always have done. We get dressed and head down to the dining hall to break our fast before Zsoka's tutor arrives.

Freya sits across from me, home for once, and I tell her about the festival last night. She laughs and grins warmly, seemingly pleased with the night's events.

"Good morning, my mate," a low voice greets behind me.

I squeak in alarm, and Alistair takes hold of my shoulders and kisses my cheek while I sit completely frozen, trying to swallow my heart back down into my chest. I can't find words to say, so I merely clear my throat and smile and stuff a piece of bread into my mouth.

Across from me, Freya watches with a wry little smile and a curious look before Alistair sits down beside me.

"Good morning, lassie, mam." He reaches over to pat the top of Zsoka's head, and she beams at him. "What d'ye have in store for the day?"

Having finished my piece of bread and sipped down some water, I finally find my voice and answer, "Zsoka's tutors should be here soon. She has lessons until noon, and I train with some of the Maeghdra soldiers in town. After that, we both help out around the manor."

Alistair makes a face and scoffs. He leans across the table to look at Zsoka and asks, "Dinna sound like much fun, now do it, my lassie?"

Zsoka just stares back at him, not quite sure how to respond. "I like reading," she says at last. "But…I dinna so's much like washin."

He laughs warmly and says, "'Tis decided then! Come! I've a gift for both o'ye."

I quirk a brow at him, and I look to Zsoka who watches him with interest.

She scurries out of her chair, standing by his side while he gets up and heads to the front doors.

He stops and throws a look back to me, warmth and laughter in his eyes.

My pounding heart stills to a content little flutter, and I smile softly, standing and following after them both.

Alistair loops an arm around me and kisses the top of my head.

I am unused to such affections, and my stomach turns in knots as I let him lead us out into the courtyard.

There, standing in the golden light of morning, is a beautiful beast with a white coat and gray spots.

My breath leaves in a rush, and I move away from Alistair to go and get a better look at the horse.

A mare, pretty and strong. She tosses her silver hair and looks to me, black eyes staring right into mine. It takes my breath away to look at her, and I walk down the length of her mighty form, my fingertips trailing over her coat with care and love.

A little sound beside me catches my attention, and I turn to see a short, golden pony stamping her feet on the cobblestone courtyard, caught in a stare with my Zsoka.

Alistair's warm laughter greets me, and I turn my head to look into his eyes. He stands there in the golden light of the sun, smiling down at us two with a softness to his gaze and a sincerity in his smile.

My heart pounds strong and hard within my chest while I watch him, watch him standing there, basking in his own love for us.

"Thank you," I whisper, and I turn to him, one kick of my boot launching myself at him. My arms go around his neck, and he gives an 'oof!' when I envelope him in my hold, squeezing him tightly. I can feel his laughter in his chest, and it warms me to my core while I hold him, nuzzling my face into his neck.

"Tank you! Tank you!" Zsoka cries, and she slams her little body into his legs, wrapping her arms around his waist and burying her face into his side.

He just laughs harder, wrapping one arm around me and laying one hand on Zsoka's back. "Ah, I'm so pleased ye like them. I'd already purchased them for ye last week when I first arrived. But they make for a fine weddin present too."

I withdraw from him enough to look at his face and find Alistair watching me, red tinting his light brown cheeks and gold dancing in his tawny hair. "They're beautiful," I tell him, pressing myself closer so that my mouth can find his, my lips dry and trembling, but his sweet and warm. My kiss is swallowed up in his own, and I sigh against him, returning each kiss until he withdraws to place his forehead gently against mine, looking down at me with laughter in his green eyes.

"Shall we take them riding then, wife?"

"Is that my new name now?" I tease him, laughing softly.

He grins and asks, "D'ye dislike it, sweetheart?"

I shake my head. "No. But I would rather hear my name from your lips."

He reaches up and gently grazes his knuckles down my cheek, and in a low and rumbling voice, he purrs, "*Scarlet.*"

A shiver rakes down my spine and robs my breath, and I think to myself it might have been better letting him simply call me 'wife'.

"Let's go riding!" Zsoka cries, thumping Alistair's stomach lightly with impatience.

He laughs and breaks away from me, grinning down at the little girl and hoisting her up into his arms. "An excellent idea, lassie! Come and let's get ye fitted with a saddle." He carts her off on his shoulders to mount up her pony and help her get adjusted in a saddle.

I smile, watching them go and feeling my heart swell with warmth. There are few things so endearing to my soul than to watch the man I love so clearly head over heels for the child I adore. With a soft laughter bubbling in my chest, I follow after them to find a saddle for my own mare. While I've ridden barebacked before, it is not comfortable and it is very difficult, even more so in a dress. A saddle would be welcome.

We spend the day riding through the country, teaching Zsoka how to stay upright on her pony and how to properly guide the creature. We stop in a little village for lunch and then continue on until just before nightfall when we return home. Cali has a delicious spread prepared for us, on which we feast with laughter and merriment. Alistair even finds his old lute and plays for us while Zsoka and I dance before the fire.

And when it comes time for bed, I take Zsoka upstairs and have her washed and in bed. Once again, Alistair is at the door, watching with quiet, gentle adoration. "Art tired, mate?" he asks softly.

I look back at him and smile wearily, giving a gentle nod.

He gives a worn smile and adds, "Wouldst prefer to stay with the wee one?"

I hesitate, feeling a lump in my throat, but I nod mutely, irritated that I am unable to find words with which to properly answer him.

He sighs but smiles at me gently and steps into the room. He cups my cheek in his hand. It is warm, and the skin is calloused. I don't mind. I lean my cheek into his touch as he kneels down and kisses my brow. "Sleep well, sweetheart."

"Goodnight, Alistair," I say softly, and he stands with a little smile and leaves the room.

Chapter Thirty Eight
Scarlet

Two Weeks Later
Maeghdra Manor, Flora

The next day, he took Zsoka and I down to the river where we skipped rocks and walked barefoot on the smooth stones, the water cold to our skin. Even so, it was nice. Alistair took us to see other towns and villages, down to a lake once, and rode with us through meadows and valleys. Each time, he would guide us home at sunset where we would eat and play music and dance. But every night always ended the same. I would take Zsoka to her room and Alistair would bid me goodnight, and he would leave to sleep alone in his bed.

I lay back against him near the fire, his back to the wall beside the hearth and one leg stretched out on it while the other dangles off. I curl up with him there, my legs both stretched out along the length of the fire, my head against his shoulder, listening to Zsoka read her new book to us. She is slow and careful when she reads, careful with her words. She struggles over some and works out the sound with care before continuing on.

When at last it is late and I sit up to go and put Zsoka to bed, Alistair leans over me and kisses my cheek. "Goodnight, Scarlet. Sleep well." I look up at him and smile softly, but my stomach twists and my heart races. I want to follow him, to go up to his room and stay the night in his arms. But the thought of it sets my heart to panic, and I withdraw from him once more, sitting on the hearth with Zsoka and watching him head up the stairs ahead of me to sleep.

"What troubles you, Scarlet?" Freya sits in a plush chair by the fire, wrapped up in her robe with her silver hair down and braided over one shoulder. She seems softer there than when she stands with her cane in hand, her hair in a tight bun and her eyes watching everything around her.

I look over to her and consider answering her, but I do not know how.

"Come, Zsoka…it's time for bed." I lead the child from the dining hall and up the stairs to her room. I help her undress and wash her face and hands before tucking her into bed. I cover her and kiss her brow and bid her goodnight.

"You're not staying?" she asks.

I smile softly and kiss the tip of her nose. "No…I am going to stay up a little while longer. Go to sleep, Zsoka. I'll be here if you need me."

I stand and leave her room, heading back into the quiet hall. I pause and glance to Alistair's room, his door firmly shut. I can see light coming in from under the door, so he must still be awake. I head down the hall and back down the stairs, climbing up on the hearth once more. I run my hand through my hair and curl up, leaning against the side wall and looking over at Freya.

"Freya."

She looks up at me from her needlework with an inoffensive stare.

I swallow. "Do you think…that I will ruin Alistair?"

Freya seems surprised, and she laughs. "Now why would you think that?"

I sigh, looking away from her and thinking quietly. "You said it once, and…I am not really—I am not a proper wife."

"Oh?"

I give a frustrated sigh and look to her with annoyance. "Aside from the fact that I have no idea how a Flora wife is different from an Inferno one I was a soldier for too long. I still have such horrible dreams. And when Alistair holds me or kisses me…I am uncertain of what to do. Things a woman should like, should enjoy—they're foreign and frightening to me."

Freya merely scoffs and gives a little chuckle. "Well…that's where you're confused," she says, and I look up at her. "Alistair didn't marry a *wife*. He married you. He married *Scarlet*. And that is all he has ever asked you to be. The rest is just excuses." She looks right at me, setting her work down and holding my gaze. "Did it never occur to you, Scarlet, that the only reason you took up a sword in the first place was to put something between you and everyone else? And now that it is no longer here, now you must actually face others…and yourself."

I breathe in a breath slowly, just watching her for a moment while the fire roars at my back.

"I think that scares you more than anything else. You must learn to look at yourself: exactly as you are. You must learn to see both the beauty and the beast, the love and the evil, and to accept all of it. Change what you can. Become better than you were. But never hide from what you see. And never run from it."

Finally, I turn my head away from her, feeling my heart pound within my chest, my mind dizzy and frantic. I close my eyes, feel the fire at my back, feel it roar and pop out from the confines to graze my skin with its loving warmth. The fire is my respite. It is my loving companion, my dearest friend.

When I feel its warmth, I am unafraid, and I am strong. Without it...I am left lonesome.

I was told once that there are two different kinds of fires—the wildfire and the hearthfire.

Wildfires burn hot and rampant, and they destroy everything in their path. Wildfires are indiscriminate killers and reckless forces. They are strong and bold and powerful, but they are beyond control and cause much harm.

Hearthfires are no less beautiful, no less powerful, no less wonderful. But they are content in their stone homes to bring warmth and light to the house. They provide life and sustenance and bring people together.

Perhaps it was my mother who once told me these things. I can no longer remember.

My pounding heart calms into a slow and steady thrum, and my mind's spinning slowly swirls to a steady halt, and all becomes calm and quiet.

"Alistair is waiting for me," I say in a soft, nonchalant way, sliding off of the hearth. I look to Freya and incline my head, smiling gently. "Goodnight, Lady Freya."

She merely smiles softly at me and takes up her needlework again. "Goodnight, Lady Scarlet. Sleep well."

"Mm." I give a single nod and leave her there before the fire, heading for the stairs. I climb them and head down the hall, finding Alistair's room with the faint glow of candlelight peering from under the door. I stop just outside of his room and wait quietly.

Slowly, I take in a long, deep breath, feeling my stomach tighten and my heart flutter nervously within me. I reach up a hand, and I knock quietly. "Alistair?"

He has not bolted his door, so when I push, it opens without complaint. I find him standing in his room in only his slacks, nearly to the door to open it for me. He stops at the sight of me. His room is illuminated only by the oil lamp burning by his bed; it casts a molten glow throughout the whole of the room, and it covers him in a golden light.

I hesitate at the door and swallow, feeling my heart pounding in my chest, my throat tight. I nearly excuse myself and shut the door and leave, but I feel frozen and unable to do anything at all. My yellow eyes study him, tall and mighty and now left bare before me except for those slacks, and he watches me with a wide-eyed look I've rarely seen in him.

Finally, my eyes go to the bed, and I smile softly, seeing letters and parchment strewn across his blankets. "Working at this hour?" I ask him, and he gives a nervous laugh, that wide-eyed look fading.

He smiles and rubs the back of his neck. "Ack, well. I was'na expecting company this hour neither."

"If I am disturbing you, I can come back in the morning," I offer, not certain if I wish for him to accept or decline.

"Nay!" he shouts, startling me, and I jump a bit. He winces a bit and laughs nervously once more, the sound shaky and uncertain. "Ack, sorry, lass. Here. Let me grab a shirt and we can talk about whatever's on your mind."

I swallow past the lump in my throat, the pounding in my chest. "No need," I tell him quietly, and he pauses from grabbing his shirt from the bed, looking back to me. I smile softly, stepping inside the room and shutting the door. I'm fairly certain he stops breathing, pinning me with those green eyes, those dark, dark eyes. When I pull the bolt on the door, locking it, he visibly swallows and lets out a breath.

"Scarlet?" he asks, his voice remarkably soft and slightly strained.

"Husband?" I return, watching his nostrils flare a bit in alarm and his body turn to face me.

I'm trembling. I can feel it. Thoughts of fear desperately try to force themselves into my mind, but I push them all away, focusing on the man in front of me, the way his golden chest rises and falls softly with his breath, the blonde scruff on his face, the curly mane of yellow hair. And those dark, emerald eyes watching me.

Slowly, I move towards him, one step and then another, my slippers padding softly on the wooden floor. I stand before him, reaching up to touch one hand to his cheek, feeling his coarse beard on my palm. I smile, stroking his cheek and going to my toes to kiss his lips sweetly.

He sighs out a breath against my cheek and puts both hands upon my hips, as if he does not trust himself to hold me. His mouth parts mine with a push of his lips. A soft sound from my throat escapes, and his fingers to dig into my hip, holding me more firmly to him. He tips his head, molding his lips to mine.

My heart pounds, and my head feels faint and swirling. My arms go around his neck, and he sucks in a breath, his tongue thrusting into my mouth, devouring me.

I gasp and cry out a muffled sound of alarm, and he hesitates to make sure I am alright. I part lips from his only to suck in a breath and then mold my lips to his again, my tongue finding his to tease.

His arms go around me then, one hand pressing my back so that I am trapped against him, the other cradling the back of my head.

He pulls a bit away after a brief moment, but he finds me smiling when he opens his eyes, and I watch him with delight, breathing a bit harder than I had been before.

"I want to stay with you tonight," I tell him, a whisper of a sound. His pupils dilate. "But…" He hesitates. "Snuff the light first."

Alistair opens his mouth, then frowns and shuts it. His green eyes look straight into mine, shifting back and forth over the sight of them, trying to read my thoughts through my yellow eyes. "Why?" he asks, his voice a husky rasp of sound.

I bite my lip, watching him quietly, my heart coming down from its rampant pace. "I do not wish for the lights is all."

My answer does not appease him, and he frowns at me, giving a soft sigh. "Scarlet, tis the matter, sweetheart?" He reaches up a hand and gently slips two fingers beneath my shoulder sleeve.

I can feel the rough imprint of his skin on my collar bone, feel his fingertips graze the smooth scars there, and I shudder faintly, feeling him push the fabric down off of my shoulder.

"No," I rasp softly, pulling the fabric back up and stepping away.

He releases me but watches intently.

"The lights first."

"Scarlet, what—"

"The scars."

He closes his mouth, watching me as I hold the cloth on my shoulder, looking away from him.

I bite my lip again, and he steps closer to me, gently placing his fingers beneath my chin and lifting my face to look at him. I finally meet his gaze, my expression uncertain. "I— the scars...I do not want you to look on them."

He reaches for me once more, placing his large, warm hand on my shoulder and gently brushing his thumb back and forth over the scar on my neck. He shifts his hand to push mine away and traces the faint bite marks of Gabriel's teeth in my shoulder. The coarse pads of his fingers send fire racing up my throat, and my breath lurches slightly.

"I've already seen them," he tells me. "At the fire in Karnei...and the princess' wedding."

My body seems frozen and solid, and I turn my head away, glaring at the ground. "Now is different."

He laughs, a loud and boisterous sound that calls my eyes back up to his face once more. Suddenly, he grabs me around the waist and tosses me onto the bed. I yelp in alarm, but he is there, looming over me, and my wide, honey eyes stare up at him with curiosity and a bit of fear—for I never quite know what Alistair will do.

"Ah, sweetheart," he says to me, leaning down to kiss my jaw, my neck.

I gasp in a breath and put my hands on his shoulders, feeling a mixture of heated desire and cold fear.

He chuckles and finishes, "The only difference," he grabs the top of my dress and grips it firmly, starting a rip at the front seam, "'tis now," he rips the dress clear from my chest to my naval, parting the tattered folds and bending his head down to my breast, "I can touch them."

My eyes fly open wide as his tongue flicks out to trace the large, white scar on my left breast where a sword cut and nearly reached my heart. My lungs pull in a gasp of their own accord, and I squirm beneath him, my face hot and my eyes wild with fear and excitement.

His touch knows no rush. His hands on my hips hold me firmly beneath him while he leans over me and runs the warm flat of his tongue over the long, white scar. Then, just when I think he has finished, his teeth scrape against the spot, and I go up in flames.

"A-Alistair!" I squeak out, unsure if I want to pull away or thrust my breast into his mouth.

A low, dark laugh rumbles in his chest, and my breath shudders into the open air. It suddenly feels so cold in the room—I feel as if I am going up in flames.

"My love," he rumbles against my skin, and he kisses my breast with sweet reverence before moving to the other. His hand slides to circle my back and pull me to him as his mouth assaults the other breast.

I whimper his name, but that only seems to drive him more.

He forces himself away from my breast and returns his lips to mine. His tongue—emboldened by its assault—devours me. He strokes my tongue and explores the cavern of my mouth in between gasps for air.

I return his endeavors with my own. My arms go around his shoulders, pulling myself into him and parting my mouth to fight his fire with my own. I never expected a Flora to burn with such heat, but even with his cooler skin, his touch only burns me all the more.

He lifts himself up to his knees and brings me with him.

I'm suddenly aware of the sharp edges of parchment—now crushed and ruined—that have left imprints on my skin, and one piece of paper that clings to my back.

We both laugh, and it fills my whole body with a hearthfire unlike any I've ever known.

I unceremoniously swipe the papers from the bed while he rids himself of his slacks. And when my eyes return to him, I am caught between awe and intimidation.

Alistair ducks his head in—is that shyness? My great and impervious Alistair blushing and timid before my eyes?

I don't dare laugh though for fear of him taking the wrong assumption. Instead, I lift myself to my knees and rest my hands upon his chest. Beneath my hands, I feel his sharp intake of breath, and his green eyes watch me with such intensity that I feel as if he has stripped me down to my inmost being.

"Art certain you're not in a half form?" I ask him.

He gives me a curious little took, and I laugh.

"You look nigh like a bear as it is. You're covered in hair." And he is. His arms and legs are shielded in thick hair, and his chest boasts a fine pattern of coarse, brown hair that trails down his stomach.

He gives a deep, bellowing laugh, and my eyes snap back to his. He grins at me, and I cannot help but smile in return. "Come here, ye wicked thing," he growls. One arm grabs my shoulders and the other my lower back, and he lifts me. There is little grace in the way he half-drags me to properly lay me on the bed, but I do not mind.

At least not until he thumps my head on the solid wood headboard when he tries to lay me down.

"Ack!" he swears, cradling me up with a guilty, worried look. "Sweetheart, I—"

"Oh, silence, rogue, and kiss me!" I say, laughing and trying to ignore the throbbing pain in my head. It took weeks to work up the courage to come here tonight, and aside from losing a limb, I'm not letting anything get in the way of it.

He obeys and lays his mouth on mine while he scoots us safely back from the headboard. He is warm, and his hair tickles my chest as he leans on me—holding me, kissing me, breathing in the air I breathe. His beard roughs my smooth chin and cheeks, but I would not for the world tell him to stop.

"Al…Alistair…" I rasp.

He lifts himself enough to look at my face properly. "Aye, wife?"

"…you're crushing me. I can't breathe."

He turns red-faced, but I laugh warmly, assuring him sweetly. He braces himself more on his arms, and I arch up to close the distance.

My lips go to his neck, one kiss after another trailing down the thick column of a throat.

He moans in approval, and I notice the subtle press of his hips into mine, a gentle rocking that he doesn't even seem aware of. I bite a little roughly at his neck; his hips buck into mine in response.

"Play nice!" he snarls.

I laugh wickedly and part my legs for him to settle his body between them. "Never."

"Ye're askin for trouble, lass." His knees scoot under my thighs and lift my legs up, pressing my back into the bed.

"I *am* trouble," I reply teasingly. My heart pounds in my chest, and I stare eagerly up at him and suddenly push my hips up to encourage him.

The action winds him, and he groans loudly and grabs my hips. "Wicked, wicked creature," he growls.

I giggle, letting myself become accustomed to his pressure.

But then his hips sink into me, and my chest fills with what I think may be my last breath. My nails bite into his shoulders, and I push my head back into the pillow and cry out a pained moan.

He freezes instantly and picks himself up.

I can see the strain on his face and how his lips are parted to breathe quickly.

"Art hurt, lass?" he asks quickly. "I'd nay mean to—"

"Shh." I breathe hard for a moment, my eyes closed, and he watches me. Even though he is the one untrained in lovemaking, it's been years for me, and I'm fairly certain that Jay'let was not so...fulfilling. "I'm alright...just...give me a minute."

Alistair doesn't move a single muscle, and I work on relaxing mine.

Slowly, I go pliant once more, and my hips shift up a bit against his.

He goes rigid for a moment, but then he slowly moves in rhythm with me. He leans over me, almost as if he's shielding me, and I wrap my arms around him and hold him to me.

"Alistair," I whimper his name into his neck, and he gives a quiet groan and nuzzles his face into my shoulder. "My Alistair."

He tentatively increases his pace, and I meet him stroke for stroke. I start whimpering as he pants and grunts with his head bowed over me. He goes still, then gives a loud groan thrusts one last time against me.

The pleasure of knowledge that he fills my womb melds with the sudden spark of pleasure, and it shatters me. I arch back with a shrill cry of alarm and fireworks splitting my muscles and striking my body in the shelter of his.

I try to move around some, and he gasps and gives an almost pained sound. "Easy, lass! Easy! Tis sensitive!"

Wearily, I giggle and fall lax into the sheets, feeling like a half-melted candle still warmed by flames and happily spent.

While I understood what he meant when he'd said that he wanted to touch my scars, I had not expected him to trace each one of them with his tongue and hands. Which—after a brief rest and sweet caressing—he most certainly did. He found every injured piece of my flesh and set it to memory with his touch until I was writhing and panting under him. I did not expect a man to have such patience, but Alistair was patient with me, bringing me almost to beg before he finally consoled my tortured body with his own.

I forced him onto his back as punishment and held him there while I controlled our pace and pleasure. He was more than strong enough to counter me, but he laid pliant to my will and willing to my control. It was all more than enough to bring his torture to completion with one of the most exquisite expressions I've ever seen on his face.

We did not last long after that.

At the end of the night and the start of dawn's birth, I lay upon Alistair's chest while he breathes slow, deep breaths: his head tipped back and his hands on my hips. Like a contented cat, I wear an arrogant smile while the oil lamp still glows and fills the room with its warmth.

And although I cannot see Alistair's face, I feel the faint impression of a smile.

Chapter Thirty Nine
Gabriel

Several Weeks Later
The Crystalice Palace, Cerulean

The dull murmur of the council fills the halls of the meeting room when I enter. I am not the last one to arrive, but Claque an older member behind me are; we take our seats quickly. The dim room illuminated by silver-blue lanterns hanging from the ceiling, making the room seem even colder. Perhaps the idea is to calm the hot tempers so often expressed.

"Good morning," my father greets, opening out his hands in a silent gesture. "I understand that the events of the princess' wedding were very terrifying to you all, and I am grateful to those of you who decided to remain on the council and return to Crystalice to continue our meetings as we deliberate these events."

He inclines his head to my mother who nods and places her spectacles on the bridge of her nose, looking down at the parchment in her hands. "Thank you, majesty. Now then, if you will all look to the first page that has been provided for you, you will see a rough account as to the names of the people implicated in the White Fang attack during Princess Denair's wedding."

"Pardon me, my lady," one of the councilors, an older gentleman, speaks up. I, sunken back in my seat and trying to banish the flashes of nightmarish images from that day, look up and sit a bit straighter. My mother is a patient woman, but she greatly dislikes being interrupted; she stares straightly at the man. The gentleman inclines his head and continues, "Forgive me, my queen, but is it not too quick to presume that this attack—terrible as it was—is the work of the White Fang? I would hate to jump to hasty conclusions."

Rage boils up in my chest as hot as the fire that blazed through Cara on that night. There is silence in the room before one of the young councilors replies in a sharp voice, "You must be mad. No—no—give me a moment. Forgive me, sir, but you must be barking mad. These incidents are becoming more and more frequent by the week. The group has claimed some of these incidents themselves, branding the ruined carriages with their bastardized emblem, painting it on the floors by the bodies they have slain. Surely we cannot still debate this."

"No, the count has a point," another counters, out-stretching his arm. "We cannot simply attribute every attack as being a part of the White Fang."

"Of course not," the other replies, "But it is simply a waste of time to sit here and deliberate the nuances of these matters. Whoever they are, whatever they are called, they *are* an organized group enacting *organized* attacks against the crown and people."

The older gentleman chuckles. Perhaps that is the final straw for me—that little laugh. The man continues, "Boy, you give them far too much credit. This is simply a band of vagabonds running a bit rampant."

"Enough."

My voice cuts clear and sharp through the room. I am rather impressed with myself that it is not a raging shout.

The councilors go quiet and watch as I stand slowly from my seat, adjusting the cuffs of my doublet as I hold their gazes. "We will not debate this any longer. I am open to disagreements. In fact, I encourage them. I want to be certain that we consider all angles and all possible opinions. But at some point, a line must be drawn between the challenging and the demented."

"Excuse me, your highness, but—"

"No." I cut my eyes to the offender, frowning at him. "You are not excused, and you do not have leave to speak." He clamps his mouth shut and stares at me, a cold rage in his eyes and a faint redness to his face.

I look away from him then and turn my attention to the council as a whole. "This council has spent the past several months, if not an entire year or more, doing absolutely nothing. We have accomplished nothing, because we have spent the entire time chasing our tails and deliberating over semantics and refusing to acknowledge and take action against what is right in front of us."

"Sir," the older gentleman cuts in. "Forgive me, but we *have* been working towards solutions. I *apologize*," he bites off, "if they are not to your liking, but the council has taken action."

"You have wasted the air within this room," I reply shortly, pinning him calmly with my stare. "I wonder, sir, how your actions might change if it had been *your* son who was poisoned, *your* sister who was nearly killed—all within the highest safety and security within *your very own home*. People have *died* at their hands. Soldiers, civilians, gentry. This is enough.

"Now, you can either sit here with us as a whole and assist in deciding *how* we are going to take action and *identify, apprehend, and prosecute* these villains, or you are welcome to take your leave, and we wish you a safe journey home."

The council for a moment is shocked into silence and begins an uproar before Petara's voice slices through the mob of anger and approval alike. "Gabriel," she calls, frowning at me. "You cannot dismiss the council. It is exists to serve as confidant and support of the monarchy, to represent the whole of Cerulean, and to be certain that all of its people are being treated fairly and equally."

"Actually, Petara," I say, standing taller and pinning her. "I *can* dismiss the council. The council serves at the king's and heir's *leisure* and are not legally required for any action the monarchy takes. At this point, they have ceased to fulfill their purpose and their obligations to the people and have *enabled* murderers and ravenous lunatics to run rampant through our country while the more common of our people suffer. And *this*, dear sister, will not be tolerated."

The room falls quiet for a moment, councilors looking between my parents and I to see if they will come to my aid or my dismissal.

I would also like to see how my parents are reacting to this disruption, but I will not break my stare from Petara to address them, and as they have yet spoken, I trust that—at least for the moment—they will hold their peace.

"If you are opposed to this course of action, Petara, and no longer wish to serve on the council, you are, of course, permitted to take your leave as well."

A few soft gasps echo through the room, and soft murmurs bubble up, but at least that is the last of the outbursts remaining.

Petara's eyes turn into slits, and even from here, I can see the silver fur rolling up on her neck. But she juts her chin up and rises with slow, measured intent from her seat—holding my gaze all the while—before turning and making for the door, her heels clicking on the floor. Kale, naturally, rises as well and follows mutely after her.

The room is silent for a moment, and I remain standing as the quiet murmurs rumbles up in debate. At last, a few more councilors rise from their seats. Some meet my eyes with fierce indignation, and others quietly gather their things before leaving the council room. The door slams on their way out.

I turn my gaze to the remaining councilors who look on me with a range from hesitant wariness to quiet approval, all waiting to see what will happen next. Roughly three-quarters of the council remains.

"Very well," I say simply and take my seat. "My queen, please forgive my disruption. Continue at your leisure."

I glance to her to find an expressionless face looking back at me.

My father, likewise, has a neutral expression—neutral in that his face is etched in its usual, disdainful scowl.

My mother gives a single, unconcerned nod and clears her throat once before continuing, "Very well. Let us continue..."

That Night

"Gabriel."

My father's voice cuts through the hall. The council meeting went on late into the night. We dined and drank while at the table, talking through the night and taking only short breaks through the day. And yet, we have accomplished more in seven hours than we have in seven months or more.

I turn my head to watch my father move towards me. Only the royal family would be heading to the left of the council room—towards our quarters. The councilors would all be headed to the right towards their own rooms. Only the four of us remain in the hall—my father, my mother, Claque, and myself.

"Sire," I greet and thump my fist to my chest in salute, bowing at the waist and rising again.

He frowns at me. "What do you mean by dismissing over a quarter of the council today? Do you have any idea what you have done?"

I incline my head. "Indeed, sir. As of today, half of our troops are being withdrawn from the assault on Inferno lands and the rest are being set up in defense of the borders. The most skilled of our soldiers will be trained in taking targeted action against the White Fang, and our mathematicians and scholars are being gathered to find the pattern to their actions and determine their most likely goals so that we can prevent future attacks.

"We are constructing new treaties with the Flora for needed food and supplies and returning their soldiers to them to strengthen their assault on the Levosa—which could enable them to end the war within the next few years if they can be convinced to revoke their edict against attack on women."

His scowl darkens, and he looms over me fiercely. "You have made *enemies*, Gabriel. You have placed yourself in a very precarious position. Now you will struggle to find support within the territories and will have to go through much more effort to either regain their trust or to otherwise replace them which could increase tensions."

I open my mouth to speak, but he cuts in, "Moreover, you have isolated a very strong ally in your sister, who now will most likely garner her own following and support as heir. She might have been more useful to you as an accomplice and not an adversary."

Once I am certain that my father is waiting for me to answer for myself, I incline my head to him again and reply, "My lord, enemies are to be expected in times of war. A lack of them shows a lack of force on needed fronts. I shall choose my battles—and my allies—carefully and to strengthen the connections that I have…as for my sister…forgive me, father, but while she is my family, she was never my ally. Petara has always had her own agenda, and I am not convinced that it aligns with my own."

My father is silent, lifting his chin nobly and watching me from down his nose, standing a good head taller than me. At last, he gives a twice-nod and growls, "Very good, Gabriel. Continue at will. Do not become too arrogant."

For a moment, I am rendered speechless, my words shoved forcefully back into my chest. Finally, I swallow and salute my father again, bowing at the waist, and this time staying leaned straight down. "Sire!" I call formally, my heart pounding within my ribs beneath my hand.

He gives a grunt and continues on down the hall.

My mother follows him at a more regal pace as I stand and look back at him. She smiles wryly as she passes me and comments quietly, "Impressive ship. Now take care that it does not sink." She turns back towards my father and follows him off to their room.

I release a gush of a sigh from my lungs once they are out of sight, and I can feel my body tremble weakly. After a moment, Claque asks, "Should I have a servant fetch some whiskey?"

"Please," I rasp, following him off to my study to finish the work from today so that we can sleep for whatever is left of the night.

Chapter Forty
Scarlet

Two Months Later
Maeghdra Manor, Flora

I am not accustomed to waking early. I do not enjoy it, either.

"Ali," I grumble irritably, rolling onto my stomach in our bed, stealing the warm spot that once had been him. "What are you doing?" Somewhere in the room, I can hear the faint sounds of cloth and armor. It is the sound of metal which calls for my attention. My eyes come open, and I yawn, sitting up in bed. The bite of cold, however, catches me, and I shiver, pulling our warm blankets up over my naked form.

The light of the late autumn morning has not yet pierced the sky, but I can faintly see Alistair dressing by the hearth which is still carrying embers from the fire in it last night. "Ack. I'm sorry, sweetheart," Alistair whispers to me. "A soldier just arrived from Gaelen. I'm needed at the border. A troop o'Levosa are trying to take the local villages."

"Let me go," I say at once, throwing my legs over the side of the bed.

"Nay." All at once, he is before me, putting his hands on my shoulders and holding me there. "Scarlet, ye're the Duchess o'Maeghdra…I need ye here, lassie. With Zsoka. Tis my place to do this."

I give him an annoyed look, shivering.

He smiles softly and nudges me back into bed, pulling the covers up to my chin. "I s'ppose ye'll nay be sleeping bare much longer, sweetheart. Winter'll be here shortly."

"Husband," I complain, sighing at him, but he just smiles teasingly. "What do the Levosa want?...perhaps I can help."

He sighs and shakes his head. "Ye canna help, lass. The Levosa are desperate and very...bitter. Few hundred years ago...when their land started dyin, Flora only had one king and only one child: a wee lassie. And this wee princess married a Griffin."

"A Griffin?"

"Aye...every offspring of a male'll have that male's form. Harpy, siren, arakocra, wyvern, and many more...But tis only one called Griffin. King o'all creature. Tis only ever one male and one female. And the Griffin wilt have only one babe. Since this Griffin was male, he would sire only one babe, and twould be a wee Griffin.

"And, o'course, since the Levosa take many wives for many children, a male Griffin would have only one mate so that other could marry and have more children.

"The Griffin—most revered o'all their kind for his might and pow'r and *Magik*, came to Flora to ask us to restore their dyin land. Many trades and deals and treaties were discussed...but tis said when the Griffin spied the Flora princess...he promised her to bind with him would give her a child of more power and wonder than could be had. And the Griffin line t'would become the guardian and defender o'Flora.

"The king agreed, and the princess was taken to Flora...and there, she was killed—she and the Griffin both. The king was left with no heir, and Flora was divided among his three brothers and remained thus."

I frown and ask, "But...but what about the Flora princess?"

Alistair gives a bitter smile. "I dinna ken. Tis been too long to ken the truth nay more...but the Flora dukes said twas o'rage that a Flora would birth a Griffin and she was attacked and the Griffin's death was an accident.

"Levosa said the Griffin was killed and the princess fled—that twas a trap to kill their greatest weapon."

"So, what's the truth?" I ask. "The Levosa and Inferno trade occasionally. They have strong metals and we have food. But we don't especially discuss each other's wars. I'm sure the king does, but among the rest of us, there are plenty rumors and fine stories, but nothing really true enough to believe."

"Aye, well..." He shrugs. "Truth o'the matter now is their land is dyin and so's their people. A great many men died when Flora stormed the mountains and slaughtered a great many o'them...whole villages. Flora'll nay make wars on women or bairns...but they did this time. Any male from newborn to ancient was killed that we could find."

He hands his head, and there are shadows in his eyes. "Twas a dark, dark stain upon the Flora to have done such a thing...people do terrible things in fear and anger...and Levosa took their revenge with a vengeance more than we ever did. And they still do.

"The women trained to fight, and they took the mountains to gain into Flora. They slaughter whole villages—men, women, and all the female babes. But the wee laddies...they still the young boys and return to Levosa with them to raise among their own."

"That's barbaric!" I cry with rage, sitting up suddenly. "To even kill the infant girls? To steal the children?"

With a tired and aching sigh, he stands to his full height and rubs his neck. "Desperate people do desperate things...the offspring o'the stolen are still avian, but the Flora blood has made their second forms stronger and more powerful."

He growls and finishes putting on his trappings. "To make it worse, Flora will'na make its wars on women. Flora men are great beasts in size. But the women are wee little things. They're nay much bigger than when they're human. The Flora will'na fight the weaker. Tis a great crime to attack or kill sommat so much weaker than ye. Even the wee laddies, we'll nay harm. Tis a matter o'pride and morality. Ye'd nay fight sommat so small when ye've such great might against them…

"*But*…the Levosa send their lassies to fight their battles…our men can fight them off…but if anyone actually killed a fighter…t'would be a great sore to him. He'd be seen as a beast, a monster. O'course, that's assumin anyone from that town lived…which they're nay likely to do…"

"What a foolish code," I tell him with a scowl. "It's going to get your men killed."

He kisses my brow. "I ken it, sweetheart… we're trying to get it changed. We will one day. Dinna fret. T'will be fine."

He stands, and I lay back in bed and watch him finish dressing and putting on his armor. He stokes the fire for me to warm up the room, and I smile softly, watching him as he tosses me a grin from the doorway. "I'll be back soon…I love ye, Scarlet."

"Mmmm be safe," I call back, snuggled up in the covers and watching him with a sinking heart as he leaves the room, shutting the door behind him. It is not the first time he has been called away in the early morning or even in the middle of the night like this, but it still makes me nervous. I toss and turn in my bed, biting my lip and thinking on his words.

If only they could change that foolish code…the Flora are much stronger. The Levosa merely take advantage of the fact that they know their enemy will take care when fighting them. I bury my face into the pillow and sigh heavily, thinking quietly. Outside, I can hear Alistair yelling and mounting up on his horse before riding out of the courtyard.

I want to jump out of bed, to run after him, embrace him, kiss him. I want to go with him. But I cannot. It would be childish and silly and would most likely embarrass him...no, he would grin and think it wonderful, but I would be embarrassed.

I roll onto my back and stare up at the ceiling.

Karnei. Karnei is the one blocking this. Alistair does not enjoy the thought of killing women or children, but he will do whatever it takes to protect his people. And the Duke of Gaelen, Craig Aaran, has no qualms with killing them either if it protects his people. He believes if they're strong enough to start a fight in his country, they're strong enough to die for it. But it is Karnei, the much aged duke, who so firmly keeps to the old traditions. I bite my lip again, feeling it bleed this time.

Suddenly, I throw the covers off of me. The chill hits me with biting breaths, the hearth having not yet warmed the room. But I hurry to the fire and throw open my chest of clothes, grabbing a cotton chemise and a wool gown with an extra layer of skirts as well. I pull on my stockings and my boots and then the rest of my clothes. As I head out of my room and down to the dining hall, I start pulling on my gloves and grab my fur-lined cloak, yanking it on.

"Where're ye goin?" Cali asks, having just finished some bread and put it on the shelf to cool. She stares at me in wonder.

I look to her and say, "To Karnei. Please pack a basket of food and supplies. I leave as soon as I can. Is Freya here?"

"Ack, no, missus. Lady Freya's on a trip t'Gaelen."

"I see." I run a hand through my hair. "Alright. I need to take Zsoka into the village to stay with one of the women there. Can you have my bags ready by then? Tell Krei to have my horse mounted and ready to go when I get back."

"Ah, yes missus. O'course." Cali seems disturbed and uncertain, but she knows better than to question me when I've set my mind on something.

I turn from the kitchens, go back through the dining hall, up the stairs, and into my little one's room.

Zsoka is still sleeping, annoyed with the dropping temperature. It'll be a long time before it's warm again, and we've not even hit winter yet.

"Shhhh, shhhh," I greet softly, going and kneeling besides her, rubbing her back to wake her. "I know it's cold. I know."

She whines and complains, giving an annoyed sound as I tug her out of bed. She sits up, slumped over, and looks to me with weary irritation. She's grown so much since we first arrived, and I smile at her, stroking her face. She will be going into her sixth year soon, and it amazes me that so much time has passed already.

"I have to go."

"Go?" she asks, looking concerned. "Go where?"

I smile faintly and then turn to start grabbing her clothes to get her dressed and warm. "I need to go to Karnei," I tell her, pulling on her skirts and then her wool dress. "I need to speak with the duke there concerning some political matters. It'll be alright."

"Why can't I come?" she asks, stuffing her arm through the sleeve of her dress and standing up so that I can straighten it out. She sits down and starts to pull on her stockings herself, now that she's awake and more lucid.

"Because I need to go quickly, and I might have to kill someone," I say flatly.

"Really?" she asks, not at all disturbed by this.

I give her a look and smile, helping her to pull on her boots and lace them up. "Quite possibly. Now let's go. I'm going to take you to the village to stay with the women there. Please behave for them."

"I'm not promising," Zsoka mutters, letting me drag her out of her room and down the stairs.

I put Zsoka and her bags up on my horse before riding into town. There, the villagers have already awoken and begun their day. I pull Zsoka down and take her to the butcher's wife who has six kids of her own, all around Zsoka's age. She has the space for Zsoka and Zsoka will be able to help her out around the shop. Even though I try to give her coins to pay for Zsoka's food and board, the woman just gives a "pish tush" and tells me to be safe and assures me that Zsoka will be looked after.

Krei is waiting for me by the horses when I return. "Krei. You really do not need to accompany me," I tell him with exasperation. "I know the way, and I can ride on my own."

"Ah, aye an' aye, missus," he says dubiously, "An' I can go ahead an' put me head up on the block for Master Alistair to wack off soon's as he finds out I let his wee wife go ridin 'cross th'countryside on her lonesome."

I glare at him and mount up on my horse. "I can take care of myself."

"Och, now *that* I believe," he says resolutely. "In fact, the last time ye took care o'yerself was in Karnei where ye damn near set half th'forest on fire."

I bite my tongue when I snap my teeth together, and I swear, adjusting myself in the saddle and muttering to myself before shooting him a nasty look. "You've gotten rather saucy with me the past few months, Krei."

"I beggin yer pardon, missus," he replies without the least bit of apology in his voice as we start riding for the edge of the city.

I huff to myself and resign myself to having a riding companion, muttering as we reach the open road, "And it was not *half* of the forest."

"Ah, ayy an' aye, missus."

Saucy wretch.

It takes two days of swift riding to reach Karnei. It will take Alistair with his company at least another day or two to reach the border. I will need to take care of my business swiftly or else my laxness could cost some men their lives or possibly worse.

Karnei is not quite as amicable to my appearance as Maeghdra is. Mine and Krei's arrival is met with wary mutters and a few uneasy greetings, wanting to know our business there. It helps that I am now the Duchess, but they have not forgotten how I scorched their homeland barely more than a year beforehand. I don't think they hate me, but I'm quite certain that they'd rather me not be here.

In the courtyard, I launch myself off my horse with little grace but at least balance. My horse is worn and tired, my pretty white and gray spotted mare. I pat her cheek affectionately and call to a squire to have her fed and watered and rested. I do not like abusing my horse with such long and swift rides, but there is no finer horse in Maeghdra who could have gotten me here so fast.

After leaving her with the squire, I hurry my way inside, out of the cold and into the hall of the Duke of Karnei. At this time of day, people are all bustling through the home. Karnei's manor is much more like a palace than Alistair's home, and it is easy to get lost in. People move in and out, and there is no real telling where Karnei is. There are also, I am certain, people here to speak with him on very important matters. But mine are very time-sensitive and I do not have the luxury of politeness or courtesy at the moment.

"Duchess Scarlet." I hear his old, tired voice before I see him, and I turn to find him emerging from a room I had just passed. Thank the goddess I do not need to go running through the halls shouting his name. That's a surefire way to convince the castle I've set something else on fire.

I smile warmly at him, breathless and impatient. "Duke Karnei. A pleasure." I go to him and curtsy, and he takes my hand and bows over it, kissing the back.

"Indeed, indeed. Always a pleasure to have Alistair's lovely bride here." He takes my hand and tucks it under his arm, patting it with old, knobby fingers. He has such a calm and peaceful way about him, like the mountains tall and strong. Or an old, sturdy oak tree.

I feel some of my anxiety and apprehension fade away as he leads me down the hall, and I am able to catch my breath.

"But come, come. I had not expected you, and so I assume your matters are of great importance." He does not ask me outright, but he guides me down the hall in a grandfatherly sort of way.

I think this is why people find it very difficult to disagree with Karnei. He is old but sharp as a tack and very kind. He has this warmth such that others desire to appease him in any way that they can. What's worse is that when he disagrees with someone, he is never unreasonable. He is simply set and solid and it is impossible to move him or change his mind. He merely says the way it is and smiles and waits patiently for agreement or at least compliance; no one has ever done otherwise.

"They are, my lord," I tell him, going into his parlor. A maid is tending to the fire, and she stands and smiles softly before curtsying and leaving, the fire now blazing.

Karnei is always considerate in that way, and thoughtful of his guests. He leads me to a small table not unlike the one we sat at a year and a half ago when I torched the woods of Karnei.

I sit, and while I wish to be hasty, I know better than to rush these matters.

Karnei is a man of etiquette and propriety, and so I let him go through his ritual of ordering tea and waiting for it to be brought.

The girl pours a cup for the pair of us, and as she does so, I think fondly upon the memory of Petara teaching me to serve tea. My heart squeezes, for whenever I think upon that place and those people, I cannot help but think of Gabriel, and my treasonous heart flutters.

I cast the thought of him and Petara's tea aside, taking the cup and sipping quietly to appease my host before I look to him and say, "May I be blunt, my lord?"

"Are you ever not?" he asks with a chuckle, sitting back and sipping his tea quietly. He watches me with those glassy eyes shrouded by silver bushes of brows and wrinkled, old lids; he wears an easy smile and a focused intention in his eyes.

I laugh quietly. "Rarely not, my lord. But what I say is of great importance."

"Then speak, my lady." He sets down his cup and folds his weathered hands on his knee, watching me.

I incline my head and begin, "Duke Karnei, the Flora code against attacking and killing a smaller enemy—even a female—is foolish, illogical, and frankly, sir, suicidal. At this point, I no longer care if it is moral or noble. Its only result will be the violation and wholesale slaughter of Gaelen's armies, and the destruction of valuable Flora cities and resources."

He seems surprised and then laughs a hoarse laugh and smiles at me, sitting back in his seat. "Ah. I see. This is about Alistair heading south to defend the borders of Gaelen."

I straighten and try to keep from glaring at him. While I do not like having my husband taken from my side unnecessarily, I find it insulting to have it insinuated that the inconvenience this causes me is the only motive for my being here. "And about the men and women and children being slaughtered, my lord. For honor."

I bite my tongue—literally—to keep from saying more. It doesn't stop me. My tongue slides painfully out from between my teeth and presses on. "They do not deserve such treatment, my lord. No one does. And by preventing them from fighting, from harming those who would hurt them…it is ridiculous. Those women are not in need of protection from the Flora. It is the Flora who need to be able to protect themselves against them without fear of losing honor and title and potentially ostracized."

He takes his cup, sipping it slowly. "Scarlet… dear girl…you are not familiar with these lands…you were not raised a Flora. You cannot possibly—"

"Understand?" I frown at him. "With all due respect, Duke Karnei, I understand that homes are being burned and whole families are being killed. I understand that very well. I want it to stop."

He frowns back at me. "Alistair is headed there now, and he will—"

"He will what?" I ask, my voice raising a bit. "Say 'oh, excuse me, lassies, but would ye mind pillagin an' plunderin elsewhere?' That's about damn near all he can do!"

He clatters his cup back down and rasps, "See here, lass."

"*Duchess* Scarlet," I snap, feeling an unhappy twisting in my gut as I continue. "And if you think that women are so weak and need such protection, then let's have a wager. My husband tells me you're quite fond of wagers and games."

He opens his mouth to speak but then sits back in his chair, idly stroking his beard and watching me. He regains the patience he had momentarily lost at my outburst and obscenities.

I tend to have that effect on people.

"What is the wager then, lassie?" he asks me.

I almost sigh in relief. I have a window. A chance. "Five, no, ten, of your men. Against me." His brows go up and I hold up a finger. "Rules: They can't kill me and they must attack only with the intent to disarm, not harm. They get only the weapons poor farmers would have—spade, pitchfork, maybe a hunting knife. That's all. I get a sword and armor and I can—but won't—kill them. These are the current rules of war your men live by. If they disable me, restrain me—the law stays. If I render each of them unconscious or unable to fight—the law is revoked and the men of Gaelen can fight to kill and can initiate attack so long as it is on Flora lands."

He watches me for a long moment, narrowing his eyes in piercing calculation before he begins nodding slowly. He sighs and says, "I do not see much point in this, my girl. Your heart is very kind, and I appreciate your care over these matters. I can tell that you are concerned for what concerns Alistair, and that makes for a good match...

"I do not like this wager of yours, and I do not think you can win...but I will allow it. If only to prove to you that our men are more than capable to do what they need to without having to use excessive force."

I say nothing, and he watches me for a moment before giving a gentle smile and inclining his head.

"Go and change. My servants will grant you armor and clothes. I'll choose my men. The fight is at dawn."

Standing, I bow at the waist and say, "Please have them also prepare your fastest horse to take the order of revocation to Gaelen as soon as the fight is finished."

He smirks at me and says wryly, "Do not get too ahead of yourself, lassie."

"Goodnight, duke," I say with a little smile and leave his room to go and rest and prepare for the morning.

I am provided a room and a hot meal during my stay, but sleep does not come easily to me. Krei and I only stopped to rest for a few hours at a local town on the way to Karnei. I haven't slept much, and I find it difficult to sleep again. Only a strict discipline of knowing that I cannot fight at my best if I am not rested forces me to visit slumber.

Chapter Forty One
Scarlet

The Next Morning
Castle Karnei, Flora

"Good morrow, lady," one of the soldiers greets me, standing out in the courtyard in the crisp morning.

I pick up my head from my focus on my arm, straightening out my gauntlets and rebuckling them so that they fit right against my forearms.

"Good morrow, soldier," I return and give a little smile.

Karnei chose his ten best men, and we all have gathered in the courtyard for a match. They're dressed simply in shirts, vests, and breeches as the men on the borders would be. I, on the other hand, am dressed in a tunic and slacks and a thick, leather vest laced up firmly. I wear gauntlets on my forearms and cuisses on my thighs as well as greaves on my calves. The rest is left open to allow for movement.

I am smaller than the men facing me, for each is a tall and broad man, like my Alistair. I will need my speed and fluidity to best them.

"Well, gentlemen," I say, unsheathing my sword and tossing away the scabbard so that it does not interfere. I inspect the blade and then look back to the ten men. "Shall we begin?"

"Och," one man says, rubbing the back of his neck, a pitchfork in hand. "I'm nay sure aboot this, missus. We'd nay want t'hurt ye." He glances behind him to where Karnei stands at one of the entryways to the courtyard.

Many others have gathered as well. Servants and peasants alike fill the windows and doorways looking out into the courtyard, having come to witness what they think will be a very quick fight.

I grin at the man and reply, "What a gentleman. Well, let us begin and leave the hurting part to me, eh? Don't you worry about it."

The man looks a bit patronized, which was partly my intention, so he sighs and the ten men all separate a bit, standing by. There are two pitchforks, four hand-spades, three hunting knives, and two men with no weapon at all.

I survey them all carefully, taking in weapon and strength and size. I decide to go for the unarmed ones first. I charge at them, and they hold their ground. They have nothing to shield them from my sword, and knowledge of that seems to register pretty quickly, for their eyes widen. I do not, however, use my sword for more than a distraction. I've no desire to kill these men and nor would I like to injure them beyond incapacitating them.

The first sidesteps my blade, and I use it to temporarily hold the other off while I rush the first, my rapier wicked sharp for being such a thin and slight blade.

The first man seeks to engage in a hand-to-hand fight, but if I'm seeking to destroy a village, I don't care for a fair fight.

I recoil my blade and slam the hilt into the man's temple, knocking him down.

Another comes up behind me with the hunting knife.

I sidestep him and dodge an attack, flicking out my blade to slice along the back of his arm.

He drops the knife, and I kick it away, rushing him and knocking him back, slamming his head into the ground to daze him. Some of these boys are going to wake up sick as dogs tomorrow. Ah well.

Three more go down this way. There are too many of them for them to all engage me at once. With five men remaining, only two of whom have actual weapons, they quickly discard their blades and shift forms.

I smirk, having expected this. They feel better in their bear forms, but Alistair taught me more than he realized on the way home from Marine. I am not stronger than them, but I am faster, and I know their weaknesses.

I call up my fire, for it will torch them faster than it will the Crystalice, and it is the greatest advantage I have.

They all five take a step back as flames lick the ends of my hair and along and tip of my blade. But it does not deter them for long, and soon one of them charges me. But he hesitates.

I smirk and start running. I dart behind one of them, sliding under his legs, and I cut the tendons in the back of his legs. He gives a cry of pain and hits the ground. The healers can use *Magik* to repair the tendons, so I am not overly concerned for them.

Another bear goes down this way, and soon I am left with three opponents, standing up in the cool autumn air and breathing a bit hard. "If I were a Levosa," I say, "You'd all be dead by now. Do not forget that they can fly."

They stand back and I watch them as they begin calling upon their earth *Magik*. The ground beneath me begins to shake and rumble, and the cobblestone cracks, the earth splitting.

I leap out of the way but vines shoot up from the earth, grabbing my wrists and my legs, holding me back. Snarling, I call upon my fire, lighting myself aflame and watching the vines burn and wither away from my form with a hiss. It slows me down enough, however, and the earth begins to pile up around me, a great dome of mud and earth forming over me.

I stand back in the darkness, my feline eyes adjusting to the low light. They think to have me captured. I scoff. Calling upon my fire again, I focus my flames upon a specific point of the clay dome, baking it until it becomes hard and brittle. The wall begins to crack beneath my fire, and I rush it with a shout of rage, kicking the side of the wall and sending it crumbling as I step out in the light of the day.

From the corner of my eye, I see the Duke of Karnei standing by with his hands folded in front of him and a frown on his face.

I smirk. I'm bleeding from my arm where one of the bears scratched me, and it throbs a bit, but at least it isn't my dominant arm, so it won't slow me down as much. I watch the three in front of me. It would be so much easier just to kill them, but I don't want to do that. Doesn't Karnei realize by now that had I wanted to kill these men, I could have done so and been finished with this much sooner? The Levosa won't hesitate.

Fire. Let's finish this with fire. They won't thank me for burning them, but it can be healed. I summon up my fire again and launch it at the nearest bear who is too slow to get away in time. It catches his heel, and soon, the whole leg is engulfed.

He roars and stops to try and put out the fire.

I rush the other two, cutting one in the groin to make him drop to all fours and then knocking him down, slamming the hilt of my blade into the side of his head to confuse and disorient him. The last one knocks me back off of his comrade, and I hit the ground hard, skidding across the dirt. I jump up and snarl, my right side throbbing and fairly certain that one of my bones is fractured at the least.

He growls back at me, giving a roar.

I charge him, and he rushes me on all fours, teeth out and ready to devour me.

He's forgotten his code. He's scared. He's angry. If he gets ahold of me, he will kill me.

I light myself aflame, so that when he comes close enough to me, he reels back at the sudden burst of fire on his muzzle and chest. When he lurches up, I strike, slicing his throat with my rapier. The sword isn't enough to kill him, but the neck bleeds badly when he crashes back down, and he roars at me in anger. I scream back at him, and with panting breaths, he considers me and then bares his teeth, growling. I brandish my sword, and he growls a low and rumbling sound before taking a few steps back and bowing his head.

He's come to his senses, and he knows that he cannot fight me without one of us killing the other.

I turn to Karnei, panting. I am dirty and my whole body aches. Part of me is bleeding and I think my arm is broken. Moreover, I now have to ride all the way to the south of Flora. All to prove a damn point. I am angry. I am tired. And I am afraid for Alistair.

"Do you see now! I am merely one woman. Had they a mind to kill me, I would be dead. You *cannot* cripple your men this way. The Levosa women won't hold back. They'll kill. They'll do whatever it takes to protect their own. You can't fight them like this."

Karnei watches me. I wonder if he will argue, try to call some sort of foul for me not actually defeating the last man or for the several who are still conscious but just a bit too dazed and unwilling to fight, their ears most likely still ringing.

Finally, the man gives an irritated sigh and snarls, "Someone bring me my parchment and seal! As of now, the Flora Code against killing women and smaller enemies on the battlefield is revoked!" To me, he mutters, "If the Levosa women mean to kill my men, then they can very well die for it."

His eyes seemed sad at those words, but a wager is a wager, and he barks at me, "You are as damn near insufferable as your husband." But he gives out a long, slow sigh. It is hard to do something against what he has believed in for so long. But still, he gives me a tired smile.

Laughing, I bow at the waist and say, "I shall relay the compliment, my lord."

Karnei heads inside, grumbling.

I find one of the servants and say, "I need my horse and I need a healer at once. I must go."

"Aye, lady. As soon as I get these men patched."

"Now," I snarl at her. "There is a battle on the borderlands, girl. I need to get moving this instant."

She frowns at me, wanting to tend to the soldiers first, but the one nearest her puts a hand on her arm and smiles, saying something quietly to her. Then she sighs and turns, hurrying off to do as I demanded.

I head inside, finally catching my breath, and the healer meets me in my room. I strip, and she checks my injuries. "A few bruised ribs an' ye'll need t'bandage yer arm—tis soundly broke. Two week's bedrest an' ye'll nay use that arm for at least a moonth," she tells me, cleaning my claw-stricken arm and stitching the claw marks closed before wrapping it tightly.

"I can't," I tell her as she wraps up my chest tightly. I wince, hissing out a breath and clenching my teeth as she works. "I've got to get to Gaelen to take the news to Alistair."

"Sommon else can do't," the woman complains, glaring up at me.

I glare back at her. "They'll take too long. Besides, he's *my* mate. I'll go."

The woman mutters under her breath and finishes bandaging me up. I hurt all over but at least I'll be sitting. The ride won't be fun, but I'll live.

I start pulling on my clothes again and strapping on the armor parts I wear, buckling them firmly. I don't plan on fighting the Levosa, but I'm not fool enough to think they won't attack me if they think I'm a threat.

With my clothes and armor fitted, I leave the room, marching down the hall to Karnei's study where he scratches on the parchment and then sits back, placing his seal upon the official revocation. I smile softly, feeling relief wash over me as I stand in the doorway.

He glances up at me and then rolls up the parchment and puts it in a sleeve for me to carry. He hands it to me. "Be careful, duchess. You like to jump in deep waters."

"I can swim—" actually, I can't "—Thank you, Duke Karnei." I incline my head, taking the sleeve.

I turn and leave him there in his study, hurrying down the hall and out into the courtyard once more.

"Duchess!" someone calls for me, and I turn my head to see a squire pulling along a sleek, brown stallion. "Duchess Maeghdra!" He reaches me, breathing a bit hard, and he grins. "Here, missus. He's all saddled and ready. Fastest horse in Karnei."

"Thank you," I tell him and throw myself on the back of the horse. My side aches in pain, and now that the rush of battle is fading, I can feel my wounds.

"Duchess Scarlet!" Krei calls, running up to my horse. He had been watching the fight and probably grinding his teeth the whole time. Any chance I had of watering down the fight to Alistair is now completely gone. My husband will be right cross with me once Krei tells him what happened. At my side, he calls, "I'll go with you!"

"Then mount up!" I order. "I'm not waiting!"

I pull my steed away from him and leave him to quickly find and mount a horse for the travels. I walk the horse out of the town to keep from trampling anyone, and by the time I have cleared the bustling city and am out on the open roads, Krei pulls up to my side with his horse. I smirk at him and snap the reigns, calling out to my horse, and he takes off. The stallion is sleek and powerful, and he carries me swiftly down the roads, clamoring towards Gaelen. I feel an urgency to race, but I'd likely kill my horse doing that, and well before I reach Gaelen. I will have to suffice with what I have.

A Few Days Later

Krei and I stop only at night, and only for a few hours to sleep and rest and heal, watering our horses and feeding them. The first two nights, we were able to find an inn to shelter us and care for our horses. It is not well for me to be out in the cold air. Already, I feel sick. My body is heavy, and my stomach churns and begins rejecting food. Even hot stews and broths and fresh, warm bread have lost their taste to me. I miss home.

The third night, however, we are nowhere near a suitable village, now most of the lands consisting of farms and fields all spread out across the countryside. The next major village will be where Alistair is, camped out with his men at the border. So Krei and I hunker down in the darkness without a fire to keep warm, not wanting to alert bandits or Levosa as to our presence.

On the last morning when I wake, I am sick, voiding my stomach of its contents and shivering miserably. I miss the hearthfire in Maeghdra. I miss the warmth of Alistair's bed. But I have been on longer and harder journeys than this, and there is no time to complain. So I get up and pack up the bags and mount up again, my arm burning and my stomach aching in pain.

"Almost there," I rasp to Krei who watches me warily in the scant morning light. "Let's hurry."

We spur our horses again, but they are tired and not as fast as when they were fresh out of Karnei. Still, they struggle to keep up and maintain a good pace, bringing us into the Flora camp shortly after high sun.

The camp isn't much. It once was a village, for there are remnants of homes and shops and even an inn and stable. Great pikes of a wall have been put up around the southwest exterior of the village, the flag of Gaelen and of Flora flying proudly from the pikes. There are horses tied up to a post not far, and the soldiers remaining are all dirty and tired in appearance.

Flora soldiers scatter as we ride in, stopping our horses and dismounting.

I slump to my feet miserably as I hear my husband's powerful voice roar, "Who's come! D'ye nay realize we're in th'middle of a war!—Krei?" He stops at the sight of Krei after breaking through the others who have gathered around, curious as to the news we bring.

I feel his eyes even before I see him. Straightening slowly, I turn to face the crowd, not quite able to stand up straight.

"*Scarlet?*" Alistair's voice is low and warning.

I've never heard of him speak to me in such a way, and to make it worse, I am slumped over pitifully with my hands on my knees while trying not to be sick in front of all of these men. I wince a bit at the sound of my name, and when I find his green eyes, they are locked on me with a mixture of terror and rage.

I look up at him with a tired smile, my face sketched in dirt and my wild, red hair tied back at the nape of my neck. "Hello, mate," I greet warmly.

He's glaring at me, his whole body tense, and I am sure his brain spinning and trying to decide just what to do with me.

I know that he is angry with me for coming, worried about me. I hold up a hand to pause whatever barrage of complaints he might have before grabbing the sleeve from my belt and opening it, pulling out the parchment from inside and holding it out to him.

"The Duke of Karnei…signed this. Obviously it'll need your seal and Gaelen's as well but…I assumed we could go ahead and move forward with this since Karnei was the only one in your way."

He takes the sleeve from me, scowling at me for a moment before pulling out the rolled parchment and unraveling it. His eyes scan across the fresh ink and clean parchment, then once more, and again. Finally, he rolls it up and hands it to a man standing by. "Give this to th'lairds up in the house," he says, and the man nods and hurries off with it.

Alistair just looks to me, watching me with wary eyes. "How d'ye…?"

"A wager," I say and grin at him. "Karnei loves a good wager. And he loves a good fight." I wince. Of all the things I should *not* have said…

His eyebrows shoot up, and he snaps, "Who d'ye fight?"

I wince. "Eh…I didn't catch their names."

"Their?" He snarls, grabbing me by both shoulders and damn near lifting me clear off the ground.

My stomach rolls, and I consider him to be a lucky man that I don't lose my stomach contents right in his face.

"How many!"

I look up at him and frown, but I am trying not to smile. Alistair is never angry with me, and I have never seen him like this. I do not know why it amuses me so. Perhaps I am merely tired. But I sigh and laugh softly and say, "Love, is it really that important right now?"

"Ten," Krei tells him, quite loudly and clearly while he starts wearily dragging our tired animals off.

"Traitor…" I mutter, casting a surly look his way.

Alistair doesn't even look at Krei. *"Ten!"* he roars at me, green eyes piercing mine, hands still gripping my shoulders and shaking me just a bit.

Goddess, I really am going to be sick…

Chapter Forty Two
Alistair

A Southwest Bordertown in Gaelen, Flora

I have never been angrier in all of my life. I specifically told her not to come. The Levosa are vicious and dangerous, and if they get ahold of her, it won't matter if she is Inferno or not. They will kill her.

Scarlet is my one mate. My only mate. Moreover, she is…she is her. I cannot lose her. I refuse.

But she seems to throw away her safety and her life as if it were meaningless, as if there are not several people in this world who would be devastated by losing her.

It infuriates me!

"A…Alistair…?" She suddenly looks a little less confident, and it's then I notice that her warm complexion is a bit pale and sallow. She doesn't seem well. "I really…would like…to…lay—" She doesn't finish her sentence. Instead, her eyes grow large and she suddenly jerks against my hands.

It's my own fault for holding onto her that she suddenly empties her stomach contents all over my nice boots, her body retching. I watch her with concern until she finishes

She gives a little sigh and wipes her mouth with the back of her hand. She must have really ridden herself hard the way down here. She looks like she barely slept, and I'm sure this late autumn weather is taking a toll on her. She should be inside by the hearth, not riding on horseback across country. Daft wee lassie.

"Ye ken these…are my favorite boots," I tell her, and that wins a half-hearted chuckle.

She looks up at me and smiles softly, dark circles under her eyes.

I tease her for her sake, but I am still trembling with anger. That is exactly why I dare not act on it. "I'll get ye back for this little escapade later, my lass. Come and rest."

She smiles softly and nods, and I let go of her shoulders to put an arm around her instead. Even with clothes between us, I can tell that she's cold, and I draw her a little nearer. My daft wee lassie…

"I won't…fight the Levosa," she says softly, her voice a bit mumbled. Behind me, I hear the shouts and cheers of the men. Word will spread fast. The Levosa have no chance now. I smile just a bit and look back to my lady with warmth in my eyes. "…if they see an Inferno attacking them…it could be very poor for my people."

"I ken it, sweetheart." I lead her to one of the fires burning and nudge her down. "Go ahead and *Shift*. Ye're stronger in that form."

She looks up at me, and for a moment, I am concerned with how dull and tired her eyes seem. I hope it is merely exhaustion that plagues her. She sighs then and starts unclasping her armaments, letting them fall away to the ground. She pulls off her vest and wool shirt before my mind catches up and I shout out in alarm, "Oy!" and grab a blanket, covering her from sight of the others. She looks up at me and gives a tired, teasing little smile before pulling off her cotton shirt and dropping her slacks and stockings before *Shifting* forms.

She gives a low groan which fades into a soft roar, her muscles ripping and the bones popping and reforming. I hear them snap like twigs, a sick, squishing sound resonating as her muscles reform and attach. Fur bursts out of her skin, covering the pale, naked flesh with a thick undercoat and her brilliant golden and red pelt. She sighs then and crawls into the bonfire, curling up around the logs. I smile a bit and grab a few more logs, leaning them against her to spread the fire over her. She cracks open a yellow eye to look at me and then sighs and falls sound asleep, her purr harmonizing with the roar of the fire.

I shake my head and turn away from her to head into camp. The men have started pouring out what's left of the ale and toasting to each other. They know as well as I do: the dawn will bring victory. The battle is already decided. The war will be won now. I glance behind me and smirk. All because of a little, red cat who stood up to a very stubborn old man.

I chuckle to myself and join in the merriment of my men. Laughing and clapping their backs as they toast their mugs.

"Oy! Master Maeghdra! Where's that mate o'yers?" one man asks.

I grin and say, "She's napping in the fire. Dinna fret. She'll be happy to dance and cheer with ye when we get back."

"Hail!" a few of the men cry, and one of them pushes a mug of ale into my hand. I laugh uproariously with them and join in a few songs and tales before changing out the watch and ordering the rest to bed.

At dawn, we rise.

The Next Morning

We hear the Levosa before we see them. Their shrill, fowl cries echo in my dreams and the nightmares of my men. We will never forget those piercing shrieks and calls and whistles. They descend upon the town just before sunrise. This harem is led by two females—two harpies, each about a third of my size and half of Scarlet's. But although they are smaller, their talons are sharp and powerful, and their grip can crush bones and skulls. Many more follow, and they darken the sky with the span of nearly a hundred wings.

Their assurance of victory almost draws me to laughter. My night watch engages them first while the rest of my men jump up and grab their blades, joining in. There is no hesitation. Arrows pour into the sky while my men unsheathe their swords and cleanse them in the flesh of the Levosa women, soaking them in the red blood of falcons and sparrows and hawks. There are cries from the women, shouts of alarm, and as half of their harem is swiftly cut down without mercy, the siren overhead gives a low and guttural cry, and the Levosa quickly break away from my men, dropping their weapons and shifting forms, taking to the sky. They leave behind their weapons and armor, their clothing, everything, taking to the skies as we chase them with arrows and spears over the border to their homeland.

"Set up a small guard in this area. We'll need to leave troops here for the next few weeks to be sure they dinna return. Send a messenger to the rest o'the border towns first," I say to my captains as we head back into the heart of the town.

"Sir!" they chime in disharmony before heading off to do as I have instructed.

I can see the little bonfire where my bride slumbers. It is smaller than it was last night, but there is still a pitiful flame crawling over a small set of logs and the sleeping tigress. As I approach, however, over the sound of the fire popping and snapping, I hear another sound. My tigress no longer purrs. Instead, I hear a low growl of a sound that every few notes shifts into a whine and whimper.

"Scarlet?" I call, feeling a sinking sensation in the pit of my stomach. Is she still unwell from her travels? I crouch down by her head to find her eyes clenched and her lips drawn up in a sneer. "*Scarlet.*"

She makes a hacking noise and then cracks open one yellow eye to look at me, giving a groan and a soft whine. She lifts her head and then collapses it again, letting it roll to the side.

Something is wrong. She is not merely tired. She is unwell, and I cannot tell by the sight of her how badly. Scarlet is not one to complain. Even in her sickness in winter, she curls up by the fire and glares at me or hisses at others who disturb her. Even in her most miserable state, she glares or growls or bares her teeth at the least. I have never seen her whimper and roll her head to the side, and as I think this, she flinches from something and begins dry heaving for several minutes before collapsing again with a pained moan.

"Scout!" I call to a nearby soldier. He scrambles over. "Get me a horse and cart. I need to take my lady home. She's very ill."

"Aye, sir!" he says and scurries off at once.

I do not wish to leave my men here until I am certain that the Levosa are gone, but with the new edict, they can fight now, and there are more than enough to deal with the attacking harems. I do not trust another to take my mate home, and even if I did, I would still worry constantly until assurance of her safety and good health reached me. I will take her myself.

"Easy, sweetheart," I murmur, reaching for the tigress and burying my fingers in the fur at her neck, rubbing gently. Her fur is hot to the touch, but most of the fire is sizzling under her belly. I rub her neck and pet her head, scratching behind her ears and down her jaw.

She makes a pitiful sound and rolls her head to the side.

My heart twists in my chest.

The man returns with a pair of horses and a cart, and I stand to go and gather a few blankets, padding the bottom of the cart and then hauling up the giant cat, getting her into the cart with some effort.

She tries to help, crawling up into the cart and dragging herself to the blankets before laying down. She curls up and shivers, hacking again as I cover her with more blankets.

"Easy, lass," I whisper, crouching beside her and petting her head again.

She groans.

"Easy, sweetheart. I'll get ye home…just rest, lassie. Ye damned fool, tearing through countryside like ye did."

She coughs.

"I've half a mind to paddle ye when we get back."

She makes a hack of a sound, something I suppose is a scoff or a laugh.

I smile softly. It's enough to encourage me for now. I leave her in the cart and go around to the horses, patting their necks and climbing up in the front of the cart and grabbing the reigns.

"I'll be back as soon as I can," I say to one of my captains when he approaches.

"Aye, sir. Take care o'yer lassie. We owe her much."

I incline my head to him and snap the reigns, clicking my tongue to get the horses moving. They toss their heads and start stomping their feet into the ground, pulling the rickety cart across the dirt road and heading back to Maeghdra.

Along the way, we stop at local inns and taverns. I try to coax Scarlet into eating, but she refuses, or when I do manage to get something into her, it always comes back up again.

Sometimes she *Shifts* forms into a woman once again and wraps herself in blankets to sit beside me on the cart. She leans her cheek against me, and I am startled by the grayness of her skin and the hollow look in her eyes.

Looking away from her and back to the road, I grumble, "I'm vexed with ye, wife."

She does not stir from my shoulder, and merely sighs and says, "I know."

Her response only annoys me more, and I do not quite know what to do with her. "I love ye," I growl, as if I can somehow communicate to her the frustration and anger and fear welling up inside of me without respite.

She opens her eyes and I feel her cheek shift as she looks up at me, but then she closes her eyes and sinks her head down again. "I know."

What took her I am sure only a few days on swift horseback takes us almost a week to return. We stop every night at local inns or at the houses of lairds and soldiers with whom I am familiar. We are always welcomed and treated with care, particularly my bride. Thus far, the only thing I have found that she can eat or drink is a mint tea, and upon this discovery, a soldier's wife made a large, boiling pot of it and set it in the cart to take with us, and I wake her often to give her a mug of it to sip. With it, she is able to eat a little more as well. It is not much, but it is more than I am used to getting into her.

We reach the town outside of my home a few hours after dawn. The townsfolk are already awake and going about their days. The baker has fresh bread and pastries filling the quarter with a sweet smell. The butcher is hacking away at a fresh kill, cutting it up between grunts and grumbles and setting it aside. The shop keepers sweep out their shops, and the inn keeper starts to wake his patrons.

The blacksmith is the first to notice us, and he comes hurrying out of the building to greet us. "Master Alistair!" he calls, coming up beside the cart. Scarlet is sleeping in the cart, curled up around the hot cast iron pot that still holds the warmth of the hot tea. I think that she is too tired to *Shift* back to her feline form even though the fur would bring her more warmth.

"Oy. Loghan."

"Master Alistair, we've heard th'news! Great blessings, milord!"

I laugh a bit and smile. "Aye an' aye. But I'm in sommat of a hurry, Loghan. Find the medicine woman. I need her at the manor."

Loghan seems concerned and asks, "Is yer mam ill, milord?"

"No, lad. My wife." I gesture back to the cart.

Loghan peers over the walls of the cart to see a small, red-headed woman curled up under blankets with soft breath and her brows pinched together in discomfort. "Ack! Poor lassie. I'll fetch 'er right away, sir!"

I incline my head and continue on, greeting the townsfolk politely but with insistence that I cannot stay, quickly making my way back home.

In the courtyard, I pull the cart to a stop and hop out, going to the back and collecting Scarlet and her mass of blankets. She lays weakly against me, murmuring something softly. I carry her inside, upstairs to our bedroom where I lay her down.

It does not take long for the medicine woman to arrive at the manor, and she shuffles into the room, shooing me out so that she can speak with Scarlet and examine her.

I kiss my lover's brow and murmur gently to her. She smiles and catches my lips in a little kiss. Her lips are cold, and it frightens me to my core. I leave her side with great hesitation, shutting the door to our room reluctantly and giving a heavy sigh. I lean back against the door, waiting for a bit, but I cannot sit still.

She is such a fool! She did not need to push herself so hard over this! We could have lasted another day, another week. She rushed herself through her travels and through her healing. She's driven herself right into the ground, and damn if it won't kill her!

With a snarl of frustration and fear, I leave the hall and go downstairs to the hearth where my mother eats and talks quietly with Karnei's mate. I give a curt grimace and incline my head to both of them before sitting down at the table as well.

"Alistair, eat," me mam scolds. "Scarlet will be fine. She always gets like this when it's cold. She's probably just exhausted. I'm sure with some rest and a hot fire, she'll be just fine."

"I'm sure ye're right," I tell my mother, but my heart is still pounding and my stomach feels sick. I take some bread and break off a few pieces, stuffing them into my mouth as the two older women talk. The bread is tasteless and falls like small stones into my stomach, offering me no comfort.

Nearly an hour passes before I hear my door open and shut upstairs. I nearly bolt up and run up the stairs, but I force myself to remain seated and hold my brass mug with both hands. I watch as the old woman makes her way down the stairs and steps into the dining hall.

"Moirah," me mam greets and smiles gently. "How fairs my lady daughter?"

"Ack," the woman barks, stairs creaking under her as she takes her dear time getting down to us. "Fine, fine. Dinna let the daft lassie go racin though th'country may more. She's worn to th'core."

I heave a great sigh of relief and sink into my chair when my shaking legs refuse to hold me up. "That is all then?" I ask as the old woman pulls up a chair across from me and takes a seat. "She's merely exhausted?"

The medicine woman gives me a sharp look. "'Tis what I said, boy? Nay. She's nay merely exhausted. If twas all twas wrong with her, I'da said so." She mutters to herself, and the hope that had once been spreading through my chest now sinks sourly in my stomach. "She's expecting, she is."

I just stare at her for a moment as me mam grins and laughs warmly.

"Marvelous! Oh what news!" Lady Karnei reaches over and grabs her hands, squeezing them affectionately.

I look to my mother, somewhat numb, feeling both relieved and horrified and not knowing why I feel either. "I-I'd nay understand," I say and look back to the medicine woman. "What's she expecting?" I'll blame my lack of sleep and prolonged fear for my wife for my addled brain.

Moirah gives me another annoyed look and says, "Art daft, boy? She's expectin a bairn!"

"A...bairn?" I repeat. A child? *My* child?

Beside me, me mam laughs at my suffering and touches my arm. "Alistair, close your mouth and go see your mate. Shoo."

She pushes me half out of my seat, and I stumble up, my chair scraping against the stone floor as I get up and look over at her. Mam just grins at me, and I stare back before my eyes go to the banister where my bride sleeps.

Getting up from the table, I move to the stairs, climbing them hesitantly back to my room. Beyond the door I push open, Scarlet lays back on the bed, awake and staring out the window, one hand resting on the little tigress at her side. When did Zsoka get home? And how did the little scamp sneak past me and up the stairs?

When I enter, Scarlet looks over at me, and her golden eyes are shining and soft. My breath leaves me in a rush at the sight of her, and I swallow hard, my heavy feet carrying me slowly inside to her.

The sight of her golden eyes clouds over, and when she blinks, twin tears roll down her cheeks.

I suck in a breath, going to her. I take her other hand and push my fingers between hers, linking our hands together as my other hand reaches up to cup her chin. "Tis amiss, sweetheart?" I plead, my voice soft and a bit hoarse.

"I'm terrified," she whispers, looking up at my eyes.

I study her for a moment, her face, her trembling lips, her wide eyes. I sigh with relief and smile softly. "Ack... aye...I think it's contagious."

She laughs, a small and pitiful sound, but it makes me smile, and I scoot her and the little one over to crawl into bed with her, kicking off my filthy boots and laying down beside her. I gather her up into my hold and lay my brow on her forehead.

She cries. I had not known what to expect from her. Sure, I had known that eventually she would be with child, but I hadn't expected so soon, and I sure as hell hadn't expected her to cry.

I'm not sure why she cries either. Does she regret conceiving a child by me? Does she fear for her health? Does she simply not feel well? Why does she cry?

As if sensing my own thoughts, she murmurs softly, "I cannot lose another..." And then I remember her story of the little babe she had carried when she was barely more than a girl, the one she had lost when her first husband died.

"Shhh," I murmur, kissing her brow. "Ye'll do fine, lassie. Dinna fret. Ye'll do just fine..."

She cries quietly for a while before she quiets and murmurs softly, "The woman said my body is trying to cool itself to protect the half-Flora babe...that's why I am so tired and sick."

"Ah..." I rub her arm slowly, a sinking feeling in my stomach. It is my fault she is so ill. Had her mate been an Inferno, she would not be nearly as sick as she is carrying my

Flora child. "I'm sorry…" I whisper, nestling my head against hers.

"Mmm," she murmurs, a soft, little sound as she sighs, fading slowly into slumber. "I am not…" She yawns and then sighs, she and the little Zsoka asleep by my side.

Chapter Forty Three
Scarlet

One Month Later
Maeghdra Manor, Flora

I stare at the letter in my hands, and I can feel my fingers trembling. Usually, a delivery from the courier brings me great joy, for it usually means that I have at least one letter to read and to spend time responding to—anything to fill my dull hours. I cannot leave my bed without assistance, and I cannot crawl into the hearth lest I possibly overheat the babe. This all leaves me in a miserable state where I cannot get well, and all I can do is wait for the remaining six or seven months for the child to be born.

I enjoy receiving letters. My favorites are from Alistair. He writes to me almost constantly, for although it is late autumn, since the edict concerning killing women in battle was passed, he has been quite busy. Karnei was not the only one who opposed the edict. Alistair has had to play politics much more than he enjoys doing, and he has also had to secure the borders with Gaelen. Moreover, the religious faction in Flora is in a fit. Since our chief deity is a female, Chelyah, many consider it blasphemy to kill a woman for any reason, but they held their peace about men killing women in self-defense. Now for Flora to wage war on the female harems of Levosa…it has been quite unsettling.

But I receive other letters as well. Gabriel still writes to me. He did not congratulate me on my marriage, saying such words would be hollow. He expressed only love for Alistair and I both and a bitterness that he asked forgiveness for. Even so, he still writes to us both, and his last letter promised that Enté would soon be joining us. Gabriel is quite insistent that Crystalice is not safe for the child and wants him in Maeghdra with me and with his *Senai.*

The letter in my hands, however, is not from Alistair, nor Gabriel, nor Dena. It is not one of my usual letters from Freya or even Lady Karnei. It is not signed, merely addressed.

On the front is written: *Knight Protector Scar*

There is no one now who calls me by that name, and it is such a foreign title. Gently, I run the pad of my fingertip across the dark brown ink that has been scratched onto the envelope, smudged and splotched in places. A shuddering breath escapes me, and I can hear my heart pounding in my chest, my golden eyes watching the envelope with caution.

Finally, I turn it over and inspect the seal. As I expected, the seal bares the mark of the Inferno Royal Crest. There are very few who are allowed to use the royal crest seal—the king and queen and their children, my father—the War Lord — and the Knight Protectors. I do not know which of them writes to me, and I find myself quite hesitant to discover it.

I break the seal with a little knife and remove the parchment within.

Knight Protector Scar

    First, permit me to apologize for the delay in my correspondence. Until recently, I was unsure as to your state of being or to your state of mind. From the moment I returned home and declared that Prince Gabriel Jan'tel had taken you on horseback, your father had you pronounced dead and established that any attempt of invading the Crystalice city for you would result only in a massacre of our best soldiers.

When we discovered that you were alive, it was with the information—which we now believe to be grossly falsified—that you were the prince's consort. It was only recently that it was decided you were neither spy, but neither were you trying to escape, at which point we established contact with Prince Gabriel Jan'tel at the border several months ago.

Allow me, again, to apologize for my severe delay in attempting to contact you in some way, Knight Protector. Let me also apologize for my bluntness, for I must ask: are you still with us?

I have heard that you are in Flora—which is susceptible to our fire—and moreover that you are staying as a guest. Now, I sincerely doubt the true meaning of the term 'guest', but I have heard rumors from our merchants that the Duke of Maeghdra has married an Inferno ward of the Ice Prince's.

I sincerely hope these rumors are false. For there is no Inferno in Flora but you. If this has been done against your will, make no mistake that we will have vengeance for you. But if it is by your consent that you have abandoned us and fled to Flora, then I will ask—no, I will demand—that you answer for yourself, Knight Protector Scar.

Have your messenger send a letter through the southeastern road. I will have men waiting to receive your word.

Knight Protector Jacob Kah'reen na La'sar Inferno

I smile despite myself. So, Jacob has become a Knight Protector after all. Sighing, I lean my head back and stare up at my ceiling, my breath slow and deep, and a tightness in my chest. What can I tell him to make him understand? What can I say? I cannot fight again. I won't. I will not take up my sword against the Cerulean, nor the Flora. I will not aid them against the Inferno...but I cannot fight them.

I close my eyes, feeling tears burn my lids and scorch my cheeks as they roll down to my jaw. My chest shudders with emotion, and I think quietly to myself. How many Inferno have fallen because I was not there to protect them? How many of my dancers' husbands and sons will never come home because I let live the men who ran them through? I clench my teeth together and turn my head away from the parchment laying lifeless in my hands, my golden eyes going to the window.

But I cannot...

Every time I try to think on it...to summon the desire to fight, to kill...it isn't there. I cannot look at a man with white hair and blue eyes and see anything—anyone—except for Gabriel and Enté and Kale and even Claque. Claque, the man who took my own brother from me. The man who, when he thinks no one is looking, will watch his now-bride with a gentle smile and will often tease her with slight, almost unnoticeable gestures. He'll tug gently on her hair or slightly poke her little waist. I've seen him smile only for her, and I remember his face the day of their wedding when his beloved was in danger, that cold and ruthless determination to do whatever necessary to protect her.

I cannot. I will not. I won't take him from her. I will not destroy that.

With a heavy sigh, I take a piece of parchment from the table by my bed. Slowly and carefully, I pull the stopper from the inkwell and set it at the edge of my table. I take my quill and dip it—once, twice—inside the bottle and then gently tap the nib on the rim of the jar. My eyes go to the blank page, and I drink in a slow and soft breath before touching the tip of my nib to the parchment...

My beloved Jacob,

*You cannot know the great joy—and the great sorrow—
it brings me to read your letter...*

Chapter Forty Four
Scarlet

Three Months Later
Maeghdra Manor, Flora

I was at last permitted to go downstairs. I cannot possibly stay cooped up in that room a moment longer. Of course, now that my stomach has actually grown and rounded some, I am in better spirits. If I am still and all is quiet, I can even feel my little one move. It's a very slight feeling, almost like bubbles where my stomach should be. But I can feel the child stir.

I was never able to feel my first little one, and the thought of it both saddens and relieves me. I cannot, now that I have felt my babe stir and move within my belly, imagine the sorrow of losing him. I could not endure such pain again. And so, although it is dull and vexing, I do as I am told and obey my midwife's orders.

Even so, I am deeply relieved that she finally permitted me to be moved downstairs so long as someone was with me. It took a long time for me to get to the bottom of the stairs. I have become very weak and very tired. Only recently have I begun to really eat as much as an Inferno woman should. I became so thin and frail in the last few months, and my body continues to cool itself for the child's sake. It was nearly to the point that Freya wrote to Alistair and bade him return home for fear that I and the child would perish.

But the past few weeks have brought with it a renewed appetite, and Cali has been shoving food in front of me every hour that I am awake. I feel guilty for worrying everyone so and for putting them through such effort, but when I consider that much of the effort is mostly for my child—Alistair's child—then I do not mind. I will let them pamper me all they wish for the little one's sake.

"Are you sure it's not infected?" Zsoka asks, sitting beside me at the table. She eyes my stomach warily, and I laugh.

"I will become even larger than this!" I tell her, leaning down in front of her face.

Her eyes get wide as if she cannot believe it.

I am really not even all that large. Winter has come and brought with it my usual moodiness and ill temper. Zsoka is frequently in bed with me as well, but for the first time, her presence produces sweating from me as my body tries to cool itself, and I am forced to put blankets between us.

"I'll never have babies," Zsoka says resolutely, turning her attention back to the hearty stew Cali provided for us. I smile and tear off a piece of bread, dipping it in the stew and then popping it into my mouth with a little smile. I must still eat small bites and slowly, but I am happy to finally enjoy food once more.

All at once, there is the sound of horses and clattering wheels in the courtyard, and we lift our heads. My heart skips a beat at the thought of Alistair returning home unexpectedly. I have not seen him more than a week here or there in the past several months.

"I'll get it!" Zsoka cries, scrambling out of her chair and going over to the door. She'll regret her decision as soon as she remembers how cold it is outside, but I smile softly from my place and watch her.

I'm not supposed to get up unless absolutely necessary, so I stay seated where I am, feeling useless and glad that pregnancy is not a permanent condition.

"Enté!" Zsoka cries, and my head snaps up. The little black-haired girl stands at the doorway. Outside, it is dark and cold, but at least it has stopped snowing. The wind howls against the back of the manor, but the courtyard is mostly spared.

"Inside! Inside!" scolds a familiar voice, and a plump, old Flora woman pushes her way into the manor, bundled up against the cold with a little Crystalice prince following behind, not in the least bit bothered—although he does seem a bit like he has just woken from a nap.

My lips stretch into a wide smile at the sight of him and Heather, and I scoot back my chair to try and stand.

"Dinna dare, lassie!" Heather scolds, glaring at me from across the room. She gives me a pointed look, and I laugh softly, sinking back into my chair.

"Cara!" Enté cries, catching sight of me and flying across the room to my side.

I laugh and receive him there.

He nuzzles his face into my side and wraps his arms around me as best he can while I am in chair.

I scoot my chair back so that he can hug me, and he looks at me with gleaming, blue eyes and a large smile spread across his face.

"I have missed you, little one," I tell him, sighing softly and pleased to feel his cold little form against mine. I lean down and stroke his hair, alarmed at how much he is grown.

He looks now like a small boy and less like a large baby. His silver hair is tipped with a shimmering teal color, and I thread my fingers gently through it. It's much longer now and a little shaggy too, curling slightly the way his mother's must have, for Gabriel's hair is mostly straight.

Enté smiles warmly at me and then looks to my stomach, and his eyes grow wider. "You're getting fat!"

I laugh at him and smile warmly. "I am."

He reaches out tentatively and pokes the little, round mound that is my stomach, and I grin at him.

"Soon, you'll be able to feel the child move." He looks up at me with wide eyes and a slightly unnerved expression.

"Ack!" Heather scoffs, moving inside as Zsoka shuts the door behind her. The old woman sighs and makes her way over to the fire to warm herself. "Dinna tell me yer here all 'lone!"

I smile softly and replied, "No, Heather. They've not left me alone. Well, not quite. A woman named Lienna is staying with me. She merely left to make a quick run to the village. She's insisting that I drink a Kjree root tea to help with the sickness. She should be back soon. Until then, Zsoka has been taking wonderful care of me."

Zsoka, who had been pouting and looking quite annoyed at being so easily dismissed as a caretaker, tips up her chin and give a cocky little smirk to Heather.

I hope I haven't taught her that.

Heather looks back at her with a quirked brow and says, "Be careful, lassie, or yer face'll get stook that way."

The child blinks in alarm and straightens up, going over to the fire as well to get warm.

Heather responds with a little smile and then says, "Well, now, where should we tell th'coach t'put our things?"

"Ah!" I can still faintly hear the sounds of men outside with the carriage. "We have extra rooms upstairs. Here, help me up, and I'll show you around."

Heather scoffs at me and says, "Pish tush! I can show meself around. Sit, sit, lassie." She waves me off and smiles softly, going to the door and calling out to the Cerulean servants before heading up the stairs. She could figure out for herself which room to take. Freya would not care regardless. Heather makes her way up the stairs and leads the servants up as well. They bring a few chests and boxes, and Heather directs them as to where to put hers and Enté's things.

"Now then," she says, making her way back down the stairs to me and the children. "I ken ye have yer own midwife, but Gabriel *specifically* said he wanted me to keep after ye. Enté's a boy now. He dinna need'na lookin after. He needs to be helpin."

"I can help," Enté says, looking up at Heather and then at me. "Oh! Oh! Father asked me to help. He gave me this. Said I was in charge of it." Around his waist is strapped a belt and on it, a pouch. He opens it and takes from inside a letter carefully folded inside. He hands it to me, and I smile softly at the familiar script with my name on the front: Knight Protector Scarlet Anita Ruairidh, Duchess of Maeghdra.

I smile gently and turn the envelope over, breaking the seal and pulling out the letter with care.

Dearest Cara,

I hope this letter finds you well. Alistair has written to me often over the past few months, and I know that he is in deep distress over your condition. I must say that news of your pregnancy reached me almost as swiftly as news of your marriage, and I am not quite adept to deal with either. But I can tell you that thought of it brings me only a deep sense of fear for you. If there is anything you or Alistair should need, please ask. I have sent Heather and know that she will do her utmost to protect you and the babe.

Please, Cara…take care of yourself. You are incredibly valuable to many people both here and in Flora. You are also stubborn and occasionally foolish. Take care of yourself and the _child. I will consider that my recompense for you marrying my childhood friend._

I smile softly at the lilt of humor in Gabriel's tone, but although it amuses me, I feel a gentle sorrow in my heart, something painful and lonely. I do not regret choosing to be Alistair's mate, but there is a quiet longing in my soul, one that I will never speak aloud—not to Alistair, nor to myself—that I had been able to stay with Gabriel. So I smile sadly because that is all I can do, and I accept his price for retribution and quietly swear that I will not remind him of the loss he has already suffered with Catherine.

As you can surely see, I have sent with this letter my son, Enté. I know that he will be safe and loved with you. Crystalice has become...very unstable even in your absence. And while there are a great many things that I suspect, there are very few that I am comfortable with writing even in this letter to you. For now, I will say only that I am unwilling to risk his life further by having him remain here.

I have, however, taken your advice and begun to spend more time out in the city with my people. They are anxious because they are so unused to my presence, and there is an air of tension and even hostility or fear when I am near. This troubles me more than I expected, and I am uncertain thus far what to make of it. I have begun expressing my concerns with the council, but again I am met with resistance. I am very near to disbanding the fools all together.

In any event, I am aware that Alistair will be going to Ocarine very soon. I will be meeting with him there for much of the winter. It is unfortunate that you cannot travel with him. The warm weather would benefit you, and I would enjoy your company. I am sorry to take him from you for so long, but there

are things we must discuss concerning our trade relations and
military. Please take care while he is gone.

There is a bit more to the letter, detailed accounts of
meetings and asking my opinion on the food shortage in
Cerulean along with the recent edict passed in Flora. The letter
is then cordially concluded with,

> *I am ever at your service, my lady,*
> *Gabriel*

I set it aside to look through more closely at a later time
when I can better reply. For now, my mind is distracted with
the two little children staring at each other mutely.

They have not seen each other since Dena's wedding
nearly a year ago, and they do not see each other often to begin
with. Zsoka doesn't smile. She merely studies Enté from her
place by the fire.

Enté hugs close to my legs, shifting a bit uncomfortably
and watching her.

I smile softly and reach out to touch the top of Enté's
head, smoothing down his hair. "Say hello to your *Senai,*
Enté."

"Hello, Lady Zsoka," he says quietly, glancing at me and
then back to her.

Zsoka sniffs the air and then scoffs, narrowing her eyes.
"Hello, Prince Enté."

Enté glances up at me and whispers, "She's scary."

I lean down with a little smile and whisper back, "Girls
always are."

"Och! Here, here! Let me put on some tea then! I want
t'hear all aboot what I've missed!" Heather calls, tromping
down the stairs again with her big, yellowed grin as she makes
her way into Cali's domain to put on tea.

I smile softly and look back to the silver-haired boy at my legs. "I missed you," I say softly, feeling my heart clench, and I stroke his hair again, as if reminding myself he is there.

Enté looks back at me with a curious expression and gentle, blue eyes. "I missed you too, mama."

Chapter Forty Five
Gabriel

One Month Later
The Training Yard at the Crystalice Palace, Cerulean

Ice crashes against ice. Ckai'ten and I join and part again and again in the field, frosted ground crunching under our feet. The frozen ice-blades in our hands collide once more, and he and I are locked together for a moment, both panting and minding our balance on the slippery ground.

We part again and circle each other. In the icy morning, my shirt is discarded over a post, and I stand in only my breeches.

Over the months, I have found a morning sparring to be beneficial. It clears my head and sharpens my skills—which have slackened embarrassingly over the years since Mit'an'av's death—and gives me the sense of strength and determination that I need to face the day—and the politicians.

"Sire!" Claque's voice cuts through the sharp chill of the morning, and I turn to him, panting for breath.

Ckai'ten and I are suddenly lurched from our spar, and we both straighten, turning to Claque.

My brother-in-law was up far earlier than I, and he has already trained, bathed, and dressed in his formal uniform. He marches towards us swiftly.

"Sire," he greets, inclining his head. "I've received some information that I believe needs to be addressed."

"Very well," I respond breathlessly, turning to Ckai'ten and inclining my head.

"Sir," he gasps, the ice sword shattering into tiny pieces and dispersing into snow on the ground. He thumps his chest in salute.

I only nod breathlessly and follow Claque, my sword turning to snow as well and remaining on the field. We move inside, but Claque does not speak. The fact that he does not even begin to inform me of anything as we make our way to our study alarms me.

Although, I suppose that we cannot be too careful as of late. With the recent tensions and the almost certain knowledge that the White Fang have on some level infiltrated the castle, we cannot afford to be heard.

Once we are safely inside of my study, I shut the door firmly behind me.

Claque wastes no time before handing me the rolled parchment in his hand and standing at attention, facing me. "Sir," he begins as I read, glancing up at him occasionally. "Our patrols noticed Inferno movement on the southernmost part of the border and pursued at a distance into Flora territory."

I frown at him, meeting his gaze and saying coldly, "Claque, the men were given strict orders to not enter Inferno territory."

He inclines his head and replies, "I am aware, sire. Forgive me. I gave permission to follow under extraordinary circumstances. The general thought it strange enough to warrant investigation."

Frowning but accepting his defense, I turn my eyes back to the parchment. "And what did they discover?"

"Due to the size and structure of their army, we do not believe that they are en route to Levosa as usual. They are keeping close to the mountains and are outfitted for battle."

I look up at him.

His voice drops faintly. "We believe that they are headed for the Skallenth pass into Maeghdra."

My heart, my breath, all of them go completely still within my chest. Everything goes cold and lifeless and vacant within me. And then it begins to surge.

"Gather a company at once," I bark, dropping my materials to leave the office and head to my own room. "Send a servant to gather supplies as quickly as we are able. We will join up with the southernmost patrol in order to form a larger party." Pausing, I add, "You will not be joining us. I need you here."

"Sire—" he interjects quickly, "I could go in your stead. You know that I—"

"I do not distrust your competency," I tell him immediately, "but I have dealings with the Inferno, and—forgive me—but this is something I must do on my own. I must be sure she is safe. I cannot stay back this time. Take my place in the meetings. I will be back as soon as I can."

Even riding swiftly, it will take at least a week to reach her. The roads are clear and favorable, and that is to our advantage, but a troop our size will not be able to move swiftly. I only pray that it is enough time. I will send word to Alistair ahead of time. Perhaps it will reach him swiftly enough to give warning, but I am not even sure if he is at Maeghdra at the moment. And anything could happen to the letter. I cannot leave it to chance. I have to go myself.

I have to be sure.

I cannot let her die.

Chapter Forty Six
Scarlet

Two Weeks Later
Maeghdra Manor, Flora

I know that it is late, but I cannot sleep. I have become used to the pain. Although the child is not due until late spring, I have had little pains all through the winter. They've become worse and frightened me often over the many months. More than once, Heather has had to counsel me out of near hysteria in fear that the child is trying to come much too soon.

The warm weather has helped. With the fading of winter and its chilling cold, the mood of Maeghdra manor has much improved. Zsoka does not sleep as much, and I do not feel quite so tired and worn. My appetite has kept me healthy, and the rising temperature gives me peace.

Even so, I cannot sleep.

Even with the warmth of spring now upon us and a letter from my husband declaring that he will be on his way home as soon as he can…I cannot rest. At first, I thought it only the pains, sharp pains in my womb giving way to dull throbs. But now, I am not so sure. I am restless and wandering the halls in front of the fire. I should be resting. I swore to Gabriel and Alistair and Heather that I would have care and rest. Usually I do. But I cannot sit still tonight.

I pace before the hearth. It is always kept burning and high, but its flames offer me no comfort tonight. I am sweating again. I can feel the cool rush of air on my damp neck and face. I rub my throat and make an unhappy sound, pausing the double over again and give a soft groan. The pain is worse than it was a few hours ago, and it is becoming more frequent ...perhaps I should wake Heather.

But dawn is several hours off still...I will try and let her rest a little longer. I will be fine.

The pain again drives me to brace myself against the hearth, and I sigh when it is finished, sitting down against the stone and leaning back, breathing hard. Alistair should be home any day now. I hope he comes soon. I do not want him to miss the birth. He would be so disappointed.

"They will be here soon."

The voice in my dining hall startles me to my core. My head snaps up, and I suck in a breath, staring at the woman not far from me.

I have never seen her before. I would know if I had. She is unlike any woman I have ever seen. Her hair is rich and black and flows down her shoulders like dark water under a midnight sky, shifting with waves and framing her slender shoulders. But her skin is like polished white marble. It is creamy pale but completely opaque. Usually even in Crystalice white skin, I can see the faint impression of blue veins underneath. But I can see nothing from her.

It is as if she isn't real at all, as if she is made of marble. It seems eerie when she moves, tipping her head slightly to watch me with blue eyes. Bright blue. Like the color of a summer sky. The color of topaz.

I have never seen anyone like her before.

But her voice. Her voice is so familiar. It rings in my head, nagging at my memory to recall it.

"The garden," says she, watching me quietly. She turns a bit, and her white-lace gown moves with her, shifting slowly off her hips and swaying to her ankles. Her feet are bare. "At the party for Bronx. I saw you there."

My eyes grow wide, and I remember then the sound of a woman calling my name before the soldier hit me on the side of my head and took me to the ground. I reach up, touching the little scar there.

"Who are you?" My voice is low and soft, but there is a warning in it. I step back from her, a protective hand on the underside of my belly. Another pain hits me, and my breath leaves in a rush. I clench my teeth and lean over, not breathing, my eyes cracked open and watching her warily.

She does not answer my question. Instead, she moves quietly to the fire and I shift away from her. She watches the flames as if they remind her of something, as if they are something familiar and loved.

"They are coming," she says to me, and I remember that is what she said the first time. She looks up at me with those blue eyes. The golden light of the fire does not reach them. They remain a still and constant blue.

"The Inferno have come to reclaim you." She straightens a bit then and half-turns from me, her eyes still on mine. "Come and see."

She moves away from me and out the back door of the manor.

Despite a tingling fear and apprehension in my chest, I cannot help but follow the woman. I carefully put my weight back on my feet and follow after her with hesitation, a hand on the stone wall to guide me.

Outside, I see her again. She is at the gazebo where I would often stand and watch the fires of Inferno from just beyond the peaks of the mountains.

I look to the peaks now; it is dark and I see no flames. But there is a light, and I turn my head.

There, just past the mountains, at Skallenth, the single pass through the mountains between Flora and Inferno. There is a red light in the forest, a brilliant glow. But the glow is on the eastern side of the mountains. It is in Flora. My heart stops.

"They have come to reclaim you," she says again, and now she is standing at my side as I look with horror upon the burning forests of Maeghdra in the distance.

"I don't understand," I tell her, feeling my eyes burn and my heart race with a wild fear. Pain clutches me again, and this time, I cry out, one knee buckling. I catch myself on the wall and pant softly, clenching my eyes and putting my hand once more to my womb.

"Who are you?" I bite out. "What do you want?"

She watches me calmly and then looks back to the burning forest. "I want many things...Mostly, I want the same things you do. As to what I want you to do...I wish only for you to do exactly as you always have." She sighs, and it is a slow and soft sigh. Her eyes seem almost...heartbroken.

"I am sorry...I have debated not telling you but...I know that you would rather know now than later."

"Why?" I rasp, the pain still seizing me. I look up at her with squinted eyes, forcing myself to breathe slow and steady past the pain.

She looks down at me with sadness and gives a rueful smile. "Because...you may be able to save more than *one* life tonight... and...so that you can say goodbye."

I watch her with confusion, staring at her and trying to understand. I do not understand. What does she want me to do? How can I save anyone? I'm certain now that the babe is coming.

I can feel the child pressing low in my womb, and the pain is getting worse and more frequent. I need to get Heather. I need to lay down.

But why would I say goodb—

Alistair.

Alistair is on his way home.

"No." My voice is but a rasp, and I turn my golden eyes to stare at the burning forest with sinking dread. I look back to the woman, but she is gone. I am alone in the darkness. My heart pounds in my chest.

"No!" Looking to the forest, I scream in panic, "Alistair! *Alistair!*"

My breaths come in ragged and terrified, shuddering in my chest. The pain fades again, and I turn, forcing myself inside. I have to go there. I have to meet the Inferno before Alistair finds them. He is on his way home from Ocarine. He will pass right by Skallenth. He will see the burning forest. He will go to them.

They will know who he is. The Duke of Maeghdra. My husband. My mate. My love.

"Alistair," I whisper his name as a quiet plea, scrambling back through the house. Pain hits me at the door, and I stumble to my knees. Groaning, I press my hand to my stomach.

"Not now. Not now!" I plead, whimpering quietly and clenching my eyes. In the back of the house, I can hear someone stirring. It must be Heather.

I shake my head slowly, pushing myself up. I grab the latch on the door and force it open. Outside, in the front of the house, all is dark. The moon and stars are veiled with clouds, and thunder rumbles in the distance. I cannot see the burning forest from here. As quickly as I am able, I push myself off the door and stumble my way into the barn, lighting a lamp with my fire.

"Grea!" I call for my horse, and I find the gray mare stamping nervously in her stall. I go to her and unlock the padlock, letting her out of the stable. She follows me to the back where a small cart is positioned. The carriage stays outside, but the cart is kept in the barn where its untreated wood will not rot. I hook her up to the car and lead her out of the barn.

"Scarlet!" Heather cries, scurrying out of the manor in only her nightgown and a shawl. "What in th'devils are ye doin, lass! Get back inside!"

"The Inferno are here!" I call to her, climbing carefully onto the front of the cart, sitting on the bench. I at least wear a robe over my nightdress, and it keeps the cool mountain air off of me.

"Get down this instant!" Heather cries, coming up to the side of the cart.

I watch her with piercing eyes. "I can't. I have to go. Alistair is there, Heather."

"Oh dear goddess…" Heather whispers, looking up at my face. But she shakes her head and pleads, "Scarlet, send sommon else. Ye'll hurt th'babe."

"I have to try," I tell her and snap the reigns. "I cannot let them die, Heather!"

Grea gives a short neigh and yanks against the cart. She has never pulled a cart before, and she doesn't like it, but she marches obediently out of the courtyard and struggles into a full gallop once we are on the road. The cart bounces and jostles, rumbling along the uneven road. I am tossed left and right, but I plant my feet firmly to stay in my seat. The pain in my womb drives me to cry out, but I merely clench the reigns tighter and hold on. I have to make it through this.

"We can do this," I rasp to my womb, unable to place a hand upon my belly to soothe the impatient child within. "We have to, little one. We can do this…"

I clench my teeth against the pain, words stolen from my throat as the horse clatters and clashes her way down the road towards the burning forest.

The rain begins to pour as the first burning tree comes into sight. I cannot tell how far it has spread, but it is reaching wide across the lands. I am glad for the rain. It should keep the fire from reaching the city and the manor. Spring rains are always hard and cold. It will dampen the fire.

"Alistair!" I scream from the cart, slowing the thundering beast into a steady walk. My robe is not enough to keep the bite of the rain off of me, and it shoots like tiny, cold daggers atop my head and cheeks, slicing my hands.

"Alistair!" I guide the cart deeper into the burning forest, but Grea does not wish to go. She screams at me and reels back in fear of the flames.

Cursing, I inch my way to the edge of the bench and climb down. I stumble at the bottom and fall, rolling so that my side hits the dirt. It is cold and wet, cushioning my fall, and I lay there breathing next to my panting and snorting horse. She watches me with black eyes as I slowly stagger to my feet and suck in my breaths, screaming again, "Alistair!"

The horse will not go with me, so I go alone. The trees are hot and flaming, and they lend me strength, destroying the biting cold of the rain and wrapping around me lovingly. I stumble from tree to tree, going deeper into the woods, to where the trees have been swallowed whole by the fire, the ones that are scarred and black and soon to crumble to dust.

"Alistair!" I scream again, a sob welling up inside of me. My hair is half wet, pressed down on my head, on my cheeks.

I push it out of my face, looking around desperately and screaming again, "Alistair!"

There is a form not far from me on the ground. I scramble to him and find a soldier, Ian, laying there. He rasps and hacks his breath, blood running from his lips. "D-Duchessss," he hisses out.

"Where is Alistair!" I shout at him, taking him by the shoulders, leaned over him and my agonized womb.

He lifts a trembling hand and points closer to the mountains. "H-Hurry…"

I suck in a breath and lay him down carefully, dragging myself to my feet. Each wave of pain is right after the other now. It seems as if there is no pause between the waves of torment.

I struggle from tree to tree, holding myself up and screaming, "Ali…Alistair!" Tears run hot down my face, and the rain pours harder, snuffing out the roaring flames into a rasping simmer hissing on blackened branches.

There is a sound to my right, a hiss and a groan. I swing my head around and find a mess of tawny, blond hair and golden skin.

"Alistair!" I shriek, stumbling towards the man barely in sight. I collapse many times, hitting my knees and crying in agony before stumbling up again and dragging my trembling legs across the ground to where he lay.

He lays on his back on the ground, breathing in slow and shallow breaths. He has his hand pressed against his stomach, and even in the pouring, cold rain, I can see ribbons of blood seeping from between his fingers and soaking his shirt.

"Alistair, Alistair," I whimper, collapsing at his side. I do not think I could have taken another step. My legs ache and tremble, the pain of my womb shooting down to my knees. I can feel it in my toes, a piercing, radiating pain that consumes my entire body.

"Scarlet," he rasps, and I can tell from his voice that he is angry. Wild, green eyes look up at me, his brows pinched together as if he cannot make sense of what he sees.

I lean over him, stroking his wet and dirty face, sobbing quietly.

"I'm here. I'm here," I whisper, my voice cracking, sobs breaking through each breath as tears run down my face.

"Get 'way," he growls at me, taking one hand from his cheek and clenching it with a trembling, weak grip. "They're here for ye...go...run."

I shake my head, my lip trembling and nostrils flaring. "No," I cry. "I can't. I won't."

"Scarlet..."

"I won't!" I scream, and as I do, the pain hits me again.

All across my womb, a stabbing, piercing pain as if my child may just rip apart my stomach in order to emerge. I can feel the muscles straining, and it feels as if they will tear. I scream. A high and stretched out scream, leaning over my womb and over Alistair's bleeding form. When it is finished, I pant hard and lay against his cold chest.

His bloody hand is in my hair, stroking gently, thumb moving back and forth.

I pant softly and gasp, "Let me—cauterize—the wound ...I can stop the bleeding." I look to him, and he is weakly shaking his head at me. "Alistair...let me try...I can—I can stop the—"

"Twill'na matter..." he whispers softly, his hand tightening in my hair. "They've run me through, sweetheart...even if—the blood stopped...tis all a—a mess— in there...I—I'm a dead man."

He gives a sardonic little chuckle, and I look at him, glaring, "Why are you laughing!" I shout at him, crying. I place my hand over his on his stomach, wanting to undo what has been done, wanting to take away the pain.

"You idiot! You fool!" I start screaming at him, and he watches me with those sad, green eyes.

They shouldn't be sad. They are always filled with laughter. Warm, beautiful green eyes that are always filled with laughter. But now they hold only sorrow despite the crooked, half-hearted smile he wears on his unshaven face.

"You stupid fool," I moan and look away from him to bury my face against his chest and scream out my pain and my sorrow as agony rips at me again.

"You stupid, stupid fool…stupid, stupid…" I thump my head against his chest, and he winces and lays his hand on my head while I cry against him.

"Shhhh…eh'salright, sweetheart," he murmurs low to me, and I pick up my head to look into his green eyes. He smiles at me, reaching out and gently rubbing the tears off my cheek. "Eh'salright…I'm here…"

I watch him, blinking furiously to see him clearly past my tears. My whole body trembles in pain, and I shudder in some rasping breaths. I clench my eyes and lean over again, squeaking out a little cry. "Alistair…the baby…"

His smile softens to concern, and he puts his arm around me carefully. "Ye should'na come…Scarlet…ye—ye got ta go—my lass." It's getting harder for him to talk. He coughs and rasps in some breaths, leaning back and staring up at the sky. He opens his eyes a little wider, too wide, as if he is afraid of closing them. I watch him in heartbreak and draw him near to me.

"I won't leave," I moan softly, shaking my head and leaning over him.

He grunts and goes quiet for a while, just breathing in short, shallow breaths, hacking weakly every now and again.

Then a moment goes by where I can't hear him, and I whimper, "Alistair?"

He sighs and gives a faint cough. "Wilt…wilt sing f-far me…lassie?"

I swallow and listen quietly to him, closing my eyes and laying my cheek against his hair. His head rests on my legs, the top of his head pressed against my anxious child in my womb. The pain squeezes my belly, and I lean over them both, groaning and crying out my pain.

"A-Aye," I choke out at last, swallowing and taking in a few slow, deep breaths.

I recall the tune my mother once sang to me as a child. Once when I was very young and very small. When I was home and my brother was still alive. When Jay'let was always by my side. Once…when war was a game that children played in the yard while supper was cooking. When death was nothing more than a long, deep sleep.

I suck in a few breaths in rapid succession and swallow again. My hand rests on his cheek, my thumb stroking gently across his skin. I swallow and reach for my swollen, broken voice.

In the low, wide hills where the skies burn red
Where the sun sinks down to the dark blue shore
There lays a little glow you shall always find
If you're still, then sit and watch at how it grows

Little star, little star, burn bright
You will always find a light
A little light that shines throughout time
It's a little glow that you always find

Deep inside your soul and mind

Swing up high, high, sweet darling
Do not fear the burning sky
Let the fire take you over and through
Where the sun sinks down to the shore

I have not felt him move since the second verse. My thumb gently strokes Alistair's cheek, and I swallow and take another soft breath. I swallow hard and lean over him, no longer containing the tears dropping from my eyes. Not a swallow. Not a breath. Not a flinch. I feel nothing from him.

"In the low, wide hills…where the—the skies burn red
Where the sun sinks—sinks down to the dark blu-ue
shore
There lays a l-little glow…you—you sh-shall always find
If you're s-still…then…sit an-and watch…at h-
how…it—it…"

The last word breaks into a soft cry, and I lean over my beloved, weeping out my sorrow in the cold, driving rain which quenches the fire on the land.

I gasp in a breath, swallowing it into my lungs, and I scream. There are no birds, no rodents to hear me. All have fled or burned away with the fire. I am alone there with him, my stomach clenching in agony, my body trembling in pain.

I scream until my air gives out, and I choke on the last of it. I suck in another breath, gasping it in, and I clench my eyes and fill my chest and scream again, a high and shrill and ugly sound stretching through the barren, broken night.

Another breath and another scream. Again, and again, and again. I spill my agony into the night, holding Alistair's cold body against me. The child in my womb fights for freedom, and my stomach spasms in pain. I gasp, sucking in a breath and arching my back, no longer able to lean over my husband. My back straightens, and my face is snatched up to the sky.

I scream again, the sound splitting through my throat and choking me.

When I am spent and the cry fades into the darkness, I slump forward, panting hard.

"Alistair…" I whisper softly, my eyes dry, no tears left within me to shed for him. "*Alistair…*" My thumbs gently stroke his cheeks, soft and pleading.

He does not move, and nor does he answer me. He is lifeless against my legs, laying there with his eyes closed and lips slightly parted. His skin is already so gray. It is usually so warm, like sunlight, warm and soft.

At any moment, I expect him to laugh at me, to smile and crack an eye open and tease me for my worry. But he lays there against me—tawny, blond hair matted with blood.

"*I need you.*" I rasp to him, something I have never said to him before. "Please…please, *I need you.* I *love* you…"

If I tell him now— even though it is so late—if I tell him then…then maybe—maybe it will be enough…

But Alistair does not stir, and I lean over him once more, a low and strangled sound in my throat, as though one who is near to death.

There is a sound.

It is low, and far off, but I hear it in the distance, and my head raises from its mute prayer for forgiveness, my golden eyes watching the dark haze of the forest.

Yes. There is a sound.

Someone is here. Someone is calling my name.

"Jacob?" I whisper. My voice is hoarse and broken. I can taste blood in my mouth. I swallow, something which brings a shooting pain down my throat, for the whole thing is swollen and sore.

"Jacob!" I call.

In the distance, I can see figures moving in the darkness. They become larger and more clear, making their way to me in the forest.

"Scarlet!"

I can hear my name on his lips, and my lips stretch into a worn and bitter smile, my beloved's head laying in my lap.

"Scarlet!"

"Jacob!"

They draw nearer and nearer—men cloaked in gold and brown and red. A man quickly jogs to me, a man who is made no more beautiful by the pretty colors he wears. He is still such a plain man. Brown skin and brown hair and brown eyes. He is dull and without any semblance of beauty. I remember this, and the memory is mine alone. He crouches down before me, his eyes wide and taking in the full sight of me. His sword is strapped to his side, and the sudden and violent thought courses through my mind that he had been the one to slay Alistair.

"What have you done?" I rasp, my golden eyes narrowing on him.

His brows pinch together, and his eyes move back and forth across mine, trying to see what he cannot understand. Trying to understand what he cannot know. "Scarlet, I—"

"What have you done!" I scream. My voice cracks, breaks, and I am left coughing and rasping again. My stomach seizes with pain, and my teeth come sharply together, barely missing my tongue. Sweat beads upon my brow and my neck. I can feel it rolling down my skin. My lungs feel so small, crushed by the little weight in my belly trying to break free.

"What have you done!" I scream again at him.

His confusion only deepens as he watches me, and I look down at Alistair, *my* Alistair. He lays limp and lifeless in my arms, his golden skin gray and his eyes closed.

It is as if a deep sleep. But I am no child now. I know better.

Death is no stranger to me.

"Look at him..." My voice is broken and wet with tears that well anew in my eyes. "Look at what you have done..."

Jacob swallows and says to me, "Scarlet...we came to bring you home—to bring you home. He was Flora and intercepted us. He—"

"He was my *husband*!" I shriek, my voice piercing the dark night. My head snaps back up, and my golden eyes lock upon him with a fury and hatred I have not felt in a very, very long time.

"He was my husband, you bastard! I loved him! And you took him from me! You killed him!" I lurch suddenly towards Jacob, and he reels back from me. I cannot hold myself up, and my form collapses to the cold, wet ground. Suddenly, there is water between my legs.

"Scarlet, I...what—tell me what to do..." Jacob watches me helplessly as I lay upon the ground, and he approaches me with a gentle hand upon my arm.

"Do not touch me!" I shriek, pushing myself up with one arm while the other goes with protective persistence to my womb. "Do not—" I grit my teeth, my whole body shaking in sorrow and rage and pain.

Slowly, I drag my chin up so that I am looking into his eyes. My golden eyes are like fire—hot and bright and furious.

"Look at what you've done!" I shriek, my voice cracking with the sound. "You and this war! This stupid, pointless thing! Look at him!"

Jacob gives a long, slow sigh, watching me with his plain, brown eyes. "Scarlet…I am sorry to have caused you pain, but we cannot allow anything to stand in our way. You know this…this is the cost of—"

"Don't speak to me of the cost of war!" I scream, and I lunge at him, grabbing him by his shirt.

He braces himself, and I use his strength to pull myself up, panting and sweating and sallow with weakness.

"Do not speak to me of the cost of war! You who have your *Dailyn* and your babies! I am tired of these death-games! They are pointless! I—"

I am silenced by another scream, and I roll myself onto my back, leaning some so that my face is tipped to the sky. I am panting, the pain making it hard to breathe.

"My babe," I whisper, choking out the sound. "My babe is-is…*here*." I groan low and clench my eyes, sinking further back.

"Cara!"

I had not expected my name upon his lips. I thought surely that I must be dreaming or else gone entirely mad to hear him here in this sick and desolate place. But I force my eyes open to see a figure of white and blue tearing through the darkness.

He is here. I've not gone mad. A furious streak of white and blue rips through the darkness with cries of vengeance and agony ripping apart the night.

Gabriel.

Chapter Forty Seven
Gabriel

In the Maeghdra Forest

I hear her before I catch sight of her, piercing screams of rage and sorrow tearing through the darkness of the night. My heart nearly stops in my chest, my knees squeezing the sides of the white horse beneath me. I swallow back a hard breath of air in my throat, my fear rising. My wrath suffocating.

But there she is. On the ground. I glimpse red and orange and golden hues. I drop from my horse and draw my sword, calling out her name.

The Inferno have noticed us by now. They shout amongst themselves and draw their bows.

An arrow whistles just past my shoulder, and as I draw my ice to me, I hear the duchess scream.

"Enough!" she shrieks, tossing a ball of fire at the man who loosed the arrow.

He glares at her, looking to his command warily.

Jacob, a man I now recognize, says nothing, but Cara clings to him and shrieks at the other man.

"Enough, you idiots! If another of you looses a single arrow, I'll bury you in the ground under ten feet of earth!"

Fire begins to sizzle from the ends of her hair, and it hisses softly in the darkness. Suddenly, however, her teeth snap together, and she doubles over, holding onto Jacob until even I can see the whites of her knuckles. She bites out a scream, choking in a breath when it is finished, her whole body trembling.

"Enough! Enough! Stand down!" Jacob puts an arm around Cara and turns his head to look at me. "You! Ice Prince! Are you of any help?"

Hesitantly, I lower my sword, and I stretch out a hand to signal for my men to do the same. I brought only a small company with me—a team of ten men.

Jacob has five with him, but I can hear others nearby. I doubt he brought less than fifty.

"Is she injured?" I ask, approaching slowly.

The archer keeps his bow trained on me, but at least the arrow is pointed to the ground and his grip is relaxed.

"She is in labor," he says shortly.

Cara leans over in his arms, panting hard and biting back cries against the pain.

My heart jumps in fear and then begins to pound in my chest. My throat feels tight, and my mind at once goes blank. I have stopped walking, and it takes a moment—and the sound of Cara's pained whimper—for me to begin moving again.

As I draw nearer, I can see a form on the ground. I barely notice it at first, my attention focused on the Inferno soldiers and then the red-headed woman crying out in pain and screaming at her once-comrades. But now I notice it. I notice the sunshine golden hair. The fine, green doublet. The gold signet ring.

I stop again.

My feet are completely still upon the ground, and the furious beating of my heart shrieks to a sudden halt.

I can't move. I can't breathe. I can merely stare at what I can see just past Scarlet. The form laying there. His skin is gray and he is completely still. Not even the screaming of his bride wakens him from that stillness.

"Gabriel!" Jacob shouts, and Cara screams again, unable to speak now.

She careens over Jacob again, choking out a sob, sweat beading on her skin.

I have never seen Cara perspire. I did not know that Inferno were able. I do not know if it is a testament to her pain or to the strangeness of her half-breed child—the precariousness of which Alistair informed me.

Either way, the sight and sound of her gets me moving again, but now I do not hesitate.

"You bastard," I snarl, storming towards her.

The archer tightens the bow again.

"Get her away from here!" I pry Cara off of Jacob and push him aside.

The man stumbles back but then quickly is up on his feet again, fists clenched for a fight as I drag Cara up into my arms, her hands on her swollen stomach.

She is soaking wet from rain and dirt and whatever else it is I smell on her.

"She cannot give birth here," I snarl at him. "Not on the battlefield where her mate lays dead." I turn my eyes back upon the woman I hold and lean my face towards hers.

"Cara, how did you get here?" I ask, my voice low but strong in her ears, demanding her attention. My heart has picked up its pace in a panic once more.

She sucks in a few rapid, shallow breaths. "H-Horse a-a-and...buggy!" she gasps out.

I nod and start heading for the main road, sure that I will find it nearby.

"Alex!" I shout, and one of my men comes forward. "Tell the men to look for the horse and cart on the main road. Then send a man on your fastest horse to Maeghdra Manor. Get the woman called Heather. Bring her here at once with anything she needs."

"Sir!" he shouts and runs off to do as I say.

I move swiftly through the woods, away from Alistair's body, away from the smell of charred earth and death. Even if we cannot find the cart, I do not want her there, laying in the dirt next to him.

Jacob barks similar orders to his own men, calling back the ones who had scattered and sending the others out. One of them finds the horse and calls out to us, bringing the mount to us about a mile from Alistair. The mare strapped to the cart is nervous and stamps her feet uneasily.

Cara screams again, arching her back and panting hard as I lay her in the cart.

"Easy, easy, Cara," I whisper to her, leaned down near her.

Jacob hesitantly climbs onto the cart as well.

I watch him from the corner of my eyes with great wariness as he settles himself beside Cara.

He watches her but does not touch her. He reaches for her once, as if he would smooth back her hair, but he stops himself and withdraws his hand from her.

"A-Alistair…" Cara whispers, cracking her golden eyes open and looking at me. Her eyes are red and filled with tears that run down pale and dirty cheeks. She feels so cool to the touch, all former warmth of her gone.

My heart sinks in my chest.

"He's…he's *dead*, G-Gabriel." She hiccups and begins sobbing again, arching up a bit and then laying down again with a soft cry.

"I know…I know." I whisper softly, smoothing back her hair and leaning down, pressing my lips to her brow.

She does not flinch from my cold touch. She cries harder, sobbing there on her back and giving a low scream of pain that climbs higher and higher.

I remember such sounds. I remember the night Catherine gave birth, and I—a much younger man—pacing in the room beside hers. I remember such screams, crying and pitiful sounds, pleading for the pain to stop, begging. For hours and hours it lasted, and I could not go to her. Men are not permitted into birthing chambers.

And yet, I cannot imagine anyone tearing me from Cara's side now.

She does not beg or plead, but the sound of her screams and sobs rend my heart and tear apart every organ in my body.

I am at a complete loss. I know that I should help. The child may not wait for Heather before trying to force its way out into the world. But I do not know how to help her. Cerulean men are taught nothing of childbirth. I would not know what to do even if I tried.

"What can I do?" Jacob asks, as if reading my thoughts, and I lift my head to find his brown eyes watching me.

You could have not killed her husband, I want to snarl at him.

My friend. My oldest companion. Dead. At his hands. The thought of grabbing my sword and running him through occurs to me. It would be easy.

But Cara bites back a shout of pain and turns her head to the side, drawing her knees up a bit and adjusting herself on the cart, trying to find whatever position her body wishes to be for the birth.

I merely stay by her side, useless. I can't kill Jacob. Not now at least. And I am useless here.

"I do not know if the midwife will make it back in time. Do Inferno men know anything of childbirth?"

Jacob growls and looks very frustrated, watching Cara's face. "Not much. But I helped with my last babe for the midwife was also late, but…"

"What?" I snarl at him.

Jacob looks back at me and says, "It is one thing for a man to help his wife. Scarlet is as close to a sister as I have ever had. If I were to help her...the shame she must already suffer at home for carrying a half-Flora child—I don't want to make it worse."

"Are you *hearing* yourself!" I scream at him, grabbing him by the shirt. "Look at her, you bastard! She is *going* to *die* here! Do you *understand* that!"

They are words I had not even said to myself, not even the quiet recesses of my mind. But when the words burst from my chest, I know that they are true.

Jacob's eyes widen, and his eyes follow mine to look at Cara.

Her face is so pale, sickly yellow. Sweat beads on her skin, and she moans and turns her head from side to side. She is so weak. Her cries are getting quieter. She isn't fighting as hard now. She's fading.

"Do you think she gives a damn about pride at the moment! I can't help her! But if you don't do something, both she and her babe are going to die!" I shake him until he slaps my hand off of his shirt and cuts his eyes to me.

"Move," he says, and I shift back out of his way. Jacob moves to sit between Cara's legs, lifting her dress and shifting her a bit.

She sucks in a breath and growls, trying to move away from him.

"Oy!" he growls at her. "*La'centa!*" A name I have heard before. He had wept the name over her when she'd first lost her fight to me. She goes very still at the sound of it, breathing hard and swift. "I am here, *La'centa....* trust me."

She stills, and Jacob sighs and goes back to his task. He swears and mutters to himself. I can see him begin to work with fire, and Cara groans in pain, arching her back and clenching her eyes.

She is moving less. Her cries have dulled into moans.

"No," I snarl at her, grabbing her head by the hair and jerking her head and shoulders up. "Cara! Not yet! Listen to me!"

Her eyes watch mine weakly.

"Your baby will *die* if you do not help! Do you hear me! *Alistair's* babe. It will die without you. Stay with me, Cara! Scarlet!"

Her eyes open just a bit more, and she takes in a deeper breath than she has in a while. Suddenly, she recoils and screams, throwing her head back.

I move to sit behind her instead, letting her lean back against me.

"Sire!" A man's cry calls for my attention, and my eyes shoot up to catch the sight of Alex on the back of his horse, hooves pounding into the dirt. He brings the horse to a sudden stop and hops down, reaching up and grabbing Heather.

The old woman stumbles a bit. In her arms, she carries a large, wooden bowl, and she wears on her back a heavy bag.

"Move, move!" the old woman hisses, hurrying to the cart. She says nothing of the Inferno man who brought her nor the one moving out from between Cara's legs.

"Ye!" she barks at Jacob, throwing the bowl into his lap. "Fill that wi'water from me bag an' heat it. Now!"

Jacob doesn't argue. He reaches into her bag and finds a jug of water which he pours out into the bowl and begins heating with his fire.

Heather moves to Cara and pushes up her dress. "Hurry!" she suddenly barks at Jacob, and she clucks her tongue and begins muttering to herself.

I can't tell what she does, but she begins working with Cara, coaxing her along.

As Heather begins shouting instructions and orders at the woman in my arms, I dip my head to Cara's ear, summoning her attention, repeating the instructions. I never stop speaking to her, sometimes demanding and cruel, sometimes soft and encouraging, whatever it takes to get her to obey whatever Heather wants.

Cara's screams from before are nothing compared to what comes. Such inhuman and nearly animalistic sounds are ripped from her chest and into the open air as the sun's light begins to break open the night and banish the darkness away. The sky is faintly gray and hinted with silver and blue as Cara collapses back into my arms.

My heart jumps and turns at the sight, and I draw her nearer to me, holding her close as she breathes.

There is no sound, only silence, and I look up with fear and a sickening dread as Heather wraps the slick, pink thing she drew from Cara's wombs in a swaddling cloth.

Heather turns her back to me, and as Cara shifts in my hold, fear of the worst comes to me. But then, a high, shrill cry breaks through the dawn, and I sigh, relaxing back against the cart.

Cara trembles in my arms, and it is only after a moment that I can tell she is crying. When I look down upon her face, there is a bitter smile stretched across her pale, pink lips.

"Hand her here," Jacob says at last, leaning back against the side of the cart and watching us both.

My eyes cut to him, narrowing in warning.

"Hand her here, I said," he snarls, reaching for her. "Let me try and warm her. If I can get her warm enough...let me try."

I cannot refuse him. I help Cara to move over to where Jacob lays, and he wraps her up in his hold.

She says nothing and limply goes where I lay her, leaning against Jacob as his body becomes at once ablaze. The fire wraps around his body and hers, and Cara draws her legs up to her chest, laying against him and shivering.

Heather moves to the back of the cart once more, looking in at us.

I draw one leg up to myself and lean my arm against it, slouching over and watching Cara.

"Ye did well, highness," Heather says to me with a faint smirk. "I've nay seen a Crystalice man e'er dirty his hands wi'a woman's labor."

I growl lightly at her and turn my head away once more, my eyes returning to the woman curled up against her childhood friend.

Heather sighs and watches her, not asking the question we both fear. Instead, she holds the child in her arms, moving to sit on the edge of the cart and giving a heavy sigh. "I sent Zsoka an' Enté t'bring th'healers an' medicine-women from th'village...they'll be here soon." She moves a bit and then offers me what she holds in her arms.

I just stare for a moment, not quite sure what she wants from me. When it finally registers in my mind—which has not slept in well over two days now—that she wants me to take the hour-old infant from her, I sit up suddenly, my eyes going wide. I reach tentatively for the bundle without complaint, taking it from her.

Inside is a little pink face and pale blue eyes, its face all fat and smushed against the cloth. It shifts a very slight bit, tiny hands drawn up to its chin. Those blue eyes look up at me, unfocused but seeing me. It frowns, and I suddenly feel quite uncertain, just watching the tiny babe in my arm as it stares at me without smiling and without making a sound.

Heather laughs softly and says, "Dinna fret, highness. She'll nay bite. She's nay got any teeth yet."

"She?" I ask, glancing up at her before looking back down at the pudgy little face, still dirty and looking as though she still has some faint feather-soft hair on her cheeks.

Heather clucks her tongue and leans back her head wearily. "Aye an' aye. A wee lassie."

I look over to the child's mother to see what she thinks of the news, but Scarlet is still curled up against Jacob, unmoving and still.

Jacob does not look at me. His arms are wrapped around her and his legs drawn up at the knee, encompassing her in the little fire he has built around them.

Being near the fire is sickeningly hot, and I scoot to the far side of the cart before finally giving up and having to climb out, moving slowly and incredibly carefully with the tiny creature in my arms.

As Heather said—while the sun began to make its appearance into the sky—more women come, another old woman like Heather and a few younger ones. They hesitate around the Inferno but then quickly move into action. The young girls take the child from me, one of them apparently a nursemaid who quickly nestles the girl to her breast to feed her. The other girl then moves closer to Cara, asking Jacob questions as to her health and condition.

Jacob lowers the fire briefly so that they can inspect Cara, and the old woman makes a mug of herbs and water for her to make her drink.

For the first time, I watch Cara move weakly to accept the drink, pressing it to her lips. Her eyes are half open, blank and empty. She does not move or think on her own. She does only what she is told exactly as she is told.

I do not know if this is from a state of her mind or a state of her body, but either of them concern me deeply. I can do nothing but sit on the edge of the cart and wait.

After an hour, Jacob pants with exhaustion and calls for one of his men. Gently, Jacob moves Cara to lay against the other soldier who in turn lights himself ablaze while Jacob climbs off of the cart to walk around a bit and then sit down on the floor, leaning over and breathing hard.

I watch him silently and then glance to the healers who talk among themselves.

The nursemaid stays with the child while Heather and the other two decide to go into the woods to look for survivors from Alistair's party.

They find none.

When they return, however, Heather moves to one of the injured Inferno and barks at him to sit down. When he does so, she takes her supplies and begins to tend his wounds.

The act doesn't surprise me from Heather, and when I glance to the local women, I find them hesitating. I am not surprised. It would not be unlikely for any of the men they found to be known to them. Not only that, but they could very well have been kin. I do not expect them to offer aid to those who assisted in killing their clansmen.

And yet, the older one moves first. She comes up beside Heather and goes to another Inferno soldier. She isn't kind, and she isn't gentle. She is crass and rude, but she bandages the man and tends his wounds. Soon, the younger healer follows suit.

Jacob merely watches, quiet and with an expression that I cannot read while those of his men who were damaged in the fight are sewn and bandaged and rested by the sister-kin of the men they slew. He says nothing but at last turns his head away and looks to Cara once more.

I know that look, and I give a humorless smile and look towards the dawn, leaning my cheek against my arm propped up on the side of the cart.

Yes…this is her doing. What you have tried to burn, she has healed.

Another hour passes, and as the Inferno's fire dies down, Jacob gets to his feet and climbs onto the cart, going over to the woman. He checks on her for a while, sparks of fire moving between she and him. Finally, he sighs and lays the unconscious woman down in the cart. There is an old horse blanket in the corner which he grabs and pulls over her.

"She'll live," he says, climbing out of the cart and moving to stand before me. He is not quite as tall as I am, but his brown eyes are piercing and firm. What he lacks in height, he makes up for in gait, and I have no doubt that a fist fight between us two would result in me on the ground.

"I'll take her home. The burning forest will heal her."

"No." My answer is immediate, and my eyes narrow. "Cara is the Duchess of Maeghdra. Her child would not survive the journey, and there is another back at her home."

His brows go up a bit, but I don't care to explain Zsoka's odd predicament to the man. "She needs to be here. Or would you, the one responsible for the death of her mate, like to be the one to explain to her why you stole her away from her home and her children?"

Jacob watches me for a long moment, unbreathing, and then finally looks back to the woman in the cart. "This place…why did she stay?"

I sigh and rub the back of my neck. "I don't know," I answer honestly. "I think…she was afraid to go home. She wanted to try and escape the war. Can you blame her? I think she thought she'd be safe here…I suppose no one is ever really safe, are they?"

I find Jacob's brown eyes watching me when I look back to him, and I meet his gaze steadily with my own. For a while, we say nothing. I don't even bother with posturing to him. I don't care how many men he has. I won't let him take her. There's no threat, no boasting, no posturing. It won't happen.

He takes a step back, looking away from me. "We'll be in touch. This isn't over." He looks back to the woman sleeping in the cart. "If she's chosen to stay, my people may view that as treason…I do not know what the War Lord will decide to do."

"Her father?" I ask.

He nods. "But I wouldn't bet on the familial relation influencing his decision. He's as strong and as old as he is because necessity has always outweighed everything else— including reason and humanity." He cuts his eyes to me. "This isn't over."

"You know where to find me," I reply flatly, and he scoffs without humor, turning away and calling for his men. Within minutes, they are up and off the main road, heading back to Skallenth and into Inferno once more, back from the hell they had come from.

Chapter Forty Eight
Scarlet

Several Days Later
Maeghdra Manor, Flora

The warmth around me cradles me as if I am light and weightless. I sigh and shift slightly within it. I can feel the fire moving over my skin, dancing and flowing as if something liquid, moving across my skin in currents of heat and *Magik*. I wonder if Alistair has placed me in the fire again? He worries too much when I wake and am too cold. Even though they worry about overheating the child, he'll occasionally put me in the hearth until my temperature rises a bit and I leave again.

I can feel the hearth beneath me as my mind slowly stirs from such a heavy slumber. It is hard and hot beneath me, the searing heat of the burning stone scalding my skin wonderfully. I sigh and lay back against it. My hearth in Maeghdra Manor. My home.

But Alistair did not place me here…

Alistair is *dead*.

Slowly, my eyes open, and my heart which had beat so slow and steady with slumber suddenly seems to pound within my chest. I stare at the chimney above the hearth, although I cannot see much.

I remember the feel of him in my arms, holding him in the darkness. I cannot remember now how I reached him or how I left. I only remember holding him there in the cold and the wetness. The smell of copper reminds me of the blood on his stomach, on my hands, matted in his hair. Even now, I can remember that smell. And the smell of death. The smell of sweat and burning, the smell of ash and smoke and lifelessness.

I did not think I would ever smell that scent again.

I remember Jacob. Gabriel.

And the baby. I remember the baby.

The racing of my heart which had slowly begun to calm jumps once more. As I begin to move, the weightlessness of dreams leaves me and reminds me that I am in fact quite heavy and quite solid and quite sore. Everything hurts. My legs are cramped and screaming in pain. My womb feels tight and sore. Worst of all are things I will not name which burn and ache and make moving such a slow and arduous task.

But with care, I ease myself around and scoot to the edge of the hearth, emerging from the flames. All around me, I can hear people calling my name and clamoring about. Gabriel is, in fact, here. It was not a wishful dream. Heather is at my side as well. And Freya.

Freya.

Goddess, forgive me…I cannot look at her.

"Mama!" one voice cuts through them all, and I turn my head to look at Zsoka. Her eyes are filled with tears, and she chokes back sobs, wrapping herself around my legs, and I sigh, focusing on her.

I expected to feel rage. Sorrow. I remember the night in the darkness. I remember screaming until my throat was hoarse and broken. Very faintly, I can remember what I felt then. I remember the panic and the desperation. I have the memory of those emotions.

I cannot feel them now.

I feel empty, broken. I know that Alistair is dead. I summon the memory of his lifeless body in my arms. I remember the sight of the Inferno and that they killed him. They *killed him.* My mate. My love.

But…I cannot feel anything.

"Where is my babe?" I ask. My voice is hoarse and rasps softly, choking over the syllables.

Heather says something to me.

Gabriel tries to coax me into sitting down.

Cali moves away, saying she'll make hot tea.

"Where is my baby?" I am more insistent now. I…I can't remember. Was the child alright? What if it didn't last the night? How long have I slumbered? I remember nothing.

"Where is my baby!"

"Here, Scarlet. Upstairs." Freya approaches me. Out of the haze of my mind, I lift my head from the still trembling form wrapped around my legs to watch her. She is dressed as regally as ever, her hair neatly combed and pulled back in a severe bun. Her eyes are dry, but I can see dark circles beneath them.

"No need to shout." She moves past me and starts for the stairs.

I watch her and slowly move away from the others and follow after her. Zsoka takes my hand and walks in step with me, but she says nothing. As I climb the stairs, I realize that I must have been changed before being placed in the hearth. This nightdress I wear bears no resemblance to the soiled and bloodied dress I surely must have returned home in.

Up the stairs, my feet pad softly on the wooden floor as Freya takes me to mine and Alistair's room. I hesitate at the door, stopping and sucking in a breath. For a moment, I entertain the thought that he is waiting inside, sitting on the parchment-covered bed again. He spilled ink on our sheets a few months ago, and I was so irritated at him for it.

But almost as soon as I fancy the thought, I see his pale and blood-smeared face in my mind.

My chest tightens and my eyes begin to burn.

Freya opens the doors, and I blink away the memories and step quietly inside.

The cradle had already been purchased. The craftsman in the city had taken great care with it, and the detail is everything that I had hoped. Slowly, I run my fingers over the delicate carvings of flowers and vines, my eyes lingering on them because I am afraid. I am afraid that the cradle will be empty.

But there, nestled onto the cushions, a little figure slumbers. She lays on her back, propped up and around with blankets. She looks so snug and comfortable, a blanket drawn up to her jutting little, round chin. Her arms lay straight down at her sides in a sure and deep sleep. Her lips are parted slightly, and I watch her in awestricken wonder. Atop her head is a fuzzy little mess of yellow hair that looks red in the faint shaft of sunlight spilling in from the window.

Behind me, I hear the door quietly close, and while I take note of it, I do not look away from the slumbering infant. I can still feel Zsoka's heat in the room, and she moves quietly to my side, peering in at the child. I glance to her, and a soft smile touches my face. Even if my sorrow had wanted to keep it from me, I cannot help but smile at the sight.

Little Zsoka with her long, black hair and big, brown eyes. She wraps her fingers around the top of the cradle and leans it slightly to peer inside. I cannot tell what she thinks of the babe, for her expression is blank and her eyes uncertain, but her lips hold a soft smile.

My eyes move from her to the infant, and I reach out to gently stroke her face.

The little one skews her face a bit, and her lips press together.

A soft rush of breath escapes me, and I smooth back her hair.

She makes a soft grunt of a sound and then cracks her eyes open, glaring at me with light blue eyes and a petulant little frown.

I reach into the cradle—selfish as I am to wake her from her slumber— I want to hold her. I want to feel her in my arms. To know that she is real and solid and safe. I draw her up out of the cradle, wrapped in cloth, and I nestle her into the crook of my arms, leaning back against the bed. She is heavier than I expected, for she seems so light and small. but her weight is heavy in my arms, and for some reason, that brings me to smile again. She is heavy and fat and healthy.

In my arms, the babe begins to squirm and cry softly.

The door cracks open.

I hush her gently, tears filling my eyes as she parts her mouth in a hungry little cry. I am blinded with tears in my eyes, and I lean over the child, touching my brow gently to hers.

She gives another cry of hunger, the space of each cry filled only with the swallowing of breath and whining of discomfort.

I hold her to me, unable to do anything else, and my whole body trembles.

When she cries there in my arms, it is as though I am released from my prison. Grief and shame and fear washes over me, and my whole body leans over the child. I bite back my sounds, soft little cries escaping between clenched teeth as I begin to sob. Tears roll down the bridge of my nose and drop onto the babe's forehead, rolling down and into her hair. I hold her and rock softly, making a feeble attempt at hushing her between my sobs.

A large, cold hand touches my arm, and I gasp in a breath, my head snapping up and golden eyes meeting ice. Gabriel is at my side. His hand squeezes my arm gently, ice blue eyes holding mine.

"Here, Cara," he says, his voice low and smooth in the midst of my chaos.

I just watch him, and my face twists into one of agony, my lips parting in a cry of sorrow.

"Shhhh. Let the nursemaid take the child, Cara…She'll take care of her," he coos, shifting to place his arms under the child I hold but not taking her from me.

"No," I argue, tightening my hold slightly. "I can do it." My voice is a low growl, although I do not even know if my breasts carry milk from how long I was unconscious. Everything is sore and feels swollen and pained. But I do not want to let her go. I am her mother. I will care for her.

"You need to rest," he says, voice barely above a whisper, and he reaches up to push back some of my hair and put a cold hand on my cheek. His chilled touch wakes me some from the fog of my mind, and my eyes seem to finally focus upon his.

"You can help her best by resting."

Slowly, my hold slackens, and Gabriel gently and very slowly takes the crying child from me and gives her to the nursemaid standing behind him.

I look to her.

She gives a soft smile and says, "I'll get the lassie fed an' cleaned up an' bring'er right back for ye, quick as can be." She ducks her head a bit and leaves the room to go and do as she had said, leaving me alone with Gabriel and Zsoka and apparently Enté—who peeks his head in from the door.

I just watch him pitifully past quiet cries, unable to smile for him when I feel so very tired and worn.

"Come rest, Cara," Gabriel says to me again, putting an arm beneath my knees and taking me from my feet.

Beside me, Zsoka hisses at him, and I watch her weakly as Gabriel carries me to my bed and lays me in it, pulling the covers out from under me and tugging them over me. Zsoka climbs up in bed as well, and nestles her warm, little body against me.

I smile softly, sadly and turn towards her, enfolding her in my embrace.

She sighs with relief and snuggles into me.

Gabriel just pulls the blankets over both of us again and leaves quietly.

I do not sleep right away. The sheets smell of Alistair. Everything is the same. The room, the scent, everything. Nothing has changed. But he is not here. He's dead.

I hold Zsoka a little tighter, and I feel her tiny fingers dig into me.

Her body begins to shake, and I hear her soft, pitiful cries against my bosom.

I wrap her up tighter, curling up around her as if I can somehow shield and protect her from the sorrow and the loss tearing apart my whole body. But I cannot. So I hold her and bury my face into her black hair and cry with her.

Chapter Forty Nine
Scarlet

Several Days Later
Maeghdra Manor, Flora

I do not remember my dreams. There is only a black emptiness. One moment, I fall asleep with Zsoka in my arms, her boney little self digging into my sore and abused body. The next, I awake with white-blue dawn light seeping into my bedroom. It is as though no time passed between the two, and I feel no more rested and healed than I had when I fell asleep.

I sit up, Zsoka sprawled out on her back with her head by the side of the bed and her heels digging into my side. I smile wearily, rubbing my face and letting my head rest within my hands for a while before I rub at my eyes again. I push my hair back, smoothing it down.

I breathe. For now, that is all I can do. I hold my hair down at my neck and close my eyes, and I breathe.

The morning air is crisp but slightly warm. It is still spring at least. I've not slept for months on end this time. Slowly, my hands slide down off of my shoulders and lay on my lap.

Carefully, I pull back the covers—or what little of them I have been left with—and climb out of bed. Although it is warmer, I still feel cold in only my nightdress in the early morning. Or perhaps I only feel cold because my chest feels hollow and empty, as if everything inside has been scraped out.

My robe is nowhere to be found, but Alistair's is laying over the back of a stuffed chair in our room. I take it, and although it hurts me to pull it around me and push my arms through the too-large sleeves, it brings me comfort as well. It smells more strongly of him than even the sheets, and I breathe in that scent quietly in the still paleness of my room.

My eyes go to the cradle in the room, and it too is still and quiet. I am afraid to draw any nearer to the thing. What will I find when I look inside? Will the child still be there? Or will she be dead as well? Will she be cold and pale and gray the way Alistair had been when I'd cradled his head in my lap as he bled out in the grass? She had come too early. What if she is too small? Too weak?

I force myself to the cradle and find that my daughter is not, in fact, sleeping within it.

The cradle is empty.

I reach in slowly and draw out the little blanket inside. It is red and blue. The colors of the Maeghdra crest. It is the first thing I ever knitted for my daughter, and Alistair had been so pleased with it, so pleased with the thought of his babe swaddled in the colors of his name.

I press the blanket to my face and smell a strange scent that I am beginning to associate with that of infants. It is a sweet and strange smell. Something new. Something untouched by the brokenness of my world. I set the blanket down again and make my way to the door.

Outside, I shut the door quietly and pad barefooted down the hall to the stairs, Alistair's long robe trailing slightly behind me. I try to pick it up some. I don't want to tear the ends of it. It is his. I don't want to ruin it. I want it to stay like this forever without showing signs of time or of wear. And yet, I cannot bring myself to take it off. It always made him smile to look at me when I had stolen his robe.

Down by the hearth, a tired Flora nursemaid leans back against the stone, my daughter suckling at her breast. The girl notices me quickly, however, and sits up, catching a yawn and giving a polite, "Good mornin, missus. Didst sleep well?"

"Not exactly," I reply softly, somehow feeling a little more clear-headed, a little more myself. I move to sit at her side, and she watches me with a little smile while I watch my daughter.

"May I?" She is my own child, so I do not know why I ask permission to nurse her, but somehow, I am hesitant as I watch her. Already, I have failed as her mother. I placed her life in danger to go out into the battlefield. I could not save her father. I have been absent in the early and most precious hours since her birth. She has barely even seen my face or known my voice outside of the womb. I am a stranger to her.

"O'course!" the nursemaid says and smiles warmly, carefully detaching the child from her breast.

The girl moves her lips as if still expecting milk and, finding them without food, begins to waken from her haze of satisfied slumber with cries. The sound at once brings a very sharp and throbbing pain to my breasts, and I take the girl from her, assured at least that I am able to feed her. After a few tries, the little babe begins nursing without complaint, and I relax, as if I had somehow faced a telling trial and succeeded.

I turn my head to watch the tired nursemaid look on with a sleepy smile, and I say to her, "I can care for her from now. Thank you for what you have done. Words cannot express my gratitude for tending my babe when I could not…but go and rest now. I will care for her."

She hesitates but then nods and says, "I kens ye still be weak, missus. I thinks ye can take cares o'the wee one jus fine on ye own but…if ye get tired or jus want'a sleep there's naught wrong with lettin sommon watch 'er for a wee bit so's ye can rest."

I look up at her and smile softly, accepting her words. "I will keep that in mind. Thank you for the offer."

She smiles and bobs her head in a nod before leaving me alone in the dining hall to nurse the little child in my arms.

There is a sacred moment there, the silence of the entire manor. In the early dawn, there is nothing but us two. I am tired and sore, but as I lean back against the stone hearth and watch my little infant suckle contently and then fall sound asleep in my arms, I am filled with a contentment and peace that for the moment overrides the sorrow and emptiness.

There is a creak of wood, and I lift my head to the banister overlooking the dining hall. At first, I see no one, but then, Gabriel slowly appears, coming out of his room and looking down at me.

He gives a soft smile and says nothing. I merely watch as he descends the stairs. He is dressed plainly in a white shirt and cream-colored slacks, his feet bare and padding quietly across the stone floor to where we sit.

As he moves to my side, I carefully pull the sleeping child off my breast and draw up the sleeve of my gown, covering myself with Alistair's robe. Such exposure would not have bothered me before. Women of my homeland frequently nurse their offspring in public. And yet, I do not want to be seen. I do not want anyone but Alistair to see me or to bear witness to the soft and quiet and intimate moment between me and the child when she nurses from my own breast.

"Do you feel better this morning?" he asks softly, mindful of the sleeping infant who has collapsed into my arms with her arms hanging limply above her head. I doubt an earthquake would wake her now, but I smile softly.

"Yes," I reply, lifting my eyes to his.

I am glad that he does not ask if I am 'alright'. I am not alright. I am broken and tired, and try as I might, my mind seems stuck and fixed upon the night I held Alistair on my lap

as he died. I am not alright. But I am better than I was
yesterday.

"What is being done with Alistair's body?" I fear that he
has already been buried with funeral rites, and the thought of
my love rotting in the earth so far from the sun's warm light
disturbs me and turns my stomach in protest.

"I have frozen his body until you could wake," he says to
me, surprising me with his words, and I look to him curiously.
He smiles faintly and replies, "I remembered something of
your kind having strange death rituals. I wanted to wait until
you woke."

I lean back against the stone, looking at nothing in
particular except to watch the pale morning light slowly fill the
empty dining hall. I have watched the dawn light fill these halls
so many times now…and yet this morning seems gray and
empty. It must be because some smoke from the burning
forest still remains and clouds the open air. But I fancy the
thought that the whole of Maeghdra mourns the loss of its
lord.

"How long have I slumbered?"

Gabriel reclines on the opposite frame of the hearth so
that he is across from me, one leg draping down and the other
bent at the knee. He watches me with a quiet, observant
expression. "Four—five days. Not long."

I nod slowly, looking back to the child again. "Burial is
disgraceful among my kind," I explain quietly. "I know that
Alistair is Flora but I would like to erect a pyre to burn him
on."

He turns his eyes to me and studies me slowly, saying
nothing at first. But then, he gives a slow and tired nod and
replies, "Flora are usually buried: they are of the earth…but I
am certain Freya would not object, and you are still the
Duchess of Maeghdra. You may do as you wish."

When I raise my eyes to his, I manage a faint but hollow smirk. "When have I ever not done as I wished?"

He gives a crooked little smile back to me. "Fair point."

But although I have the ultimate decision…I would not wish to place further sorrow upon Freya if it disturbs her greatly. I know what it is to lose a child.

"I do not mind." I thought I had imagined it, but Freya's low and scratchy voice draws my attention from the stairs. She dismounts them with a heavy sigh, and somehow. She seems older now.

I watch her straighten up at the bottom of the stairs, the dawn's white-blue light making her skin seem more gray and deepening the dark circles under her eyes.

She frowns and walks quietly towards us. "Alistair is dead. What does he care if he is buried or burned? If it gives you peace to burn him, then do so. I ask only that I may still place a headstone in his honor at the burial grounds."

I incline my head to her, watching quietly as the aged mother who now has lost both husband and son sinks slowly into her green, high-back chair which is stuffed and threaded with silk. "Of course," I say softly, watching her.

Freya notices my staring and looks back at me, her pale eyes studying mine and her frown never changing.

I wonder if she blames me for this. The Inferno who killed her son were only here because of me. Had I never come…Alistair would still be alive.

"She is a pretty baby," Freya says at last, startling me out of my thoughts.

I give a small start and look down to the sleeping infant with a slight smile. "Aye…she's a pretty lassie."

Freya sits in silence for a while, watching me and her granddaughter there upon the hearth. "She's not yet been named. Did you and Alistair decide on anything?"

I shake my head. "Alistair said it was bad luck to name a child before she was born. He would not even speak of names lest it tempt poor luck. But…I had often though…to give her the name of my mother." I give a bitter smile, tears in my eyes.

I swallow them back and whisper softly, "… Estaire." I give a sad smile, stroking her face. Her bottom lip quivers with a breath, and she sighs. My smile widens faintly. "Estaire…Estaire ne Maeghdra Flora…my little fire."

I sniffle and lean back my head. I cannot look at Estaire without crying, and I know that if I surrender to another fit of tears, then I will be too weak to stay awake, and I wish to hold my daughter a little longer.

"What will you do now, Cara?" Gabriel calls.

I raise a weary brow, rolling my head a bit to the side to look at him because I am too tired to lift my head.

He sighs and explains, "Despite Alistair's death, you remain the Duchess of Maeghdra…you may remain here with Freya and continue your duties as the duchess until either a new duke is named or Estaire is of age to take your place."

I do not know exactly what he wishes for me to say, so I remain quiet and watch him.

"Maeghdra is a peaceful place and although Jacob warned me of your father's intentions towards you…I think that you can remain here with relative ease. Close the pass through Skallenth. Continue here. Now that the edict is passed, the Levosa will quickly become less of a problem; it is a life of peace and comfort. That is what Alistair has left for you."

Swallowing the ache in my throat, I close my eyes for a long moment. All I can do is focus upon the warm weight within my arms and listen to my own slow, deep breaths. "And what if I do not wish for a life of peace and comfort?" I open my eyes to find him watching me with confusion.

"You are asking me to hide, Gabriel. Pretend that your people and mine are not still killing each other at the borderlands. Pretend that the White Fang are not ravaging your country and that your people are not starving. You are asking me to forget that my own people—a man whom I considered my *brother*—ran my mate through all to reclaim me from these lands."

He opens his mouth to speak, but I shake my head.

"No…I was not born for a life of peace and comfort. If I had been, I'd have been born as a *Drakkon* far to the north or as some *Fae* to the west where lands are filled with rich fruits and vines of green and no blood has ever spilled upon their soil."

I drag in a long, slow breath, and my lungs feel so sore and tired. "But I was born here—to the daughter of the War Lord, the captive of the Ice Prince, the mate of the Duke of Flora. I cannot run, and I won't. I tried. I ran away here so that I would not have to return home, so that I would not have to face your people. And see what has happened?"

"Cara, what happened to Alistair was not your—"

"Fault?" I give a bitter laugh. "Were it not for me, my mate would still be alive. Do not insult me by suggesting otherwise." My voice is biting and sharp, and Gabriel will not meet my eyes. "Perhaps it is my fault, perhaps not. Regardless it *is* my responsibility. I won't hide anymore.

"How many Inferno men have died while I have not been there to protect them? How many Cerulean have lost their husbands and fathers and sons because I could not help your people understand my own?"

I give a sardonic smile, looking down at my little daughter, my child who already has known so much of pain and death. Her father dead hours before her birth, her first moments hungry and alone and nursing from a woman whose smell and whose voice were strange to her. Already such suffering she will know.

"Perhaps I am a fool to think it can be stopped, but I cannot hide. It may be that it will kill me…and perhaps I will suffer far worse than I do now." I look up at him, meeting the ice blue gaze that watches me. "But I will not hide."

I shift against the stone and watch him.

Gabriel drums his fingers upon the stone hearth, watching me and thinking quietly to himself. He does not share his inmost thoughts with me. He merely watches my face, looking for something that I cannot name.

"What will you do then?" he repeats, ice blue eyes on my golden ones.

Now that, I do not entirely know. I am tired, and I am worn.

All I want is to take my daughter and crawl back into bed. I want to keep waking up with the scent of my mate surrounding me. I want to taste Cali's bread every morning and go and gather red pears with my daughter. I want to ride our horses in the meadow at sunset, and each morning, I want to go out to the gazebo and stare out at the burning forest beyond the mountains.

I want to wake up in Alistair's arms.

But for now, I just want to sleep. Beyond that…beyond that, I do not know.

"I think that you should return to Cerulean with me."

My eyes lift back to Gabriel's, and I frown, watching him calmly from where

I lean back against the hearth.

He continues to hold my gaze, unmoving and studying me all the while.

"Are you mad?" I reply flatly.

He cracks a small smile and gives a slow shake of his head. "Alistair left a life for you here—a good life. One where you would be safe and well cared for…but I think you should return to Crystalice. You said yourself that you were not made for an easy life. That is all that waits for you here."

"So, I should go and seek out death, then?" I challenge. "I said that I would not run. I did not say that I would charge blindly to my death and leave my children without father and mother."

Gabriel winces and looks away from me, sighing and considering his words for a long moment before looking back to me. "The choice is yours, Cara. If you do not wish to return, then stay here. But…I do not think this is what you want." I open my mouth, but he continues, "You *do* something to people. Out in the forests of Maeghdra, I watched Crystalice and Inferno soldiers band together to find your horse and your healer and help you deliver your child. I watched Flora nurses go and tend to injured men who may very well have killed their kinsmen.

"When people are near you—when people follow you— they do *incredible* things… things that they could not have done otherwise."

I watch him quietly, and he studies my face. I do not particularly know what he wants me to say. "I think you put far more faith in me than you should; people do what they must in a single moment in order to achieve a goal."

"Their *goal*," he replies, "was to bring you home dead or alive. Their *goal* was to kill anyone who stood in their way. That had nothing to do with their *goal*. You changed that, Cara."

Freya barely moves and does not speak. Her hands are folded neatly in her lap as she quietly watches the flames beside us both. She takes in a long, slow breath as if she had not done so for some time and then looks to me, her pale, green eyes studying my golden ones. "Scarlet…Alistair believed in you; he respected you and trusted you. He never hid from anything, and he would not want you to either, not for his sake. Go where you are needed. I can continue to manage Maeghdra from here. I will assist you in Flora matters if you can work with the Cerulean for our sake and their own."

She hesitates then and adds, "Or…you could go home."

"What?" Gabriel snarls at her.

Freya has strength enough left to scowl at him. "She could," the old woman says. "Let her go home. She has suffered enough. She's been half-killed Chelyah knows how many times. She's been beaten and tortured. Her husband has been killed. She has no family here and few friends. I think she's earned the right to go home, Gabriel."

"I can't."

They both pause and look back to me.

I give a slow, sad smile, my eyes filled with tears. "I am a Knight Protector. Titles…titles have great meaning for my people. You do not *cease* to be a Knight Protector; I would be expected to take up the sword again and fight. No one ever 'retires' from war. They fight until they die. If they are unable to fight, they go to the battlefield to build weapons or tend the horses. The Inferno fight until they are dead. Those who are completely useless for war are put to death nobly by a family member."

Freya seems more than a little horrified, and I know that it must seem barbaric to them.

I stare up at the ceiling. "How can I go back? Take up a sword against my own people? My own Flora? I may as well cut off my own arm." I closing my eyes. "And even so…how can I go home? How can I go home to the people who stole my husband from me? The people who left me to die in Crystalice? My heart is betrayed."

The room is still and quiet for a moment, and then Freya echoes, "Then go to Cerulean. There you have a chance to end what violence began…so that all swords may be laid down…so that no more sons and husbands die."

I open my eyes once more and watch Freya for a very long moment.

Her eyes are hollow and bleak, but she stares straight at me without fear and without weakness. I wonder if I will ever look so. She who has lost lover and child and who can still walk tall and with her head high, unafraid of the world before her. Had it been Gabriel who protested, I could have argued against him. And if ever he pushed me, I know exactly what I can say to cut him to the quick and force him to leave me alone.

But Freya...

I turn my head away, her words echoing quietly through my ears. Surely...surely Alistair would want me to stay. He would want me to remain in his homeland, to raise his daughter here, to teach her of love and laughter and warmth, not of war and of fear. But then I smile softly and hang my head.

Fool.

I know better than that. Alistair chose me because I know what it means to have lost those I love. I know what it means to have stared down death and walked away not entirely whole. And even though he knew that pain, he walked towards it each time it called. He never backed down. He never gave in. He chose a mate who could do the same.

And so, I roll my head back and lay it wearily against the stone wall, looking back into the Ice Prince's eyes.

Gabriel watches me, and I can tell from his expression that he actually does not want me to agree.

In Crystalice, there is cold, there is fear, and there is suffering. We will have to pick up the sword again that we had set down when I left.

It will not be easy and it will not be enjoyable. It will be a life of trial and of suffering for both of us.

I smirk.

It seems my Gabriel managed to lose his humanity as well. He is putting his people before his heart. Finally.

"I will return with you."

A look of regret crosses his eyes, and he waits a moment as if giving me a chance to change my mind, but Gabriel inclines his head in a small bow and says, "Very well, duchess. As Crowned Prince and Heir of Cerulean…I formally invite and request your stay at the Crystalice Palace."

One Week Later
The Burial Grounds of Maeghdra, Flora

My fingers slide slowly over the ice. It is perfect; clear and without flaw. Within its deadly grasp, my beloved lies lifelessly, cold and pale and as if in slumber. The ice burns my fingertips. The pain races up my hand and into my arm. And yet I do not mind. It is the most I have felt in a week since I have awoken. The burning agony of it trembles up my body until I cannot stand it any longer and pull my fingertips away from the ice. The pads are a dark purple. The skin will harden and slough off and be replaced with new skin in a few weeks.

It will be slow and painful, but they will heal.

The day is a bright one. The spring is something warm and lovely. With the fire came the rain, and once the rain passed, the skies became clear and beautiful. Freya had a pyre built out at the gravesite, and Gabriel brought Alistair's body.

"Mama." Zsoka's voice is small and frail, and I forget that she is young and most likely does not remember the death she had known years before when she'd gone running into the battlefield to find her father.

I turn my gaze to her now, standing there and watching Alistair's frozen form with fear and horror.

Children know what death is. But until it takes from them, until it reaches into their soul and leaves them open and raw when it pulls away, they do not truly understand it.

Zsoka is beginning to understand now.

I cannot pick her up. I am still healing, and my body would not be able to hold her. Moreover, my newborn daughter is in my arms, sleeping soundly, completely unaware of what lays before her. And so all that I can do is lay my hand upon her back, some small and pitiful comfort that I can offer her in a time when her entire world is being shattered…once again.

Gabriel approaches the crystallized form and places his hand upon the ice. It melts away slowly at first, and then faster, leaving Alistair upon a stone table which had been brought out to hold his form. Then, two of the servants carry him carefully up to the top of the pyre and climb down again.

The entire country has gathered. The dukes, the lairds. Thousands of people have come to witness this day even with so little warning. They came at once and without hesitation. That is what Alistair inspired in others. That is what he moved in me.

"Scarlet?" Gabriel calls my name, and the full length of it sounds strange on his lips.

I turn my eyes to him, watching him and wanting to say something, but I am left with no words. I feel as though I am a doll pulled along by strings, but I move forward one step at a time and approach the dais. I lift my hand, raising it in a last goodbye to my friend, my lover, my husband, my mate.

Alistair.

Tears roll down my cheeks freely and without shame.

Fire bursts forth from my hand and engulfs the top of the pyre. The flames roar and hiss, quickly catching on to the wood. They seem confused at first by the body atop it which is still most likely wet and cold. It hisses and pops and sizzles, steam rising up from the pyre. But then the steam is replaced by smoke. A thick, curling snake of black smoke that rises up from the pyre to cloud the brilliant mid-morning sky.

I watch the black smoke, watch it slither up from the pyre.
That damn pyre.

Chapter Fifty
Scarlet

Several Hours Later
The Burial Grounds of Maeghdra, Flora

I stand before the pyre. The sound of the fire fills my ears, and when I close my eyes, it is almost as if I am back at the Den.

I open my eyes, and I stand before the darkening Flora sky.

"Cara." There is no one left now, and Gabriel quietly approaches me.

The sky has turned dark, and yet not quite dark enough to see the stars. Everyone has either gone home or to the inn or back to the Maeghdra manor where they will sit around a hearth and laugh and talk and tell stories of my love who is dead and who is gone.

I have no desire to join them. I turn my head when Gabriel calls to me, coming up slowly to my side and giving a tired smile.

"You should come inside, duchess. It is getting cold out…and the pyre is all burned away."

I look back at where the pyre had been and see, in fact, that he speaks truth. I do not know where the day went, but the pyre has all been eaten away by the flames, and there is nothing left to be seen of my Alistair. There is no need to stay here any longer.

Alistair is gone.

I close my eyes, and a cool breeze spills over the mountain sides. The wind tangles in my hair and drifts over my face. For a moment, I can imagine the feel of my lover's fingertips across my cheek.

I drag in a breath—long and slow—as if filling my lungs for the very first time…

> "…Swing up high—high, sweet darling
> Do not fear the burning sky
> Let the fire take you—over and through
> Where the sun sinks down to the shore…"

ABOUT

A HEART OF STONE

A Heart of Stone is a story very near and dear to me. Many of the struggles Scarlet experiences in this story are ones that I have gone through myself. Writing this story unearthed raw emotion and old memories that I had to work through on my own throughout this sequel.

The feeling of finding yourself is something almost entirely universal. The desire to belong and the desire to have the security in who you are. Scarlet had placed all of her identity in being a soldier and in hating others. She did the same thing many of us do—define ourselves by our jobs, our spouses, even our children. And when that thing is gone, she is at a loss as to who she is and she has to struggle to redefine herself by something stronger and unmovable.

We read about Scarlet struggling through the death of her first husband in *A Heart of Ice*, but now we have to watch as she again must face down her own sorrows and come out alive. Before, she managed to hide from her pain by masking it with hatred and with anger so that she didn't have to face her grief. But now she can't do that and she has to learn to stare death in the eyes and not back down.

Her struggles are real ones that I see people face every day. My young students grapple with their identity and their place in the world. They learn how and by what to define themselves. Many of them also struggle with almost insurmountable trials of pain and loss, and as they struggle and fight through their own heartbreak, I watch them emerge as beautiful and incredible individuals.

I wrote this story for them.

For the ones who don't know who they are and the ones who have lost more than words can say.

This story belongs to you.

As a side note: this book was finished July 2017… *but*, as I was finishing the cover, the file became corrupted, and I lost the entire file and had to redo the cover…I also had life completely and unrelentingly explode on me. Personally, professionally, financially, everything. I am just proud of myself for having gotten out of bed each day and not just giving up. So, thank you for your patience!

Another side note: Chapter 46 still makes me sob any time I read it…

ABOUT THE AUTHOR

Phoenix lives in Atlanta, Georgia with her husband, their crazy German Shepherd, and their beautiful daughter, Rhea. She grew up in the South and from an early age developed a love for reading, writing, and teaching.
Phoenix loves working with middle school and high school students. She hopes to teach English Language Arts both in the U.S. and in other countries as well, specifically Kenya, a place very dear to her heart.

Check us out online at
www.PhoenixBriar.com

www.ingramcontent.com/pod-product-compliance
Lightning Source LLC
Chambersburg PA
CBHW030541020726
47494CB00005B/1443